"MYOBU HAS TRAINED ME WELL. I AM A GEISHA."

Jessica slid off his legs, her hands now guiding him over onto his back so that he could see her.

Longarm gazed at her lovely features. The gold-and-red tendrils of her hair sparked desire so strong it made him throb with anticipation.

"Lord above, woman," Longarm gasped. "What fine tricks Myobu has taught you."

"There are no tricks, silly," Jessica laughed. "The geisha's art lies not in playing tricks, but in knowing how to surrender..."

LONGARM AND THE LONE STAR LEGEND

TABOR EVANS

AND THE
LONE STAR LEGEND

A JOVE BOOK

LONGARM AND THE LONE STAR LEGEND

A Jove Book / published by arrangement with
the author

PRINTING HISTORY
Jove edition / August 1982

ISBN: 0-515-06225-1

Jove books are published by Jove Publications, Inc.,
200 Madison Avenue, New York, N.Y. 10016.
The words "A JOVE BOOK" and the "J" with sunburst
are trademarks belonging to Jove Publications, Inc.

PRINTED IN THE UNITED STATES OF AMERICA

LONGARM

AND THE
LONE STAR LEGEND

★

Chapter 1

It was nine-thirty in the morning on a gray day in Denver, and Longarm, his steel-blue eyes bleary, was wondering just how many fried eggs and slices of ham he was going to have to watch Billy Vail eat before the man explained why the hell they were having breakfast together. Not that Longarm and his boss, the Chief United States Marshal of the First District Court of Colorado, weren't friends, but Billy's usual style was to summon his deputies to his Federal Courthouse office up on Capitol Hill, growl out his orders, and then send his men off with a boot in the ass.

But not this morning. This morning, Vail's pale-faced young clerk, Henry, had left his typewriter in the front room of the marshal's office long enough to skitter his way across Cherry Creek, over to the unfashionable part of town, to Longarm's rooming house. The knock on Longarm's door had brought the lawman awake, his big right hand finding his double-action Colt .44 in its place beneath his pillow. His groggy-sounding "Who is it?" nicely covered the sharp double click of the Colt's hammer being pulled back.

Henry had identified himself and called out Vail's invitation through the room's closed door. Longarm had eased

1

down the Colt's hammer as he told the clerk that he'd meet Marshal Vail presently, and then swung his six-foot, four-inch frame up and out of bed.

He'd stared into the old mirror above the dressing table, viewing his reflection in between the black spots where the silvery stuff had been scraped off the glass over the years. His longhorn mustache and close-cropped hair, both the brown, lustrous color of well-oiled saddle leather, had been tended to just yesterday by a barber over on Colfax Avenue, so Longarm had figured he could get through the day without a shave. Over on the washstand, a bar of soap floated in a china basin three-quarters filled with tepid water. Having decided that being able to see the basin's cracked bottom vouched well enough for the purity of the water, he'd frothed up some suds, dipped a washrag into them, and scrubbed himself down. The friction of the rough cotton against the hide of his lean, muscular body had soon banished the last remnants of the previous evening's tour of Larimer Street's saloon row.

So much for the outer man, Longarm had thought. He'd picked up the bottle of Maryland rye he kept by the bed, pulled the cork with his teeth, and aimed the bottom of the bottle toward the grimy plaster of the ceiling. One big swallow later, with the rye stoking a fire in his belly, Longarm had felt ready to face the day.

He'd dressed quickly, shrugging on a clean gray flannel shirt, fumbling his shoestring tie into place, and tugging on his cotton longjohns and skintight brown tweed pants. After hauling on a pair of woolen socks and stomping his feet against the threadbare carpet of his room to get his low-heeled stovepipe boots on snugly, he'd turned his attention to the important parts of his wardrobe. His gunbelt was a cross-draw rig, and he wore it high, just above his narrow hip bones. Retrieving his Colt Model T .44-40 from where he'd left it on the bed, Longarm had slipped the sixgun, butt forward, into the waxed and heat-hardened holster on his left hip. He'd positioned himself in front of that tarnished

2

mirror, and had then reached across his belt buckle with his right hand, drawing the weapon in a whip-fast, rock-steady, single motion. Yep, the gun's polished walnut grips were just where they ought to be...

Longarm had next turned his attention to the Colt itself. He'd cleaned and oiled the weapon and then checked all five of its cartridges—only a fool neglected to let the firing pin ride safely on an empty chamber—late last night, before turning in. Lucky for Marshal Vail that he had, Longarm had thought to himself with a grin. It could've been the President of these United States, Rutherford B. Hayes himself, waiting breakfast for him—Longarm *never* started the day without first seeing to his revolver. He'd paid his respects to the grave markers of too many fellow lawmen *ever* to neglect the main tool of his trade.

The Colt had a barrel cut down to five inches, eliminating the front blade sight as well, and good riddance to it—a front sight could cost a man a precious instant of drawing time if it snagged the lip of an open-toed holster. A handgun was for close-in work. If a man needed to sight-aim, he'd best turn the job over to Mr. Winchester's saddle gun.

Returning his Colt to its place on his hip, Longarm had then put on a vest cut from the same brown tweed as his pants. Next came his ace-in-the-hole. He'd scooped up his Ingersoll pocket watch on its long, gold-washed chain. The other end of the chain was clipped to a ring in the butt of a double-barreled .44 derringer. The watch had gone into the left breast pocket of his vest. The derringer—that ace—had gone into the right. As always, the gold-washed chain draped between the two, like a wide, innocent smile.

He'd slipped into his brown frock coat, patting the pockets to be sure they held some spare .44 cartridges, his wallet—inside of which was pinned his silver-plated federal badge—a pair of handcuffs, and a bundle of waterproofed matches. On the way out of his digs he'd grabbed his snuff-brown Stetson from its nail on the wall. After locking his door, he'd pulled out one of the matches and broken off a piece of matchstick, then wedged it into the crack between the door and the jamb.

Longarm considered himself a generous man. He liked to give surprises, not receive them. If the match splinter had been dislodged when he returned, he'd know somebody had been in the room. Or was *still* in it, waiting for him.

He'd crossed the little sandy wash of Cherry Creek, leaving the cinder path behind as he headed up Colfax Avenue, his boots clicking on the brown sandstone sidewalks they'd installed here on the better side of the city. Up ahead, the gold dome of the Colorado State Capitol glittered against the overcast sky like a fine piece of jewelry nested in folds of gray flannel.

Nodding good morning to the Front Range of the Rockies, fifteen miles to the west, but looking like they were close enough to topple over and crush a man, Longarm had begun to turn into the Federal Courthouse before he'd remembered that Marshal Vail wasn't in his office upstairs, but was waiting for his deputy down the block, in Hodder's Cafe.

Breakfast had proceeded at a leisurely and—for Marshal Vail—very subdued pace. The big-gutted, red-faced, balding marshal was normally about as quiet and easygoing as a Kansas twister. This morning, or at least so far, all Billy did was make dumb small talk.

But something was up. Longarm had sensed it. He'd been a lawman too long not to know when a man had something on his mind but wasn't yet ready to speak it plain. The cafe was still crowded, so Longarm had figured that Billy was waiting until these stinkwater dudes had drained their teacups, gathered up their legal briefs, and then wandered off to do battle along the marble corridors of the State House and the Federal Court.

At about nine-thirty, the large group sitting at the table just to the right of Longarm and Vail had lit up their cigars and pipes, paid their check, and left. Vail had watched them

4

go as if they were the James gang on their way to the nearest bank.

Longarm leaned back in his chair and tucked the end of a cheroot into the corner of his mouth. He didn't light it, and not just because Billy was still working on his *second* plate of ham and eggs. Longarm had been trying to quit the damned tobacco habit for a long time, and his latest ploy was a vow not to light up a smoke before noon.

The waitress, a pretty little redhead whose sky-blue eyes had been sending smoke signals Longarm's way since he'd come in, came around to their table to refill their coffee cups. As she passed behind Longarm's chair, her cool fingers caressed the back of his neck. Not a word passed between them, and then Longarm was watching her walk away, her shapely behind doing a soul-stirring, rhythmic dance beneath the snug expanse of her skirt, which was stretched even tighter by the big, puffy bow of her apron . . .

"Why don't you ask her if she's on the menu?" Vail grumbled as he pushed his cleaned-off plate away.

"Chief, that line stopped getting women when you were still young enough to want them," Longarm drawled, knowing that Vail could take a joke. The marshal had long ago been roped and branded by a fine woman. Like most lawmen smart enough to survive, Vail had waited until he'd taken a desk job before taking a bride.

Vail signaled for more coffee and the check. "I don't want us to be disturbed while we talk," he told the pretty waitress. Longarm breathed a sigh of relief when Vail paid for the meal. Fifty-five cents for two breakfasts was robbery, even if this eatery was a Capitol Hill hangout! He'd not had a raise since '78, and everybody was saying that 1880's inflation was going to be the worst ever.

Longarm eyed Vail, wondering if now was a good time to bring up the question of his raise. It was funny how a man might be able to measure his opponent when it came to a fight, and yet be as skittery as a mustang when it came to jawing about money matters.

"You're most likely wondering why I didn't want to talk to you in my office," Vail began once the waitress had scooted off with their money, giving them both a big smile of thanks for their generous tip.

"It had crossed my mind," Longarm replied, chewing on his cold cheroot, trying to keep his mind off that waitress and on what Billy Vail was saying. She'd settled down at a table on the far side of the now nearly empty dining room, taking a break now that the morning rush was over. She was counting up her tip money as she sipped at her own mug of coffee. Every time she leaned forward over her sums, her fine, full breasts strained the buttons of her bodice, threatening to pop over the demure white piping of her uniform as if they too wanted to witness the count.

"Fact is, I've been issued orders from the Justice Department not to let anyone but the deputy I'm assigning hear about this case," Vail quietly explained. "I've sent you out to investigate murders before, but this time I've got something a mite rarer for you, Longarm." Vail took a deep breath and looked his deputy square in the eye. "This time I'm sending you out to unravel an assassination. You remember the killing of Alex Starbuck?"

"Hell, everybody remembers the Starbuck shooting," Longarm said. "He was one of the wealthiest, most powerful cattlemen in Texas. But why all the secrecy? Usually we're either in a case or we're not, depending on whether any federal laws have been broken. What's Justice's angle on this one?"

"A lot of angles," Vail muttered into his coffee. "But the one that scares me is that we've been *unofficially* ordered in." He sighed. "Maybe I'd better start from the beginning. At the time of his death, Starbuck was in his late fifties." Vail reached down for a manila folder that had evidently been propped on his lap throughout breakfast. He opened it and removed from it a photograph, which he handed across to Longarm. "Got this sent to me from San Francisco. Big newspaper there had it in the files."

It was a well-detailed, full-front, formal pose, showing a tall, barrel-chested man with a full head of gray hair. The man was dressed in a fine suit, obviously custom-tailored, and probably from one of the shops in San Francisco. Once, while on a case that had taken him to the West Coast some years before, Longarm had visited such a shop. Even then, a suit like that worn by Starbuck in the photograph would have cost Longarm half a year's salary. He flipped the photograph over. "According to the date written here, this was run pretty recent. Whatever they were writing about him, it wasn't his obituary. How did a Texas cattleman rate a picture in a San Francisco newspaper morgue?"

Vail smiled. "You ain't been reading the financial pages."

"Where you've been sending me, there's no newspapers. I did run across one of those telephone contraptions a while back, in the Sand Hills..."

"Well, if you did read a paper once in a while, you'd know that cattle were the least of Starbuck's fortune, and the most recent addition to it," Vail replied, tapping the manila folder. "He got into beef just in time to reap the profits of the bad harvests and political troubles in Europe. He made his real fortune back in the fifties. Starbuck happened to be one of the sailors on Perry's fleet, when the commodore used his gunboats to convince the Japans to open up their ports to the United States. Hell, that was around '50, I'd reckon—"

"It was 1853 to '54, Chief," Longarm grinned from behind his cheroot. "I read me a book about it once that some fellow wrote," he added in an attempt to damp down Vail's slow burn.

"Anyway," the glowering marshal continued, "Starbuck might have been just another sailor boy, but he saw his opportunity. As soon as he was discharged back home, he gathered up every penny he could borrow and got himself passage back to the Orient. He stayed there for a while, learning the language and such, and then returned to San Francisco with a sizable piece of the Japans' import-and-export trade in his pocket."

Longarm nodded ruefully. "Then he was in the right place at the right time. San Francisco's harbors were just being dredged for foreign trade, and the transcontinental railroad was getting itself into one piece to carry his goods to the East."

"Today, the Starbuck empire stretches all across the country," Vail agreed. "But we ain't here to jaw about the man's good luck. What we're concerned with is the one instant when he was in the *wrong* place at the *wrong* time."

"Starbuck was murdered in Texas, right?"

"Right."

"Well, Texas is a state," Longarm said. "One of the thirty-eight. They got all kinds of solid law down there. One more lawman shoves his badge into Texas, the state, big as it is, is going to sink like an overloaded rowboat. And I still don't understand what all the secrecy's about. It sure as hell ain't a secret that Starbuck's dead—"

"Keep quiet and let me get there," Vail ordered. "First off, there's no local law big enough to investigate Starbuck's death. Hell, Starbuck *was* the law in his part of North-Central Texas. His hands did a damn fine job of keeping things peaceable, from what I've been told. The governor is a sissy who spends most of his time in Washington, sucking up to the federal politicos. Word is, *he's* got his eye on a Senate seat. That must have been all right with Starbuck, as he was the one who paid for the governor's election."

"I'm starting to get the idea," Longarm drawled.

"Then get this. President Hayes has personally taken an interest in this case. The worry is that without Starbuck's restraining influence on the area, vigilante groups will form, and then it'll only be a matter of time before range wars break out as the various groups start shooting each other up for killing Starbuck."

"Hell, Billy, I didn't think any man *but* the President was so all-fired important."

"Starbuck was also the head of the Cattlemen's Association. It was his money that allowed his neighbors to build up their own herds. Starbuck lent them that money to bring stability to the state. His death has shaken Texas's stability. His killers have got to be brought to justice."

"And that's where I come in," Longarm nodded.

"Wrong," Vail spat. "That's where the army comes in."

"The army!" Longarm groaned. "They can't do this sort of snooping-around work. Everybody knows that the army's method of smoking out a rat is to burn down the whole barn!"

Vail shrugged. "Everybody but President Hayes, it seems. The various spreads in that part of Texas are about to start their big roundup, driving their combined herds to the railhead. They'll fatten those steers up in the feed pens of Kansas and Nebraska, but they breed 'em and birth 'em in Texas. The nation needs that beef, and President Hayes has promised millions of pounds of it to England and the rest of Europe. The President aims to keep his promise to those countries, and it's his feeling that what Texas needs is a good dose of martial law to keep things quieted down."

"How do we come into it?" Longarm asked.

"Secretly. I told you that the governor has friends in Washington. He's afraid that flooding the state with soldiers might make him unpopular, come the Senate elections."

"Makes sense," Longarm mused. "If the army comes into the proud Lone Star State, the governor's career would be finished. He'd be out on his ass."

"Now the Justice Department wants the credit for solving this case, so between Justice and the governor's friends, the President's orders to the army have gotten 'lost.' For the

9

time being, at any rate. You've got a week, Custis, maybe a day or so more, but not much more," Vail warned. "If you can wrap it up by then, we'll both of us have earned ourselves a pat on the back from Justice. If you fail, it'll likely mean our jobs."

"You sure about that, Billy?" Longarm asked softly. "Damn, that don't hardly seem fair—"

"I'm sure."

Longarm looked into Vail's seamed, care-worn face, and saw that he was. He himself would get along just fine if he lost his badge. He was still on the friendly side of forty. But Vail had spent his entire life as a lawman, and was counting on his pension to support him and his wife in their old age. Damn—It was always the good and true men, men who had ridden out their lives in the cause of the law, men like Billy Vail, who had to suffer the consequences for the dumb actions of a bunch of politicos who'd ruined more lives with a stroke of their pens than any outlaw *ever* had with a sixgun.

"I drew up all your papers and travel vouchers myself," Vail was explaining. "I didn't want that rules-and-regulations clerk of mine controlling the case records on this one. I picked you because you keep that badge of yours pinned in your wallet, and flash it only when you have to. You know how to be...dis-*creet*—" Vail blushed—"and, Jesus, that's what I need this time around. If word gets back to Hayes before you're ready to make an arrest—"

"First I've got to find the killer, and *then* I've got to find a federal angle, else all I can do is point my finger for the local law—"

"I know that!" Vail snarled. "I was making arrests when you were still wearing short pants—"

"Sorry, Chief." Longarm grinned. "Well, reckon I've got me a cattle baron's murder to solve."

"Assassination."

10

"Now there you go throwing that word around again, Chief." Longarm glanced at the pendulum clock hanging just above the blackboard that announced the day's blue-plate specials. He sighed and placed his still-unlit cheroot into the ashtray, where he could eye it wistfully. Still two hours before noon. "What makes you so all-fired sure Starbuck wasn't cut down by a spurned woman, or an envious neighbor whose loan was coming due, or maybe a passing rustler or two?"

"Because Alex Starbuck had seven rounds in him, and from the looks of the spot where he'd been ambushed, at least thirty rounds had been fired." Vail's features softened with joy over the fact that he'd been able to tell Longarm something the man hadn't already known. "The Texas officials put a lid on any of this going out over the telegraph lines, again at the behest of the President. At least fifteen men had to have been involved in the ambush, and they'd been lying in wait for Starbuck to pass."

"I guess he never knew what hit him," Longarm mused as he glanced down at Starbuck's photograph.

"Guess again," Vail said. "He lived for a couple of hours afterward. Tough old buzzard."

Longarm didn't answer, but just stared down at the photograph. The print was sharp enough for him to make out Starbuck's characteristics—the sorts of things an experienced lawman could tell about a man from glancing at him. Longarm could tell that Starbuck was no greenhorn. Despite his fine clothes, he had the hard, callused-looking hands of a man who had roped his share of cattle and thumbed back his share of Colt hammers. Longarm could only wonder: What sort of soul was this who had conquered the Japans, built up an empire, and then, as dessert, tamed Texas until it had trotted at his feet like a hound at heel?

"Starbuck's daughter—her name is Jessica—was the only one at her father's bedside when he died. Maybe she'll

11

know something. Starbuck's wife passed away long ago. Jessica is the only heir. It all belongs to her now—lock, stock, and barrel."

"Maybe *she* killed him." Longarm winked and reached into his pocket and came out with a match, which he struck against the table. "Her and her fifteen boyfriends." He brought the flaring tip of the match up to his cheroot, and puffed it alight.

"Well, get on to Texas and find out, dammit," Vail growled.

"On my way." Longarm smiled, grateful that Vail's usual nasty disposition was coming back. It meant the old boy was growing less worried.

"By the way, I thought you'd told me that you weren't going to smoke those two-for-a-nickel stinkweeds of yours until noontime," Vail taunted as his deputy rose from the table. "Ain't got the willpower, is that it, old son?"

"Sure I do, Billy." Longarm exhaled a great stream of blue smoke, the expression on his face blissful. "I just figured I ought to commemorate the event. It's not every day a deputy marshal gets to investigate an *assassination.*"

Longarm left the cafe and swung around the side of the building to the alleyway behind it. Once he'd passed the long rear expanse of the courthouse building, he could save himself some time by shortcutting to yet another alley that would lead him to the livery stable, where he could collect his McClellan saddle and Mexican bridle. His plan was to gather up his gear, then haul it along to the railway station, which was just about halfway between the stable and his rooming house. Longarm's years as a deputy marshal had taught him the railroads' schedules. He knew he had little more than an hour before the Kansas Pacific's local huffed its way out of Denver toward Pueblo, the site of his first transfer—that was, if he wanted to leave today, and he did. He had just about a week, and ahead of him were several train changes and a few days of travel by rail until he reached his jumping-off point.

The baggage clerk would watch his gear while Longarm went back to his rooming house to get his saddle bags, bedroll, and Winchester. He'd be back at the station, waiting for his train, in plenty of time. All of his travel papers were already tucked away in his frock coat, along with his authorization to borrow an army mount. He'd pick up the horse at an army remount station located on the New Mexico side of the border. It would cost the Justice Department a bit more for Longarm to transport the mount via the railroad, but that was better than sparking curiosity inside Texas by flashing his badge and papers at some Ranger post.

Be discreet, Vail had warned him. Well, Texas Rangers were fine men, but they considered any business in Texas *their* business.

He could ride the railroad all the way to Sarah, one of the newest cow towns in that region. Starbuck had built the town, persuaded the railroad to run a spur into it, and contracted with cattle buyers in the East to have holding pens built. Sarah was the place where the Old West's cattle drive jumped into the next century, where drovers wearing chaps came in from the range to turn their cows over to men wearing ties, who kept their herds in ledger books. Sarah was the site upon which Alex Starbuck had built his empire.

Overhead, the sun had poked holes through the fuzzy gray blanket of clouds, so that the sky now looked like an old bedroll that had been worn out by hard use on the trail. It was just a little after ten, but the air was already stifling and still. It was going to be a true Denver dog day.

But it wasn't the heat that was making Longarm feel uncomfortable; it wasn't the breakfast in his belly that was causing that flutter in the pit of his stomach.

Longarm continued on his way down the deserted alley. He ambled—quick, but easy—his boots making hardly a sound on the hard-packed dirt beneath them. He was chan-

13

neling all of his awareness into his sense of hearing now, and any sound he himself made might just muffle the crucial sound.

As he passed a clapboard building, the front of which housed a stationery store, a crow loitering in the building's eaves squawked in outrage over being disturbed. A covert glance told Longarm that the crow was no longer watching him but had focused its beady, sideways glare on the alleyway behind him.

The crow squawked again, and as it did, Longarm used the distraction to casually brush back the left side of his frock coat, clearing the butt of his Colt. But he kept on walking, resisting the urge to look back over his shoulder.

The crow had been confirmation, but Longarm had already known he was being followed—and had been, since he'd left the cafe. The real question was by whom. And why?

The end of the alley loomed before him. When he cut over, he'd only have a short stretch of the second alley to go before he reached the street, where there would be people, where the stable was located. If his shadow was planning on doing some shooting, now was the time.

Still, Longarm kept on walking, not looking back, trusting instincts born of long years at this sort of work to get him through. It just didn't feel like a gunplay situation to him, and Longarm didn't want to be the one to provoke gunplay by spooking his tail. For one thing, Vail would hit the roof if his deputy had to spend the rest of his morning filling out papers on a corpse, thereby missing his train.

That he would be the one standing over a corpse, and not the corpse himself, Longarm had no doubts. He knew that he could take whoever it was. Hell, if the fellow was twice as good with a gun as he was at trying to follow somebody inconspicuously, he'd still be tenderfoot-lousy.

The end of the second alley loomed before him. Longarm concentrated, ears straining for the faint metallic click of

14

gun mechanism, which would be all the warning he'd have before it was time to get out of a bullet's path. Then he was out of the alley.

The tail hung back as Longarm crossed the street, dodging the weekday traffic as he did so. Inside the livery stable it was dark and still cool, the air fragrant with the honest, pleasant smell of oiled leather and healthy horseflesh. Several horses whickered in their stalls as he walked by them to the rear of the building and the storage shelves.

"Morning, Deputy Long," the stable boy beamed. He was a gangling fourteen-year-old, looking like a scarecrow in his baggy union-suit shirt and too-short, obviously hand-me-down britches.

"Morning, son, fetch me my gear, would you? I've got a train to catch." Longarm flipped the boy a shiny dime, which the youngster caught even as he headed off to do the deputy's bidding.

"Take a look at what we got in stall six, Deputy," the boy enthused as he wrestled down Longarm's McClellan saddle from its place on the wall.

Longarm did so and whistled softly in appreciation at one of the finest specimens of Virginia walking horse that he'd ever seen. "Mighty fine, boy." He reached out to lift the chin of the horse, watching the animal's muscles tremble with life beneath the sleek dappled gray of its hide. "Whose stallion is this?"

"Judge Bing had him shipped in," the boy answered, lugging Longarm's saddle to a sawhorse just a few feet away from where the lawman was standing. He set the McClellan across the sawhorse and then paused before going back for the bridle. "The judge already has himself a few fine mares, and means to get into the breeding business. He'll be taking this fella home tonight." The boy gazed with undisguised admiration at the horse. "Wouldn't you like to call him your own, sir?"

Longarm smiled. "That I would, son."

15

Like most working men in the West, Longarm had never owned a horse. It was a hell of lot cheaper—even if the government didn't pick up your expenses—to take the train to where you wanted to go, and rent a horse when you got there. "Hope that fool judge has more sense than to try and ride this fellow home."

The boy giggled as he headed back to the rear of the stable. "Wouldn't that be something?" he called over his shoulder. "That old judge holding on for dear life, his black robes flapping, while his fine stallion does it to the milkman's old mare—"

The stallion gave a nervous whinny, its massive head bobbing up and down as its eyes showed white and rolled toward the stable's front doors. The other mounts—geldings all—seemed undisturbed, but something was spooking the stallion. Longarm remembered his unseen follower.

He walked to the rear of the stable. "Boy, I want you to run an errand for me," he began. "Get on to my rooming house, and tell my landlady that I said to let you into my room to pick up my saddlebags, bedroll, and rifle. I keep that stuff all packed up and ready to go. Bring it all back here for me, all right?"

"Gee, Deputy . . . I don't know, sir. I'm supposed to watch over that stallion—"

"You git," Longarm ordered good-naturedly, handing over some more change. "Reckon that horse can't have a better guard than a federal marshal. I aim to wait right here for you."

"That's fine, then," the boy laughed, relieved that he didn't have to give up the money.

Longarm gave the boy his address. "Hold on," he called thoughtfully as the boy headed toward the front doors. "You go out the back way, son, through the corral. And shut those two old doors behind you as you go."

The boy peered up at Longarm's face. "Sir? Is there something up?"

"Go on now," Longarm said absently. "And if you should stop off for a soda on the way, I don't aim to tattle to your boss."

The stable boy ran off. Longarm waited until he was sure the kid was well away, and then began to make his way silently toward the front of the stable. The stallion was pawing the ground, huffing and snorting, as if agreeing with Longarm that the tail was hiding behind the front stable door, which was still swung closed.

Longarm considered climbing up into the hayloft, the better to get the drop on his adversary, but decided against it. It was a hot day, and this fellow's bumbling attempts at trailing him had put Longarm in a bad enough mood as it was.

Longarm leaned against the tall sawhorse that held his saddle and waited, watching. The door was nothing but a bunch of old boards nailed to a frame. Sunlight streamed in through the various chinks and knotholes. Whoever it was on the other side, creeping along to the door's edge, standing between the sun and those chinks, he was evidently too dumb to realize that Longarm could chart his progress by the way his form passed from chink to chink, blocking one sunbeam after another.

As the tail's fingers curled around the door's edge, Longarm sprang forward, locking his big hand about the other's wrist. He gave one solid yank, and almost followed the trajectory of his own arm as his adversary came flying in to tumble onto the stable floor. The jasper was sure a lightweight...

"Owww!" bawled the mysterious form, in a high, unmistakably feminine voice.

"I'll be damned." Longarm kicked open the stable door to let the sunlight flood in. Sprawled across the floor, with her skirts up around her thighs, was the waitress from the cafe!

"My God, Deputy," she pouted, her fingers gingerly

rubbing her wrist. "I think you came awfully close to break-ing my arm." She extended both arms to him. "Help me up!"

Longarm did as he was told. Placing a hand on each side of her slender waist, he picked her up, setting her on her feet. "Sorry about hurting you. But how was I to know it was you stalking after me like the wolf after the lamb?"

"I might have been doing the stalking, but I surely hope you've got that wolf-and-lamb stuff backward, Deputy," she laughed.

"Never mind. What *are* you doing following me?" Long-arm asked sternly. He tried to keep his eyes on her face, but as pretty as it was, with her big blue eyes blinking at him as wide and seemingly innocent as a newborn babe's, his own eyes kept wandering back to her bodice. Her breasts were rising and falling, obviously over the excitement of being hauled into the stable.

"Well, answer me!" Longarm demanded, but the waitress just smiled, and took a step closer.

"It's a long story. I'm sort of new in Denver. I only arrived here, from back East, a few weeks ago. I don't hardly know *anyone*," she complained, brushing a tendril of her copper-colored hair off of her face. The tight bun in which she had been wearing it had come loose during her tumble. Now wisps of her hair hung down, the strands clinging to the hot, moist nape of her neck. "Not knowing anyone really doesn't bother me, because that just means I get to save more of my salary. I intend to open up a dress shop in just a little while."

"That don't explain why you were following me."

"Hush. I'm getting to that. You see, Deputy, coming out West, leaving my parents, was a big step into a new way of life. So when I saw you in the cafe—and I *knew* you saw me—um, well, I have a couple of hours before it'll get busy again, and so, well, I decided to come meet you and—" Here she blushed, cat-grinning at the same time,

18

her bright white teeth flashing like a bunch of daisies in a field of pink rose blossoms. "What can I say, Deputy? A girl only lives once. This is sort of like moving West. I thought maybe you and I could—"

Now it was Longarm's turn to grin. He thought about scolding her for trailing him, about pointing out to her that those who wanted to stay healthy ought to make it a habit to approach both lawmen *and* outlaws from the front, but somehow this didn't seem like the right time.

"My name's Maggie Henders," she said, and then waited. "And you're Deputy...uh...?"

But Longarm seemed not to have heard her. He was still watching her breasts. Maggie smiled knowingly, as if she'd witnessed such reactions on the part of men before. "I should point out that while this *is* my first time out West," she continued demurely, "This will *not* be my first time, um, you know..."

Longarm just had to chuckle. Something about this young lady made a man feel like it was springtime. "Custis Long, ma'am. At your service."

"Oh, I hope you are." Maggie's eyes glinted merrily.

"Well, now, Maggie, we've got ourselves a little problem on that score." Longarm sighed, thinking that she was a fine woman, and certainly an experienced one who knew what she wanted and how to handle it after it was given. "I've got a train to catch in about one hour, and that means there's no time to get to my rooming house between now and then."

"Well, what about right here?" Maggie challenged. "We're alone, and there's piles of nice, soft hay in the loft." She took another step closer and slid her hands around his waist, her palms caressing his buttocks beneath the tightly stretched tweed of his britches.

Brazen as she was, Longarm could feel her trembling as he pulled her to himself and found her lips with his own. Their tongues did a fine mating dance, and Longarm felt as if the crotch of his pants had suddenly shrunk in size as Maggie rubbed herself against him. He noticed that she was still wearing her waitress's apron.

"Oh, *let's*, Deputy Long," she breathed, pecking moist kisses up the curve of his jaw while fingering the solid bulge behind his fly.

Longarm thought about it and then decided, Why not? The stable boy was gone, and he'd told the kid to take his time.

"Folks generally call me Longarm, Maggie."

"Well, *I* won't," she teased. "Not until you prove it."

Longarm untangled himself from her grasp long enough to hurry to the stable door and swing it halfway closed. The light that filtered in made the stable's interior agreeably dim.

"Is this your saddle?" Maggie asked, running her fingers along the smooth leather curve of the McClellan. She'd already begun to get undressed, the two halves of her unbuttoned bodice parting like curtains before the proud swell of her fine round breasts. As Longarm feasted his eyes, her nipples stiffened to attention. "But Deputy"—she frowned, a look of puzzlement suffusing her lovely features as she stroked the front part of the saddle—"where's the—the *thing?*"

Longarm had already taken off his coat and gunbelt, and was unbuttoning his shirt, which he would keep on, along with his loosened vest. That way his derringer would remain within easy reach. It was one thing to be a fool in love, quite another to be a loving fool... "You mean the saddlehorn, Maggie? This here's a McClellan saddle. It doesn't have a horn." He kicked off his boots.

Maggie winced at the thought of a male crotch sliding along that saddle. "If there's no horn, how do you protect your... *things*? she asked wide-eyed as Longarm peeled off his pants. "Oh, I hope they're *all right,*" she whimpered

20

as he kicked off his longjohns. "Oh, they *are!*"

Longarm laughed as he gathered her up in his arms for another kiss. She was still wearing her skirt and apron, but she placed a hand under each of her breasts and lifted them for Longarm's approval, as if she were right now fulfilling her waitress's role, presenting two sumptuous globes of fruit.

"Deputy, I know just how I want to do it," she giggled. "Oh, you'll think me shameless!" She reached behind her to unhook her skirt, then wiggled out of it, the pert, round cheeks of her bottom finally bouncing free and bare. She skipped over to the saddle and stood on tiptoe to drape herself belly-down across it. "I'll keep my apron on to protect my belly from all these nasty brass fittings, Deputy Longar— Oops! I almost said it." She licked her lips. "But you haven't made me yet!" With that she lowered her head and raised her bottom in invitation.

Though Longarm did fleetingly wonder if she'd left her underwear back East, along with her folks, he couldn't remember when he'd gazed at a finer sight. Her long legs and full, soft buttocks were a lovely white and pink against the brown leather of the saddle. And above it all was the crisp white bow of her apron, its knot resting right at the small of her back, just an inch above where her buttocks began their soft, full swell. It reminded him of the twitching, white cotton-ball tail of a female bunny in heat.

As he rushed toward her, she parted her legs and arched her back, tilting her hips in order to draw him in. He toyed his rigid member along the crevice between her thighs. "Lord, are you wet," he laughed. "Good thing you're wearing that apron, Maggie, else you'd be soaking my saddle!"

"Soak *mine!*" she bawled like a cat, and before she could say another word, Longarm slid into her to the hilt, withdrawing slowly and then sliding back to set an easy, slick, incredibly pleasurable rhythm, like that which a cow-pony might set as it loped along the prairie. Like that cow-pony, Longarm knew that this was a pace he could easily keep up for a long, long time.

Maggie's cat-bawling had now become something that sounded more like a coyote howling at the moon. As she wiggled and twitched to meet his thrusts, she slipped forward across the saddle, so that her toes left the ground. She was helpless now, draped across the expanse of leather as if she were a set of saddlebags. Longarm gripped each side of her hips and impaled her again and again, each thrust making her yelp and kick her legs uselessly and wave her arms in the air, until he began to worry that someone outside the stable might think a murder was taking place.

Her hips, beneath Longarm's fingers, began to rock and buck, while her juices gushed out of her, rolling down the sides of her legs in beaded trails. "Oh, God!" she sobbed, arching her back. "Oh Deputy, I'm dying—"

"What's my name?" he teased, quickening his pace, driving her to her climax with short, sharp strokes.

"Ahhh! Longarm!" she sang. "Longarm! *L-o-n-g-a-r-mmm!*"

All tension left her as she collapsed limply across the saddle to shudder through orgasm after orgasm. Longarm, his muscles corded, threw back his head to growl his pleasure as he spent himself deep inside her.

As he withdrew, she shimmied off the saddle to spin around, throwing her arms about his neck as she locked her legs about his waist. Longarm felt the wonderful wetness of her center pressing against him as she kissed him over and over, murmuring endearments.

"Best that we start getting dressed," Longarm said gently.

"Oh . . . can't we *again?*"

"We *can*, but we *won't*," Longarm laughed, rubbing her bottom. "Maggie, we can't expect to keep this stable to ourselves forever, you know, and I've got a train to catch."

22

"But we can when you come back, right?" Maggie asked earnestly.

"I promise, ma'am."

Nodding happily, Maggie let go of him and began to gather up her clothes. Suddenly she stopped and, pointing at one of the stalls, called out delightedly, "Oh, darling! Look at the boy horse!"

Longarm whirled to look at the stallion, and then began to roar with laughter. The big gray Walker was reared up on its hind legs, its nostrils flared, and its total, equine attention transfixed by Maggie's delectable form. *No wonder*, Longarm thought. No wonder the stallion, of all the mounts in the stable, was the one to become agitated by the approach of the mystery adversary! All the other mounts were geldings. But the big Virginia walker was a stud, and on this warm, still day, he'd focused on what it took Longarm longer to get to: a female in heat!

"Ohhh," Maggie sighed as she stood with her legs apart, absently stroking the tousled wet fur between her legs. "Look at *his* thing..."

Still laughing, Longarm walked over to her and slid his arm around her shoulder. The stallion's long, slender member stood out, a trembling, bobbing rob. "Yes, ma'am, Maggie," he mused. "Just look at it. It sort of makes a man stop and think..."

Maggie spun around to gaze up at him with adoration in her eyes. "Some men, maybe. But not you, Longarm..."

He scooped her up under one arm and headed for the ladder that led up to the hayloft. As Maggie giggled with delight, and squealed with certain knowledge of the joy to come, Longarm thought: *What the hell, that old local to Pueblo is always late!*

23

★

Chapter 2

Longarm stretched out as best he could across the red plush seat toward the rear of the Texas & Pacific passenger coach. The train was crowded, but there were plenty of cars. Even if there hadn't been, Longarm would most likely have kept his Stetson tipped over his eyes. He was in no mood for company. Trains had been his entire world for the last forty-eight hours, and he was feeling ornery as hell. Well, all he had to do now was get through the night. They were scheduled to reach Grassy Bow, a jerkwater town in New Mexico where the army remount Station was located, in a few hours. He'd pick up his horse, and then, by tomorrow afternoon, they'd be at Sarah, Texas.

Longarm felt himself drifting off into a doze. He wasn't worried about being disturbed, since folks tended not to trouble fellows wearing double-action Colts. As he drifted toward sleep, his mind returned—as any man's would—to that last time with Maggie, up in the hayloft. Besides, thinking about Maggie might just serve to take his mind off the stale sandwiches he'd eaten for dinner, peddled to its captive clients by the railroad.

"Tickets! Tickets!" droned the old conductor as he stumbled down the swaying aisle. He was dressed in his regulation blue suit and cap, with its black, duck-bill visor. This train made more stops than an old hound had fleas, and an eternity ago, when Longarm had first boarded, the conductor had grumped about how impossible it was to keep track of who had paid their fare and who had not. "Hope you stay settled in one place," the conductor had muttered as he punched Longarm's federal vouchers. He'd made it sound as if asking a man not to get out of his seat for more than a day and a night were the most reasonable thing in the world.

Longarm had figured that the conductor probably considered him a sort of fellow civil servant. What a railroad man thought he had in common with a deputy marshal was beyond Longarm, but the old conductor had insisted on talking shop, complaining about the fact that he was the only conductor on board, and there were just too many folks riding the trains these days...

Fortunately the old codger had been too busy tracking down fare evaders to chew the rest of Longarm's ear off during the journey.

Now Longarm lifted his hat just long enough to watch the conductor disappear through the door at the front of the car, which led out to the open platform between this coach and the rear of the next. *Crazy old coot*, he thought, and then lowered his hatbrim, letting the murmuring drone of the other passengers conversing among themselves send him back into his reverie.

The rocking and swaying of the train on its track reminded him of the rocking and swaying he and Maggie had done up in that loft. They'd had a fine time together, but Longarm had to admit to himself that the best memory he would take from the experience came after their loving was over, and they'd descended back down to the stable floor. Longarm had dressed quickly, and Maggie had dawdled, standing slightly spread-legged, still totally nude, so that her sassy rump and proud breasts were jutting out in all their glory. She'd been standing in front of that stallion's stall. She was so transfixed that she evidently didn't hear the squeak of the rear stable door, or the soft footsteps of the stable boy across the scattered hay.

"Deputy!" the boy had begun. "I've got your gear—*holy cow!*"

Maggie'd given a little scream as she whirled around to stare wide-eyed at the boy, whose own eyes were about the size of saucers. She'd blushed about the color of a strawberry from head to toe, as both Longarm and the boy had ample time to see, as she darted this way and that, gathering up her clothing, and finally dashing into an empty stall to get dressed.

Longarm had kept an eye on the boy. That little fellow had grown up about five years' worth in the time it had taken Maggie to find a place to hide. Longarm had pushed the youngster out of the stable, muttering something about giving a lady time to make herself presentable.

"Yes, sir, I understand," the boy had said, doing his best to keep the top half of his face respectful, even though his mouth had been wearing a shit-eating grin wider than he was tall.

Even now, on the train, the sight in his mind's eye made Longarm chuckle. Most likely that stable boy's interest in horses was about to shift over to another kind of filly!

The door just behind Longarm swung open, and the deputy, out of habit, turned his head to see who was entering the coach. It was another conductor, this one much younger than the other, although his face wore a three-days' growth of glossy black beard. *Now why didn't the old codger know about this fellow?* Longarm wondered.

"Hey, Conductor!" called a man sitting on the aisle two rows up from and opposite Longarm. He was a rough-hewn laborer of some sort, according to the story told by his clothes. He wore a ragged chambray shirt, bib overalls, and a straw hat. The man waved his ticket in the air, saying, "The other conductor didn't punch it."

"No time now," rasped the conductor. "Get the other fellow to do it."

But the man in the straw hat wasn't taking no for an answer. He reached out to grasp the conductor's coattails. "Punch my ticket!" he demanded.

The conductor pulled away, nervously smoothing his jacket. "Shut up afore I punch *you,*" he snarled.

Up ahead, a matronly woman tried to ask, "What time will we—"

"Dunno," the conductor cut her off. "Pretty soon."

Straw Hat, meanwhile, had been looking to his neighbors for sympathy. "Didn't punch my ticket," he moped to Longarm.

"Well, old son, I'd say he's a pretty strange bird to be a railway man."

"Ignorant sumbitch," Straw Hat agreed.

And he's no damned conductor, Longarm thought. The uniform was correct, right down to the man's black shoes, but a uniform was easy enough to fake. It was what was *under* the uniform that gave this man away. Even before the fellow in the straw hat had inadvertently lifted the conductor's coattails to reveal the snout of a protruding weapon, Longarm had spotted the bulk of iron hanging from beneath the fellow's armpit. The conductor's suit jacket had fit him funny, and that was clue enough for a lawman.

Longarm waited until the conductor had disappeared through the front door of the car before quietly sliding out of his seat to follow. Even granted that the railroad had decided to arm their employees, no conductor would dare risk his job by walking around with several days' worth of scruffy beard. The railroad had a separate washroom where employees could shave. Most passengers, of course, did not bother.

28

As Longarm trailed the conductor, hanging back about a car's length so as not to be observed, he pulled out his wallet to remove his badge so that he could pin it to his lapel. Something nasty was about to occur, and since the other fellow was cloaked in the authority of the railroad, Longarm wanted all trigger-happy bystanders to realize that *he* was the law.

He caught up to his quarry in the next car. Standing as solidly as he could in the swaying coach, Longarm called out to the man's back, "Federal Marshal! Stop where you are!" Even as he spoke, Longarm saw the phony conductor—now there was no doubt that the man was bogus; a real conductor would have obeyed the order—unbutton his jacket and begin to spin around.

Dumb bastard is going to draw, Longarm groaned inwardly, even as his Colt found its way into his own hand.

But the conductor did not draw. Instead, in the fraction of the time pulling a handgun would take, he swung up from out of his unbuttoned jacket a sawed-off, double-barreled shotgun, suspended from his right shoulder by some sort of leather loop.

Longarm did not fire, but instead hurled himself face-down in the aisle. He stayed there, praying that the man would not fire his awesome weapon, but instead make a break for it, as all around Longarm, the coach's passengers erupted into screams. They began to rise out of their seats. Exactly the worst thing they could do, Longarm mourned.

Fortunately the phony conductor held off pulling his dual triggers, instead choosing to back-pedal his way down the aisle and out through the end door. Longarm, breathing a sigh of relief, sprang to his feet to continue the pursuit. It had not been concern for his own personal safety that had kept him from shooting that bastard, but rather concern for the safety of the other passengers. A sawed-off shotgun was the evillest weapon on the face of the earth. It was totally unsuited for killing any sort of critter except the human kind. A blast from that shotgun would have killed or maimed half a dozen of the passengers crowded into seats between the conductor and Longarm.

As Longarm raced through the coach door and onto the platform, he saw the man raise his shotgun to fire right through the next coach's door. As the blast thundered, punching through the door's windowpane, so that shards of glass were now added to the cloud of twelve-gauge shot coming his way, Longarm swung out and off the train's platform, so that he was hanging on only by the grip of his left hand's fingers on a grab-iron, and the leverage provided by his boot tips dancing on a greasy bolt overhanging the platform's flooring. He fought to regain the relative safety of the narrow space in between the cars, almost losing his Colt in the process, while all the while the hot, dry New Mexico wind buffeted him.

"One barrel down and one to go," Longarm muttered to himself as he pushed through into the next car, trying to get past the confused, milling passengers blocking the aisle. He could see the blue expanse of the phony conductor's back disappearing through the far door. This was getting serious. It was only a matter of time before his quarry ran into the real conductor, and that old coot was just rambunctious enough to try and *argue* with a double-barreled sawed-off. And there was the little question of the whereabouts of the rest of the outlaw gang. Nobody tried to hold up a train all by his lonesome . . .

As Longarm hurried along, his eyes flicked from right to left, searching the parallel rows of seats, trying to guess which of the passengers was planning on rising up as soon as Longarm had passed, in order to blast his back. But no one did rise up, and Longarm began to understand what had been the phony conductor's plan.

Entering the next car, Longarm saw his adversary waiting for him. The man was braced at the far end, but he was

30

still close enough for his shotgun to do its dirty work, either to Longarm or the people caught in the middle between them.

"Thought so, old son," Longarm called. "Thought you were about out of time to play around with me."

"You—you're the one out of time, Marshal," the outlaw excitedly shouted back. "Throw down yer pistol!"

Between them, one of the passengers began to rise, his movement attracting the snout of the shotgun. "Get back down!" Longarm commanded, and the passenger, looking into the twin stare of the shotgun's barrel, and suddenly thinking better of his initial impulse towards heroics, obeyed.

Time for a bluff, Longarm thought. "See here now, we both got guns in our hands," he began.

"Yeah, but mine's bigger than yours," the phony conductor leered. "You shoot me, Marshal, and this here scattergun of mine is gonna take a lot of these citizens with me."

So much for bluffing. "Throw it down or I'll shoot you where you stand!" Longarm growled. At that moment the door behind the outlaw began to open.

Feeling the wind on his neck, the man with the shotgun began to turn, but then paused in mid-movement, stuck in between the two distractions the way a mule can get paralyzed between equidistant piles of hay. The outlaw's head swiveled desperately from Longarm to whatever was coming in behind him, and in the couple of seconds it took for all of this to go on, two more things happened: there was a sharp report, the sound like that of a dry twig being snapped in two, and the outlaw slapped at the back of his neck, as if he'd been beestung. The squat shotgun rose up a few inches—

—and a few inches were all Longarm needed. In one movement he swung up his .44 and fired, the round taking

31

the outlaw just above the ear, lifting the top of his head beneath its cap in a spray of red mist as the car erupted into shouts and screams.

The outlaw tottered on his feet, the shotgun slipping from his grasp to swing like a pendulum from its shoulder loop. Then he fell to the floor, revealing behind him the tiny form of the real conductor. The old codger was dancing in place like a randy rooster. Gripped in his right hand was a small pistol.

"We got him, Deputy! We surely did!" he crowed as Longarm walked up the aisle, ignoring the panicked queries of the passengers.

"That we did, friend," Longarm calmly agreed. He reached out for the conductor's weapon, and then examined it. It was a diminutive .25-caliber Smith & Wesson revolver. It had tape holding its grips to its butt, and deep nicks and scratches along the cylinder and barrel. It looked as if it had hammered more nails than bullets.

"Bought me that there belly-gun in a pawnshop," the conductor winked. "Did it when they transferred me to this here New Mexico-Texas run. Outlaws, boy! I knew there'd be outlaws, and I was right! Shot this one dead, I did!"

Longarm decided not to spoil the old man's fun by reminding him that the outlaw most likely could have picked that little bitty .25 slug out of his neck like it was a thorn, and that it was the man-sized piece of lead from his own .44 that had settled the train robber's hash. "You see any other suspicious-looking passengers along the way you came, Conductor?"

"Not a soul, Deputy." He removed his cap to scratch at the gray wisps of hair plastered across his bald dome. "That's a good point, though. Did this hombre expect to hold up my train all by hisself?"

"Not hardly," Longarm muttered. "Reckon he was aiming to use his conductor's suit to bluster his way into the locomotive crew's area. Then, once his gang started riding alongside the engine, he'd force the crew to stop the train. Don't imagine most men would say no to that shotgun of his."

"You mean we're going to be ambushed?" the conductor asked as Longarm handed back his little gun.

"Let's get this fellow out of sight of the ladies," Longarm suggested. "Then you and I will talk."

Two male passengers volunteered their services, and the corpse was hoisted up. As Longarm held open the coach door, the conductor said, "Throw him off the side, boys!"

"No!" Longarm said. "We'll put him in the baggage car, and leave him at the remount station in Grassy Bow. I figure that's the closest thing there is to authority in this part of New Mexico Territory."

"Damn, I forgot!" the conductor said. "The reward! You reckon there is one, Deputy?"

"If there is, it's all yours," Longarm said. "Federal lawmen ain't allowed to accept rewards."

In the baggage car, Longarm thanked the two men who'd helped, and waited until they'd left before asking the conductor to help him strip the suit jacket off the dead man's body. He explained that since the outlaw had been making his move when he died, the rest of the gang could not be far away.

As Longarm stripped off his own frock coat and replaced it with the regulation blue suit jacket, the old conductor beamed. "I get it! You're planning on taking this hombre's place!"

Longarm nodded. "It's getting dark. If we don't nab these fellows, they'll just try this stunt again. I'm hoping that being all nervous about the holdup, the gang will see what they're expecting to see. In the dark, with this man's outfit on, I ought to be able to fool them long enough to get the drop on them."

"What do you want me to do?" the conductor asked.

"Lend me your cap. The one this poor soul was wearing

is a mite messy." He reached into the pocket of his folded frock coat and came out with a fresh cartridge to replace the one he'd fired. "And make sure you keep the passengers from lending a hand. Should shooting start, my two advantages will be the darkness and the fact that everything in front of me is fair game."

Patting the suit jacket's pocket, Longarm found spare shells for the shotgun. He loaded the spent barrel of the weapon, pulled off its rawhide shoulder loop, and headed for the locomotive. His badge was back in its usual place, pinned inside the fold of his wallet, which itself was tucked into his hip pocket. Not that he seriously expected that he'd have to show it. The gang would either give up when he said he was a lawman, or they'd start shooting. No, the only men who might want a look at his symbol of authority were the locomotive crew.

He spent a nervous quarter of an hour with them, the noise of the engine precluding any attempt at conversation as the four pairs of eyes—Longarm's, the engineer's, the brakeman's, and the stoker's—scanned the rapidly darkening, rugged terrain. It was Longarm who spotted the three horsemen atop a low, mesquite-studded butte, their forms silhouetted against the last glimmer of a sun that had long since dropped below the horizon.

The horsemen seemed only to be watching the progress of the train. Longarm wondered fleetingly if he was supposed to send them some signal that he was in control, perhaps a series of toots from the locomotive's whistle. Well, better no signal than the *wrong* one; that way, the gang might just figure their man on board had forgotten.

"Brakeman! Now!" Longarm commanded. The crewman pulled his levers, and the world around them erupted into sparks and one long, banshee-like scream as locked metal wheels filed shavings off the tracks. Its boiler-head bleeding steam, the big locomotive's pistons slowed until they were barely moving. The train jolted several times, then came to a stop.

Longarm watched the three riders spur their horses down the treacherous incline of the butte. As they reached the level prairie they broke into a full gallop toward the stalled train.

One of the riders was leading a saddled horse, obviously the mount that their confederate aboard the train was to use for his getaway. This rider came toward the locomotive, while the other two rode toward the baggage and mail car in the center of the train. Longarm realized he had to take out this first outlaw, then get the other two before they discovered their comrade's corpse—or else the jig would be up. Fortunately the baggage car was unattended, so no unarmed clerk would have to absorb the outlaws' wrath.

"Get your hands up!" Longarm hissed to the crew as the rider reined up beside the locomotive.

"How'd it go, Walt?" the rider asked, his own gun out.

"Fine," Longarm said, doing his best to approximate the raspy voice of the late Walt. He had his conductor's hat pulled low, and tried to keep to the shadows of the engine's interior.

The rider dismounted and reached up with his free hand for his comrade to give him some help in climbing up onto the locomotive's platform. Longarm reached out a hand and helped pull the outlaw up, at the same time slamming the butt of his shotgun into the man's face. Knocked cold, the outlaw fell back to sprawl motionless in the dust. Longarm jumped down to retrieve the fallen man's gun. It was a big old Colt Dragoon rechambered to take brass cartridges. Tossing the hogleg to the first pair of hands that appeared over the side of the engine, Longarm whispered, "Watch him, and if he comes to, keep him quiet, but don't kill him. He's unarmed."

That done, Longarm began to run in a low crouch along

35

the length of the train, toward the baggage car. The old conductor was doing his job well, maybe too well. The passengers were acting as unconcerned as if this were a scheduled stop. With any luck it would all be over before the remaining pair realized something was fishy.

Longarm heard the squeak of the baggage car's side door sliding open. He ran faster. He *had* to get the drop on them before the two found that body. As he ran, he snapped back both hammers of the stubby shotgun.

The rider who was still mounted twisted in his saddle, bringing his handgun around to point in Longarm's direction. Longarm quickly straightened up, holding his shotgun to port, relying on his outline in the darkness to fool the outlaw.

The outlaw lowered his pistol. "I told you to stay up front," he shouted angrily. "And you screwed up on the whistle signal we'd agreed on. What's wrong with you, Walt?" he demanded.

The other outlaw appeared in the baggage car's open side door, his own gun in his hand. "Walt's in here dead!" he cried.

Longarm muttered a curse under his breath. It was too late to give these fellows fair warning, as he was expected to do. He just pointed the shotgun toward the car's open doorway and let fly with both barrels, blasting the outlaw back into the darkness of the car's interior.

"What the hell?" the mounted gang member swore as he shot fast three times, his gun erupting flame, his three slugs kicking up dirt where Longarm had been standing. Dropping the empty shotgun, Longarm had crabbed sideways, drawing his Colt as he did so. As the mounted man tried to get a bead on him, Longarm fired twice. The outlaw fell backward out of the saddle as his horse bucked in fear. He landed heavily on the ground and lay still.

Longarm checked him. Both of his rounds had taken the

36

man in the chest. He was dead. Boosting himself into the baggage car, Longarm struck a match to check on the other one. The shotgun hadn't left much to check. Longarm flicked out the match and jumped to the ground to get away from the grisly remains, and to get a breath of fresh air. He felt a little weak-kneed now that it was over—

A deep boom came from the front of the train. Longarm had heard that boom a lot fifteen years ago, during the War. It was the sound made by an older-model sidearm—like a Colt Dragoon, for instance.

Longarm repeated his run in reverse, going toward the engine. When he got there he saw, by the flickering light of a lantern, the brakeman holding the outlaw's smoking Dragoon in both of his trembling, white-knuckled hands. His face was pale and a trifle green around the edges.

"I had to, Marshal!" the young man wailed. "When he came to, I told him to lay still, like you said, but he just laughed at me. He got to his feet and went for that rifle there on his saddle!"

The other crew members nodded in agreement, and Longarm glanced at the body stretched out on the ground, a hole a half-inch across in the center of the man's back. The outlaw's horse was just a few steps away; obviously it had shied at the sound of the shot. As if in mute testimony to the brakeman's story, the outlaw's saddle gun, an old Henry repeater, was hanging half out of its boot.

"You ain't gonna arrest me, are you, Marshal?" the brakeman asked fearfully. "I didn't want to shoot—"

"Quiet now," Longarm soothed as he holstered his Colt. "You had no choice, old son. You surely did the right thing."

The brakeman looked down at his hands, and as if surprised that he still held the revolver, he quickly tossed it to the ground. "I never killed anyone or anything before, Marshal. I was too young for the War, and—" He clamped both hands over his mouth and scrambled down from the locomotive platform. Falling to his knees, he vomited in the dust.

A crowd of passengers, led by the conductor, had gathered around the scene. "Anybody have a flask or bottle on them?" Longarm called. "This boy could surely use a drink."

One of the men approached the sobbing brakeman. From his hip pocket he pulled a silver flask. "Drink up, boy," he ordered softly. "No sense carrying on like *you* was the dead one."

"Well, it all happened like you said it would," the conductor told Longarm. "How'd you figure it so neatly? This sorta thing old hat to you?"

Longarm laughed. He patted the pockets of his coat for a cheroot, realized he was still wearing the phony conductor's garb, and stripped the garment off, letting it fall to the ground.

"Like I told you before," he began, "it wasn't likely that the fellow with the shotgun was going to try and keep watch over the crew for too long." He pulled the stub of a cheroot out of his vest pocket and fired it up. "And they had to make their move this side of the New Mexico-Texas border. New Mexico being only a territory, there's no real law to chase after them."

"Except for that army remount station at Grassy Bow," the conductor pointed out.

"Right, but that meant they had to make their move now, before we reached that station. We're still an hour or so away. Robbing a train in the army's backyard would've just about guaranteed them a cavalry troop riding up their asses."

The old conductor cackled with laughter. "Sure as hell wasn't their lucky day when *you* boarded, Deputy—what is your name, son?"

"Custis Long. Folks call me Longarm. See here, Conductor. You got your train back now. See that these bodies and horses are loaded up. We've got to drop 'em off at the remount station."

"Yessir!" Chuckling to himself, the spry old conductor snatched up the lantern and began waving it in the air as he walked the length of the train, calling out, "All aboard! Let's go, folks! We're behind schedule! All aboard!"

Longarm was the first to obey the conductor's command.

★

Chapter 3

That night, while Longarm slept, his train crossed the border into Texas. It paralleled the Rio Grande for some forty-odd miles before veering east to cross the Pecos River and then slice through the baked brown crust of the Llano Estacado, the Staked Plains.

A few hours after dawn, the train began its descent into the north-central plains, crossing the Colorado River. The mesquite, yucca, and their brother cacti gave way to buffalo grass and little bluestem. The buttes turned into hills, and then even softer hills, and then woodlots of pecan, walnut, and hickory, lorded over by massive oaks. And carpeting the thickly grassed prairie everywhere was a dusting of wildflowers—bluebonnet, just now giving way in early summer to asters, daisies, and goldenrod.

But most important, as the train made its way from the Staked Plains to the north-central prairie region, the mountain sheep and mule deer, the jaguarundi and bobcat, gave way to cattle. Magnificent herds of steers basked in the warm sunshine of the Lone Star State—the cow nursery of the world.

Longarm had spent time in many cow towns in his day, but none had prepared him for Alex Starbuck's cow town of

Sarah. Once the train had pulled into the station, he'd led the chestnut gelding he'd borrowed from the army remount station to a quiet place alongside the now-empty cattle pens and loading ramps. His gear—saddle and bridle, saddlebags and bedroll—had been carried for him by a pair of boys, just two of the multitude of young scamps who made pocket change by transporting baggage from station to hotel. The only thing Longarm carried was his Winchester. He didn't believe in letting others handle his firearms if he could help it.

Last night, for example, the old conductor had offered to clean Longarm's Colt for him. Longarm had politely thanked the man, but informed him that that was the sort of job he always did himself. As he'd tended to his weapon, using kerosene, a small brush, a soft rag, and then sperm oil for lubrication, all of which Longarm carried in a kit in his saddlebags, he'd had to suffer the curious looks of just about every passenger on the train, every one of whom just sort of happened to stroll by his seat. Never for the life of him could Longarm figure out the fascination of his fellow man for those who had the misfortune of having to kill others. Blessedly, things quieted down once they'd left Grassy Bow. Longarm had filled out a few forms for the army detailing the events that had led up to the triple shooting, sympathized with the old conductor when it was learned that there was no reward for this particular gang, and arranged to borrow his mount.

His gelding was a good one. A veteran of several shooting campaigns, the animal was not in the least fazed by the tumult of the station. Once his horse was saddled, his bags in place, and his Winchester tucked into its boot, Longarm rode the short distance to Sarah's main street.

Longarm liked to get the lay of a good-sized town, which Sarah was, before he began an investigation. Sarah's wide, regularly sprinkled Main Street had several general stores, a bakery, two gunsmiths, a bank, a telegraph office, and—

obviously the showplace of the town—a magnificent, brightly painted, three-story mansion. Above the wide, golden-oak double doors, there hung a sign painted in gilt script that read: SARAH TOWNSHIP CATTLEMEN'S ASSOCIATION.

As Longarm walked his horse along the avenue, he saw raised wooden sidewalks on bóth sides of the street. Clustered together were several saloons and cafes, and next door to them, as if keeping watch like a stern parent, was a combination jail and office labeled TOWN MARSHAL. On the saloon side of Main Street, the buildings were more ramshackle, and were mostly devoted to the day-to-day business of tending to cowboys and their mounts. A few blocks down along this side of town, the railway holding pens and ramps began. Nearby he saw canvas tents being erected by workmen.

Walking his mount around to the residential neighborhood behind the Cattlemen's building, Longarm explored rows of brightly painted clapboard houses, each with a picket fence, and many with gardens, and trees planted in horse-trough-sized planters. Here there were two schools— a primary and a secondary one—and a fine church. The golden bell in its tall steeple gleamed against the deep blue, cloud-studded sky.

Longarm rode up to the one hotel in town, around the corner from Main Street, and tied his horse to a hitch rail in front. Inside, he inquired about a room. The clerk, dressed in a blue velvet suit, despite the eighty-degree heat, was polite but adamant.

"We can lodge you just for tonight, Mr."—the clerk spun the register around to read Longarm's scrawl—"Mr. Long. Beginning tomorrow, we're completely booked up. Lots of folk from the East are arriving for the round-up, you see."

Longarm nodded, sighing. "I didn't notice another hotel. I don't suppose there are any?"

"I'm afraid not," the clerk sniffed. "You might try Canvas Town—"

"Where?" Long asked.

"Oh, that's our area out by the railway spur. Every roundup, tents are set up to house and entertain the hands who sign up temporarily at the various cattle outfits hereabouts. Check at the Cattlemen's Association. You'll find bulletin boards there that carry announcements concerning who's hiring and who is not." The clerk's brow furrowed beneath the slicked-back thatch of his hair. "You are in town to work as a hand, I presume?"

"Exactly right." Longarm nodded, thinking that this clerk was indeed an imbecile to imagine that a man dressed the way he was even faintly resembled a working cowboy. "You certainly are a fine judge of character," he added.

"Thank you," the clerk replied, beaming. "It comes with the job."

"I know what you mean. Say, I've got a horse out front. Can you recommend a good stable?"

"Oh, we have our own stable," the clerk said. "For an extra charge, we'll care for your horse."

"Good enough," Longarm said.

"But you must be out by noon," the clerk reminded him.

"Actually, I'll be out very early in the morning," Longarm told him. "Why don't I pay now?"

"That'll be three-fifty, including the stable charge," the clerk replied, and in answer to Longarm's wince of surprise, he added, "Tomorrow it goes up to five dollars." He said it like a boast. "Do you have any luggage?"

"Just my saddlebags," Longarm said. "Send a boy around for my horse, would you?"

"Right away," the clerk said. "Here's your key."

Longarm took it and went outside to fetch his bags and rifle. The clerk eyed the Winchester as Longarm reentered the hotel, but said nothing.

After stashing his property in his room, Longarm went back downstairs and out to visit the town marshal's office. It was fast becoming early evening, but Longarm wanted to gather whatever information he could, so as to be able to start out bright and early the next day.

He had to cool his heels awhile outside the marshal's office. Several deputies were receiving some instructions before beginning their rounds of the town. Longarm knew he had to reveal his identity as deputy U.S. marshal to Sarah's chief law officer, but he'd prefer that the several deputies not know who he really was. There was most likely a small newspaper office stashed away somewhere in Sarah. A loose-lipped local deputy would be all it would take for the news of Longarm's arrival to make town headlines. After that it would only be a matter of time before word got back to those officials in the Nation's Capital who were in charge of the case.

Once the deputies had left, Longarm entered the marshal's office. The marshal, a big-bellied man—what was it about desks and bellies that seemed to go hand in hand?— had his head down and his eyes fixed on a report written on yellow paper.

"Be with you in a minute," he grumbled, his voice a Texas version of Billy Vail's.

Longarm used the time to look around the office. A door to the rear, just behind the marshal's desk, led to the cells. Along one wall was a rack of rifles and shotguns, all securely locked in place by a length of chain threaded through their trigger guards. On the opposite wall hung a motley assortment of wanted flyers, from the federal government and neighboring states, as well as from private organizations like the Pinkertons. Several straight-backed chairs stood scattered about, but Longarm, who had done more than his share of sitting during the trip, preferred to stand. As the marshal tended to his desk work, Longarm read over the duty roster that told which deputies were supposed to be on patrol, and where.

"What can I do for you?" the marshal finally asked.

When Longarm turned to face him, he saw with some satisfaction that the town marshal was staring at him with narrowed eyes. Unlike the hotel clerk, the lawman probably knew how to judge a man.

"My name's Custis Long, and I'm a deputy U.S. marshal, working out of Denver," Longarm explained, pulling out his wallet and flipping it open to show his badge.

"My name's Farley. Pleased to meet you, Deputy," the town marshal said, standing up to shake hands. "Guess I know why you're here," he said shrewdly. "Though I'd thought the army was going to handle this."

"Well, sir, I was passing through the region, and got sidetracked to take a look-see around," Longarm fibbed. "Incidentally, I'd appreciate it if you kept my job to yourself. I can work easier that way."

Farley nodded. "Whatever you say. Grab a chair and tell me what I can do to help."

"First off, I'd like to know the results of your investigation of Starbuck's murder," Longarm said, turning a chair around and straddling it horse-style, folding his arms on top of the back rest. "If you've got any reports I could borrow to read—"

Farley cut him off gruffly. "No reports."

"Why not?" Longarm asked, surprised.

"Damn it, you're federal, Long, so you ought to know that my jurisdiction ends at the town limits. The shooting took place on Starbuck's spread. That makes it a job for the Rangers."

"I understand, Marshal," Longarm said quietly, as Vail's words echoed in his mind. *This case is too big for any local law* ... Any law officer who stuck his neck out by getting involved in something as serious as the Starbuck assassination risked having his head cut off for incompetence if

46

he failed to find the culprits. It made perfect sense that Farley was less than anxious to involve himself with a hot-potato case like this one.

"Don't get me wrong, Marshal," Longarm continued, "but the Rangers—and they're good boys—are better suited for stomping a range war or shooting it up man-to-man with a bunch of cow thieves. Investigations ain't their meat."

"My jurisdiction ends at the town limits," Farley repeated stubbornly.

"Yes, sir," Longarm said wearily. "How do I get to where it happened?"

"That's easy," Farley said, obviously relieved. "Just take Main Street out of town past the Cattlemen's building. It becomes a trail that cuts across a creek a few times. That's Goat Creek. It, along with Goat Lake, is fed by an underground spring hereabouts. Anyway, you just follow that trail for about two hours. You'll see a number of cutoffs that lead to various spreads, but stay on the main trail. Eventually you'll hit a granite outcropping, and alongside it a wooded rise. You're on Starbuck property at that point, and you're also where it happened. Mr. Starbuck was riding past that outcropping when they all fired down on him."

"You really believe fifteen men shot him up, Marshal?" Longarm asked skeptically.

"See for yourself, Deputy," Farley muttered. "Everybody else in Sarah has. Place has become a regular sightseeing spot. Reckon they'll run tours out to it once the Easterners start arriving tomorrow," he added in disgust.

"You haven't answered my question," Longarm persisted. "What's your opinion? From one lawman to another."

Farley shrugged. "Starbuck lived big his whole life. It makes some kind of sense to me he would *die* big as well." The marshal shrugged. "Hell, Long, hand me a guitar and maybe I'll write a ballad about it," he chuckled.

"Sarah's a strange name for a Texas cow town," Longarm said, to change the subject.

"That was the name of Starbuck's wife. She died long ago, over in Europe it was. Alex Starbuck built this town. Figure he had the right to name it what he wanted." Farley tugged a pocket watch out of his pants and glanced at it. "I'm due somewhere, Deputy. Anything else I can help you with?"

"Just one thing," Longarm said, getting to his feet. "Point me toward a place to fill my belly."

"Best grub in town is at Leda's," Farley smiled. "Two doors down from the Union Saloon," He rose. "I'll walk you down since I'm going that way."

"Thanks just the same, Marshal," Longarm said. "But I'd just as soon not attract attention by being seen with you."

"I get it," Farley replied with a wink. "Go on, then. Don't worry. My lips are sealed."

Longarm thanked him and left the office, strolling down the block past the Union Saloon, to a small cafe with LEDA'S painted across the window. Inside, he had a decent, uneventful meal of steak and eggs, despite the fact that beef was the most expensive thing on the menu. It made Longarm smile. No cattleman liked the taste of his own beef—not when that very slab, shipped on the hoof to the East, could put dollars in his pocket.

After dinner, Longarm stopped at one of the saloons and bought a bottle of Maryland rye, which he took with him back to the hotel. Once in his room, he undressed, and after scattering a few balled-up sheets of the hotel's stationery between his double-locked door and his bed, to give him some advance warning should an unannounced visitor try to enter, he stretched out upon the crisp, fresh sheets of the fine four-poster, and took a few sips off the top of his bottle.

Five minutes later, Longarm was sound asleep. Maryland rye was not as sweet as a mother's lullaby, but for Longarm it worked just as fine.

★

Chapter 4

Dawn's first flush broke pink, as radiant as a pleased woman's blush, before that rosy glow bled down into the pearly gray that marked the real start of the day. Longarm walked silently down the stairs, so as not to disturb the other guests. The hotel seemed to rise and fall with the rhythmic breathing of so many sleeping people.

His saddlebags over his shoulder, and his Winchester in the crook of his arm, Longarm stopped off at the desk to hand his key to the weary night clerk who was about to go off duty. Then he left the lobby and walked around the side of the hotel to the stables.

The young kid who was supposed to keep watch over the mounts was sleeping curled up on a bale of hay. That was fine with Longarm. He'd rather saddle his own horse anyway. Saddling your own horse was like buying somebody a drink: it broke the ice between two old boys who wanted to be friends.

The stable boy stirred in his sleep behind Longarm as the tall deputy finished fitting his Mexican bridle into place over his gelding's nose. As Longarm tied his saddlebags to the brass fittings of his saddle and slid his Winchester into its boot, the boy woke up.

"Sorry, mister," the kid yawned, rubbing his eyes. "I was supposed to do that for you."

"No problem." Longarm handed him a nickel just so the kid wouldn't feel bad, and began to lead his mount out past the stable doors.

"If you wait a bit, mister, there's coffee," the boy called after him. "The pot's all ready to go on the stove. I've just got to start the fire."

"No thanks, I'm in a hurry," Longarm replied. A hot mug of black coffee would have been just the thing to wash out of his bones the last syrupy remnants of sleep, but Longarm was concerned over Farley's remark that the site of Starbuck's shooting had become a tourist attraction. If that was true, Longarm wanted to get there nice and early, so he'd have an hour or so to poke about the site undisturbed.

Longarm kept his gelding to an easy trot during the ride out. It was going to be a warm, sunny day, and since Longarm had no idea where he and the horse were going to spend that evening—except that he knew for sure that Canvas Town was out of the question—he did not want the horse exhausting itself. He didn't mind the possibility of camping out for the night, and in fact he sort of relished the idea. He had dried beef, flour, coffee, and salt, to go with a compact little cook set in one side of his saddlebags, and he had his bottle of Maryland rye. There was plenty of water from old Goat Creek available for both him and his mount, and he figured the gelding could make it through the night without starving by grazing on the fine grass that covered the prairie in a thick carpet.

During the couple of hours it took to reach the site, passing the cutoffs Farley had warned him about, and splashing through the creek as it cut across the trail, Longarm actually began to look forward to a night under the stars. The groundcloth wrapped about his bedroll was all the shelter he'd need for the coming warm, rainless night.

The ground all around the granite outcropping had been

stamped down by the hooves of countless horses and the iron rims of buckboard and wagon wheels. Farley had been right. The place looked as if everybody in Sarah had taken a ride out to the spot where Alex Starbuck had met his end.

Longarm dismounted, merely dropping his horse's reins to the ground. The army mount had been trained to stay in place when its reins trailed.

"Well, fellow," he told the horse, "maybe this ride out was a waste of time after all." Longarm stood with his hands on his hips and shook his head. The place was as dirty as a street gutter back in Denver.

Cigar butts and chewed-up, dried-out plugs of tobacco littered the ground around the boulders, while candy wrappers had been jammed into the crevices and fissures veining the rocks. Over on a flat surface of granite, some cowpoke had chiseled an endearment to his sweetheart.

But there was one piece of evidence that no amount of gruesome touristing could erase or deface. Longarm ran his fingers across the wide swath of nicks and scratches gouged out of the boulders by the hail of bullets that had ended Starbuck's life. From their number, it did seem that the assassination had been the work of a small army of bushwhackers. By studying the angle of the scratches, he tried to determine the direction from which the deadly fusillade had come. He tilted his hat to one side and laid his cheek against a boulder, sighting along one especially deep gouge.

He found himself looking at a high, wooded rise a little distance from the outcropping. He straightened up and squared his hat on his head, pondering. There was no sense in looking for rounds that might have ricocheted off the rocks. Any such bits of lead would long since have been taken as souvenirs by the local folk. But it would be a long, hard, sweaty climb to the top of that hill. Longarm couldn't be sure, but he'd lay fair odds that no sightseers had troubled to haul their asses up that slope on the off-chance of finding a few cartridge cases. Farley and his deputies might have

51

thought of doing that, if they'd bothered to ride out and take a look around, but they hadn't.

As the first lawman to poke around the scene, Longarm figured he had a good chance of finding a slug casing—or a bunch of them, assuming that a number of men had participated in the ambush. Of course, there was always the chance that the murderers had cleaned up after themselves, but remembering to do something like that took cool logic, and such things usually fled a fellow's mind after he'd murdered a man.

Yep, it was time to climb, Longarm decided grimly. "Don't go running off to do anything interesting without me," he told the gelding as he untied the flap of his saddlebag, extracting a pair of leather gloves to protect his hands during the climb. The gelding tossed its head and then lowered it to resume its stoic stance, as if Longarm's unneeded admonition had hurt its feelings.

It took Longarm a half hour to reach the top of the rise. He'd left his frock coat down below, but he'd nevertheless soaked through his shirt and vest as he threaded his way through clumps of post-oak and blackjack, and scrambled on all fours over wide belts of crumbly sandstone and slick marble. Finally he reached the top, which was a surprisingly pleasant area, thick with soil and studded with dense groves of hickory. There was brush everywhere and—thankfully— a cool gurgle of pure water slithering out from between two boulders, so that Longarm could slake his thirst and douse his sweaty head.

Refreshed, Longarm began his search for those shell casings. He sighted down at the granite outcropping, using his own gelding to give him some perspective. It was just about a hundred yards to where Starbuck would have been, certainly an easy enough shot for a band of men armed with rifles. Longarm was surprised that so many of the rounds they'd fired had gone off target...

He kept his eyes fixed on the ground as he ambled from one side of the likely ambush area to the other. Grasshoppers fiddled away, playing their sleep-inducing song, and from somewhere in the trees a mockingbird lived up to its name, its callous laugh seeming to suggest that anyone who would bother to come up here without the help of a set of wings was a damned fool...

And then Longarm found the shell casings. Except that what he found was just plain, damned crazy.

There, within a two-foot radius, were some thirty shell casings, almost as if they'd been piled up, neat as you please! Longarm bent to pick one up. He examined it, and then another, and a third. All were small caliber, .25's, and all had—

Longarm was startled by the dull, thudding rush of a pair of warblers taking off from a stand of brush. He turned his attention back to the cartridge casings as some small part of his mind registered the fact that the grasshoppers had suddenly grown quiet...

He threw himself to the ground as the report of a handgun echoed. The round ricocheted off a rock, which would have been spared its wound by Longarm's head if he'd been a fraction of a second slower in reading the warning given him by the birds and bugs.

The rocks had distorted the sound of that gun, so that Longarm didn't know where his attacker was firing from. He hauled himself to his feet, his Colt in his hand, but still feeling as naked as a newborn babe, standing out in the open, with his ambusher hidden from view.

Another shot thwacked into the rock just behind Longarm, flecks of granite stinging his cheek. Then, out of the corner of his eye, to his left, he saw movement: a man's hatless figure dashing from one stand of trees to the next.

Longarm snapped off a shot in the fellow's direction, not really expecting to hit anything, but simply to let his adversary know he was mad. He began to move in that direction, thinking that as fast as that man had been, he had gotten a good look at him. The man had not been holding or wearing a gun—

Damn decoy, and I've fallen for it, Longarm chided himself, even as he heard the noise and twisted his head to his right, in time to see a blue-denim-clad blur streaking toward him. Before Longarm could bring his gun around, the blur rammed into the backs of his knees, sweeping his feet out from under him. Longarm fell hard. His Colt went clattering off somewhere.

He was flat on his back when the blue-denim man sat squarely on his stomach. Longarm bucked him off, but not before realizing that the fellow he was bucking was a *her*—he'd had enough womanly bottoms straddling his belly to know another when he felt it.

"Just hold on," Longarm managed to shout as he rose to his feet, but not before the *other* one, the hatless, gunless man, came at him. Longarm brought up his fists to meet the attacker, but was totally unprepared for what happened next. The fellow jumped about five feet off the ground to snap out a barefooted kick at Longarm's head!

Whip-fast as Longarm's reflexes were, the kick still grazed the side of his skull. He fell back, dazed, but awake enough to jam his boots into the other fellow's rock-hard stomach as the man dove toward him. Longarm kept his knees locked as he jackknifed his legs, sending the man sailing past. He was pleased with this old-as-the-Virginia-hills "wrassling" move, but disappointed at the way his attacker managed to land as lightly as a robin on the soles of his feet. The girl, meanwhile, was crawling rapidly on all fours toward the revolver that had fallen out of her holster.

These two might just manage to kill him, Longarm realized, before he even got a chance to arrest them. He reached into his vest pocket and came out with his brass-plated, double-barreled, .44 derringer. He thumbed back the hammer of the little gun, the metallic click freezing both of his attackers.

"Just hold it, you two," Longarm muttered as he scooted around on his butt to lean back against a rock, in that way managing to get his wind back while keeping them both within his field of fire.

"Do you plan to murder me the way you did my father?" the girl spat.

"Jessica Starbuck," Longarm said, smiling. "Pleased to meet you." And he was. Lord, she was lovely! She'd straightened up to stand with her hands on her hips. Her angry green eyes flashed daggers Longarm's way. Her hat had fallen off during the struggle, to reveal a tawny mane of honey-blond hair, glinting with a hint of copper beneath the strong Texas sun. She was in her twenties. She was long-legged and had high, full breasts, a slender waist accented by the gunbelt she wore, and a firm, pleasantly rounded bottom. None of her figure was in the least hidden by her tight denim jeans and wrangler's jacket. The clothes fit her like a second skin. "Miss Starbuck, you've got things a mite backward," Longarm continued. "I'm not one of your father's murderers. I'm the law."

"The hell you are!" she snarled.

"Easy, Jessie," soothed the fellow with her. "There is time. We will listen to what he has to say."

Longarm glanced the man's way. He'd been standing so rock-still that Longarm had almost forgotten he was there. *Probably what he wanted me to do,* Longarm scolded himself. "My name is Custis Long. I'm a deputy U.S. marshal, working out of Denver. I've been assigned to investigate your father's death, ma'am."

"How do I know that?" Jessica asked skeptically. "I don't see your badge."

55

"Damn," Longarm swore. "My damned badge is in my damned wallet, which is in my damned coat, which is down with my damned horse."

"What were you doing up here?" she demanded.

"Just one minute, ma'am," Longarm said, his temper rising. "I'm the one holding the damned gun, so I'll ask the damned questions." He cooled down as he saw a glint of laughter in the girl's eyes, and before he knew it he found himself grinning back at her. "Sorry to lose my temper, but I tend not to take kindly to being ambushed."

"What do you think, Ki?" Jessica asked her companion.

The man shrugged. "He has the gun, what need would he have to lie? He could have killed us by now, if that was his purpose."

"Thank you, Ki," Longarm laughed, getting to his feet. "Strange name, but then you're sort of a strange fellow, ain't you?" Longarm trailed off, examining the man. He was around thirty, and tall; about six foot two, Longarm estimated. The man had brown eyes and thick, straight, blue-black hair, worn longish just past the tops of his ears. He was dressed in well-broken-in, well-fitting denim jeans, a blousy, pullover collarless shirt of cotton twill, and a loose, many-pocketed leather vest. Longarm peered at his face. It was a white man's face, except for the eyes, which were almond shaped. *He's half Oriental,* Longarm told himself. He looked down at the man's feet. "You don't seem to be in the habit of wearing shoes or boots, Ki," he remarked.

"My feet are quite tough," the man said in a calm voice.

"I know they're tough, old son," Longarm said. "And you ought to *know* that I know. You seem to disremember the fact that you were scraping one up alongside my skull a few minutes ago."

This time Jessica Starbuck laughed out loud, the sound rich and throaty. "Oh, I hope he really *is* a marshal, Ki,"

56

she drawled. "I hope he really hasn't anything to do with my father's death. It'd be a shame to have to kill him."

"I guess that's a compliment," Longarm acknowledged dryly. "Now that we're all being friendly, I think I'll put my little pacifier away." He uncocked the derringer and slipped it back into his vest pocket. "Now what say you pick up your gun, and holster it, Miss Starbuck. I'll do the same with mine, and Ki here can keep his damned feet on the ground where they belong."

"Folks hereabouts call me Jessie," she said as she bent to retrieve her gun. "Friends do, anyway." She eyed Longarm speculatively.

"Folks tend to call me Longarm," he said. "And I reckon we three best be friends if we're going to get to the bottom of who it was murdered your daddy."

★

Chapter 5

"Just what were you two doing up here?" Longarm asked again, once he and Jessica Starbuck had gathered up their revolvers under the watchful eyes of Ki, and had walked a short distance to sit under the shade of a hardwood tree.

"Marshal Farley rode out late last night to let me know that a fellow had stopped by his office to ask about what was known concerning my father's murder," she began.

"I told him I was a federal deputy," Longarm said, frowning. "And I showed him my badge."

"He mentioned that, of course," Ki interrupted. "But it is nothing to say one represents the law, and badges can be easily forged. We wished to watch your actions. A man's actions, when he thinks he is alone, are much more revealing than his words or credentials."

"I trust my actions have convinced you," Longarm said. "I've been assigned to this case sort of on the sly. It won't help me find Alex Starbuck's killers if everybody in Sarah knows a federal lawman is on the job."

"You mustn't blame Marshal Farley, Longarm," Jessica said. "He was a good friend of my father's. And telling *us* who you are doesn't mean everyone in Sarah will know. Your real identity is safe with us." As she spoke, she

59

shrugged off her denim jacket. "Today's going to be a hot one..."

Longarm tried not to stare. She was wearing a pearl-colored, thin silk blouse, with nothing at all on underneath it. Her nipples were tantalizingly visible through the sheer material.

Making an effort to maintain his composure, he said, "Yes, ma'am, it seems as though it's going to be hot indeed." He longed for his frock coat, and for the sun to be directly overhead, signaling noon. That way he could banish the randy thoughts he was having by tucking a cheroot between his lips.

As if she could read Longarm's mind, Jessie pulled her revolver out of its holster, but only to extract the spent shells. Longarm peered at the handgun with surprise, which Jessica evidently noticed. She handed him the weapon, saying, "My father taught me how to shoot. He used a double-action .44, the Colt Model T. Just like yours, unless I miss my guess."

"I'm impressed," Longarm admitted. "Not many females know their way around either firearms or horseflesh."

"I'm a special sort of female, a Starbuck," Jessie explained. Her bewitching green eyes sparkled, but there was also something straight-on, no-nonsense serious about the way she said it. "Anyway, the .44's recoil was just a hair too strong for my hand. During one of his business trips back East, my father visited the Colt factory in Connecticut. He commissioned that weapon as a gift for my eighteenth birthday. It's bored and chambered for .38 shells, but mounted on a .44 frame. The recoil's been reduced to the point where I could squeeze off all five of my pistol's rounds—and accurately too—before my father could fire his own .44 three times."

Longarm was silent as he examined the weapon. Her gun was indeed a double-action Colt, finished blue-gray, with grips of polished peachwood. *What money won't buy,* he thought to himself. As far as Longarm was concerned, the jury was still out on Jessie Starbuck. Her daddy had bought her this toy. Longarm hoped her daddy had taught her how dangerous it was, and how one had to be responsible with it. She'd shot at him twice before even knowing who he was. True, she hadn't hit him, but was that because she hadn't *wanted* to, or hadn't been *able* to?

"Isn't it beautiful?" Jessica asked. "The color reminds me of the Texas sky at dawn."

"Just like a woman to go prattling on about how pretty a handgun is," Longarm chuckled, handing back the revolver.

"There is nothing foolish about seeing beauty in an exquisite weapon," Ki said suddenly. He tossed his head to flip back the glossy mane of his ink-colored hair. His almond eyes traveled from Jessica's form to Longarm's face. "What is foolish is to ogle obvious beauty, forgetting one's manners in the process." Though his expression was impassive, there was a hint of warning in his tone.

"Uh, yeah," Longarm muttered, thinking, *Careful! Jessie might be this fellow's woman . . .* He didn't cotton to muscling in on another fellow's claim. "I notice you ain't armed."

"I don't often carry a gun."

"Mighty dangerous, lying in wait for murderers with no weapons—"

"I said I did not carry a gun," Ki corrected him. "I did not say I was weaponless."

"What clue had you found when we made our move on you, Longarm?" Jessie asked.

"You mean when you almost *killed* me, young lady," Longarm said sternly.

"Oh, Marshal, if I'd wanted to kill you, I would have," Jessie announced. "I don't miss unless I want to." She patted the revolver resting in its holster of cordovan leather. She wore it riding high, just behind the shapely curve of her

61

right hip. "I don't often strap this on," she said. "I don't think it's right for a woman to go strutting around wearing a gun. That can cause needless trouble. But when I do pull a gun, I know how to use it."

"Yes, ma'am," Longarm said. "Reckon you just wanted to distract me so as to take me alive, which you did. I have to give you that, though I got myself out of it. But the fact remains that you came up here fully intending to administer justice to a man you thought had something to do with your daddy's murder."

"What's wrong with punishing the men who killed my father?" Jessica asked, eyes flashing.

"The *law* will punish them. And *I* represent the law," Longarm cut her off, his own steely gaze flashing fiercely. "Vigilante justice is worse than no justice at all. Now I know this here part of Texas is considered Starbuck country, but it's also federal country. As a federal lawman, I'm telling you that if you try to take the law into your own hands again, I'll punish you, and I don't mean by taking you across my knee, which I'm starting to think you need, young lady. I'm talking about taking you off to jail. Is that clear?"

"Get hold of yourself, Longarm," Ki growled.

"You get hold of yourself, old son," Longarm snapped back. "You're so all-fired keen about seeing beauty, try and see authority when it's staring you in the face."

Ki nodded. "You are correct, Marshal. I accept your admonition."

"And you?" Longarm turned his gaze on Jessica. "Is what I said clear to you?"

"Yes, sir," she pouted.

"Fine. Now maybe we really can be friends," Longarm said, softening his tone.

"What was it you found back there, Marshal?" Jessica asked again. "You can tell us now that the smoke has cleared, so to speak."

"Shell casings, Jessie." Longarm climbed to his feet. "Come along, you two, and I'll show you."

He led them to the pile of casings he'd found earlier, before all the excitement had started. Jessica picked one up and held it to the sun.

"These are .25-caliber casings," she sighed. "My father had .25-caliber rounds in him."

"I was going to ask if you knew that," Longarm said uneasily. "At first I thought these had been left by a hunter. Odd as hell, this low-powered a round being used to ambush a man."

"That's what I thought," Jessie said. "But it's true. After my father died, I removed the seven bullets in him myself."

"That must have been hard on you," Longarm remarked, surprised.

"Hard or not, it had to be done," Jessie answered quietly. "I didn't trust the doctor in Sarah to do it. Oh, he's a fine physician, but an old-fashioned man. I was afraid he wouldn't tell me what he'd found." She nodded meaningfully at Longarm. "Like most of his sex, he has no idea what a good woman is capable of."

"Not me," Longarm replied quickly. "I remember the capabilities of every good woman I've had the good fortune to know." He noted with satisfaction the blush he'd brought to Jessica's lovely features, as he knelt down to gather up the pile of shell casings.

"Did you group them all together like that, Longarm?" Ki asked.

"No sir. You thinking what I'm thinking?"

"That one, or perhaps two rifles, did all the shooting?" Ki shrugged.

"That can't be," Jessica broke in. "Willie said he heard all the shots fired in just a few seconds."

"Who's Willie?" Longarm squinted up at her. "You mean there was a witness?"

"Sort of," Jessica said slowly. "He didn't exactly see

63

anything. Willie's an old hand at my spread, Longarm. He and my father were good friends from the old days, when I was just a little girl. My father and Willie would go riding together. Willie doesn't have any duties except during the roundup, when he acts as cook; he's sort of on pension at the Circle-Star outfit. That's our brand. Anyway, he and my father were together the day it happened. Willie was off chasing a stray calf when he heard the shooting. He said it sounded like a string of firecrackers going off on the Fourth of July. He said it only took him a few moments to ride to my father, and by then the shooting was over." Jessie shook her head, perplexed. "There's no way one or two men could have levered off thirty-odd-rounds in that short a time."

"There's something purely crazy going on here," Longarm mused. He lined up three of the cartridge casings between his thumb and forefinger, holding them up for examination by Jessie and Ki. "See it?" he asked.

"A long scratch running along each one," Ki said. "The scratch is identical on these three. Are they all like these?"

"Every one that I've found," Longarm said. "Yes, there's something crazy going on, all right. Reckon I'd better have a talk with your Willie. How far is your spread from here?"

"About three hours' ride," Jessie answered.

"Five hours, all told, from town!" Longarm exclaimed.

"Yep," Jessie said proudly. "We're just at where my land starts, right now. A soul could ride for two days and not leave Starbuck land."

"Texas and Texans." Longarm grinned. "Would you mind if I camped out on some of this here Starbuck land? It would kill a day to ride back and forth between your spread and Sarah."

"Marshal Farley said you were staying at the hotel."

"Only last night. They don't have a room for me as of today. They're all booked up because of the roundup."

"Well," Jessica smiled. "You are certainly not going to

64

sleep outside. You'll stay with us." She winked. "That's Texas hospitality."

"I'm obliged," Longarm said. "Where are your horses?"

"Down below, on the other side of this rise," Ki answered. "We'll travel down to get them, and then ride around to meet you by the outcropping." Ki paused to lock Longarm's eyes with his own. "You have some theory about what has taken place here, do you not, Longarm?"

Longarm ran a finger along both sides of his longhorn moustache. "Friend, the first thing a lawman learns is to keep his mind open to all sorts of theories, meanwhile collecting the facts. Then you fit your theory and the facts together, and if the two halves balance, you just may have an answer."

Ki grinned. "A warrior once said, 'To open one's mouth indiscriminately brings shame.'"

Longarm shrugged. "I just believe in eating the apple one bite at a time."

"Longarm! You are a poet!" Ki's strong, even teeth flashed white as he roared with laughter.

"Don't know about that, old son," Longarm smiled. "But I do think you and I are finally starting to understand each other."

★

Chapter 6

It was past noon before the trio reached the Starbuck spread, so Longarm took advantage of the hour to light up his first blessedly sweet cheroot of the day. He offered one to Ki, who politely refused. Despite Jessie's smile, Longarm decided that it wouldn't have been proper to offer one to a lady, even if she was packing a .38.

During the ride, they passed small herds of cattle tended by Circle-Star hands. To a man, the cowboys touched their hats and called out, "Morning, Miss Jessie," as she rode past.

Longarm was impressed. He himself had spent some years as a hand, and he knew that unless cowboys truly respected a person, they could be taciturn to the point of rudeness, even if that person was paying the bills. These hands were clearly experienced men who could write their own tickets with any outfit. The fact that they addressed Jessica Starbuck with the respect usually reserved for a foreman said a great deal about the way she managed her outfit.

Longarm was even more impressed when he caught his first glimpse of the Starbuck house—or *mansion*, rather. It was built of stone, with the main, middle section looking to be three stories tall. One-story wings jutted out from either side. There was a bunkhouse for the hands, and a stable nearby. Trees were plentiful, lending a cool, shady feel to the home spread.

As Jessie and Ki rode up to the veranda of the house, a young boy in denims appeared. He was one of the green hands fulfilling his apprenticeship by working for the spread's boss wrangler, the experienced ranch veteran who was in charge of the outfit's stable of horses. The boy gathered up the reins of Jessie's and Ki's mounts, and then looked inquiringly at Longarm's.

"See that this man's horse is well cared for," Jessica ordered. "He'll be staying with us for a spell."

A shape detached itself from the shadows beneath the veranda to reveal itself as a huge, hulking man, standing at least as tall as Longarm, but outweighing the deputy by at least twenty pounds. None of that extra weight looked like fat, either. He was dressed in a suit, complete with a string tie in place down the front of his grimy white shirt. "Hold it, boy!" the man snapped out at the young wrangler, countermanding Jessica's orders. "Just who is staying with us, Miss Jessie?"

"This doesn't concern you, Higgins," Jessica said.

"As foreman of there here outfit, I guess it'll be me who decides what concerns me or not. With all due respect, Miss Jessie." He grinned, his smile yellow-toothed and resembling that of a grizzly just before it cracks open a beehive. He ambled over to Longarm's horse, patting its flanks as he looked the gelding over. "Fine animal. Don't often see a hand with his own mount." He turned to stare at Longarm. "You signing on as a hand, boy?"

"I'm signing on to dig your grave if you call me 'boy' again," Longarm told him. There was the sound of guffaws swiftly choked off. Four more men stepped out from the interior darkness of the veranda to lean against the railing.

Longarm looked them over. They were wearing expensive Stetsons and shiny Justin boots, though the rest of their clothes were broken down and dusty. Their gunbelts were cracked and scuffed, cinched tightly about their waists. Longarm didn't have to examine their weapons to know that they'd be single-action weapons, working hands' weapons—not the kind of guns that man-killers carried. They were a wolf pack following their big bad he-wolf, Higgins. They could be troublesome when drunk, all of them against one man in the dark, but they were nothing but wind when stared down in broad daylight.

Higgins, however, glancing back at them, did not appear sorry to see them. "You son of a bitch," he said to Longarm.

"Easy, boss," one of the men on the veranda warned.

"Shut up, Ray," Higgins glowered back over his shoulder. He looked back at Longarm. "I called you a son of a bitch."

"Now that ain't much better than 'boy,'" Longarm drawled. "Try again, else I'll have to fetch me a shovel."

Higgins flushed red. He whipped off his Stetson to wipe at the sweat dewing his brow. He was bald. His hatband had pressed a red ridge across his ivory pate. "You get your horse," he snarled, "and ride off this spread."

"Whether I stay or go is up to Jessica," Longarm explained. "That's *Miss Jessie* to you," he added.

Higgins unbuttoned his suit jacket.

"Easy, old son," Longarm cautioned. "I can see you're carrying your gun in a shoulder rig. You ought to realize there's damn little chance you can outdraw me."

Higgins, his hand hovering in midair, seemed to think that what Longarm had said was good advice.

"This has gone far enough, Higgins," Jessica fumed. "Now get back to work."

"Your daddy made me foreman, and it's my job to take care of you," Higgins argued.

"Your job is to take care of this spread, period," Jessica said.

69

"Now don't go getting all riled, Miss Jessie." Higgins winked slyly. "You know I only got your best interest at heart."

More men have their eyes on this filly than Texas has cows, Longarm thought to himself. Plain as day, Higgins saw himself as Jessica's beau, regardless of how Jessica saw it.

"Just get back to work," Jessie said disgustedly.

"First I'll take his gun," Higgins replied, pointing at Longarm. "I'm doing it for you, Miss Jessie. With your daddy being shot dead and all, we can't have no strangers being around you armed."

"Higgins, I'm warning you—" Jessica began, but Higgins waved her aside as he strode down the steps of the veranda.

"Hush now, girl. Your daddy would want me to do this." He advanced upon Longarm, his hand outstretched. "Give me your gun, boy. Else you'll have to outshoot me *and* the four behind me."

Longarm prepared himself for trouble, but just then Ki glided between the deputy and the burly foreman.

"Miss Jessica has given you an order, Higgins," the unarmed man said in his soft voice.

"Get out of my way!"

Ki was now less than a yard away from the foreman. He seemed dwarfed by Higgins's hulking form. "You are not being polite to our guest, Higgins."

"Now that Mr. Starbuck is dead, maybe there's no room for you on this spread," Higgins snarled. "What do you think, boys?" he called over his shoulder.

"Get rid of him, boss," one of the men called.

"Bust his hole," another chortled.

"That tears it." Higgins grinned. "Run along, Chinaman—"

Before he could say another word, Ki struck with a roundhouse kick. His torso bent sideways as his leg came around straight and true, his foot catching Higgins beneath the chin.

The foreman rose about six inches in the air, and then fell, to land hard on his butt. By then, Ki was back in a relaxed, standing position. The whole kick and return had taken less time than a rattlesnake takes to strike.

"I am of Japanese ancestry, not Chinese, Higgins," Ki said, staring down at the foreman. "But you needn't grovel in the dirt. Merely apologize."

Higgins lumbered to his feet. He was swearing and spitting in rage. He tugged out from beneath his jacket a blued-steel Peacemaker. But before he could even thumb back the hammer on the single-action weapon, Ki moved in fast. He swatted Higgins's gun with the edge of his right hand. The Peacemaker went flying off in the direction of the Texas Panhandle as Higgins yelped in surprise and clasped his wrist.

"Shoot the yellow chink!" Higgins shouted in frustration to his men.

Longarm quickly moved toward the veranda, drawing his Colt as he did so. "Let's all stay out of this, boys. What do you say?"

The four men stared at Longarm's Colt. They noticed that its barrel had been cut down to five inches, and that it lacked a front sight. They looked at the cross-draw rig, and then back at the gun trained rock-steady upon them. "He's a gunslick, we can't do nothing!" one of them said. Gradually they lifted their hands toward the pitched roof of the veranda.

"Then I'll kill you myself, chink. With my bare hands," Higgins huffed, now truly resembling a grizzly. He moved warily around Ki, who stood motionless, not even bothering to turn as Higgins attacked from behind.

As the foreman looped both brawny arms around Ki's neck, the smaller man thrust his elbow into the other's solar plexus. Higgins gasped in pain, his arms going limp, now encompassing nothing but thin air. Ki slammed his elbow

71

into Higgins's ribs, and the foreman staggered like a pole-axed steer. Ki swept Higgins's boots out from under the heavy man, using only his own bare foot, but that foot was like a broom sweeping away litter. Higgins landed on his knees, and then toppled all the way to the ground. He rolled over on his back, his breath coming in agonized rasps as he clutched at his chest and side.

Light as a feather, Ki knelt beside him. With one hand he tilted Higgins's chin to expose the foreman's throat. "If I struck here," he said, his finger gently tracing Higgins's Adam's apple, "you would choke to death on your own crushed throat."

"Please . . ." Higgins gasped, his eyes rolling white. Ki's rigid grip had arced his neck back at an impossible angle. Higgins resembled—in more ways than one—a chicken with its neck stretched across the chopping block.

"Or here," Ki continued, ignoring Higgins's plea. He touched the foreman's nose. "If I struck here, shards of bone would drive themselves into your pig's brain. Your life would bleed out of your ears into the dust—"

"Ki," Jessica called. "Don't. Let him go."

After a moment, Ki smiled and nodded. "Higgins, am I Chinese?"

"No . . ."

"What am I, Higgins?"

"Japanese . . ." the foreman gurgled, and then moaned.

"*Half* Japanese," Ki remarked. "But close enough, Higgins, close enough." He rose to his feet without apparent effort, as if he were a puppet wafted into the air by strings attached to his head and shoulders. "The mistress of this ranch gives you back your life, Higgins. *I* give it back to you. Take it now, and flee with it." Ki paused a moment, waiting, as Higgins stared up at him, paralyzed, a bird bewitched by a serpent.

"You are fired," Ki said.

Wincing in pain, Higgins tottered up onto his feet, and stumbled off toward the bunk house.

Ki turned to the four men held at bay by Longarm. "You are all fired as well," he announced. "Get off Circle-Star land." Silently, the four began to do as they were told. Ki watched them shuffle off in the direction Higgins had taken.

Longarm holstered his Colt as he stared at Ki. "That was something . . ."

Ki smiled. He flipped back the blue-black shock of hair that had fallen across his forehead, and stood with his powerful hands resting on his narrow hips. "He called me Chinese. That was an insult."

"Absolutely," Longarm said.

"The Chinese and the Japanese do not mix."

"Don't mix," Longarm agreed adamantly.

"Oil and water," Ki added.

Longarm gazed at the man's slender form. "You didn't hardly work up a sweat with that big bruiser, did you?"

"Hardly," Ki agreed.

"If there had been maybe a half-dozen more of him against you," Longarm said thoughtfully, "it wouldn't have made all that much difference, would it?"

Ki shrugged. "Not much difference at all."

"How?" asked Longarm. "I mean, you never even made a fist."

"It is called *te,*" Ki interrupted. "In your language the word roughly translates as 'hand.' Long ago, in a faraway land known as Okinawa—"

"That's a chain of islands off the Japanese mainland," Longarm remarked.

"Longarm!" Ki laughed. "That is twice today you have delighted me! The Okinawans were conquered by my own people, the Japanese, and as their overlords, my ancestors forbade the Okinawans the honor of owning weapons. The Okinawans are a proud people. To have the ability to defend

73

themselves they developed the art of *te*—empty-hand fighting, in which one's body becomes the ultimate weapon."

"Is that what you meant before, up on the rise, when I asked if you were unarmed, and you said you had weapons?"

"To a degree," Ki smiled. "But I am armed in ways other than *te* . . ." Turning his gaze toward the stables, he added, "We will speak of that another time, my friend. I wish to make sure that Higgins and his followers indeed leave as ordered."

Longarm watched Ki stride away. "Quite a strange bird, that one . . ."

"That's an interesting way to put it," Jessica smiled.

"He seems mighty devoted to you."

"It's a long story," Jessica walked to Longarm's side. "Thank you for helping. I mean keeping those others out of it."

Longarm shrugged. "I wanted to keep it a fair fight. 'Course, that was before I knew that Ki could beat up the whole damn bunkhouse if he had a mind to. Sorry about causing you the trouble in the first place. It looks as if my arriving here has cost you your foreman and a bunch of hands. And at roundup time, as well . . ."

"Things were coming to a head anyway, Longarm," Jessie said. "Higgins was one of our top hands. A few weeks before my father was killed, he made Higgins foreman. I guess you know that on a spread of this size, the foreman's job is pretty much taken up with desk work, with balancing the books. Higgins was good at it. He took to wearing suits, like my father. Like a businessman. He got rid of his gunbelt and took to that shoulder-holster rig, thinking it was more dignified. Now don't get me wrong," Jessie added, her pretty green eyes serious. "There's nothing wrong with a man wanting to improve his station in life. That's what this country and Texas are all about. It's just that once my father was gone, Higgins started to think *I* came along with his job. That somehow the fact that he was foreman made him the man I'm supposed to marry. Why it all came to a head with your arrival is beyond me."

"I could see that he considered you a stray heifer ripe for his brand," Longarm mused.

"Painful analogy." Jessica rubbed at the seat of her jeans and pretended to wince. "But apt, nonetheless."

"Forgive an old cattleman, ma'am," Longarm smiled, his eyes dancing merrily.

"You're forgiven," Jessica answered. "But I must say, Deputy, you can't know very much about women if you think the way into their hearts is with a branding iron." She took his arm and led him up the steps, across the veranda, and into the house.

"A man has no business trying to brand a woman as his own," Longarm agreed thoughtfully. "Though a red-hot poker does have its place," he chuckled.

"It does indeed," Jessica laughed with abandon, and Longarm thought that unless he was careful, he'd have to add his own name to Jessica Starbuck's list of admiring beaus.

★

Chapter 7

That night, Longarm, asleep, tossed and turned in his bed. It wasn't his fault the Springfield had jammed. There was just too much mud. Too much blood.

At Shiloh!

The Springfield had jammed! Custis Long's panic grew by the moment. He was defenseless against the enemy marching upon him.

Against the boy marching upon him! The bullet hole Custis Long had just put into the boy's chest seemed to have no effect. How could that be? The boy was only fourteen or so; A .51 was way too much bullet for such a skinny stripling... but the bullet hole just glistened there on the boy's chest like some ghastly boutonniere of flesh. The boy wore it proudly. He'd take it home to show his mama, his papa, his girl. The boy was leering and laughing as he fixed his bayonet and broke into a dog-trot charge directly at his murderer...

His murderer, Custis Long, brought his useless Springfield up like a club. As he prepared to repel the attack, he felt the rifle crumble into dust, spilling across his now-empty hands.

The boy laughed. The boy's chest wound laughed. It said, *"He's a gunslick, but he can't do nothing!"*

Custis Long's panic was greater than the whole muddy field, greater than the entire limbo that was Shiloh. Amid dying men's cries, the sky became a huge chest wound, ragged and burning, blood-crimson wet, urine-yellow, urine-stinking...

Custis Long stood frozen in place, waiting for the keen edge of the boy's bayonet. All around, the Springfields and Spencer rifles chewed their bites out of men. All around, a *new* sort of gunfire emerged. The sound was like a string of firecrackers going off in quick succession. The sound signaled a change in the odds. The sound changed the battlefield from limbo, where, after all, there was some hope of redemption, into *hell*—where there was no hope at all...

Longarm woke up and came to his senses a split second before he began to fire his Colt into the dark corners of the room. He was slick with sweat, disoriented; despite the room's open windows he felt suffocated. A moonbeam, a softly glowing shaft of light, angled into the room. Longarm's eyes focused on it in desperation.

The Starbuck spread, he realized. In a bedroom in the Starbuck house. It had been a dream, but what a dream!

With shaking fingers Longarm struck a match, one of the bundle lying on the bedside table, and held the flame to the wick of the kerosene lamp. The flickering light banished the last of the nightmare from the room, but not from Longarm's mind. The damp bedsheets were wound around his legs like swamp grass. He kicked his way free and got out of bed, to pad across the room to where his saddlebags were draped across a chair back. He extracted his bottle of Maryland rye and took a healthy swallow. And then another swallow.

And then a third swallow. For the boy.

Longarm's nightmare had stacked the deck against him. Hell, the war was fifteen years ago. He'd just been a boy himself at Shiloh, where he'd killed for the first time. That time he'd killed the boy—he was no gunslick back then . . .

It had been just one boy—himself—against another. That damned fool kid had shouted some brave nonsense as he'd charged into the sights of that other youngster's Springfield. Longarm still remembered the impact of the rifle's butt against his shoulder as the Springfield spat blue smoke and gray lead the boy's way.

"Kid must of thought he was going to live forever," Longarm muttered out loud to break the oppressive silence in the room. "Well, he found out how short 'forever' could be."

Longarm stretched out on the bed to let the fragments of the dream drift back to him. Nightmares had a way of shuffling—as well as stacking—a deck. Nightmares shuffled time, for example. In his dream, that firecracker sound filled the air at Shiloh, but Longarm knew he hadn't actually heard the unique, chattering noise of a Gatling gun until just after the War, when the carpetbaggers flooded into the South, and the Union Army was ramming through the once-Confederate states, hunting down the scattered bands of defiant, bitter rebels who refused to pledge their allegiance to the Stars and Stripes. And so they were branded outlaws, and hunted down—one way or another . . .

The big, carriage-mounted Gatlings were often used by the Union Army to intimidate those stubborn rebels who would not surrender, and execute the ones considered too damned ornery to tame. It seemed to Longarm that just such a weapon had been used to murder Alex Starbuck.

But how?

But Alex Starbuck was riddled with .25-caliber bullets, and shot at from a high rocky crest, a crest from which the ambushers had managed to escape—with their weapon—within minutes. No Gatling had that sort of mobility, and no Gatling was chambered for .25's. And yet it had happened, somehow. Happened to Alex Starbuck the way it had happened to so many poor, bullet-riddled bastards just after the War...

Longarm sighed to himself. It was bad to have the War and its aftermath on one's mind. Well, by morning's light he'd go to talk to Willie, the old hand now turned cook, who was with Alex Starbuck the day he was murdered. *It sounded like a string of firecrackers going off on the Fourth of July,* Willie had told Jessica. Chances were, old Willie knew something about Gatling guns. Chances were, old Willie had what he'd witnessed just after the War on his mind, as well...

It was just too hot in the bedroom. Longarm needed air. He slipped on his trousers, scooped up his bottle, and left the room on the second floor of the house.

Though this part of the house was three stories high, there were only two floors. The second-floor bedrooms opened out to a corridor, one side of which was a railed balcony that overlooked a huge combination dining and living room. The dark-stained roof rafters soared above this room, which had polished wood floors, and a magnificent slate fireplace. Comfortable furniture was arranged about the room, and off to one side, in a generous space of its own, there stood a massive mahogany dining room set. At this table Longarm, along with Jessie and Ki, had earlier eaten a delicious dinner, prepared and served by an elderly, diminutive Oriental woman—a Japanese, Longarm was quite sure.

The big room was dark now, except for the moonlight filtering in through a brace of curtained bay windows. The idea of wandering alone through someone's house did not appeal to Longarm. He was about to return to his own room when his sharp eyes caught a flicker of movement by the fireplace. He strained to see in the dim light, and called out softly, "Is there someone there?"

"Longarm?" Jessie called back. "What are you doing awake?"

"Same as you, I guess," Longarm laughed.

"Quiet," she scolded. "You'll wake the others."

Longarm walked to the end of the corridor and felt his way down the steps, his bare feet silent against the sturdy wood planks. As he reached the ground floor, he squinted against the bright flash of a match as Jessica lit a candle on the mantelpiece. The tiny flame dimly illuminated the portrait mounted above the fireplace. It was of a lovely, red-haired woman dressed in a green gown. The dress's hue exactly matched the woman's emerald eyes.

Although he had noticed the large portrait earlier in the evening, he had not had the opportunity to comment upon it. As he approached the soft circle of steady light thrown by the candle, Jessica saw that his eyes were fixed on the painting.

"That's my mother," she said proudly. "She died when I was very young."

"I'm sorry," Longarm said. He did not mention that the file Billy Vail had given him back in Denver had such information between its covers.

"Some say that death is just awakening from the dream that is life," Jessica murmured.

"Did Ki teach you that?" Longarm asked, thinking of boys killed in wars, and of dreams of such boys.

"No," Jessica smiled, turning from the portrait, to face Longarm. "My father taught me that."

So close to her now, close enough to breathe in the fragrance of her hair, Longarm could see that she had been weeping. Her eyes were red-rimmed, her cheeks tear-stained. Tears had also stained the front of the long robe she was wearing. The robe was of sheerest silk, colored pale lavender. Her feet, beneath the hem of the robe, were bare. Was she bare as well, beneath the robe?

Jessica gestured toward Longarm's hand. "What have you got there?"

He looked down in surprise. He had forgotten he was

holding the bottle of Maryland rye. He held it up to the candle's light so that the amber whiskey's color would please her. "Take a drink," he coaxed, "and tell me why you were crying."

"It's nothing . . ." she began tentatively, and then stopped to shake her head, as if at the foolishness of such a statement. "If it's nothing, then why am I crying over it, I know, I know . . ."

Longarm chuckled. "Took the words right out of my mouth. Look, problems can be solved." His head was full of what he was sure was worrying her. She'd lost her foreman and a bunch of hands. The roundup was coming, and the running of such a huge spread had to be the cause of her anxiousness. "If you'd like, tomorrow we can ride into Sarah together, to see who's available to be hired. If you think about it, one of your top hands right here might be able to handle the job."

"You're very kind to be concerned," Jessica said. Before the fireplace was a fur throw rug in front of a sofa. She sat on the sofa with her back against the armrest and her legs curled beneath her. Patting the sofa, she said, "Sit down and give me your bottle. I think I will have a drink." She tilted the bottle, taking tiny sips from it, as she explained that she'd already appointed one of her hands as foreman, and that the Circle-Star had more than enough men to handle the roundup. "My father taught me to shoot and ride and rope, Longarm, but he didn't neglect my brain. Maybe it was because he'd always wanted a son, I don't know . . . Anyway, I know all about how the cattle business works, as well as all the other businesses my father owned, which I've inherited. I fully intend to run them all myself," she trailed off. "Someday . . ." She stared at the fireplace, cold and empty as a mineshaft. "I wish it were fall. I could do with a roaring fire. I could do with being able to gaze into the flames."

"Why were you crying?" Longarm persisted. "Why must

you wait to take control of your father's empire?"

Jessica looked at him. "I have to answer your questions with some of my own, but be patient and answer me honestly, and you'll find out what you want to know. Longarm, suppose you capture the men who killed my father—what happens then?"

Longarm shrugged. "They'll stand trial, of course."

"And if duly convicted they will be hanged." Jessica nodded. "But what if they were merely the muscles that pulled the triggers? What if the brain that ordered them to do the deed belonged to someone else?"

"You folks in Texas sure have a funny way of talking," Longarm muttered. He reached for the bottle and took a swig. "Reckon what you're asking is, what if this gang has a boss that sent them out to do their dirty deed? If that's the case, I'll arrest the boss as well, if I can dig up the proof that links him to the gang."

"And what if that boss has yet another boss? A boss far away? What if *that* boss can't be touched?" Her smile was warm. "Not even by a federal lawman?"

"I think you've got more than a 'what if' situation on your pretty little mind," Longarm said. "What you're talking about is a conspiracy."

"What's on my mind, Mr. Longarm of the law, is not at all a conspiracy, but a *war*. A war in which my father was a casualty." She paused. "And not the first."

"Tell me why you were crying, Jessie."

"Because they think that killing my father has ended the war. It hasn't, Longarm." She stared into his eyes, her expression in the candlelight both fierce and beautiful. "I'm crying because I've got to prove to them that the war isn't over, and that means I've got to do some things—live my life—in a way I'd never planned, in a way I don't really want. It means I've got to fight, and kill, even though those things are *not* what women are meant for."

"What are women meant for?" Longarm asked.

"For love," Jessica whispered, her eyes now bright, liquid, emerald-hued as her mother's. "But before I can love," Jessica finished, "I must hate."

Longarm was silent, pondering what he'd been told. Finally he said, "Two things are on my mind. Number one, I'm sorry for saying that your mind was pretty and little. That just sort of slipped out. Your mind is certainly not little. The second thing on my mind is"—he grinned—"I haven't got the slightest idea what you're talking about. Why don't we eat this apple—"

"—one bite at a time!" Jessie chimed in before giving vent to her rich laugh. "Oh, Longarm"—she reached out to squeeze his hand—"I'm glad you're here. I might have gone insane if you hadn't showed up."

"Well, you going to start from the beginning?"

"From the beginning," Jessie declared. "From the first bite of the apple."

"Whoa now . . ." Longarm chuckled. "That's a little *too* far back. As I recollect it, that was Eve who took that bite."

Jessica Starbuck didn't laugh. "That's true. That first bite out of the apple came about because of temptation. Temptation brought about the start of the trade wars between my father and his enemies."

"I assume the start of your father's troubles was in the Japans?" Longarm asked.

Jessie nodded as she rose to fetch two glasses from a sideboard. "Would you prefer brandy to your bottle of rye?"

"This here suits me fine, thank you."

"I'll stick with the rye as well," she said, and then continued to tell her story as she returned to the sofa. "You have to try and picture what the Japanese were like when Commodore Perry's fleet sailed into their harbor. The Japanese had kept all Western influence out of their country for two hundred years. Two hundred! Think about it, Longarm. They'd conquered the Okinawans, as Ki told you. But he neglected to mention that they were, for all practical purposes, the overlords of the Chinese as well. They were the masters of their part of the world, and they thought that because the rest of the world was beneath their interest, their paradise would be left undisturbed."

"Paradise for the Japanese, maybe," Longarm pointed out. "But not so wonderful for the Okinawans and Chinese under the Japanese thumb."

"Spoken like an American." Jessica grinned. "Like a lawman. But that's how it was, at least, for the Japanese. Then America steamed up to their front door. My father was just a sailor, but he saw his chance, and fate was kind to him. By the time he'd returned to our own West Coast, and convinced enough wealthy businessmen to lend him the money he needed to buy up import and export rights, the civil war in the Japans was in full swing."

"I reckon there were fellows in the Japans who were all for tossing us foreigners out on our ears. Those Japanese fellows were most likely the fat cats. They had things sewed up nice and neat. Then along comes America and Europe, wanting a piece of the pie."

"A samurai—that's a warrior, a man a lot like you, Longarm—once said, 'If you understand on situation, you understand all.' You've proven him right. The Japanese civil war was fought by a group of conservative men who had everything to lose if the traditional order of things was changed. To be fair, they were also concerned about losing their heritage." She paused. "Heritage is very important to the Japanese. To the samurai, especially," she added sorrowfully.

"But the old order lost, as it did in our country's Civil War?" Longarm interjected.

"Yes, the Shogunate was overthrown by an alliance of progressive-minded lords and samurai fighting under the banner of the young Emperor Meiji. A city called Edo became the nation's new capital, and was renamed Tokyo to commemorate the nation's change."

"And your father rode the Japans like a man rides and breaks a bucking horse."

Jessica stared into her glass. She had drunk too much. The whiskey had loosened her resolve, allowing the memories she'd kept locked away to rise. She remembered her father when he was young and strong. In her heart she saw him the way he must have been during that wonderful time when his thick blond hair had blown in the wet winds coming off Tokyo Bay. Her father had brought her fine silk kimonos and painted fans like jewels—trappings more exquisite than any princess's adornment pictured in the storybooks of her childhood. He had told her about houses built of paper, and about warriors who made fierce faces and crowed like ogres as their glittering blades flashed through the clear blue sky like lightning bolts. Since her father's death she had banished the memories of the way he had held his small daughter upon his knee, regaling her with tales that allowed her to see and smell the pink cherry blossoms falling like snowflakes, and taste the sweet plum wine...

"Jessie?" Longarm whispered. "If it hurts you to talk about it, let's not." He poured himself more rye. "Memories can hurt."

She shook herself. "My father *did* ride and break the Japans," she began again. "He branded his presence onto that land the way a hot iron sears the hide of a steer, or an artist's brush sweeps across white canvas." She glanced at her mother's portrait. "During that time, while back in America, he met my mother and they married. I was born in San Francisco. That's where the original Starbuck office was established. Things went very well. Not only for my father, but for other American and European businessmen. The British built miles of railroad in the Japans. The French and Germans had a fair share of commerce as well."

"There's no such thing as a fair share when you're talking business and commerce," Longarm said. "Two men might be working their claims on opposite sides of a mountain, all of a sudden one figures half a mountain isn't nearly enough, he wants the whole pile of rock for himself."

"And he'll try and take the whole mountain if he thinks he can get away with it," Jessie agreed. "The trouble began in the late sixties. The depression of the seventies was just beginning, and money was growing tight. My father was overextended. The men who had lent him money were beginning to feel the pinch so many Americans would soon feel. He and my mother were in danger of losing everything for which they had worked so hard."

"Of losing what they were trying to build for you?" Longarm asked.

"Yes." Jessie blushed. "Of course my future was weighing heavily upon their minds. Remember, I told you that like Adam and Eve in the Garden of Eden, my father's troubles began with temptation? Well, in those days he owned no clipper ships of his own, but leased ships from others. A group of European businessmen, Prussians, approached him with an offer. They were willing to sublease from my father all of his ships, at a price three times what he had been paying. The profit was enough to get him out of his immediate money problems. He accepted the Prussians' offer." Jessica's voice began to tremble. "There was, of course, good reason for the Prussians to be willing to pay my father so much. Their cargo was very precious. The Europeans were shipping slaves to America, Longarm. Chinese slaves, stolen from their homeland by the Prussians with the help of certain Japanese warlords."

"Your father knew what he was contributing to?" Longarm asked.

"Of course not. The manifests the Prussians supplied my father with listed the cargo as bolts of silk and other goods. Once he found out what was going on upon his ships he put a stop to it, but oriental philosophy says that a man is not excused from blame because he is ignorant of his part in some wrongdoing." She looked away.

"Well, my philosophy says you can't right a wrong till you know about it," Longarm scolded. "Your father did no more business with them, right?"

"He tried not to, Longarm, but once the Prussians had their claws into him they refused to let him go. They needed my father's cooperation to establish themselves in America. They considered our country ripe for the taking, and they believed in taking what they could. That's what you've got to understand about these men," she pleaded, her voice grown strong and intense. "They believe that a few men are destined to rule all men. They dismiss as foolishness the idea that men are created equal. They want to rule the world as they've ruled parts of Europe for so long, and they will do anything to get what they want!"

"Like murdering your father, Jessie? Or having him murdered?"

She smiled grimly. "One bite at a time, Longarm, remember? When my father refused their advances upon his business, they began to strike at his interests in the Orient. Old friends of his were at first coerced, and then, if they refused to listen out of loyalty to my father, they or members of their families were killed. My father, meanwhile, had branched out into Europe, and began to give as good as he got," Jessie added proudly. "Ships were hijacked on both sides. Private armies sprang up. Trade wars uncondoned by any government, but just as bloody as those between countries, were waged. The battles were fought with violence, paid for and protected with money. Nobody interfered. Nobody could. Nobody dared. Money bought silence. Men fought and died and the world was none the wiser. It might have gone on like that forever, just another expense to add to the profit-and-loss sheets, the lives of a lost crew memorialized by a few ink marks in a ledger." She paused. "My father has done many wonderful things, Longarm. But please understand that what I've told you about him tonight is not something I'm proud of."

"Men make mistakes in their lives, like I told you, Jessie," Longarm said quietly. "If your father did some bad things, so be it. He's dead now. I reckon that ledger you were speaking of shows he had more marks on the credit side of the page." He longed for a smoke, but he dared not leave the room to get one, thinking that if he left Jessie's side, the spell would be broken and she would pull back into the shell she'd built around herself in order to survive. "You said the war, the sea and land battles, the hijackings between the two sides *might* have gone on forever. What happened?"

"I now know that in a war, everyone is fair game," she said bitterly. "My father didn't understand that, but then he'd had little experience in such matters. For the Europeans it was old hat. They bided their time, waiting for the proper moment to strike. It came when my parents voyaged to Europe on business and for a holiday. I was too young to make the journey with them, of course. The authorities there said it was an accident, and my father, for all of his power, was far from home. He could not make them change their ruling. My father and mother were crossing a street. A carriage came from around a corner. Supposedly it was out of control. It careened into their path—four maddened horses dragging behind them steel-rimmed wheels. My father suffered minor injuries, but my mother . . ." Jessica looked at Longarm and smiled sadly. "Thinking about it, it seems so naive of my parents to have traveled into the lion's den, so to speak. But in those days—and even until the day he died—my father was a curious mixture of shrewdness and innocence. And back then, when it had happened, the idea of rivals striking at one's immediate family—well, even if my father had *wanted* to live his life in a fortress, my mother would not have allowed it." Jessie looked up at the portrait above the fireplace. She gazed at the women whose spirit seemed to live in her own green eyes. "My mother was not the sort of woman who would allow herself to be caged."

"Her murderers went unpunished?"

"You don't—*didn't* know my father if you can ask that," Jessie declared. "The actual assassins, the men who did the deed for money, were beneath my father's notice. He found out which of his Prussian enemies had ordered the attempt. The man who'd hatched the plot, a count, had a son, a young man in his twenties, who would fall heir to his father's holdings and power. The boy was a fop, a lover of high society and nightlife. On the eve of his sailing back to America, my father, all alone, trailed the young man until he came upon him on a secluded street. With his bare hands he snapped the boy's neck, leaving the body in the gutter. Several days later, as the count mourned his loss, a package came to him via courier. It was the boy's handkerchief, embroidered with his family's crest. Tucked inside the cloth was my father's business card. On it he had written, 'With my compliments'—"

"Sweet Jesus," Longarm murmured, when he could find his voice.

"There was an uproar, of course," Jessie continued. "The count demanded justice." She laughed. "But by then my father was back in America. Back in *his* territory. The shoe was on the other foot. The death of the count's son went unavenged."

"But surely not for long?" Longarm began.

"Yes," she nodded. "Things calmed down. Maybe the shock of my father losing his wife and one of his enemies losing his son spoiled their taste for further violence. In any event, there were fewer battles. Business interests on both sides enjoyed undisturbed prosperity. Things remained that way up until the day they'd finished what they'd started on those European streets. Up until the day they murdered my father, here on his own ranch." Jessie tilted the bottle, pouring the last inch of rye into her glass. "We've drunk it all, I'm sorry..."

Longarm smiled and shook his head. "This was thirsty talk, woman." He thought about things for a moment, then said, "How do you know that your father's murder had anything to do with what you've told me? I don't mean to be unfeeling, but what proof do you have linking his European enemies to the shooting?"

Jessica stared at Longarm, her eyes narrowed and her lips pursed, as if she were evaluating him and, at the same time, weighing an important decision. She rose from the sofa. Longarm saw the outline of her long, lithe body traced by the shimmering silk as she reached out to take his hand. "Come with me. I'm going to show you something." She held his eyes with her own. "Because I trust you."

She lit another candle, and by its light they walked down a hallway to a room that turned out to be Alex Starbuck's study. Fine leather-upholstered armchairs and sofas furnished the big room. The walls were lined with book-laden shelves and glass-windowed cabinets of gleaming, expensive firearms. In the air was the cherry scent of aromatic pipe tobacco. Longarm didn't have to ask to know that the humidor would be regularly replaced to keep that scent fresh and strong. This was Alex Starbuck's room. It always would be, while this house stood...

Jessica went to a shelf and removed a leatherbound volume. Wedged in its pages was a small key. This she took to an old, scarred, and battered oak desk. Its massive bulk dominated the room.

"This white elephant was the first desk my father owned," she said fondly. "He bought it secondhand, when he'd just started out. Then, it was all he could afford. He never used another. It was shipped here from San Francisco when we moved to Texas." She took a small, black leatherbound notebook out of the opened drawer. "With the exceptions of the circumstances surrounding my mother's death, and

91

the fact that my father knew what sort of cargo the Europeans wanted to ship in his clippers, the history of my father's business was known to me since my adolescence. My father felt I had to understand its birthing if I was someday to run the empire. While on his deathbed, he told me about the slaves, about my mother, and about this book."

She handed it to Longarm. Inside, written in a careful hand, were a series of names and places. Beneath each heading, cryptic notes detailed that individual's business or position in government.

"After my father had returned from Europe, he waited for his enemies to retaliate. He hired private detectives on both sides of the Atlantic to ferret out the links between his enemies in Europe and their minions in this country. He wanted plenty of targets, you see, and he wanted his enemies to know that he was collecting such potential targets. This was the only way he had to protect me. It was his hope that his enemies would think twice about striking at his child if they knew that Alex Starbuck had tracked down their children, as well as their vital interests—both legal and illegal—in America."

"These European folks have illegal operations in America?" Longarm asked sharply.

"Through blackmail alone they own lawmen, congressmen, business tycoons—" She stopped, and grinned from ear to ear. Holding out her hand, she said, "Give it back, Mr. Longarm of the law."

Like a cat watching a canary get locked up in its cage, Longarm watched the black book get locked back up in its drawer. "Reckon I would need a court order to confiscate that juicy little diary." He was joking, but his tone was rueful.

"Reckon you would, Marshal," Jessie mimicked, giving his bare belly a playful poke. "But don't you see? Even if you did have the book, it would be useless to you. The men and women in it are above the law."

"Nobody's above the law. I told you that once." Longarm growled. He'd have been growing hot under the collar, if he'd been wearing one.

"Damn it, Marshal," she argued, "in many cases, the folks I'm going to track down *write* the laws!"

Longarm stood silent, his hands on his hips. "You can't be judge and jury all by yourself. It doesn't matter what your father did in Europe—"

"It does matter!" Jessie insisted. "It was the only thing he could do. Answer me truthfully. How long would you be a federal marshal, how long would your superior back in Denver keep his badge, if you started sniffing around the tracks of a crooked congressman?" She gave him a second to ponder that, then said, "Come on, Longarm, let's get ourselves a nightcap."

Back on the sofa by the fireplace, with snifters of brandy before them, Longarm added, "What you do concerning that book of names is none of my concern. But remember that I've warned you once that while I'm investigating the murder of your father, you're to stay out of the way and let *me* do the dirty work."

"And I've said that your point was clear to me."

"Fine," Longarm said. "How do you know those names in that book are even current?"

"Well, as I told you, there was no retaliation from abroad, so my father was content to let things rest. Losing my mother tore a whole lot out of him—out of his spirit, and he had me to contend with. Anyway, he kept his detectives on the case through the years. Up until his death he kept crossing out those who had died, adding in those newly recruited. I've kept the investigators on the payroll. Now their reports will come to me."

Longarm nodded. He yawned and stretched. It was late, and his body was thick with sleep, but his mind was wide awake. He needed sleep, knew he ought to get some, for tomorrow promised a hard day of riding to find Willie, the

93

only witness to the Starbuck shooting. The old hand was acting as cook for a bunch of Circle-Star hands rounding up a distant herd on Starbuck land.

"What's wrong?" Jessica suddenly asked.

"Who said anything's wrong?" he smiled.

"You did," she said. "You told me something was wrong in the way your voice sounded when you called down to me from the second floor. Your eyes told me something was wrong when I first looked into them tonight. You've no shirt on, so I could see the tension in your body." She smiled warmly. "You see, Longarm? You're telling me something is wrong in every way possible, without actually using words."

He shook his head in wonder. "Damn, woman. What a lawman you'd have made."

Jessie slid off the sofa to kneel on the soft fur rug in front of the fireplace. "Come, lie down on your stomach, here, on the rug. Let's see if I can rub the tension out of your shoulders."

Jessica, beside him, ran her fingers along the taut cords of his neck. With a feathery touch, she first stroked, then gently kneaded the thick masses of muscle and sinew padding his shoulders and upper arms. "Relax," she crooned, bending to him so that her lips were just inches away from the shell of his ear.

Longarm tried, but it was no use. A new worry was nagging at him...

Jessica sat back crosslegged. "You're too strong for me," she scolded lightly. "Your muscles are too developed for me to force them to relax." She raised one leg and bent it at the knee. The gown fell open, revealing the splendid curve of her thigh and calf.

Longarm colored, but her beauty was such that he could not look away. *If only...*

Sensing his unease, Jessica covered up. "Have I offended you?" she asked.

94

"No, ma'am," he said forcefully. "Hardly that. I think you're lovely, and what I'd most like to do is slide that silk thing off you and start rubbing the tension out of you. It's just that—"

"What?" Jessica demanded.

"It just doesn't seem right." He glanced up at the portrait above the fireplace. "I mean, with your mother looking down on us and all."

Jessica laughed in delight. "You really are a samurai! Gallant, and a gentleman to the very core!"

"I don't see what's so funny," Longarm said, disgruntled. "Just because a man has a sense of what's right and wrong—"

"Hush," she giggled, pressing her finger to his lips, and then, as if to make sure he obeyed, she pecked a cool, delicious kiss against his mouth. "Lie back down. On your stomach. That's an order," she said sternly.

Longarm obeyed, somehow not at all surprised by the fact that Jessie was unbuttoning his trousers and then peeling them down over his buttocks, past his thighs, and then off. He heard a soft rustling sound, and turned his head to see the silken gown fall to the floor, the folds dropping in on themselves so that the garment resembled a stream of plum-colored liquid splashing down. When he tried to look at Jessica, she placed a hand on either side of his head, her palms acting like blinders.

"No, you're not to look at me. Not until I give you permission," she teased. "You must lie on your stomach with your eyes closed while I massage your back. Just relax and listen to what I have to tell you."

Longarm felt his erection grow rock hard, and his heart begin to pound, as Jessica straddled him. She gave her bottom a little shake as she settled down on the small of his back, light as a butterfly. As her fingers began to do their dance down along his shoulders and spine, Longarm became mad with passion. Her trick of touching him without letting him see her had a way of driving a man loco! Where had she ever learned such a wonderful love-game?

"I've told you that my parents were unusual people," Jessica said. "Part of that came from their love of the Orient. They had always planned to retire in the Japans someday, but after my mother was killed, my father knew that to return there without her would be much too painful. What he decided to do was bring a bit of the Japans to America. Instead of hiring an American woman to be the ranch's housekeeper and my nanny, he arranged for Myobu to come to our country, and to take over those duties."

Longarm thought of the small old woman, so graceful and polite, who had prepared and served the fine dinner earlier in the evening. "Did your father know her?" he asked.

"In a manner of speaking," Jessica laughed. "Longarm, do you know what a geisha is?"

Longarm chose his words carefully. "Reckon you might describe one as a very high-priced, uh, lady of the night."

"A courtesan, to be sure," Jessie agreed in amusement, "but please understand that things in the Orient are not the same as they are in America. In the Japans, body and soul are not considered two separate things. Here, women are hired by men to tend only to their physical cravings. In the Japans, geishas cater to men's bodies, but also to their souls. The word geisha best translates as 'artist.' She is trained from childhood to be skilled in music, art, and literature, the preparation and serving of fine food, and finally, if she has proven herself worthy, she is taught the skills and abilities that are the keys to a man's soul. A geisha is not only an artist, but also a sort of priestess. Through her body, a man can experience enlightenment. For the brief time a man spends with a geisha, he is one with the universe. This frees the geisha's soul, as well."

"And Myobu was such an . . . artist?" Longarm marveled.

"Many years ago, she was one of the most famous geishas in the Japans," Jessie told him. "She had an honored place in the Emperor's court. She was one of the most powerful women in that nation."

"Do geishas become rich?"

"Oh, yes," Jessica said, her fingers rubbing the last drops of tension out of Longarm's body. "And along with monetary wealth comes public respect, and a high, honored place in society."

"Then forgive me for saying so," Longarm frowned, "but it strikes me as powerful sad that such a woman has to end her life as a housekeeper, happy as she is here, I'm sure..."

"Oh, she didn't *have* to, Longarm," Jessie explained. "She still has her wealth, most of it transferred to this country. She could live well, anywhere in the world."

"Then why did she choose to become a housekeeper and nanny for a Texas tycoon and his daughter?"

"During the time he was in the Japans, long before he met my mother, Myobu was my father's geisha. During their time together, she guided my father as he melded his mind and spirit into what we in this country call our soul, and then she guided him through the process in which the soul and physical body become one. That is enlightenment. In addition, Myobu, who already had extensive business holdings, taught my father much that was to help him later on, while building his own business in his own country."

"I still don't understand," Longarm interrupted. "If all that's so, why did she consent to work for him?"

"After my mother was killed, my father wrote to Myobu. She was older, and her time of being an active geisha was coming to an end. In the Japans, it is traditional for such an older woman to open a *ryu*, a school in which worthy young girls are initiated and then taught the various aspects of becoming geishas. My father explained to Myobu that he would never again marry, which meant that I was to be the sole heir to all of his holdings. Accordingly he wanted me to have the benefit of the finest education in the world.

That meant tutors and, later on, university schooling, but it also meant that from childhood on, I was to have that special guidance that would allow my soul to blossom, and later to join together with my body—guidance and training that would prepare me for the awesome responsibility of ruling the Starbuck empire. Myobu considered herself my father's mentor. When his request came to her, she considered it her destiny, her *karma*, to accept. She had favored the father who built the empire, thereby beginning the circle. Now she would train the daughter who would complete the circle. The chance to do such a thing, the honor to do such a thing, could only come to a geisha as fine as Myobu."

"But to do the cooking and cleaning . . ." Longarm shook his head, perplexed.

"Don't you try to look at me yet," Jessica warned him as she slid down to straddle his thighs. Gently she caressed his lower back, her touch now sending velvety pulses of pleasure through his body. How he longed to turn her over and kiss her! But he didn't move.

"A true geisha will cook and clean as expertly as she will play an instrument or manage her business affairs," Jessica was murmuring. "She doesn't concern herself with the relative status of a task. All tasks that are honestly performed will bring honor. A geisha is an artist, and life is her art form."

"Earlier you told me that women weren't meant for hate but for love—" Longarm started to say, but Jessica cut him off.

"I've been given a very different, special sort of destiny. There is the art of negotiating one's way through the world, and the art of loving one's way through it. In these two aspects of life, Myobu has trained me well. I am a geisha." She slid off his legs, her hands now guiding him over onto his back so that he could see her.

Longarm gazed at her lovely features, suffused with passion. By the flickering candle glow he watched the nipples of her full, lush breasts tighten, as if they could actually feel his eyes' loving caress.

He reached out for her, his fingers gently locking about her arms, and pulled her down upon him. As she let herself fall, she dipped her head so that her shimmering tresses brushed across his chest. The touch was like fire, but a pleasurable fire. The gold-and-red tendrils of her hair sparked desire so strong it made Longarm throb with anticipation.

As they kissed, Jessica pressed her soft, flat belly against his erection, blanketing it with sweet warmth. She slid up to lock and squeeze his member between her thighs, allowing him to touch and tease her center, but never quite enter. She planted a hand on either side of him to support herself, and stretched and arched her back, catlike, brushing her pubic hair against him again and again. Her teasing forced him to grow harder, to swell and swell.

"Do you feel what is happening?" Jessica breathed into his ear between long, wet kisses. "Do you feel it?"

Longarm felt himself grow dizzy. Up above, their tongues were intertwined, and down below, his erection was kissing the moist folds between her thighs. Between one kiss and the next, Longarm rolled over onto his side. He pulled Jessie in tight against him, and buried his face in her mass of fragrant hair, his palm gliding the length of her curled body. Her skin was far softer than even the silk robe she had worn. His fingers rode up the curve of her hip, to cup and stroke the hemispheres of her buttocks.

"Lord above, woman," Longarm gasped. "What fine tricks Myobu has taught you."

"There are no tricks, silly," Jessica laughed. She watched his face as she licked and lightly bit his nipples. Her fingers stroked his erection and cupped his scrotum, making him moan. "The geisha's art lies not in knowing how to play tricks, but in knowing how to surrender."

Longarm buried his face in the warm valley between her

breasts. He inhaled her woman-scent. He flicked his tongue around and around the dark rosettes of her breasts. Quickly he moved from one to the other, at first licking and sucking, and then using his teeth to barely rake her swollen nipples, until her pleasured purr rose to a sob of joy.

Jessica's legs parted then, and as she rolled over onto her back, she drew him into her. They moved flesh against flesh, sliding and rocking together against the soft fur of the rug. Longarm kept her cradled in his arms as he swung his hips up and then plunged down, each thrust seeming to take him deeper and deeper. It went on like this for long minutes. All barriers between them now fell. Neither had any thoughts, but lived only in those parts of their bodies that touched. Those were the only parts that mattered.

Longarm slowed his movements each time he felt his orgasm growing near. Jessica rubbed her bottom against the rug as her inner muscles squeezed against him. Finally, moaning uncontrollably, she dug her fingers into Longarm's buttocks and pressed him in to the hilt, all the while gyrating her hips in an endless circle. Helpless in that luscious embrace, Longarm felt his orgasm build and build until it burst forth. At that moment, Jessica locked her mouth to his as she came, so that their love-cries were exchanged as their kisses had been.

Longarm stayed nested inside her as they talked, punctuating each exchange with kisses. Soon her silken, rippling contractions brought him blossoming forth, newly hard, and more ravenous for her than he had been before. This time their lovemaking was slow and playful—after all, now they were old friends. They exchanged gifts of love. Jessie gloated each time she was able to make him beg for mercy, for a moment's rest. This time when they came, Jessie threw her legs up around Longarm's back. His fire spread into and through her in ever-widening circles. Waves of rapture washed over her, her eyelids fluttered, and her mouth formed a perfect circle. She clutched at Longarm like a woman about to drown, and she didn't let go until he had carried her to their passion's limit.

They had only a few hours until dawn, so they went up the stairs to Jessica's bedroom, to sleep wrapped in each other's arms. As Longarm dropped off, while his lips nibbled absentminded kisses across the nape of Jessie's neck, he thought of the diminutive, elderly Myobu, of her small round face, cracked and yellowed like ancient porcelain. He thought of her laugh, tinkling like wind chimes, and of her eyes flashing brightly, like those of a young girl's.

Listening to Jessica's soft, regular breathing, pressing his length against her, Longarm remembered what this woman in his arms had said about destiny, about *karma*. He wondered what was going through wise Myobu's mind tonight. How much did the frail geisha's soul know about what had gone on between this woman and him?

When Longarm finally slept, his dreams stayed far from the Shiloh battlefield, where death came too soon, to boys too young. Instead he dreamed of the Japans, and geishas, and women everywhere—women meant for love.

Chapter 8

Longarm awoke a few moments before dawn. He slipped from Jessica's embrace and padded silently to his own room, where he groomed and dressed himself for the day.

As he left the house and walked toward the stable, his Winchester in hand, he spied Ki sitting crosslegged on the ground, facing the rising sun. His back was ramrod straight and his hands were placed in his lap. He had his eyes half closed and was breathing in a deep, regular manner, almost the way a sleeper breathes.

Longarm knew instinctively not to disturb the man. It was some kind of praying that Ki was doing, or not praying exactly, but the sort of thing that goes on in church when the pastor calls for a moment's silence.

In the stable he found his gelding already saddled up and ready to go. The only other person awake was Ki, so Longarm wanted to thank him on the way out, but when he led his horse out of the stable, Ki was nowhere in sight.

It was full morning by the time Longarm reached the range area where Willie and the other hands were supposed to be. The hands had long since ridden out for the day, and Willie was stacking up the other men's bedrolls before he started the day's cooking chores.

The little fellow looked to be in his late sixties. He had a gray, close-cropped beard covering his chin and cheeks, maybe to make up in part for the lack of hair on his head. He was dressed in baggy jeans and a ragged flannel shirt. His boots were low-heeled, as befit a man who did more wagon-sitting and walking than riding. He wore no gunbelt, but an old Colt Peacemaker hung from its trigger guard on a nail pounded into the chuck box.

As Longarm rode up, Willie pulled a cloth cap out of the back pocket of his denims and perched it on his bald head.

"It's my cooking hat, and gives me something to wipe my hands on," he told Longarm by way of greeting. "Now who might you be?" Before Longarm could answer, the old cook turned his attention to stoking up a cookfire.

"Can you keep a secret, Uncle?" Longarm asked Willie's back. He dismounted and let the gelding's reins trail.

The cook straightened up, grimacing, and then spat into the fire. "Sonny, I forgot more secrets than you'll ever have the pleasure to tell. Now if you can get me a little drunk while you're telling me, I can surely forget what I heard." He looked hopefully at Longarm, his pale blue eyes twinkling.

"Damn, I don't have a bottle with me, Uncle," Longarm apologized.

"Shoot, then we'll have to drink mine," the cook said disgustedly. "And my name's Willie. You keep calling me 'Uncle,' folks gonna think I'm old, boy . . ." He rummaged around in the chuck box and came out with a bottle of bourbon. "I keep this about for cooking purposes, you understand." Willie winked at Longarm as he pulled the cork with his teeth. "Can't cook for shit unless I'm half sloshed." He gulped a big swallow, and handed the bottle to Longarm. "Now who the hell are you, boy? This here's Starbuck land. What are you doing here?"

Longarm took a tentative swallow of the bourbon, and liked what he tasted. "Willie, I was going to spin you a tall tale concerning the who and why of me, but I need your help, and if I'm asking for a man to help me, least I can do is tell him the God's honest."

"Well said, sonny." He kicked the last bedroll under the awning jutting out from the side of the chuckwagon, and looked back at the fire, which was sputtering and crackling now as the seasoned wood caught flame. A sudden, short breeze sent the smoke his way, and as he turned, coughing and swearing, rubbing at his eyes, he spied Longarm about to take another pull off the bourbon. 'Here, sonny!" he cried, lunging for the bottle. "Don't drink too much, else you'll fry your brain!" He beamed a moony look at his quart, took a long drink, and then smacked his lips. "Now who the hell are you, boy?"

"I'm a deputy U.S. marshal, and my name's Custis Long. Folks generally call me Longarm. I'm here to look into Alex Starbuck's death. I'd appreciate it if that could stay between us, Willie."

The old-timer nodded sagely. "You be the fellow they call Longarm?"

"Yep," Longarm smiled.

"The lawman?"

"That'd be me."

"The *federal* lawman?"

"The very one." Longarm knew what was coming.

"Never heard a' ya!" Willie cackled. He slapped his thigh and hopped about, cackling like a chicken that just laid a turkey egg. "Ah, my, still as sharp as the day is long," he complimented himself as he wiped the tears from his eyes. "Reckon you want to talk to me about that fateful day. Yessir, many have, many have. You could say that I've become sort of a famous person in these parts as the man who knew Alex Starbuck best. I taught him what he knew about cattle, you see. He'd often said to me, 'Will'—he called me Will, you see—'Will, I owe everything I have to you—'"

"Care for a smoke?" Longarm asked. He'd hoped to wait the windstorm out patiently, but Willie showed no signs of blowing until next day's dawn.

Willie plucked the proffered cheroot out of Longarm's fingers. "Smoke it later," he explained, tucking it behind his ear. "No good, a fellow smoking while he cooks," he announced. "Ashes might get in the grub." He headed for the rear of the wagon, where the chuck box was firmly bolted into place against the tailgate. The box was about four feet tall and a yard wide, with its outer wall hinged at the base so that it could be swung down to form a sturdy work table supported by a leg. The leg was itself hinged so that it could be folded flat when the box was closed. "You want to ask me stuff, go right ahead, Longarm. But I gotta keep cooking while you talk. Some new hands came in last night from Sarah. We're signing on hands faster than I can make biscuits." He reached into the chuck box, rummaging around in the various partitions and shelves built into it, to come out with a small keg of sourdough, a sack of flour, and salt and baking soda.

"Can't get over Mr. Starbuck naming a cow town after his wife," Longarm said as he watched the cook work. "Cow town's a rough place to carry a woman's pretty name."

"You didn't know Alex, so you can say that, Longbow."

"Longarm."

"Right," Willie replied. He filled a large, pockmarked tin pan half full of flour, poured some of the sourdough batter into that and threw in some soda and salt. "Sonny, fetch me that skillet over yonder," he asked Longarm.

Longarm wandered over to where a black cast-iron skillet's handle was poking out from the rack of pots and pans beneath the wagon bed. He carried it over to Willie, who instructed Longarm to dribble some of the bacon grease it contained from the morning's meal into the batter.

"Like I said, you didn't know Alex, so you can say that." Willie began to knead the dough against the floured surface of his cook table. "Starbuck admired cowpokes. You see, he felt he had more in common with independent men than with rich ones. A honest hand makes his own way and answers to no one but his foreman, and if he and the foreman don't get along, he collects his pay and moves on. That's a hell of a lot better life than wearing a pinstriped suit and having a slack belly, breathing stale air, and getting a hump in your back from bending over your figuring—"

"I get it," Longarm cut him off.

"Anyway, we got fine schools in Sarah. And a church— not that I've ever been inside it," Willie cackled. "Fetch a Dutch oven and pour some of that bacon grease in it, will you? We got the railroad, and flowers and trees—*that's* Sarah too. There's a doctor and a dentist. In Sarah, kids will grow up healthy and knowing how to read. *That's* what Alex left for his wife."

Longarm watched the cook pinch off eggs of the dough and place them in the greased Dutch oven. "I guess he loved his wife very much."

"You might say that, Longbow."

"Longarm."

"Right again, sonny, right again." He put a lid on the filled Dutch oven, and had Longarm set it in the summer sun, so that the biscuits would have time to rise before being baked on the fire. "Alex built an entire town to carry on Miss Sarah's memory. Beats a bunch of flowers at a stone grave marker. Flowers die, but a town goes on forever." He paused a moment to smile at Longarm, and then squinted up at the sun. "Guess I'd better start on the meat. Them peckerheads will be riding in for dinner soon enough. I tell you, boy, cooking three meals a day, it's surely just and

107

fair that a cook gets paid better than the top hands."

"No argument there, Willie." Some of the worst meals he'd ever eaten had been chuckwagon prepared, Longarm remembered. But when well made, no fare on earth was tastier. "Where did Alex bury his wife?" he asked out of idle curiosity.

Willie shrugged. "No one knows. Alex took her back from that there Europe, and buried her himself, with a little help," he chuckled as he began slicing steaks from a haunch of beef hauled from the wagon's cool, dark interior. "Don't matter where Miss Sarah lies, the town's her monument." Willie set several skillets on the fire and began to fry the flour-dredged beef filets in hot fat. He put the biscuit-filled Dutch oven on the fire, and piled coals on its lid to create an even, baking heat. "Ain't you going to ask about where Alex himself is buried?" he asked as he prodded and poked the sizzling meat with a long, two-pronged fork.

"Reckon he's with his wife in some quiet, wooded grove." Longarm smiled. "I don't want to know where the graves are, Willie. I want to know about what you heard and saw that day Mr. Starbuck was shot and killed."

Willie was silent as he transferred all the cooked steaks to one skillet and moved it off the fire. He set a lid on the pan, to keep the meat warm and free of dust. When he finally looked at Longarm, there was suspicion and self-doubt in his pale blue eyes. "Don't rightly think I've the time to jaw with you anymore, sonny. I've got to make the gravy and un-crock the stewed fruit and—"

"You said the shooting sounded like a string of firecrackers going off," Longarm cut him off.

"And the other boys laughed at me. Said I was getting senile." He spat out the word like it was a piece of foul food. "They said I made it up to get free drinks. That I made up everything about me and Alex being trail partners."

"I believe you, Willie," Longarm said quietly, sincerely. Willie squinted at him, trying to see if he was being joshed. When he spoke it was with an emotional, trembling voice. "All them others had me senile so many times, maybe I got to believing them. I don't want to talk about the day Alex was cut down. I'm afraid Miss Jessie will lose patience with me. Decide she's got no place for an old hand."

"You've got a home here till you die, Willie," Longarm assured the old man. "Miss Jessie herself told me so. She said you've got a pension here. She couldn't imagine running the place without you."

"Fine girl. What a fine girl," Willie muttered, turning back to his work table, so that Longarm could not see the film of tears glossing his eyes. "What a tussler she is!" he exclaimed in that hoarse tone of voice some men use when their feelings of love grow too strong. "Just like Alex. What a tussler!"

To get the conversation back on the right track, Longarm said, "You know, when I heard the firecracker remark of yours, it reminded me of a sort of shooting noise I'd once heard."

"Yeah?" Willie mused, his eyes growing shrewd. He carried a small sack of flour and a box of salt over to the fire. "Now where might that have been?" He poured the meat juices from all the skillets into one pan and threw in a handful of flour and a pinch of salt. This he stirred until it became a thick gravy.

"I heard it well over fifteen years ago, Willie. Now it don't matter if we were side by side during that time, or if we were facing each other. I've learned that it's best for a soul to disremember whether he rode for the blue or the gray." As he spoke he took a handful of the .25-caliber shell casings from his pocket and stood them on end, like a line of soldiers, along the edge of the work table.

Willie ambled over, attracted by what Longarm was doing. He picked up two of the casings and compared them. "Same damn gun fired them both, sonny. These two long scratches prove that much."

"I know," Longarm said. "How many shots did you hear?"

"'Bout thirty." After a moment's pause, Willie asked, "How many did you find with that long scratch?"

"About thirty."

"Damn!" Willie gleefully slapped his thigh. He was almost hopping up and down in excitement. Longarm had to remind him that the gravy was going to burn if left untended much longer.

After a moment's stirring of the thick sauce, the old man put down his spoon and turned to face Longarm. "Sure as I live and breathe, I'll never forget the first time I heard that noise. I was a wild fella back then, hanging around with a bunch of toughs who figured that despite the surrender, the War wasn't nearly over yet, not for *us*. We raided Union outposts, waylaid carpetbaggers—" Willie scowled, but good-naturedly. "Never you mind where, and when, federal lawman. I guess we thought we were small potatoes. We swaggered and bragged about how we were making the bluecoats pay, but I don't think we ever really thought the Union boys would bother to get after us."

"The way they looked at it, they had to make examples," Longarm said.

"Well, they surely did make us into them examples, boy," Willie murmured sadly. "We was closing in on a supply wagon, but it was a setup, an ambush. All of a sudden the canvas tent on the wagon dropped, and this big old cannonlike thing began chewing us up. It just kept on firing. It was like we had stepped into a yellowjackets' nest. You know? The mean ones build their nests in low bramble, or beneath hollow logs... I just threw myself off of my horse and kissed that there grass like it was a ten-dollar whore. The boys with me were jumping and twitching just like beestung dogs, 'cept that it wasn't bugs tearing into them, it was lead. They were dancing in the air, dead already, but so much lead was being pumped into them that it was keeping them on their feet. The rounds that didn't hit flesh chewed up the ground. Clods of earth and tufts of greenery went flying. And all the while I was hugging the ground and shitting in my pants, I was listening to that string-of-firecrackers noise. It grew in my ears until it sounded loud as thunder. I knew I would never, *never* forget it."

"I never forgot what it sounded like either, Willie." Longarm's nod was doleful. "I never forgot what it could do to a line of good men."

The cook retrieved his bottle of bourbon. He took a swig and handed the bottle to Longarm. "You and yours, me and mine. Lot of good boys never made it past those awful years. A drink to them."

"To them," Longarm agreed. After the whiskey had begun its slow burn in the pit of his belly, Longarm asked, "Was it a Gatling gun you heard back during that raid? And on the day Starbuck was cut down?"

Willie sighed. "It was, sonny, but if we're agreed on that, it causes more problems than it solves. These here casings you gathered are .25 caliber. They've got more in common with a range hand's coyote gun. Hell, the Gatlings I saw after the War fired .42s. They looked like artillery. Weighed as much, too. They were big, heavy contraptions mounted on field carriages, and pulled along by teams of horses.

"Long-gun, I tell you true," the old cook admonished. "I was by Alex's side—at the very scene of the ambush— within seconds of the time they opened up on him. You climbed the rise to gather up these shells, so you know how steep it is. No way in the world ten men could carry a Gatling *down* such a slope, let alone *up* it in the first place. No way horses could haul it, either, not within the space of an hour, let alone moments."

111

"And even if we could figure out the way they got the gun up there," Longarm sighed, "we'd still have the fact that these here shells are .25s."

The cook said thoughtfully, "Be a real nightmare if they'd had a Gatling, say, small enough for one man to carry. That one man would be the equal of ten. Speaking of one man against ten, I've got a fine story for you. You're a lawman, you ought to appreciate a story about a good fight. You see, Alex and I were down by the Mexican border, and we ran into a gang of these here desperadoes. This goes back a few years, now—"

"Willie, save it for next time," Longarm said. "I'll bring a bottle of rye along with me, to keep our throats wet." He swept the row of shell casings into the palm of his hand, and slipped them into his coat pocket.

"Just as well," Willie said. "I got to lay out this here dinner for the boys."

"Remember, Willie," Longarm warned him as he mounted up, "this little talk we had, and my job in these parts, goes no further."

"I ain't gonna tell them peckerheads nothing," Willie cackled. "Why *should* I? I'm *senile*, for chrissakes." He turned back to his pots and pans, calling, "See you around, Longboat!"

"See you around," Longarm laughed, and rode off. After a mile, and just before he rode over the crest of a rise, he slowed his gelding and twisted in the saddle to look back at the camp. The hands were just riding in. Soon they'd be eating and laughing, and teasing Willie about the quality of his grub. After dinner the hands would return to their work, and then the few men left behind to day-herd could ride in for their midday meal. Willie would keep their food hot. He knew his job.

Longarm rode on, back toward the Starbuck spread. Jessie would be around, and he looked forward to seeing her. It was always hard to say goodbye to a fine woman, but bidding Jessie farewell when the time came was going to be the hardest yet. Longarm wondered if he even wanted to say goodbye. He only had a few days to get to the bottom of this case before the army came stomping in. Old Billy Vail was probably going crazy with worry back in Denver. Sending his boss a progress report over the telegraph wire was the way it usually worked, but this time around, Longarm didn't want to chance the Denver clerk intercepting it. He could send the wire directly to Vail's home, of course, but for now Longarm decided that he didn't have anything worth the cost of the wire to report anyway. According to Jessie and Willie, Alex Starbuck was murdered by Europeans with a weapon that didn't exist. Vail would not be pleased to hear that. He was a mite old-fashioned concerning murders, Billy Vail was; he liked his criminals to be one-hundred-percent American boys, just right for American courts of law. Billy was pretty much a meat-and-potatoes man when it came to murder weapons, as well. He'd take a sixgun or, in a pinch, a Winchester over a Gatling gun anytime.

The pocketful of shell casings jingled as Longarm rode. Their weight pressed against his side all the way back to the Starbuck spread.

★

Chapter 9

Longarm cut through a stand of tall pecan trees to come around to the wide, dusty trail that led to the Starbuck residence. About three hundred yards from the house, Longarm reined in his mount. In the front yard sat a brougham hitched to a two-horse team. There were other mounts around the closed buggy, and several men.

Longarm unstrapped one of his saddlebag flaps and poked around until he came up with a small brass spyglass. He extended the segments of the battered telescope, spat on and polished the scratched lenses, and, squinting one eye, peered through it at the scene. The brougham was displaying a flag. As Longarm watched, a breeze fluttered the square of cloth. It was the flag of Texas: on the left, a broad, vertical band of blue with a single white star in its center, on the right, two horizontal bars—white above, red below.

Longarm shifted the spyglass's narrow field of vision to the men around the brougham. There were three of them. One was obviously the buggy's driver, while the other two were escorts. They were mean, hard-looking men who appeared as if they needed both baths and shaves. The only things they didn't seem to need were more guns. They all wore two pistols holstered butt-forward in crisscross gun belts, and Winchesters were tucked into the saddle boots of the two mounts. One of the men had some sort of badge glittering on his chest. No matter. Longarm had run into men like these before, and knew that they were lax about everything but fighting. They were Texas Rangers.

Longarm kneed his gelding into a slow walk toward the bunkhouse and stables. The Rangers glanced his way, but Longarm knew that at this distance they could only assume he was one of the hands coming in early. At the stable he turned his mount over to the wrangler on duty, informing the kid that the horse would be needed later in the afternoon. Winchester in hand, Longarm walked around the back of the stables, by the corrals, to avoid any chance of being spotted by the Rangers. He had a good idea who the visitor to the Starbuck spread was. If he was right, there was no problem, although he would still want to keep from revealing himself to the Ranger escorts.

His plan was to rest up on one of the empty beds in the bunkhouse. There'd be cool, fresh water there, for washing as well as drinking. Longarm intended to ride into town for the evening and make a tour of the saloons. It had been his experience that the best thing a lawman undercover could do was to go trawling for information, and there were no more fertile fishing holes than the saloon row of a cow town in the middle of roundup fever.

He was about to enter the bunkhouse when he caught movement out of the corner of his eye. Some distance away he spotted Ki, partially hidden within the shadows of a grove of leafy hardwoods. Ki spotted him at the same time, and waved. Longarm strolled over.

"You're practicing archery, I see," Longarm said by way of greeting. "Funny-looking bow, though. It's crooked, ain't it?"

"Hello, Longarm," Ki said. "This is a Japanese bow."

Ki was shirtless, his torso filmed with sweat from the

heat of the day. Longarm considered him very unusually built for a man who had been powerful enough to toss about the much larger Higgins during their fight. Ki's muscles were long and slender. His biceps bulged very little when he strung his bow. But lean of build as Ki was, and without an ounce of excess fat on him, the rippling pattern of his belly muscles and the cords of his shoulders showed clearly.

Longarm had to smile. If he were a betting man, he'd still have put his money on Higgins during that fight, and sure as hell, he'd have lost his cash. It was a simple fact that Ki looked skinny by Caucasian standards, which preached that there was no such thing as strength without bulk.

"Do you not wish to meet our esteemed governor?" Ki asked. He selected an arrow from the leather quiver by his feet, and fitted the notch to the string.

"Thought it was him. I spotted his flag on his buggy. Who else would rate three Texas Rangers as babysitters?" Longarm glanced overhead. The sunlight was filtering through the thick foliage of the grove. He tugged out his pocket watch. Eleven-thirty. Close enough. He took a cheroot from the breast pocket of his coat and lit up. "The governor come all the way from Austin to see Jessica?"

"More or less," Ki said. "He came by rail to address tonight's Cattlemen's Association meeting in Sarah. The meeting will be held late, after the day's work is done. A tally boss will be voted on. The various outfits are ready to combine their herds."

"Seems a mite unusual for a state governor to take an interest in something like picking a tally boss," Longarm remarked.

"There is more to it, of course. Alex Starbuck lent the cattlemen a great deal of money. He cared for their well-being in other ways, as well. Jessica is not the only individual in these parts who feels as if a father has been lost."

"So the governor is here to reassure them that all's well?"

"No." Ki seemed amused. He flipped his long hair out of his eyes and rested his bow, along with its notched arrow, against his hip. "If the governor did try to reassure them, who would believe? He has not brought the army, his only source of power, knowing full well that Texans would not be happy if he had done so. No, my friend. The governor is here to convince Jessica Starbuck that she must reassure her neighbors. As heir to her father's holdings, it is she who can extend the notes on the land, defer payments on the loans for cattle, and pledge the Circle-Star hands to keeping the peace and protecting the big main herd."

"Will she do it?" Longarm asked. "Whatever it is the governor wants?"

"Of course!" Ki threw back his head and laughed heartily. "She will do so much more than he wants. The governor will be very surprised. He expects to comfort a trembling, frightened, frail female, to offer her a masculine shoulder on which she can cry. You see, he does not really know Jessica. The governor thinks that all that he had once owed to Alex Starbuck has been canceled out by the man's death. He is about to find out that Jessica controls the payment schedules to those debts of honor, as well." He swung his bow up into position.

Longarm looked the way Ki's arrow was pointing. One hundred yards away, a two-by-four post stood vertically planted in the bright sunshine. "You forgot to mount your target," he said. "And I still say that bow is lopsided." It was about five feet long, with several asymmetrical bends and curves in it. Ki gripped the bow a third of the way up from the bottom.

"All Japanese bows are shaped in this manner," Ki explained. "Although some are considerably longer." He pulled the notched arrow back to a point well behind his ear.

Longarm nodded silently, in respect. The strength it took to keep the bow flexed to that degree was clearly enormous, but Ki's arm and hand were rock-steady. "You still forgot to mount your target on that there post," he reminded the archer.

"That post *is* the target," Ki murmured absently. He turned his head as if he were shunning the distant two-by-four. He released the string, the twang of the hemp cord turning the bow a full one hundred and eighty degrees around in Ki's left hand. The bow was now pointing at the archer.

The method and style of Ki's shooting was so different from that of Indians, that Longarm forgot to watch the arrow's flight. When he thought to look, he saw that its head was firmly embedded in the two-by-four.

"How the hell did you manage to hit that itty-bitty stick without looking?" Longarm demanded.

"The arrow hit the target. All I did was prevent myself from getting in its way." Ki's soft voice was slightly slurred, and his dark brown, almond-shaped eyes were halfclosed. He resembled a man more than two sheets to the wind on fine whiskey, but there was nothing drunken about the way he selected another arrow from the quiver. "With the proper mind, or *zanshin*, Longarm, there is literally 'no way' I can miss even the smallest target. It is, as Westerners say, 'as easy as hitting the broad side of a barn.'"

"What kind of arrow is that you've got?" Longarm peered at the projectile's head. Instead of a point, or series of barbs, the arrowhead was a crescent-shaped wafer of steel. "May I look at it?"

Ki handed it over, warning, "Do not touch the edge. It is razor sharp. In my homeland, this sort of arrow is called the 'cleaver.'"

"What's it for?"

"For severing ropes or, say, the harness binding together a team of horses. In my own land, such an arrow was often used to cut down the enemy's battle flag, and in that way demoralize his forces." He took back his arrow, and notched

119

it. In one smooth motion he raised his bow, drew the string back far past his ear, looked way from the target, and let the arrow fly. Without even watching it, he turned back to his quiver to select a third arrow.

Longarm, meanwhile, watched the 'cleaver' bury itself an inch or so beneath the first arrow. "Lord, the way you bend that bow, I'd think it would snap."

"A Japanese bow does not snap," Ki explained patiently. "Look." He turned the bow sideways, to show Longarm a light-colored sort of wood sandwiched between two layers of another kind. The layers were glued together, and wound at several points with a red-colored, silken thread. "This bow's core is held between two pieces of a wood called bamboo. The bamboo has been tempered by a special fire treatment. It's flexibility, lightness, and strength are unsurpassed by any bow devised by Americans."

It took Longarm a moment to figure out what Ki had meant by that last remark. "You mean by Indians, right?"

"I am an outsider," Ki shrugged. "Are not all people born here Americans?"

"It depends on who you ask, and how you look at it," Longarm said ruefully. "Someday maybe all folks will be considered just plain Americans. At least we can hope."

"You *should* hope," Ki said adamantly. "To remain strong, a nation must not divide itself. It is a bad thing to be an outsider in one's own nation." The arrow he was about to fire had a head as twisted as a corkscrew. "This is called the 'chewer.' It is designed to be fired into the midsection of the enemy so that it can rend and chew his bowels."

"Nice," Longarm said with a grimace. He watched as the arrow went whizzing on its way to join its brothers. "Seeing as you don't need to spend much time on aiming, do you mind if I ask you a couple of personal questions?"

Ki's eyes crinkled with amusement. "Actually, I have

spent long years in aiming, without ever firing an arrow, but as to your questions, you may certainly ask."

"But you may not answer, that it?" Longarm finished for him. Ki did not answer, but only shrugged as he bent to his quiver. "Well, we'll cross that bridge when and if we come to it," Longarm decided. He flicked an inch of gray ash off the glowing tip of his cheroot. "I'm interested in why you're not up at the house with Jessie and the governor. Don't you care about what's being discussed? It could concern the future of this spread."

Ki sighed. "You know so little of me, Longarm. Be careful. In my homeland, ignorance is no excuse for compromising another man's honor."

"I'm just curious as to where you fit in. Are you Jessie's partner?"

Ki smiled at Longarm like a man looking at his dinner. "I *help* Jessie. I help her *accomplish* things."

"Ki, you're a man with a shitload of surprises up your sleeve. You've got all kinds of unusual weapons." Longarm dropped the stub of his cheroot to the dirt. Before he could grind it out with his boot, Ki did it for him, with the sole of his bare foot.

"Alex Starbuck was killed with an unusual weapon, was he not?" Ki asked.

"He was. That makes you a suspect, Ki." Longarm waited for the other man's response.

"In my homeland—" Ki began.

"We ain't in your homeland."

"In my homeland," Ki raised his voice to override Longarm's interruption, "a man who even *accidentally* brushes against another's blade must be prepared to pay for this dishonor with his life. But you do not even realize the dishonor you have done me."

"I'm still waiting for your answer, Ki." Longarm swept his coat from the butt of his Colt as Ki let his bow slide to the ground and shifted his weight onto the balls of his feet.

"Withdraw the question, Longarm, or I will kill you," Ki said matter-of-factly.

"Reckon we're at that bridge I mentioned a minute ago," Longarm said sadly.

"It is a very narrow and delicate bridge you bid us to travel," Ki whispered. "The bridge will only allow one of us to survive this journey."

Longarm watched Ki carefully. He'd seen this before, in Mexicans and Indians. They didn't bluster and fume the way a white man did when something got his dander up. They just got quieter and quieter. Maybe they would even smile. But finally there would come a moment—faster than the eye could see, faster than thought—and woe be unto the one who'd insulted or riled them...

Longarm decided it was time to defuse this situation, before things got past the point of no return. He brought his hands up to chest level, palms forward. "Easy, my friend," he said. "You don't have to answer my question. You already did. No guilty man who was smart would show that he was so upset at being accused. You got to realize it's my simple duty to pry into the business of anyone involved in any way with a crime."

For one measured moment, Ki stood silent, his eyes as if he were listening to distant sounds too faint for Longarm's ears. Then he smiled and relaxed. "We are not in my homeland. Your authority is the relevant point of this... discussion we are having. You are still my friend, Longarm."

"Glad to hear it," Longarm chuckled.

"I am not at the house because I am not concerned with wealth. I care only about Jessie's well-being."

"That I do believe, old son," Longarm interjected quietly.

"You must also realize that the agenda the governor has planned for today is, well, *known* to us. Jessica has been well trained in many aspects of business, but especially in

122

the art of negotiating, an art the Japanese take very seriously.

"The governor will suggest that she give him power of attorney, that he sell off parts of her holdings. He will suggest that it is all too much for a young woman to comprehend. 'Don't you want to enjoy life?' he will ask. Jessica, meanwhile, will ponder what she has been taught, and do her best not to insult the governor by showing her boredom. They will dine together this evening, and then the governor will offer his protection as an escort to tonight's meeting. She will accept, of course, out of politeness, but she will have her horse towed along by one of the Rangers, so that she will be able to ride back with us."

"With *us?*" Longarm asked innocently. He tried hard to keep his amusement hidden.

Ki smiled to show that he understood the joke they were acting out. "Of course, *us!* Sarah has filled up with drifters and strangers working for the roundup. I know quite well that you must have planned to circulate around the town to see what you can learn. I intend to do the same."

"The governor isn't staying here?"

"Jessica could not bear that," Ki laughed. "He will stay at the hotel."

"That place didn't seem fancy enough to me to be fit for a governor," Longarm kidded.

"Oh, he will have a much nicer room than the one they gave you," Ki remarked innocently.

"How would you know? They let in folks *barefoot* in that place?"

Ki, his dark eyes sparkling, held up another arrow. "This is called 'death's song.' The bulb you see fitted just behind the head has a hole that catches the wind and, in that way, sings the last song the enemy will ever hear. Would you like to hear it?" he asked politely.

"Just a couple of opening stanzas," Longarm warned.

"Of course." Now Ki was grinning like a wolf. "In any

123

event I advise you not to miss the Cattlemen's meeting. It will be a treat to see Jessie..." His voice faded as he notched the arrow and let it fly.

Instantly the air around them was filled with a high, sharp keening sound. To Longarm it sounded like a combination of the world's biggest mosquito—one with murder on its mind—and a violin's strings being tortured to their breaking point. The arrow's pitch would have made a dog howl. The nightmare sound ended with an abrupt *thud!* as the 'death's song' found its target post.

Throughout the arrow's flight, Ki had stood as if mesmerized. "Once I heard that sound multiplied by several hundred. I was just a young boy, not yet in my teens. The army of archers were all accomplished masters of *yugamae.*" In answer to Longarm's look of puzzlement, he added, *"Yugamae* is the term used to describe the correct etiquette with which to approach *kyujutsu,* the technique of bow and arrow. The battle taking place was one between rival warlords. The force for which the archers fought was badly outnumbered, so their warlord decided on the strategy of intimidation. He ordered his archers to being the technique of *inagashi,* the style of archery in which the bowman sustains a rapid rate of fire—fifteen arrows per man, let us say, accurately shot as fast as you could fire fifteen accurate rounds from your Winchester. As intimidation was the object of the attack, the 'death's song' was fired exclusively, with the exception of one 'cleaver' arrow, fired by the chief archer, to cut down the enemy's flag. Think of it, Longarm! The sky darkened by the hailstorm of so many arrows. The world was filled with the sound of 'death's song!' Now the warlord was careful to instruct his men not to hit any of the enemy, for if intimidation brings about anger in the adversary, it has failed in its purpose. No, all of the arrows landed in the same area to prove that the archers had the ability to control their weapons, but none of the arrows drew blood." Ki stared into Longarm's face to make sure he was understood. "They did not have to draw blood. At this warning chorus of 'death's song,' the enemy soldiers and warriors threw down their arms and clapped their hands over their ears in terror. Their warlord had no choice but to surrender to his opponent. His men had been intimidated. The battle was over, with not one drop of blood spilt, except for the vanquished warlord, of course, who committed *seppuku*. That is suicide, Longarm. It was the only way he could expunge his shame at being defeated."

"That's quite a story," Longarm said after a few moments.

They both stood silent for a while, until the vivid images the story had raised began to fade.

"Ki? Why did you come to America?" Longarm finally asked. "Did Starbuck send for you, the way he sent for Myobu?"

Ki looked at him sharply. "I was not sent for, but came here to seek my future. I stowed away on a clipper bound for San Francisco. Later I learned that the ship belonged to Alex Starbuck. It seemed to me to be an omen—I was to seek out and offer my services to the man upon whose ship I found transport. There were other reasons, of course. I felt that my *karma* was linked to those Americans who plucked their nourishment from my homeland. More about that I will not say... After some time in San Francisco, I found my way to Mr. Starbuck's offices. I was fifteen years old."

"And you actually got to see him?" Longarm asked, amazed. "You were just a boy, and you got past all of his clerks and assistants?"

"I had grown up in a house where English was spoken, so I had the language, though that would not have mattered, since Mr. Starbuck spoke fluent Japanese." Ki smiled faintly. "As for getting past his security provisions, I considered that to be my employment test. In any event, I offered him my services, and he accepted."

"What do you mean by 'services,' Ki?"

He shook his head. "Here the stream that is my story flows into the Starbuck River. I cannot tell the rest without Jessica's permission."

Longarm nodded. He did not want to strain their fragile friendship by revealing that Jessie had already told him her story. "You haven't mentioned why you decided to leave the Japans in the first place. You sound to me like a very homesick man."

Ki bowed. He placed his palms on his thighs and bent from the waist. It was a gesture of politeness, but not one of obsequiousness. During the entire maneuver he held Longarm's eyes with his own. "I mean you no disrespect, Longarm, but there are things I cannot discuss."

"Was it your father or mother who was Caucasian?"

"Forgive my silence, Longarm."

"I understand." Longarm looked away from the pain he saw in Ki's eyes. "Good enough." He picked up his Winchester and headed back toward the bunkhouse. "See you in town."

As Longarm walked away, Ki chose another arrow from his quiver and blindly notched it. He brought up the bow, pulled back the string, and fired. His eyes, blurred by tears, could not see the target, but his ears told him that he had hit it. His raging heart had not ruined his aim.

Ki nodded to himself in grim satisfaction. That was honorable if not excellent.

★

Chapter 10

Longarm approached Canvas Town on foot. It was like approaching the seashore at night. The roar, like the thunder of the surf, grew louder as he drew closer. If Sarah's high white church steeple and her schools embodied the spiritual and moral fortitude of Sarah Starbuck, the section beyond Main Street, the section called Canvas Town, embodied her fiery red hair, bedroom eyes, and hot, sensual femaleness. The proper side of Sarah immortalized a fine woman, but Canvas Town was that woman by night, sparked by her man's embrace.

In Canvas Town there were no street lamps—no streets, for that matter. Longarm went from the glare of the brightly lit tent entrances to the pitch-black, grassy fields in between. Ambling about, he listened to the squeak and groan as the tents swayed against their ropes in the night breeze. There rose everywhere the sound of tinny piano music and the hearty laughter of men who were tired, but not so tired that they might give up their fun. Voices would swell out of the darkness only to fade as shadowy forms blundered past, drunk, night-blind, or a little of both.

The hissing kerosene lanterns by each tent entrance were surrounded by fluttering moths, and farther out, by the railroad tracks, other tents with faintly glimmering red lanterns attracted a different sort of moth to flutter and beat its wings before burning up in a flame far, far too hot. How could this honkytonk, carnival atmosphere, this wild abandon just a street away from the gas lamps and whitewashed picket fences, not remind Longarm of the two sides of every woman's personality?

The sharp tang of cheap whiskey, and the smoky grease-smell of even cheaper food both attracted their share of cowboys. In one relatively well-lit area, gunsmiths, saddlemakers, clothiers, and cobblers peddled their wares from small booths or the tailgates of wagons. Competing for the cowboys' hard-earned dollars were the stalls that offered games of chance. These lured their marks with a pretty girl standing by the entranceway. Only the greenest lad could think that he had any more chance of winning the woman outside than he did of winning the game inside, but still the hands streamed in, not caring whether they won or lost, only looking for a good time.

By morning's light, Canvas Town would look sordid and dreary, Longarm knew. But that was tomorrow. Tonight the shadows and kerosene glow only softened and beautified, and the whiskey did not punish but instead rewarded the drinker with sharp wit and boundless energy. Come morning, both Canvas Town and cowboy could lick their wounds and swear never again—until nightfall.

It would all last as long as the roundup lasted. Sarah had no need for tent hotels and soft-roofed saloons once the free-lance hands had drifted from the area. The tents owned by the town would be taken down and folded up for another season. The peddlers would hitch their swaybacked teams to their gaudy wagons and slowly head for other parts, other gatherings of men with time and money on their hands.

Longarm entered a saloon tent and bellied up to the bar—which happened to be a couple of planks laid lengthwise on a trio of high sawhorses. There was no floor to the tent, and consequently no floor to the saloon, except for well-trampled grass, but there were tables and chairs, lit by candles stuck into empty whiskey bottles, or by small, hissing lanterns. Behind the bar were beer kegs and a motley assortment of half-filled bottles.

"What's yours?" the bartender asked in a weary, punch-drunk voice. He had a day's worth of beard on his cheeks, purple shadows beneath his eyes, a cigar clamped between his yellowed teeth, and, incongruously, a shiny, brand-new derby, about one size too small, perched like a bird directly on top of his bald head.

Longarm gave the bottles a quick perusal. Sure, he could order Maryland rye, and the label would probably even assert that it *was* Maryland rye, but what would he get? "I'll take a beer," he told the barkeep, who filled a mug with the draft, and then gave Longarm his change from a leather purse strung about his ample middle.

As the bartender performed his services, Longarm noticed him scanning the tent with ever-watchful eyes. The place was crowded and rowdy. The bartender carried no gun, but when he turned around, Longarm saw the braided leather handle and wrist loop of a blackjack sticking out of the back pocket of his pants. Behind the bar, in a corner, a fellow with a double-barreled scattergun sat and watched the crowd from a high-chair contraption.

Longarm took his mug to a nearby vacant table. Toward the rear of the tent, two liquored-up hands began to fight over which way a deck was stacked. The bartender pointed to the two men and hollered, "Quiet down, there!"

The hands ignored him, of course. Longarm lit up a cheroot, sipped at his beer, and leaned back in his chair to watch the show.

The fellow in the high chair climbed down, scattergun in hand. He wasn't very tall, but he was well built, with thick forearms and large, capable-looking hands. He was wearing a sleeveless undershirt, and a derby that seemed the identical match for the bartender's. Maybe they were brothers.

The scattergun was more than likely a means of intimidating the patrons rather than blowing their fool heads off. Usually such fearsome-looking weapons were loaded with birdshot. A rowdy cowboy might end up enduring the taunts of his friends as he searched out a doc to pick the pellets out of his backside, but he'd heal up pretty soon. It would not do for any saloon, permanent or canvas-roofed, to earn itself a reputation as the sort of place where a patron could be killed by the help. As the man passed Longarm's table, he saw that in addition to the scattergun, the fellow wore a .44 derringer in a tiny stitch of a holster, high up just behind his right hip. In the unlikely event that killing should be required, the tiny handgun's range was adequate in the close confines of the tent.

Both cowboys quieted down as the bouncer approached their table. Longarm could not hear what passed between the bouncer and the rowdy pair, but he did see one of the cowboys make a grab for the scattergun, a stupid move in any case, but especially stupid against such a handy opponent. The fellow with the derby stepped nimbly back, swinging the barrel of his shotgun as he did so, to crack the steel against the other's outstretched fingers. The cowboy howled and let his injured paw hang limply at his side. His buddy scrabbled for the revolver crammed into the waistband of his jeans—the fellow was plainly no gunslick—and was rewarded for his clumsy efforts by having the twin barrels of the scattergun shoved hard into his belly. The cowboy doubled over, his revolver falling out of his pants to thud against the grass as he did so, and the fellow with the derby spun him around and booted him right through the doorway of the tent.

Throughout the short-pitched battle, the bouncer had kept on his face the relaxed but alert look of a seasoned veteran. That expression signaled to Longarm that the fellow knew that nine out of ten bar brawls ended in low comedy, like this one had, but every once in a while there was one that could suddenly burst out of control, like a forest fire in woods gone too long without rain.

The cowboy with the swollen hand scurried after his drinking partner. The derby-wearing winner of the fight tossed the fallen revolver after the two, then sauntered back to his lookout post behind the bar. The din of conversation and clinking of bottle against glass went on as it had before and during the confrontation. As far as Longarm could tell, he was the only man who had even bothered to look in the direction of the commotion.

Longarm sent blue wreaths of smoke toward the pitched cloth ceiling. Canvas Town was an interesting place to while away the hours, but its pace and commotion were such that no information or gossip could be gleaned. For his purposes, Longarm needed a quiet saloon where the barkeep had time on his hands and was grateful for company, paying or otherwise. The bartenders in Canvas Town were just passing through, like the cowboys themselves. The place was too fleeting a phenomenon for anybody to learn much about anybody else.

Longarm would have spent his time at the Union Saloon, the largest of the permanent watering holes in Sarah, except that Ki had warned him off, saying that the place was stodgy and stiff, that nothing ever happened there because it was on the regular patrol of Town Marshal Farley and his deputies. Longarm decided to head over that way anyhow, since he'd tied his horse up in front of the Union. Besides, there he could get himself a drink of bona fide Maryland rye.

Longarm was finishing off his beer when he felt a heavy hand clamp down on his shoulder. He twisted around in his chair to see that he was bracketed by two men.

"Howdy there, gunslick. 'Member us?" one of them said.

It took Longarm a second to place them. The one who had spoken had a wispy, billy-goat beard. "Sure. You're the fellow named Ray. Both of you were Higgins's boys. You still with him, now that he's out as the Starbucks' foreman?"

"Now we're with *you*, gunslick." Ray grinned, showing broken teeth. "Or should I call you by your name? Longarm. Musty, get us some chairs. Us and Mr. Longarm is gonna have a drink."

While Musty did as he was told, Longarm checked the two cowboys out. They were still each just a pair of gleaming Justin boots, an expensive Stetson, and a long, dusty road in between. They smelled of horseshit, and their guns jutted out from their right hips like the hammers in a workman's belt.

They sat down, one on either side of Longarm, so that they were positioned more like three men abreast than facing each other. Longarm thought about the danger of the situation, but he figured he was safe from being shot here in the saloon with the bouncer watching over everything from his high vantage point. The one named Musty, a youngish, curly-haired man with pale gray, squinty eyes and sun-reddened cheeks, pulled out a plug of tobacco and bit off a chaw. He set the plug down on the table.

"How'd you boys find out my name?" Longarm asked, not that he really expected them to answer, but you could never tell with horse turds like these two. "Pretty slick of you, anyway, I'll give you that." He poked Ray in the ribs, pleased at the angry glare the poke provoked.

"Never you mind, lawman," Musty mumbled around his mouthful of chewing tobacco.

"Who said I'm a lawman?" Longarm asked, casting his bait.

"Not just a lawman, but a federal marshal," Musty replied.

"Fetch us both a drink, Musty," Ray growled disgustedly. "Longarm here don't need one. He's still got an inch of warm beer left in his glass."

"You two are real sports," Longarm grimaced.

"We can't be buying you drinks." Musty indignantly spat a long, brown stream of tobacco juice on the trampled grass. "We lost our jobs on account of you snooping around—"

"The drinks," Ray barked.

So they not only know my name, Longarm thought, they know why I'm here. That eliminated the possibility that his being recognized was just a bit of bad luck brought on by his being spied by some jailbird he'd arrested in the past. That sort of thing happened all the time to undercover men. You took the time to build a painstakingly exact cover, and then, from out of the blue, some joker who saw you strolling down the street pointed his finger and sang out, 'He's a lawman!' to anyone who had reason to be interested in such news.

But an ex-convict, or any outlaw, would have no way of knowing *why* Longarm was in Sarah. Town Marshal Farley might have spilled the beans, but it also could have been either Jessica or Ki. Right now, Longarm had his money on Farley. But why would any of the three who knew his business talk about it to men like these?

Musty returned with two shots of whiskey and two mugs of beer. The men tossed off their drinks and then chased the rough liquor with cooling swallows of brew.

Longarm watched, pleased. They were trying to drink their courage, of course, but more alcohol would also loosen their lips. "Buy you gents another round?" Longarm began to rise, but he stopped as Ray, on his left, snaked his right hand beneath the armrests of their side-by-side spindle chairs. Longarm looked down at the six-inch blade Ray was holding against his vest, just about where his heart would be.

"You just sit back down, Longarm, 'less you want me to pop your pump," Ray said jovially. "It wouldn't be no trouble at all on my part."

Longarm realized that Ray's knife was out of sight of

anyone else in the saloon. Amid all the noise and confusion, Longarm could be stabbed dead and left for a drunk sleeping it off in his chair, and no one would be the wiser.

"You gonna sit, or you gonna bleed?" Ray softly insisted.

"Bar's a little crowded anyway," Longarm said, and sat back down.

Musty reached over and plucked Longarm's Colt out of its holster. He was about to slip it into his own waistband when Ray ordered, "Give it here, boy."

Musty did as he was told, scowling all the while. Ray held the double-action weapon up to the lantern light. "Fine gun, Longarm. I promise to think of you every time I plink away at a coyote with this here Colt."

"Hey, you!" came a shout from behind the bar. It was the bouncer, the man with the scattergun, high up on his tower-chair, addressing himself to Ray. "You want to stay in here, put that piece away."

Ray tucked Longarm's Colt into his gunbelt. "Musty, take his wallet, see if he has any papers that could help— No! Wait a minute, that bastard with the shotgun is still watching us," he grumbled. "Longarm, real pleasant-like, you take out your billfold and lay it down on the table."

"I'd be careful with the likes of him, Ray," Musty warned. "He could have another gun stashed in his coat."

"Hmm, do you, Longarm?" Ray coaxed. "Iffen you do, think on this. I'm no gunslick like you, but I've spent a lot of time around campfires with nothing better to do than practice with my knife. There's no gun on earth that can be drawed and fired before I'm able to push these here six inches of steel between your ribs."

"Except one gun, maybe," Longarm suggested as he slowly removed his wallet and placed it on the table. "The kind of gun that shoots .25s?"

"But you ain't likely to have one beneath your coat," Musty guffawed.

"Shut up about them guns," Ray snapped at his partner.

"Give me the money in the wallet."

"There's no papers in here but travel tickets and the like," Musty said. "Hot damn, here's his shiny badge."

"Hold on to it, and the wallet," Ray said. "That way they'll find a corpse with no identification. We'll all be long gone by the time they figure out that a lawman's been killed, and not just some drunk got himself involved in a knife fight."

"Let's get it over with, Ray," Musty whined.

"I guess I'm a dead man, eh, boys?" Longarm made his voice rise high and trembling, the way Henry, the clerk in Marshal Vail's office, sounded when Billy began roaring and fuming over some misplaced report.

"Keep your voice down," Ray hissed, anxiously eyeing the bouncer surveying the scene.

"Lord, I hate the idea of it's being a knife." Longarm reached into his pants pocket, the action bringing Ray's glinting blade close by, just like a cat will pounce at the first sign of movement around a mouse hole. "Easy now," Longarm soothed. "Here, see?" He held up a double eagle. "I just thought Musty could fetch us all another round. I know I sure could use a shot. What do you say, boys?"

Musty snatched up the money, as Longarm had known he would. The nineteen dollars and change would carry an out-of-work cowboy quite a ways. Poor Musty! He wasn't even smart enough to figure out that Ray would never let him keep a cent. Not that Ray was going to profit for very long from this little exchange. "I suppose you boys know more than you're telling concerning the murder of Alex Starbuck?"

"Plenty more," Ray boasted. His knife hand rested on the seat of Longarm's chair, although the blade was still tickling Longarm's ribs.

"What you know doesn't seem to be paying you very well," Longarm observed.

"The ransom hasn't been collected yet," Ray shrugged.

"When it is, we'll get our share. Higgins said so."

"You boys believe *that?*" Longarm mocked.

"Shut up! We'll do all right. We already got your money, lawman. And after tonight's Cattlemen's meeting, the whole town will pay off. Too bad you won't be around by then," he laughed, as Musty returned with three shots of whiskey.

"Reckon that meeting will be starting in just an hour or so," Longarm mused. "Well, let's drink up, boys."

"And then get the other part done with," Musty added meaningfully as he tilted his head toward Longarm and shifted his mouthful of tobacco to one cheek to give the rotgut an unobstructed chute down his gullet.

Longarm felt Ray's knife blade momentarily lessen its pressure against his ribs as the man lifted his glass and knocked back his drink. Slamming his own left hand down upon Ray's right, so as to pin the knife in place, Longarm shouted at the top of his lungs, "Don't stab me, boys! Please!"

"Christ, Ray!" Musty gasped. "Get it done!"

"I'm trying, dammit!" Ray's face contorted with effort.

"Help!" Longarm shouted, doing his best not to break out laughing. He pressed down with all his strength as Ray's sweat-slippery fist slipped another fraction of an inch closer. Now the man redoubled his efforts to stab Longarm, but he just couldn't make that last crucial inch.

"Here now! What's going on?" It was Mr. Derby, with his scattergun. He'd climbed down from his chair and was coming over to see what was the matter. Just as Longarm knew he would.

"Ah, shit," Ray moaned. "Can't stab him with this bird watching."

"He's going to throw you two out," Longarm chortled. "Just as well, I've gotten to like you two jokers. It'd be a shame for me to have to kill you both."

"All right, you two," the bouncer growled, his scattergun hovering ominously. "This here gent was sitting peaceably enough, and then you two come in and start a ruckus. Out of here, now!"

Ray and Musty exchanged anguished looks. "Please—" Ray began.

"I said now!"

Haltingly, both men rose. "Aren't you coming with us, old pal?" Ray coaxed Longarm. The knife had somehow disappeared from sight.

"No," Longarm drawled. "I think I'm staying right here. This is a fine establishment that knows how to look out for its patrons." He beamed at the bouncer, who smiled back.

"Come on now, Longarm." Musty tried to laugh. "Come with us!"

Longarm looked at the bouncer. "Weren't you throwing these two out?" he asked innocently.

"That I was." He tilted his derby forward and cocked both barrels of his scattergun. "Now git! Both of you."

Like two boys being sent to the woodshed, Ray and Musty began to trudge away. The bouncer turned and began to head back to his chair. Musty took the opportunity to spin around and spit a glob of chewing tobacco squarely against the back of the bouncer's neck.

The fellow almost lost his derby as he clamped his hand against the thick sludge. He turned, his face at first pale with anger, but his expression soon changed to aghast horror as the shit-brown, sticky mass began to run down beneath his undershirt. His fingers came away with gruesome webs of the stuff stringing down. "Who?" he managed to say, his voice shaking with fury. "Who did it?"

Without a word, Musty pointed to the plug of chewing tobacco still on the table where Longarm sat, and then at Longarm himself.

"All right, you son of a bitch! You go with your friends!"

Longarm was about to argue, but when the bouncer shoved the scattergun into his belly, he decided that now was not the time to claim he only smoked cheroots.

137

As he stood up, Ray put his arm around Longarm's shoulders. "Let's go, old pal!" he said triumphantly.

"I would have missed you fellows, anyhow," Longarm sighed. As they walked toward the tent saloon's flap doorway, Longarm realized that the knife had materialized once more in Ray's right hand, and that its blade was once again against his ribs. As before, no one could see what was happening, not the way Ray had his left arm around Longarm's shoulders, and his knife hand buried beneath the tails of Longarm's frock coat.

"Once we're outside," Ray whispered into Longarm's ear, "once we're in the dark, I'm going to cut your heart out!"

As the bouncer returned to his chair, Musty took up a position on Longarm's left, but when they reached the flap doorway, he had to fall back behind the other two.

Longarm made his move. He brought his left hand around to grab hold of Ray's knife, but not before he felt the icy bite of the blade slice through his vest and shirt to pierce the skin across his ribs. Ignorning the pain, he brought his right fist up in a short, stiff uppercut. The force of the blow drove Ray back, although the cowboy still kept hold of his knife. Longarm's hand snaked out to pluck his double-action Colt from where it was dangling in Ray's belt, but before he could get a shooting grip on the gun, Ray pressed his attack. His knife came around in a deadly windmill motion to slash down toward the point where Longarm's neck joined his shoulder.

Longarm threw himself backward to the ground, managing to send two shots Ray's way before he even hit the grass. Out of the corner of his eye, Longarm saw Musty draw his Peacemaker. There was nothing he could do about it in time. Longarm prepared to take at least one of the young cowboy's bullets—

There was a loud boom, and Musty screamed. His gun fell as he dropped to his knees, his shirt in tatters, his back peppered with birdshot. The bouncer, from his high vantage point, had sent his swarm of pellets over the heads of those in the crowded tent.

Longarm looked back at Ray. The man's knife lay in the grass, forgotten, as Ray concentrated on the two holes the .44 slugs had punched into his chest. He rocked on his legs like a seasick landlubber experiencing his first sea storm, and then fell forward, his head coming to rest between Longarm's boots.

The bouncer was making his way toward the scene, trying to get through the gaping crowd, as Musty.—still on his knees—picked up his Peacemaker and pointed it at where Longarm lay sprawled.

"Don't do it,. boy," Longarm warned him, but Musty wasn't listening. Longarm brought his own gun around.

"Gonna kill you!" Musty babbled. He clicked back his revolver's hammer.

Longarm fired first. He aimed high and to the left, to put his round into Musty's right shoulder. The bullet's impact knocked Musty backward, off his knees. Longarm rode the .44's recoil up, then brought the gun back down into position as Musty wailed in agony, his pellet-peppered spine scraping against the rough turf. Still he held on to his cocked Peacemaker.

"Please!" Longarm begged. "Drop that damned gun!"

Musty slowly brought up his revolver. He was holding the Peacemaker in both hands now, to steady his wavering aim. "Gonna kill you—"

Longarm fired again, an instant before Musty squeezed off that one damn shot he'd been working on. Longarm's shot went true, thudding into Musty's heart. As the young cowboy died, his own bullet ploughed a furrow through the grass just a foot in front of him.

"Throw it down!" the bouncer demanded. He'd exchanged his scattergun for his derringer. Longarm guessed that was his way of saying he was serious.

Longarm set his Colt down on the grass. His side was slick with blood and stung like the devil, but he didn't think it was a deep wound. Christ, he hated a knife! "I'm a federal marshal." He told the bouncer, thinking that his cover was blown to shreds anyway. His wound hurt, and the Cattlemen's meeting was due to begin and Longarm wanted to be there to see or hear whatever Ray had expected to happen.

"If you're a lawman, where's your badge?" the bouncer asked craftily.

"My badge is in my wallet," Longarm sighed; he'd been through this routine before. He gestured toward Musty. "That one lifted it." He'd underestimated these two cowboys, it seemed, and it had almost cost him his life. Longarm dabbed gingerly at his side with his pocket handkerchief.

"How come you spit at me if you're a lawman?"

Longarm pointed at Musty, his bloodied handkerchief balled in his hand. *"He's* your damned spitter, not me!"

"Then how do I know he isn't the marshal as well?" the bouncer roared triumphantly, to the general approval of the crowd. "Somebody go get Farley!" he shouted. "And you—"

"Long's the name."

"You, Long, you sit right there and wait for the *real* law."

Sighing to himself, Longarm got comfortable on the grass. It looked as though he wasn't going to get to stop off at the Union Saloon before the meeting, after all.

★

Chapter 11

Ki surveyed the action from his vantage point at the Union Saloon. He was standing shoulder to shoulder with others at one end of the fifty-foot, polished mahogany bar. He had one foot on the brass rail—a booted foot. As Longarm had remarked about the hotel, the Union was not the sort of place where they let you in barefoot.

Poor Longarm, Ki thought. He felt a little guilty about fibbing to the lawman, telling him that the Union Saloon was a dull place, and that the best area to snoop around was Canvas Town. The truth of the matter was, Ki wanted to stake out the Union himself, and didn't want Longarm around to attract attention. Well, at least Longarm would stay out of trouble in Canvas Town...

Several bartenders were being kept busy by the crowd in the saloon. They drew mugs of draft from built-in taps decorated with ornate metal spigots, or poured shots from the extensive display of bottles on the backbar beneath a wide, gleaming mirror.

Ki stared into the mirror. He was, of course, known in Sarah, and had been recognized by several people, but there were enough out-of-towners in for the roundup for Ki to blend in. Those who knew him tended not to say more than a few words to him anyway...

He was, after all, a 'chink' to those who were American, just as he was a 'round-eyes' to the Japanese. He belonged to no race, no country—but then, he never really had.

Ki stared into that mirror behind the bar. He was wearing a blue-gray tweed suit, a sky-blue cotton shirt, and a black shoestring tie. His Stetson was steel blue. On his feet he wore black, ankle-high Wellington boots. The low cut of the boots gave his feet the freedom they needed . . .

All around him, reflected in the mirror, people went about enjoying themselves. Ki watched them, or their reflections in the glass, but he felt as much apart from them as he would have staring at aquatic creatures below a pond's flat, gleamingly clear surface. The saloon, the oldest and largest in Sarah, was a cavernous place brightly lit by gas lamps. Gaming tables, including a wheel of fortune, took up half of the room, with tables for drinking taking up the other half. Leading up to the second floor was a wide, red-carpeted staircase. If a man wished, one of the saloon's "hostesses" would escort him to one of the many rooms on the second floor, and there she would entertain him in private.

Ki turned around to lean against the bar. He hooked his fingers in his gunbelt. Wearing a firearm was a nuisance, but it was his experience that to blend in, a man had to look like everybody else. Not wearing a gun invariably attracted attention in these parts, so he wore one.

It was not that Ki was unfamiliar with firearms, or with any weapon. The study of weaponry, of killing, had been his life's work. His life had been decreed worthless on the day he was born. The only path of honor open to him had been the path that led to his becoming a warrior.

Ki sipped at his scotch, neat. Over the years he'd developed a taste for the spirits imported from Scotland in exchange for Texas beef. Once, scotch had been hard to come by, but now imported foods and distilled spirits from Europe were becoming commonplace in the larger cities and towns of America. He sipped at his whiskey, and remembered the past...

His mother had been high-born, a member of an aristocratic family in Japan. She was beautiful and full of life—the exquisite product of centuries of culture and high, fierce, Nipponese blood. When the Yankee barbarians forced their way into Japan, his mother fell in love with one of the American adventurers who came to take his fortune from the island nation originally dubbed *Jibon* by the conquered Chinese. *Jibon,* literally meant "origin of the sun."

Against all warning, and totally realizing the horror she was causing her family, his mother took the Yankee barbarian as her husband. The family disowned her in disgrace, society shunned her in disgust and contempt. To Ki's mother, all this made no difference. So completely and totally did she love her husband that she willingly made plans to leave her homeland and journey with him to America. Ki—but that was not his name then—was born to them a year later. He was to be their only child.

For six years the child's father labored, and then, finally, his business in Nippon was done. The long years of loneliness for the mother and son were soon to turn into a future of great adventures. Both mother and son had learned English, for they had no company other than barbarian company; the Nipponese shunned them totally. The child was only able to attend school because of his father's mighty influence, but even then, Nipponese children would have nothing to do with him. It made no difference that he claimed his heritage, for he looked like a Yankee, a barbarian.

It did not matter, the child told himself countless times, every day. It did not matter. A new world waited, his father's world—surely, in the fantastic land called America, the land his father had lovingly told him about, surely in such a place a soul would not be judged merely by how he or she looked? Surely in America he would belong!

Only a month before they were due to set sail, the child's father took sick. The finest physicians were sent for, but they could do nothing. 'A disease of the blood,' they'd said, shaking their heads. A disease of the blood; the little boy who would grow up to become Ki had always thought that funny...

His father died in Nippon. His mother, heartbroken, did not know what to do to protect herself and her son. She was a simple woman, for all of her noble heritage. Her husband's holdings were looted by rival businessmen in Nippon, and in America she was totally dismissed by her husband's relatives as a bizarre anomaly in the man's past. Without his father's patronage and funds, the little boy was soon expelled from his school. Soon after that, his mother died of a broken heart.

Her funeral was attended by the curious only, for no one would consent to mourn her. "This is what comes of the barbarians," the curious laughed at her funeral. "This is what comes of foolish love..."

But the hecklers at his mother's funeral would not consent to mourn. The five-year-old hoped that his lone mourning would be enough to soothe his mother's *Kami,* her spirit...

Ki grinned to himself as he sipped at his whiskey. Never had he blamed his mother for falling in love. Never had he taken from his origins the moral others had taken: that love could be wrong, a foolish thing. Love could be impossible, love could be doomed never to blossom—Ki knew firsthand about such love—but this did not taint it with foolishness. A man's love was like a wild horse, like a powerful animal that had to be controlled, but could never really be broken or tamed. One could not let love interfere with one's duties, with one's vow of service. Love had to be kept in its place, but never was love foolish.

Of course, such high-flown thoughts belonged to him now, but in the days following his mother's death, the little

144

boy that he was then had no thoughts except for thoughts of fear...

His mother's relatives had disowned her, and so they had disowned him. He did not exist for them. He went with the other urchins to sit outside the monastery gates, as was the custom for orphans. Most were, of course, turned away by the priests who taught spiritual matters and who conducted *ryu* in which the *bugei,* the martial arts, were taught.

Ki sat with the other orphans. He sat with them at gate after monastery gate, traveling with—but never befriended by—those who were successively turned away. When it came Ki's time for an interview, the results were always the same.

"It is not that you are lacking in any spiritual, physical, or intellectual capacity," the priests would intone serenely, sitting in their fine silk robes, their shaven heads glistening like ivory carvings in the lambent glow of a thousand candles. "It is because your blood is impure that we must turn you away. Despite your mother, you are not Nipponese, you are the son of a barbarian. You must go."

The little boy would trudge from the light and warmth of the monastery, to try the next one. And then the next.

And then there were no more. What the little boy had once dismissed as childish taunts, he now realized were in fact a prophecy...

"Mongrel!" his schoolmates had jeered. "You are a cur, fit only to scavenge in the gutter!"

Months passed. His clothing became rags. He fought the dogs—his fellow mongrels—for the garbage tossed in the back alleys. He dodged merchants' sticks, criminals' knives. At night he solemnly prayed that his ancestors, and especially his mother and father, were not suffering disgrace and humiliation as they looked down from heaven at his poor circumstances.

It was during his wanderings that the boy stumbled across

a blind alley buried deep in the heart of the city. Here there was a shack, and in front of it, a large, strong-looking man of fierce expression. His possessions were few, as far as the little boy could tell, and most of them were shabby, except for the man's gleaming, obviously well-tended collection of blades and weapons. This man, the child knew at once, was a *bushi,* a warrior.

The man sat on a thin, threadbare *tatami* mat. His hair was long and lacquered in back, shaved in front, as was the samurai's custom. The man's clothing was of thin, threadbare cotton. The little boy stared in awe at the man's arms and torso, marbled with muscle. Off to one side was a cooking pot over a small fire. Steam rose from beneath the lid of the pot, the fumes rising toward the heavens like incense, and oh! didn't the aroma smell just as wonderful! The little boy's senses had grown quite sharp since he'd lost his home, as sharp as the constant pangs of hunger in his belly. There was chicken cooking in that pot, and pungent vegetables—

The samurai looked the little boy over. "What do you want here, termite?" he growled. "Begone, you with your big eyes staring at my dinner."

The little boy took no step back or forward, but just stared, and wondered how to ask. Dinner meant little to the boy; how many times had he gone without it, or lunch or breakfast, for that matter? What the little boy wanted to ask...but how could he ever hope?

"Get out of here!" the samurai shouted. "Go, or else, instead of looking at my dinner, I'll cut you up and cook you with it!" The samurai pretended to start to get up, hoping to frighten the boy away, but the ruse didn't work. He settled back on his mat, to glower darkly at the little snip.

"It's not your food I want, noble warrior," the little boy began, but then he lost his nerve.

"Not my dinner, eh?" the samurai grumbled. "What,

then? Money?" He waved away the boy in disgust. "I have no money. You wish money, go beg the *bushi* who have it, those who call themselves true warriors, and yet disgrace themselves and the warrior's code by teaching the martial arts to any student who has the coin to pay for the lessons. Once, before the cursed barbarians came to our land, there were plenty of excellent wars for a samurai to fight! Now it's gotten so a warrior can't make an honest living, unless he wants to open a stall next door to the flower-arranging teacher, and the tea-ceremony teacher, and the music teacher! Never! I for one, Hirata Soko, will never dishonor the *bugei,* the martial arts, by revealing them to a bunch of spoiled brats. Nor will I degrade them by turning them into what is being called these days *budo*—"Martial Ways," indeed! Just a rationalization so that dishonorable samurai can make money!"

"It is neither food nor money I wish, noble samurai," the little boy replied.

"Samurai!" the man snorted derisively. "I am no samurai!"

Startled, the boy replied, "Then what—?"

He was silenced by a wave of the man's hand. "I *was* a samurai, once. But a samurai is a warrior who serves a great lord. I serve no one! And what is a servant without a master? A *ronin,* a 'wave man,' blown here and there like the waves of the ocean, owning nothing, owned *by* no one."

Abruptly his fierce manner changed, and he beckoned to the boy.

"Come closer," the *ronin* said. "Come on! Hirata will not hurt you. I was only joking about cutting you up and putting you in the pot."

"I know," the little boy said bashfully.

"You know, do you?" Hirata laughed. "Tell me, how do you know?"

"I'm too skinny to eat."

At this the man threw back his head and roared his laughter. "Come closer, boy. Your voice is like the squeak of a mouse, I can hardly hear you." Hirata peered and squinted. "My eyes aren't what they once were, but you do seem strange to me, boy. Come closer, I'll not say it again..."

"Samurai!" the man snorted derisively. "I am no samurai!"

Startled, the boy replied, "Then what—?"

He was silenced by a wave of the man's hand. "I *was* a samurai, once. But a samurai is a warrior who serves a great lord. I serve no one! And what is a servant without a master? A *ronin,* a 'waveman,' blown here and there like the waves of the ocean, owning nothing, owned *by* no one."

Abruptly his fierce manner changed, and he beckoned to the boy.

The little boy slowly came forward, within an arm's length of the huge *ronin.* The child had to stare up to look at the man's face, even though the warrior was seated cross-legged. The boy felt like he was standing next to a boulder of a man, a mountain of a man. Inhaling, he could smell, mingling with the food's aroma, the *ronin's* man scent, the smell of brute animal.

"How can it be?" Hirata exclaimed. "You are a barbarian child!"

"My father was...barbarian," the little boy said, lowering his eyes. "My mother was high-born..."

"And what is it you wish of me, boy?" the man growled, his ill humor revived by this living reminder of the rape of his homeland.

The little boy took a deep breath. He sent a prayer to his parents in heaven to prepare the way for him should the warrior chop off his head in a fit of anger brought about by his arrogant request. Fully expecting to be slain for his impetuousness, the boy said, "I beg that I be allowed to pledge myself to you as your servant and apprentice, that you teach me—"

That was all he got out. With a flick of his wrist, the

148

man swept the boy's feet out from under him. He placed his hand across the boy's neck to pin him fast. Such was the breadth of Hirata's hand that he was able to place thumb and little finger on the ground, with his palm across the boy's windpipe.

The boy stared up at the fearsome face of the *ronin*. He was pinned fast, but so thin and scrawny had he grown that he felt no discomfort beneath the *ronin's* hand. The boy was about to beg for forgiveness, and to be allowed to wander on his way, but before he could, the man began to berate him.

"How dare you ask to be taught the *bugei?*" the warrior spat scornfully, his words causing the boy more pain than could any of his assortment of razor-sharp weapons. "You are not even fit to learn the *budo*. You are tainted with barbarian blood! You are impure! A—"

The boy closed his eyes, and allowed his soul to wander through the depths of his own anguished heart deep as a cave, so that the taunts and jeers of the *ronin* grew muffled and distant. Shame and guilt for his predicament fell from him. Lying on the ground, pinned by his tormentor, the boy felt anger and defiance wash over his frail, tiny body. The boy opened his mouth, and made a sound...

Just as the eerie howl of the wind is the aural manifestation of the terrific potential force of moving air, so is the *kiai*—the shout of spirit—the aural manifestation of *ki,* the all-encompassing, indefinable spirit of the universe, focused through the body and will of the master of *bugei*...

At that moment the little boy felt just that power grow in him. Another boy might have cried out in surrender, in a plea for mercy; in *this* boy it was a shout of utterly fearless determination.

It was the *kiai,* the shout of spirit. The boy sounded it as his tiny fist the size of a butterfly struck the *ronin's* massive forearm.

Hirata unpinned the boy at once. Awed, he stared at the

place on his arm the boy had struck. The blow did not harm him, of course, but it did astound him, and touch his heart. This child's body—to be sure, a tainted body—housed a soul stripped pure and clean by adversity. This soul had been pitted against the world from birth. It *had* to tread the warrior's path.

"What is your name?" Hirata asked, and after the boy had told him, the *ronin* said, "Yes, I have heard the story of your mother's marriage. It is a well-known bit of gossip." He pondered the pale, frightened, but stoic lad lying sprawled before him; as he did so, love, pity, and sympathy flooded his heart, for the *bugei's* code decreed that such emotions must live in every true warrior. Corrupted *budo* be damned, Hirata thought. Here, at last, was a worthy protege to whom Hirata could teach the strict, stern *kakuto bugei*—the true samurai's way. The boy *had* to tread the warrior's path, there was no other path for him to follow . . .

All of this the little boy did not then know, of course, but Hirata told it to him toward the end of their ten years together. As the little boy grew in both stature and strength, he learned the *kyujutsu, kenjutsu, bojutsu,* and *shuriken-jutsu*—the arts of bow and arrow, sword, staff, and throwing-knife—and all the other fighting arts. The two of them, mentor and protege, had many talks about duty and destiny and how those two guiding principals had merged on the day of their fateful meeting, during the ten years that the boy spent becoming a warrior . . .

Ki's keen ears picked up a strange-sounding voice. Instantly it seized his wary attention, hauling him back from the reverie into which he had drifted, floating on whiskey. The voice, with its European accent, catapulted him into the present, and his duty toward the woman he had sworn himself to protect, Jessica Starbuck.

A stranger had entered the Union Saloon, to take a table near the bar. The man looked to be in his thirties. He was

150

tall and fit-looking, with close-cropped blond hair the color of goldenrod, and eyes as heartlessly pale blue as the sky during a Texas drought. The man's handsome looks were marred by a thin red scar running the length of one cheek. He was dressed in a suit of black, but wore no hat. Beneath the man's long coat, Ki could see the bulges made by a brace of pistols.

Ki stared at the man from his own place at the bar. It was not the stranger's thick Germanic accent as he harangued the bartender for service that had tipped Ki off. It was the way the man carried himself. There were, after all, many Europeans who visted Sarah on legitimate business. The Scottish cattle barons were buying up ranches, as were the English and others, from the Continent, but this blond, scarred, pistol-packing stranger was no cattleman. Ki knew that it was quite possible that the stranger would sense him in the room and turn in his chair to stare at him. Instantly a silent sort of mutual recognition and acknowledgment would flow between them, even though they had never before laid eyes on each other. They would recognize each other not as men, but as warriors.

It was the *ki,* the focused energy, or perhaps just the faint heat of it, that warriors could sense in one another. Ki had felt it radiating from Longarm that first time they'd met, up on the rise overlooking the place where Alex Starbuck had died. In Longarm, the fierceness was tempered by mercy and honor. Ki knew that Longarm suffered a tiny bit of each death he brought to his adversaries. Longarm was a warrior who still fought the most important battle, the battle to maintain a hold on his humanity while he lived by the sword—or gun. This was a battle Ki still fought as well. The first thing Hirata had taught him was that all of a warrior's prowess could turn into a thing of shame rather than pride if his soul was weak and he surrendered to the thrill of spilling blood.

Yes, Ki nodded to himself. He had instantly recognized

151

this European stranger for what he was: a warrior, but not one like Longarm or Hirata, a warrior who had given himself over to dishonor, who plied his trade not out of duty and destiny, but for the dark and addictive joy of killing.

The bartender brought the stranger a bottle and two glasses. Ki watched and waited. When the stranger's drinking partner arrived, he would be distracted. Then Ki could perhaps move closer without tipping the man off. He would like to hear what this European killer had to say. Ki only hoped the conversation would be conducted in English. Unlike Jessie, he did not have a command of German, Spanish, French, and Italian. He could speak only English and, of course, his own Nipponese.

As the stranger looked about the room, Ki pulled his hat down over his eyes, so that the other could not see them. It was the eyes, mostly, that gave away a man's secrets. Even the most experienced warrior could not keep his eyes from telegraphing a warning to his adversary a moment before he struck his killing blow. Hirata had always taught that this did not matter, that the aim of a *bushi* was to strike a blow so perfectly executed that his adversary could not block it, no matter how much advance warning he had received.

Ki had never fully accepted this teaching, and that had been the only source of disharmony between himself and his teacher over the ten years of his apprenticeship. Hirata was proud and pure-blooded, after all. There was no question as to his place and stature in Nipponese society. He had been samurai, like his father before him, and his father's father. The only question was, how excellent a samurai. The ancient *bugei* tradition decreed that a warrior walk loud and proud, and in that way give lesser beings an opportunity to scurry from his path. Should a man even accidentally touch the scabbard of a samurai's *katana,* his long sword, that man could be instantly slain; the samurai's code demanded that the guilty party be cut down then and there. Hirata's way of handling this particular situation that Ki now found himself in would be to stride up to the blond stranger, demand to know what his business was in Sarah, and then kill him, then and there, if the man refused to say, tried to defend himself, or, in Hirata's estimation, attempted to lie.

This Ki would not do, just as he would not carry or willingly use the *katana*. Ki had often thought that it was this decision on his part that had finally broken the bond between himself and his teacher, effectively ending his ten-year apprenticeship.

"I simply do not understand," Hirata had shouted. The *ronin* had grown older and grayer over the years, but he was still a mountain of a man with hard stones for muscles and tree trunks for limbs. "The *katana,* the long sword, is a divine weapon, a badge of honor that links a warrior to his noble ancestry." They were sitting in front of Hirata's shabby house, situated at the end of the blind alley. As always, every evening, the cookfire was burning, and the pot of food the two would share was quietly bubbling away, the puffs of fragrant steam rattling the lid. "For the life of me, I cannot understand why you are so stubborn about using it!"

The young man only smiled. "Honored teacher, it is precisely for the reasons you have mentioned that I refuse to use it, even though I have practiced and mastered its techniques."

Hirata drew his *katana* from its scabbard, as if to seduce the young man with its exquisite, deadly beauty. The fine steel's lovingly polished length caught the fire's reflection. *Hirata* turned the blade this way and that, so that the flame's reflection glittered, captured in the gleaming sword, reminding the young man of precious gems, of the jewellike Siamese fighting fish in their crystal bowls, of the light in a woman's eyes when she is joined in blissful sexual union with a man...

"Honored teacher," the young man began, "you have

described the *katana* as the link between a warrior and his noble ancestry. For this reason I turn my back on it."

"Explain yourself," Hirata growled like a tiger, and lifted his hand as if to cuff his pupil. He restrained himself only because it had been his experience that some unlikely seeds of wisdom had a way of sprouting from this half-breed's mind.

The young man, meanwhile, had not flinched from the threat of the blow. An apprentice can learn nothing until he trusts his teacher, and the ultimate sign of such trust in the world of the warrior is for the pupil to calmly await any sort of strike from his master, knowing that an expert *bushi* can perfectly control the force and intensity of the attack. "How can I carry a symbol of noble ancestry?" the young man explained, not even looking at Hirata's unpraised ham of a fist. "Society has shunned me, and even my mother's own family has denied me my birthright."

"Ah . . ." Hirata sighed, and looked away from his pupil. What the young man had said was, of course, quite true. The *ronin* felt his heart grow heavy with pity. The young man had an indomitable spirit, a spirit that had not been broken by the stigma of his barbaric sire, but oh, how that spirit—once so tender and vulnerable—had been scarred! "I did not mean literal ancestry," Hirata said gruffly, "but *spiritual*, my boy. This spiritual link you have with all the great warriors of the past, despite your unfortunate parentage."

"That I understand," the young man said. "That I believe, just as I believe you are my spiritual father."

"Ah . . . go on, now," Hirata sputtered, turning eyes grown liquid away from his pupil. "None of that, else I *will* cuff you . . ."

"But despite the spiritual link, honored teacher, I will not carry the *katana,*" the young man continued. "I would have to kill far too many men who I suspected were scoffing at my pretensions. No, I will make it a point to use the *sai,* the *bo* staff, the *nunchaku,* and the small, deadly *shuriken* throwing blades and stars. I will use the weapons perfected by our homeland's vanquished foes, the weapons of China and Okinawa, the weapons of the downtrodden, the underdogs. If I am to be a samurai, honored teacher, I will not be samurai to the noble class, as you were. I will be samurai to those who suffer through no fault of their own, in the land where my father was born."

"To this vow of yours I have no answer," Hirata replied softly. He sheathed his sword, then reached out and took his pupil's hand. "Tradition compels me to reprimand you, and yet the barbarians have taken over our country. I, once a noble samurai, have been reduced to living in a hovel. I have my pride, my strength, my *katana,* and my honor. But each day I grew a little older. Soon my strength will be gone. How then will I sustain my pride? What then will become of my honor?"

"You are the last true samurai," the young man answered. And then he smiled. "You are the last because you would not degrade the code by teaching *budo*. You would not take on a student for money."

"And I never did," Hirata smiled back. "I took on the last true pupil. In you I have been able to turn the wheel of my life one complete cycle. Now that I have taught you all I know, you must go off to wherever your vow shall take you."

"When?" the young man asked.

"Now," the old *ronin* answered. "Come back in a little while."

"I understand," the young man said, very, very softly, taking care to keep his tone totally neutral.

"Of course you do," Hirata chuckled. "You were my student."

The young man rose, bowed to his teacher, and then walked off to a quiet park in the city, where he meditated for an hour. When he returned to the old shack that had been his home for a decade, he saw the still, lifeless body of Hirata. The master was slumped over, his two hands still holding the hilt of the short sword lodged in his abdomen. The young man did not have to examine the body to know that his teacher was dead, just as he did not have to examine the long, self-inflicted horizontal and vertical slashes in his teacher's belly to know that the cuts were crisp, clean, and totally excellent. Even in dying, the old man had remained true to the ancient spirit of *bugei*. In recent times it had become the custom among samurai committed to *seppuku*— suicide by ritual disembowelment—to appoint a second who would stand by, prepared to lop off the suicide's head as soon as he had made the first thrust with the short sword, thus sparing him the agony of the two long, deep cuts. Typically, the noble Hirata had shunned this cheapening of the samurai's ultimate act of courage.

The young man turned to where his belongings had been neatly stacked. On top, in its scabbard, was Hirata's *katana*. Smiling, the young man drew the sword, and with it saluted his teacher. Smiling he slid the blade back into its scabbard. He did not thrust it through his sash, as was customary, but holding true to his vow, he wrapped it in his clothing and carried it on his back as he left Hirata for the final time. He brought the blade with him to America. He kept it clean and sharp, and when he was sure he was alone, he practiced with it, hearing Hirata's whispered instruction in the singing of the sword as it sliced through the air.

But he never used the *katana* in battle. In battle he used the common weapons of his culture and background, for he had declared himself samurai of the common man. Accordingly, when he journeyed to America, he told no one of the aristocratic background from which he sprang. Had not both "noble" families—his mother's and his Yankee father's—disowned him? America was to be the starting place for his new life, and so he chose for himself a new name. In America he would be known by a name that symbolized the unifying spirit of all men, all creatures. Some he met, men like Alex Starbuck, understood, while others did not, but Ki was sure his ancestors, and Hirata were pleased.

From his place at the bar, Ki watched a short, fat man approach the blond stranger's table. The newcomer's blue crushed velvet suit, his red and gold paisley silk vest, only emphasized his girth.

"I've been looking all over for you," the fat man said in a clear, American-accented voice. "It's going to be wonderful! The town is packed with people!"

"I've been waiting here for fifteen minutes," the blond man said. Ki could see the arteries in his neck pulse with anger. That almost made him feel a more positive kinship with the blond European. How difficult it was to suffer all the fools in the world! Truely, avoiding a fight was often the most difficult test a warrior could face...

"I *told* you I would meet you here," the blond man growled through clenched teeth. Then, calming himself, he stood up to shake hands.

"Lord, I suppose I forgot," the fat man laughed.

"Well, sit down now, and have a drink. You technicals are in the clouds, yes? Absentminded..."

"Scientist, not 'technical,' my friend," the fat man corrected him, careful to keep his voice good-humored and his manner polite. "And I will have a drink."

Ki looked the new man over, grateful that their exchange, so far at least, was in English. The man looked to be about fifty-five. He was bald, with gray tufts of dry hair sprouting on both sides of his head, just above the ears. He wore steel-rimmed spectacles with thick lenses. If he was carrying a firearm, it was small enough not to make a bulge in his snug-fitting clothes. The blond man had already identified his friend as a scientist. If he hadn't, Ki would have guessed that he was a barber, merchant, or town mayor. Only two things about the man belied his soft-looking image. Ki noticed that his fingers were blunt and callused-looking, the nails either missing or blackened. Whatever work this man did, it took its toll on his hands.

The other odd thing about the soft-looking, fat man was his *smell*. It was smoky and crowded in the saloon, but Ki's sharp olfactory sense picked up the odor immediately. Emanating from that suit of crushed velvet and that silly vest of red and gold silk, was the unmistakable scent of cordite, the eye-stinging pungency of spent gunpowder.

The two men were talking more softly now. Ki began to wander toward them, but was foiled in his attempt to eavesdrop when several drunk and rowdy cowboys beat him to the only nearby vacant table.

Ki stood rooted to the floor, totally frustrated. Not only did he risk discovery if he attempted to get any closer to the quietly conversing pair, but now the rowdy cowboys were making so much noise that Ki could only pick up an occasional word coming from the two men.

". . . twelve men, all with coffee grinders . . ." the fat man beamed, but the rest of what he said was drowned out by the shouts of the cowboys for more beer. ". . . both sides of town. It'll happen at . . ."

Three of the cowboys broke into a chorus of a filthy ditty currently popular with the hands, and Ki gave up in disgust. He returned to the bar and ordered another drink. He sipped it slowly, and about the time he was finished, the two men stood up to shake hands. The one in the velvet suit hurried out, while the blond man signaled a hostess—a pretty little brunette—whispered something in her ear that made her giggle, and put his arm around her as they headed toward the staircase, and up to the second-floor rooms.

Ki gave them a few seconds' lead, and then followed, to slip unnoticed up the stairs. At the head of the staircase the second floor branched out into two wings, but Ki had seen the girl lead the blond man to the left. He carefully and silently hurried that way. The downstairs noise decreased dramatically once he entered the corridor. All he could hear was an occasional thump, and a steady but very muted drone rising up through the carpet.

Ki cat-crept down the long, narrow hallway. He hoped he wasn't too late to catch a glimpse of the blond man and the woman as they chose a room. It would make things more difficult if he had to begin peeking through every keyhole.

He turned a corner and quickly jumped back. The blond man was standing in profile just a few feet ahead. Fortunately his attention was fixed on the girl's backside as she bent to fiddle with the lock on the room's door. Finally she got it open, and the two went inside. The door shut, and then clicked locked. Ki was alone in the still, quiet hallway.

It would be exquisitely difficult, Ki thought as he approached their door. He began to wait patiently. Soon they would be engaged in lovemaking. Then he would silently pick the lock, enter the room, and render them both unconscious before they could have a chance to see him or even sense that he was there. Once that was done, he could go through the blond man's belongings. He'd be gone by the time they came to. The blond man and the girl would think they had dozed off. What else could they imagine? A Nipponese would, of course, comprehend immediately what it was that had happened. One of Ki's fellow countrymen would know that he had been overcome by a *ninja*.

Ki smiled as he leaned against the far wall of the hallway, watching the door in question. He doubted that there was anyone else in this part of the world who could accomplish what he was going to do. Not even Hirata had known much of *ninjutsu*, the art of the "invisible assassin." The samurai's way was to bluster upon the enemy, dealing death to whoever got in the way.

While serving as Hirata's apprentice, Ki had, without telling his teacher, practiced *ninjutsu* until he was as proficient in it as he had become in the other, "nobler" arts he had learned from Hirata. It had not been difficult for a student like Ki; in fact, Hirata could easily have mastered the necessary skills, but he, like all other samurai, considered them beneath his position as a member of that exalted class. This had served as a warning to Ki that even the greatest of warriors have blind spots born of foolish prejudice.

For example, there was *atemi,* the use of pressure-points on an opponent's body. Through the use of *atemi,* Ki would be able to render this couple unconscious quickly, silently, painlessly. Hirata could have learned *atemi* in a day, but he considered the art beneath contempt. Why deign to touch the enemy with one's bare hands, when one could touch him so much more effectively with one's blade? Even such limited *te* techniques as Hirata knew were to be reserved for those times of last resort when, for some unthinkable reason, a samurai found himself without his noble *katana,* or without any weapons at all.

Ki watched the thin ribbon of light gleaming from beneath the door. Suddenly it blinked out. Excellent! If the lamp or candle had remained lit, Ki would have had to extinguish it, but he'd known the chances were good that the room would already be dark when he attacked. For some bizarre reason, Americans and Europeans preferred to make love to their partners in the shadows. Well, there was no accounting for taste.

Ki smiled and listened to the murmurs coming through the door. He approached, tossing his hat to the carpeted floor, then pressing his ear against the wood. At the same time, he began to regulate his breathing. His inhalations and exhalations were now very shallow. Someone watching would say that Ki was not breathing at all, for where was the rise and fall of his chest?

There was no chest movement, no physical movement at all, as far as the eye could tell, but if Ki had been shirtless,

160

a palm pressed against his stomach would have felt the rhythms of his diaphragm beneath the thick bands of his belly muscles. For a few seconds the roar of his own blood rushing through his veins filled his ears, but then the internal noise of his own body receded, and his sense of hearing seemed to reach out to encompass the room, the hallway, and even the corridor around the corner. Now Ki did not need his eyes. He could focus them on the lock, let them puzzle out the intricate task of picking the mechanism silently. His ears could hear everything, and what they heard told him that he was alone, safe from discovery, and could proceed with the attack.

From one of the many pockets sewn into the lining of his coat he removed a thin, needlelike *shuriken*, or throwing blade. He inserted it into the lock, and begin the series of tiny movements, mere vibrations, that would coax the tumblers open. On the other side of the door, the key—forced from the lock by his pick—fell to the carpet. Ki heard it thud down like a sack of potatoes. The blond man and the girl in his arms had not heard it at all. Another movement of the pick, another twist and careful shake, and the lock was open.

Slipping the *shuriken* back into its pocket, Ki reached out for the doorknob. He prepared himself. Once the door was opened, there could be no retreat. Light from the hallway would shine in. Both the blond man and the girl would have a moment to turn toward the light before the door was closed again, plunging them back into the darkness. They would not have even seen Ki's silhouette. He'd be no more than a foot off of the ground, slithering toward them on his belly like a snake. The crawling technique was even named after the serpent—Ki could move forward that way faster than many men could run. He'd slide to their bed and then up the side. He would reach out . . . and it would be done.

He could hear the creaking of the bedsprings, as steady as the beat of a song. It was time—

Ki froze, his hand still on the doorknob. Someone was coming down the corridor. He bent to scoop up his Stetson just as a woman turned the corner to confront him.

"Oh! What are you doing here?" she demanded, obviously startled. She was a pretty little honey blonde, with a pert hourglass figure beneath the thin white cotton dress she was wearing. "You're not supposed to be up here alone!"

Ki straightened up, his hat in his hand. He hurried toward her to keep the conversation from being conducted where the blond man and the woman he was with could hear it. There was a coal-oil lamp affixed to the wall several feet behind her. The wick was turned up fairly high, and by its bright light Ki could see right through the gauze of her dress, see her figure in shadowy but clearly delineated silhouette, see the lovely shapes of her legs as they rose up, the space between them ever narrowing, until his eyes finally came to rest upon the slimmest sliver of light so softly diffused by the soft hair covering her womanhood.

The blonde followed Ki's eyes down her own front, and once she saw where he was gazing, she smiled and said, "I guess it doesn't matter how you got up here all by your lonesome. Something hot in your eyes—and something hot filling out the front of your pants—tells me you're not planning on being lonesome much longer." Then her own eyes, a delicate shade of lavender, narrowed as she looked at Ki's face. "You're a handsome one, aren't you, darling, but your eyes—" She brushed back the black, shiny hair from Ki's forehead, and tilted his head down with the touch of a light, cool finger. "Lord above! You're—"

"I am partly Japanese, as you see," Ki smiled.

"Well, you're a beautiful man, whatever you are." She smiled back at him and licked her lips. "I've never had an Oriental fellow before. I'm on my own time right now. What do you say?" Her fingers tickled down the length of Ki's fly, to brush against his hardness. "Well! You don't have to say anything, you *lovely* man."

162

Before Ki could protest, she'd gripped his hand and led him to the nearest room. While she fiddled with the door, Ki glanced back over his shoulder at the room he'd been about to invade before he'd been so sweetly interrupted. For a moment he considered placing his forefinger at the side of the girl's neck, pressing ever so gently, and then catching her before she had a chance to collapse on the carpet.

He *could* do that to her. But, truth to tell, Ki couldn't get the memory of her figure—so delectable, glimpsed through the wispy cotton of her dress—out of his mind. Granted, he felt like squeezing various portions of this female's anatomy, but *atemi* pressure-points were not on that list.

As she pulled him into the room, Ki looked back at the other door for one last time. The stranger in there was not likely to go anywhere soon. And considering the grip this little honey blonde with the eyes like violets had on him, he wasn't going anywhere, either.

If he wanted to stay up here without causing a fuss, it fell to him to satisfy this girl's curiosity about Oriental ways of lovemaking. So be it.

As Hirata had always taught, a true warrior ran from no confrontation, but always marched resolutely toward battle, his mighty sword unsheathed. Clicking the door shut behind him, Ki tried hard not to laugh.

★

Chapter 12

The room she had brought him to was small and scrupulously clean. In one corner stood a pitcher and washbasin upon a stand. The open window in the far wall let in a cool, steady breeze. Pale blue wallpaper and a tan carpet made the room seem larger than it was. The brass bed was large, fitted out with crisp-looking, clean white sheets. If this room was indicative of the others on the second floor of the Union Saloon, the place would have made a very comfortable hotel. Of course, the proprietors were making much more money on the place by using the second floor as a cathouse.

Ki kept an ear cocked toward the door. There was little extraneous noise up here, except for that dull throb rising up through the floor from the saloon. He was sure he would hear the blond man leave his room. If that happened, Ki would have a few extra moments to intercept him. If he was at all like others, he would pause at the bar for a drink to refresh himself after his activities up here.

The girl had undone the bow that kept her dress pulled together at the front. She'd loosened the ties and was about to slip the garment off. She turned and caught Ki looking at the door. "I told you I'm on my own time, so you won't have to pay," she said, misunderstanding the cause of his unease. The white cotton dress had slipped down off her shoulders, but she kept it bunched up in front of her, protecting her breasts with her crossed arms.

"Yes, I know." Ki smiled. "Thank you," he added, meanwhile thinking that this obsession Americans and Europeans had over whether or not they "paid" for sex was a curious thing indeed. Sexual pleasure was always paid for; the unlucky paid with guilt, the majority with money or protection, and the few who understood paid for pleasure by returning that pleasure to the giver. The only woman he had ever met who understood this was Jessie . . .

"Being with a man on my own time always makes me nervous," the honey blonde whispered. "Now don't you smile like that, because it's true!" she scolded indignantly. "My name's Celine, by the way."

"Celine, my name is Ki." This woman was beginning to interest him. Her spirit was strong, and in some way kindred to his own. He slipped off his coat and hung it over the back of a chair. "Tell me why you are nervous," he said softly, genuinely intrigued. He unstrapped his gunbelt and set it down.

"It's kind of like when I wanted to be an actress," Celine said. "When I was on stage playing a part, I wasn't me, so I didn't have to worry about what people thought of me. Now, when I'm with men, um . . . when it's my job"—she blushed, not quite able to look Ki in the eye—"well, then I'm just like an actress. Usually I'm acting for the man . . ."

"Let me see you, Celine," Ki commanded gently.

She let her dress fall to the carpet and stood before him in a slightly pigeoned-toed, bashful stance. If there came to her face a slight blush, it was as nothing compared to the peach-pink flush of shyness and arousal that suffused the large round globes of her breasts, the seductive curve of her belly, and the moist juncture of her thighs beneath the honey-colored fur.

"You are lovely," Ki said, beckoning her to come into

his arms. "You are indeed fit for the stage, where all can admire your beauty."

Ki's words brought a happy sigh from Celine. "Thank you, but those dreams are long gone," she said. "The new one is to own a place like this, someday." She turned to blow out the candles, but he stopped her.

"The light sets fire to your golden skin," he told her as he shed the last of his clothes.

Her violet eyes danced the length of his body, feasting upon the sight of his thick shoulders and long, sinewy arms, his hard, rippling belly, and the cords of his calves and thighs. "Anyway, this job does have its benefits," she said merrily. "I'm glad I'm the one who found you wandering around up here. I've never seen a man like you before . . . not like you . . ." She reached out tentatively to touch the hard curve of him jutting out from his center like the spar of a sailing ship. Her tongue slid absently from between her lips as she giggled in nervous expectation. "You sure don't talk much, do you?"

Ki enfolded her in his arms and kissed her, before she could fill the room with her nervous chatter. He captured her tongue beneath his own, as he felt her trembling, satiny body pressed against him like a fluttering bird upon his palm. Now she could not speak at all, but only sing high notes as his fingers stroked the length of her spine, playing along it like a keyboard.

"Lord above," she finally breathed. "This is some sort of magic." She sucked and nibbled her way along his chest, taking satisfaction in the way the lightest touch of her tongue and lips upon his body could make him dance and jerk in place.

Ki arched his back in pleasure. His hands cupped her posterior and lifted her up. She locked her legs about his waist to squirm and buck against him, whimpering all the while. She was so hot and wet that he slid easily into her.

"You're so strong," she marveled between groans. "I'm

167

like a feather in your hands." She painted steamy kisses across his neck and face as Ki stood rock steady, meeting her wildly gyrating hips with perfectly synchronized thrusts. "Oh, I'm coming already," she moaned. "I've never started so quickly before!"

Ki began to run his tongue around and around the dark aureoles of her breasts. Perspiration, wrung out of her by her passion, beaded in her cleavage. His tongue lapped up the salty taste. Her nipples became hard nuggets of flesh. He chewed them ever so gently, while his hands supported and massaged her twitching bottom.

She began to wail, softly and faintly. Her legs, scissored around his waist, clamped together like a vise.

Ki only laughed. "Woman, I have hardly begun with you. Go ahead and take your pleasure. It is only the first of so much more to savor."

Celine delighted in the challenge. "I bet I can make you come too," she cooed into his ear. "Like this, and this!" Her silky furnace gripped and stroked the length of him, embedded inside of her. "You'd just better come, or else!" She tilted her pelvis so that her backside stuck up and out, in that way pulling herself back so that now only the tip of him was still in her. "Are you going to come, or are you going to be left out in the cold!" she crowed in triumph, her tongue teasingly licking his face.

Ki grinned, his dark eyes locking with her lavender gaze. "Before my worthy adversary declares her total victory and issues her ultimatum, she had best look to her rear . . ."

In order for Celine to pull her hips away from him, she'd had to jut out the twin globes of her bottom. Her buttocks were now splayed wide apart, her anus totally defenseless and vulnerable, as Ki's fingers tickled the length of her backside's cleft.

"Ooh!" she squeaked, involuntarily pressing closer to him, taking in fully half of his member. "Oh! Ooooh!" Her ass danced and bobbed as he lightly pressed against her opening. "You wouldn't dare," she whimpered, coaxed by Ki's prodding finger into the preliminary throes of her orgasm. "You wouldn't dare!" But the tone of her voice, and the sparkle in her violet eyes, told him that he certainly should dare!

Ki brought his finger up to wet and lubricate it in the pool of sweat that had collected in the small of her back. Then, as she began the long slide toward her climax, he slid his finger deep into her anus.

Celine threw back her head and sang like a bird. She came like a summer's cloudburst, her bottom sizzling against Ki's hands as tremors ran through her limp body.

Ki, still as hard as a stick of marble, carried her over to the bed and laid her down upon it. He began again, running his fingers through her silky, honey-colored tresses as he kissed the flush of sexual abandon that had spread across her nose and cheeks. His mouth tirelessly worked its way down her neck, breasts, and belly until he was by her side, on his hands and knees, and then he lowered his head between her spread legs, to nip and lick the tender flesh of her inner thighs.

Celine was so paralyzed with pleasure, with delicious sensation, that she could do nothing but stroke and palm his erection, delighting at the way his hardness cavorted beneath her touch.

"My pet..." she giggled, giving his tip a squeeze. Her nails tickled and scratched at his groin, forcing a long, low moan from Ki as he darted his tongue between her parted, glistening inner folds.

"Ohhh!" Her cry became an unintelligible garble of noise as Ki's tongue flicked and flicked and flicked like some tiny whip of love against her very core. Her hands became claws pulling him away, and then around to enter her. As he buried himself in her steaming body, she bent her legs to press her calves against the backs of his knees, pinning him down.

169

Ki worked his hips like a steam locomotive's pistons. He felt his climax rising up from the soles of his feet, coursing through his loins to spin like a deep whirlpool in his groin. He began to shudder as the silvery hot ball inside of him sent drips along his spine.

Celine felt him grow and swell until she thought he might burst. She was tottering on the edge of yet another cascading climax, but before she lost the power of speech, she languidly slid her hand down Ki's broad, muscular back, to press a finger meaningfully against the swell that marked the start of the cleft of *his* rear end.

"Ahhh," she said between kisses. "I've got *you* right where I want!"

Fully delighted to play out this most wonderful game, Ki pretended to plead, "Oh, don't!" He angled up his groin in order to rub his tip against the most sensitive area of her sex. He sawed back and forth, delaying his orgasm for just one more moment, as Celine writhed below him.

Suddenly she slid the sweat-slick tip of her index finger into his anus, and gave a little push, the movement propelling his hips, now turned to hot jelly, forward so that as he came he was locked within her to the hilt. Their voices blended into a chorus of love-sounds as their bodies bucked together mindlessly, their climaxes slowly fading, to leave them breathless and faint.

As they cuddled together, Celine drawled, "Well, I never..."

Ki waited a moment, and then said, "You never what?" But still there was no answer. He glanced at her face. Her eyes were closed, and her breathing had become regular. A moment later her lips parted, and she began to snore.

Laughing, Ki untangled himself from her grip, and quietly went to the washstand to bathe. He dressed silently, but he must have made some noise, for Celine suddenly awoke.

"Where you goin'?" she mumbled sleepily. "Stay..."

"I have duty I must attend to, sweet woman," he whispered.

"Maybe I could help you," she pouted. "I want to help you a lot," she added dreamily.

"You may help me by remaining very quiet," Ki instructed.

"Wel-l-l," she drawled. "I don't know . . . you may have to bribe me . . ." She held out her arms and spread her legs.

She leaves me no choice, Ki thought calmly. Saying nothing, moving toward her, he focused the energy within him, sending all of it flooding into the fingers of his right hand. This was the force behind the unarmed combat system of *te*. It was what allowed a man to split a board, shatter a brick, or finger-slice through a man's chest to burst his heart. Ki had done the first two of these things many times—and that last thing once. Now, as he approached Celine's unsuspecting supine figure, he prepared himself to apply that same force to a far different task.

"Ki? Why are you smiling like that?" Celine asked. She shuddered, and tried to rise.

Ki pinned her down with his left hand firmly planted on her belly. He pressed the nail of his steel-stiff index finger against the core of Celine's sex, and then vibrated his digit to send waves of pleasure through her pelvis. In seconds she was caterwauling in the grip of yet another orgasm, her legs flailing in the air as she bucked like a wild horse. She floated in the ever-widening rings of warmth for another blissful minute before her eyes closed, and her snoring began again.

Ki kissed her feather-softly upon her brow before letting himself out of the room. He hoped she was in good with her boss. After that last trick—in Nippon it was called the 'vibrating beak' technique—women usually slept through the night.

Back in the corridor, with his gunbelt slung over his shoulder, Ki once again approached the door behind which the blond man had been taking *his* pleasure. Once again Ki made himself ready for his *ninja* attack. He set his gunbelt down, regulated his breathing, composed his mind, and reached out for the doorknob—

But once again his plans went awry. Before his own fingers could touch it, the doorknob began to turn. Somebody was leaving the room!

Ki flattened himself against the hinge side of the doorjamb. Out of the room came the brunette. He silently wished the American geisha an apology for what he was about to do. After all, the world was a strange place, and the spinning wheel of *karma* that controlled all people's lives could just as easily have ordained that this woman be his sweet Celine. Ki took one soundless step to synchronize his rhythms with those of his victim, and then rushed up behind her, one hand gently covering her eyes while the other found the *atemi* point at the side of her neck.

The frightened woman stiffened, but before she could find her voice, her knees sagged and she collapsed like a rag doll that had lost its stuffing. Ki swept her up into his arms before she could hit the floor, and carried her into a nearby vacant room. He set her down on the bed and then hurried out to retrieve his gunbelt, strap it around his waist, and enter the blond man's room.

The stranger was stretched out nude upon the bed, his double gunbelt draped over the head of the brass bedstead, the grips of his revolvers within easy reach. All looked natural: a man, sexually exhausted, sleeping in a dark room. All *looked* natural—

But a *ninja* knew the difference between what was real and what only seemed real. Ki could tell the difference between real and faked sleep. A person truly dreaming is absolutely still. His bones and joints do not creak, and his snores are uneven. This man, Ki realized, was pretending to be asleep in order to get the drop on him. Nevertheless, Ki pretended to be fooled by the ruse. It would be entertaining to experience the outcome of this little contest, for each man was an expert in some aspect of warrior hood, and each had an advantage over the other. The blond man had eyes grown accustomed to the darkness, and his nearby pistols. Ki had the quickness of wit to pretend to be fooled, and his *atemi* skills.

Of course, the blond stranger lying so quietly might only be pretending to be fooled by Ki's pretending. Ki was within three feet of the bed now. Another step and his adversary would be within reach.

With lizardlike speed, the blond man snapped out his right hand to pull a revolver from his gunbelt. Ki moved in to slam the edge of his palm against the stranger's wrist. It was the *shuto-uchi*, the "knife-hand strike," and its force sent the pistol skidding across the carpet before a shot could be fired.

"Scheiss!" breathed the man as he sat up. He brought his arm up and around to catch Ki in a headlock. The man was strong and knew how to use leverage. He twisted to pull Ki off balance and over the man's lap. His fist caught Ki twice against the side of the head, and made him see stars.

Ki jackknifed his legs up and over, to lock about the blond man's neck. Then it was *his* turn to twist, and the blond man was forced to break his hold on Ki as he went somersaulting toward the foot of the bed. The man's hands reached out to break his fall, in lieu of breaking his neck, and Ki's stiff fingers punched at a point just above the man's collar bone and to the right of his Adam's apple.

The blond man managed a last feeble jab at Ki's ribs as he faded into unconsciousness. The whole fight had taken less than ten seconds, and had been totally silent except for the light thud of the gun upon the soft carpet, the man's one whispered curse word, and the creaking of the bedsprings.

Gingerly rubbing at the bruise on his temple, Ki lit a

173

candle and began to go through the blond man's belongings. The first thing he did was extract the other pistol from the gunbelt. If the blond man came to, Ki did not want him to have a gun within reach.

Ki carried the weapon over to the candle's flame in order to examine it. He'd never before seen such a weapon. The nickel-plated handgun looked to be a .38, but was smaller than a Colt of comparable caliber. Instead of wood or hard rubber handgrips, the pistol had a long, slender, rounded butt of filigreed metal. Ki searched for the catch and then broke open the pistol to extract its six shells. Then he closed it and experimentally worked the action. There were diagonal groovings on the outside of the revolver's cylinder. As the pistol was cocked and dry-fired, a pin in the frame moved back and forth, riding in these zigzag grooves, rotating the cylinder.

Ki tucked the emptied weapon into his gunbelt, at the small of his back, and continued his search through the man's clothes. There was nothing in his pockets or wallet to identify him, but Ki did find a yellowed, tattered newspaper clipping, folded into quarters and tucked into the watch pocket of the man's vest.

There was a photo pinned to the clipping. It was of the short, fat man whom Ki had earlier seen drinking downstairs in the saloon. Ki couldn't make out what the article was about, for it was written in German.

What he'd found were slim pickings, but intriguing ones. Perhaps Longarm could garner some clue from the unusual revolver; Jessica could certainly translate the German newspaper article.

Ki slipped out of the room and down along the corridor. He ambled down the stairs, keeping his hat pulled low and his eyes on the floor, meeting no one's gaze—assuming anyone was bothering to look at him—as he cut across the saloon and out the batwing double doors.

He began to walk down the wooden sidewalk, toward

the Cattlemen's Association. He sensed a presence behind him and had begun to turn when he felt the cold, hard barrel of a gun thrust behind his ear, and froze in his tracks.

"That's right, chink," rumbled a familiar voice. "Thought it was you. We were having a drink when we saw you leave."

"Hello, Higgins," Ki said. His eyes flicked right and left as two of the ex-foreman's men bracketed him on both sides. "It's no use pleading, you know. You will not get your job back."

"Just start walking, and turn into that alley coming up," Higgins snarled, careful to keep his cocked .45 pressed against Ki's head. "Once we're off the street, we'll see who does the pleading, boy."

Ki did as he was told. The street was deserted. At this hour, those not already in the Cattlemen's building for the meeting were whiling away the time in the Union or over in Canvas Town. Ki could not hope that a passerby, seeing what was going on, might help, or alert the town marshal. He was on his own against three men who had the drop on him.

The alley was narrow and dark; it snaked around behind the Union Saloon to end where a high wooden fence separated the saloon's property from the building next door. There was no first-floor back door into the saloon, but a wooden staircase led up to the second floor. Ki supposed this was built so the more illustrious members of the community could partake of the pleasures offered up there, then slip away unnoticed.

Higgins marched Ki up to the fence, then retreated a few paces, his two men on either side of him. He lowered his Peacemaker and said, "Turn around, chink!"

Ki turned slowly to face the three men. His back was against the fence. A beam of light spilling out of a window upstairs illuminated him as if he were in a spotlight. There was no place to run, and certainly no place to hide.

"I noticed you're wearing a gun, boy." Higgins grinned like a man who has dealt himself a winning hand at poker. "I ain't never seen you wear one before, but seeing that you are, I figure it's plenty legal for me to call you out on account of that beating you gave me the other day." The big man glowered darkly. "You did that to me in front of Miss Starbuck, too." He gestured at his two men. "These fellows here will testify to old Farley that it was a fair enough shootout."

"But your gun is already in your hand," Ki observed quietly.

"Well now," Higgins chuckled. "Seeing as how I'm wearing a shoulder rig, and you've got your gun in a waist holster, I figure my holding my gun down at my side like this makes it fair enough." His two cronies smiled and shifted their weight from leg to leg like a pair of watchdogs straining at their leads.

"I cannot draw on you, Higgins," Ki said.

"Why not? You scared, boy?"

"You're so quick and all, you know, Chinaman?" one of the other men guffawed.

"If you're scared, you better start pleading." All traces of humor were gone from Higgins's face and voice. "I'll give you a few minutes to plead with me, on your knees . . ."

"I am not frightened," Ki said, folding his arms across his chest. "It is that my gun is not loaded. I only wore it so as not to attract attention to myself."

The men on either side of Higgins broke out into nervous laughter. "That's just too bad," the one who had spoken before said scornfully.

"Loaded or not, how was I to know you were telling the truth? Especially since you drew on me first. Right, boys?"

The two men nodded meaningfully, their eyes on Ki, their hands hovering near their own holstered Peacemakers.

Ki was amused by their agitation. "Tell me, where are your other two hounds, Ray and Musty? Just three of you against me seems like you are taking an awful chance..."

"They're taking care of that nosy federal marshal, Long-arm," Higgins said. "Getting him out of the way, just like we're going to get you out of the way. Miss Jessie will be all alone. That'll make Danzig's job that much easier."

"Who is Danzig?" Ki asked, but he thought he knew. "That name sounds German," he mused out loud, noting with satisfaction Higgins's surprised look of unease.

"Never you mind who he is," the ex-foreman grumbled, clearly off balance.

"Very well," Ki said agreeably. "How did you find out Longarm was a federal marshal?"

"That was easy," Higgins boasted. "I checked out his horse the day he rode in with you and Miss Jessie. That gelding was carrying a U.S. brand. The Rangers got their own horses. That made Longarm either army or a federal man. I bet on the last, since he didn't carry himself like he was army." Higgins's eyes narrowed. "The time for talking's over, chink."

"Listen to me carefully," Ki addressed the one man who had remained silent throughout the entire exchange. "It is too late for Higgins, as I have already spared his life once."

"You'd do better to use your last time on earth praying to them ancestors of yours," Higgins interrupted angrily.

"And it is too late for this other," Ki continued unperturbed, "for he had insulted me, but you have said nothing. You may go, but you must leave now."

All three men only shook their heads in amazed disbelief. Ki still had his arms folded across his chest. His hands were nowhere near his gun.

"I'll say this for you," the man Ki had spoken to snorted in disbelief. "You're a brazen son of a bitch."

"He's a dead one!" Higgins spat, his voice thick with hate and tension as he brought up his .45.

Ki slid his arms apart so that the inner sides of his fore-arms and palms of his hands rubbed together. The smooth

177

motion forced the two *shuriken* throwing blades out of the hidden sheaths sewn to the insides of his sleeves. His hands rose up, the blades—four-inch knives without hilt or handle—glinting in the light as they left his fingers.

The men on either side of Higgins spat blood instead of screams as Ki's *shuriken* flew to their throats. They were falling to the ground as Higgins fired.

The .45 thundered as the big slug chewed a splintery hole through a fence plank. Ki had somersaulted forward, to rise up in front of Higgins before he could recock his single-action revolver.

At first Higgins didn't even attempt to fight, but turned on his heel and ran back down the alley, toward the street. As he ran, he spun around to back-pedal a few steps and snap a shot at Ki.

That was Higgins's final mistake. His shot went wild as Ki reached into his coat to extract another *shuriken*, this one a disc in the shape of a six-pointed star. The disc looked like a spur-wheel, except that the *shuriken* was four inches across and forged of high-grade steel. Ki snapped his wrist to send the lethal star on its journey toward its target.

Higgins saw the metallic thing glitter as it left the circle of light in which Ki stood, to come whizzing and swooping his way like some razor-edged bat. He screamed, dropping his .45 to the dirt as he turned to run furiously for the street. He heard the deadly whir of the throwing star, and uselessly fluttered his hands behind him in an attempt to protect the back of his neck.

The *shuriken* sliced through three of Higgins's spread fingers before burying half of its diameter in the base of his skull, instantly severing his spinal cord. He fell forward, his own momentum carrying him, so that his face plowed a furrow in the dirt before he came to rest. His body twitched and jerked in muscle spasms even as his staring eyes began to glaze.

Ki retrieved his two throwing blades from the throats of

the other men, wiping the steel off on their clothes. He walked over to where Higgins lay, and with some difficulty pried the throwing star out of its niche of skull-bone. He cleaned it on the lining of Higgins's coat, put it back in its pocket in his own coat, and stared down at the corpse.

"I never make a man a present of his life twice," he said out loud, so that Higgins's Kami, should it be hovering near the body, could take the message along as it began the journey into the destiny long ago decreed for it by the ex-foreman's *karma*.

Ki stepped over the body and made his way to the street. If anybody had heard Higgins's shot, or his scream, they were certainly lying low.

Ki would report the deaths to Town Marshal Farley as soon as possible. The marshal was most likely at the Cattlemen's Association.

Ki strode in that direction. The meeting was where he'd been going before these three had temporarily delayed him.

And Jessie would be waiting for him, Ki knew. He quickened his stride. He'd begun to feel lonesome and just a tiny bit sad. It was the way he always seemed to feel whenever he was away from Jessica Starbuck for very long.

The Cattlemen's Association building was lit up like a Christmas tree. Inside the large meeting hall, the leather armchairs and fine antique side tables had been haphazardly stacked against one of the wainscoted walls, to make room for the rows of backless benches brought in to seat the crowd. The benches filled the room except for a narrow aisle down the center, and the speaker's platform at the front.

The crowd filled the benches. The womenfolk had been left at home, but the cattlemen had brought their foremen and top hands for moral support and physical protection. After all, if a man like Alex Starbuck had been shot down like a dog, who was safe? The agitated voices of the cowboys and their bosses created a general din that echoed in

179

the room and spilled through the open windows that faced Main Street.

Ki stood in the rear of the hall, watching the governor try to call for order. The governor was a tall and stately man, as befit his position, and was dressed in a blue pinstriped suit. He stood ramrod straight, and had a lion's mane of gray hair brushed straight back from his high forehead.

Ki, watching him pound his gavel in a futile attempt to command the room's attention, thought that the fellow looked just like a governor ought to; it was a shame that nobody was paying any attention to him.

The brace of Texas Rangers who stood slouched against the wall behind the governor looked embarrassed. The governor's mouth was opening and closing, but Ki could not make out the words being intoned. Too many people were shouting and carrying on.

"Where's Jessica Starbuck!" a man yelled.

The governor flushed red and pounded his gavel.

Another of the ranchers jumped up on his bench to address himself to the entire room, totally ignoring the podium as he yelled, "We've got to face facts! Everybody here owes the Starbucks!"

"Please!" the governor shouted, attempting to drown him out. "Let's have order!"

"If Jessie's the new head of the Circle-Star spread, she's the only one who can call the roundup on or off!" the man continued. Now he turned to point his finger at the podium. "If things are all right, Governor, where's Jessie?"

There was a chorus of supportive yells, and a smattering of applause. The speaker, pleased, looked as if he were about to continue, but a number of hands reached up to tug him down from the bench that had been his impromptu platform.

Ki, for his part, thought that the man had asked a good question. Just where was Jessie?

While the governor endlessly, impotently pounded his

gavel, Ki, spying Farley's rotund form, began to shoulder through the crowd at the rear of the hall in order to make his way to the town marshal's side.

Farley saw him coming. His eyes were red from fatigue, with dark circles beneath them. Before Ki could say a word, Farley sighed, "She's over at Dr. Brown's office."

"What has happened to her?" Ki demanded, gripping Farley's arm.

"Easy!" Farley winced.

Ki let go, and fought to compose his emotions. "Tell me," he said quietly.

"She's all right!" Farley groaned, rubbing at his bicep. "Damn that grip of yours! Anyway, she's just there to hold Longarm's hand while he gets himself stitched up. He got into a ruckus with two hands you fired recently. Anyhow, one of them sliced Longarm's ribs up some—nothing serious—before he shot them both. I had to go over to Canvas Town myself to straighten it all out. Hell, it's been a long day." Farley shook his head. "I'm satisfied it was self-defense," he added as an afterthought.

"Marshal Farley, I am sorry, but I must make your day even longer," Ki began. "Those two that Longarm shot worked for the foreman we fired, a man named Higgins."

"Yeah, so?" Farley looked suspiciously at Ki. "I've seen Higgins around. What of it?"

"Higgins and two others of his men are lying dead in the alley behind the Union Saloon."

"Oh, no..."

"I had to kill them," Ki said apologetically. "It was self-defense."

"That's what Longarm said. I swear, you two are starting to remind me of each other."

Ki only shrugged. He had no intention of telling Farley the obvious connection between the two attacks this night. Higgins had been working for Danzig, the blond man whom Ki had encountered upstairs at the Union, but this was information for Jessica and perhaps for Longarm, but definitely not for this town constable who had refused even to investigate the Alex Starbuck murder.

"Well, let's go clean up your mess," Farley muttered, walking. He looked back at Ki, who had not moved. "I said come on!"

"I think not, Marshal," Ki said absently. "I will remain here, to wait for Jessie."

"Now you listen here, son," Farley said, his temper rising and a note of warning creeping into his gruff voice. "I've got no patience for your high and mighty ways. I said you're coming, and that means—"

Ki cut him off, his black eyes flashing with amusement. "Marshal, I have been living in these parts for fifteen years. Do you really think I am going to hightail it out of town, or Texas, because I was forced to defend myself against three armed men in an alley?"

"I suppose if I insisted that you come along, or tried to pull my gun on you, you'd kill me," Farley demanded furiously. "Is that what you'd do, Ki?"

Wondering if the marshal meant to be funny, Ki merely said, "Of course not, Farley." He paused. "I would probably only sprain your wrist."

"I believe you. Thanks for nothing!" Farley groused. "Well, you wait here, then."

"Yes, Marshal."

Farley whirled at what he had initially taken to be a sarcastic retort, but Ki's tone and expression seemed totally innocent and respectful. The marshal glanced dubiously at Ki's gunbelt. "How'd you kill those three? Surely not with that?" He pointed at Ki's holstered revolver. "Well?"

Ki gazed at Farley and blinked like a cat. "With blades," he said pleasantly. "Throwing knives."

"A funny fellow, just like Longarm," Farley mourned. Maybe that's why Jessie has taken such in interest in that deputy marshal.

Ki flinched.

"But at least Longarm has blood in his veins," Farley added in farewell. "He isn't a cold fish like you."

Farley wandered away, muttering imprecations beneath his breath. Ki did not notice. He was too busy thinking that the marshal's last hurled accusation had been ironic indeed! If he was such a cold fish, why was his blood just now boiling, his heart threatening to break in two at the thought of Jessie's being with Longarm?

And what right do I have to feel this way? he raged silently at himself. *I am pledged to defend her honor and her person . . .*

Just then, Jessie entered the hall, with Longarm at her side. The tall, broad-shouldered federal marshal was walking stiffly, but he seemed fit enough. Ki composed himself, gathering up the reins of his stampeding emotions. His duty had to come before his feelings. There was some sadness, and a little pain in that, but Ki could live his life no other way.

★

Chapter 13

The doc had not had to stitch the shallow wound on Longarm's side, but merely plaster down the raised flap of skin with a taped square of gauze. It was more of a scrape than a cut. Longarm had already tested his draw and found it to be unaffected. He'd be healed up in a week or so, and until then he'd just have to put up with an occasional twinge of soreness.

A week or so. Longarm pulled a cheroot from his coat pocket and stuck it into the corner of his mouth. He did not light it, but absently chewed on the end. In a week the army would be patrolling Texas, and he and Billy Vail would be looking for new jobs. Longarm was no closer to finding Alex Starbuck's murderers than he had been when he'd first arrived in Sarah. If the agitated mood of this crowd of cattlemen was any indication, martial law and a flood of bluecoats were just around the corner for Texas.

"There's Ki!" Jessica Starbuck said, and hurried off that way.

She was wearing a green tweed riding jacket, and a skirt made of the same material. Longarm felt himself stirring as, following along behind her, he watched the swaying of her hips. Damn, but the effect of this woman on him was purely magical! Her long, reddish-blond tresses had been pinned up on top of her head. Wisps of hair hung down

185

from beneath her brown Stetson hat. Longarm found himself growing warm as he gazed at the nape of her neck, remembering how it had felt to press his lips against her soft skin during the height of their sexual abandon.

"We ran into Farley on our way in," Jessie blurted to Ki, taking his hands in her own. "Are you all right?"

Ki smiled. He found himself staring into the green pools of her eyes, and then glanced down to see her delicate hands sheltered in his own strong fingers. "I am unhurt," he said quietly, savoring the touch of her, and then letting go. He turned his glistening black eyes on Longarm. "You were wounded, I understand?"

Longarm shrugged. "Hell, my vest and shirt took more of a licking than I did," he remarked absently, still pondering the expression that had been on Ki's face when Jessie had touched him. "Doc Brown is about my size, and was able to lend me a fresh shirt." His vest had been ruined, so he'd transferred his watch, with its gold-washed chain, to a pocket of his frock coat, tucking his unclipped derringer behind the large square buckle of his gunbelt. It wasn't the best place in the world to stash an ace-in-the-hole, but it would have to do until Longarm could replace his vest.

"I am very pleased that you survived tonight's trouble," Ki said evenly. He turned to Jessie. "I must speak with you."

"Reckon the fact that Higgins's gang split up to come at us *both* this evening was no coincidence," Longarm mused.

Ki ignored him. "Jessie?" He reached out to pull her away.

"You just don't let anything happen the easy way, do you old son?" Longarm swore softly. "So here it comes the hard way. Anything you found out tonight comes under the heading of official business."

Ki, said stubbornly, "Jessie, come with me."

"Son," Longarm warned, his eyes narrowing. "I don't have a lot of time to fool with you."

"Careful, Longarm," Ki seethed.

"And I don't have a lot of time to get to the bottom of this damned case. I don't intend to allow you and this young lady to withold evidence."

"You have no choice in the matter, Longarm," Ki declared, his dark eyes flashing with fury barely controlled.

"I could arrest you, and get what I need to know out of you by making you cool your heels in Farley's jail."

"Incorrect, Longarm." Ki smiled thinly. "You could merely *try* to arrest me."

"Blustery talk, old son, but unless those fast hands of yours can stop lead—"

"Stop it! Both of you!" Jessie commanded, her hands on her hips. "Men! You're both acting like bulls pounding their skulls together to get command of the herd. And you're both as stupid!"

Longarm blushed, recognizing the truth in her words. But he also wondered how she could be so wise and so blind at the same time. *It's you Ki is wanting to impress, girl*...

"I haven't forgotten the wild-goose chase you sent me on in Canvas Town, Ki," Longarm said sullenly. He wasn't really all that angry; he would have done the same thing in Ki's position, but he wanted a concession from the man, and he was starting to understand how Ki's value system operated.

"Yes, I apologize." Ki looked down at his boots.

"Farley filled me in." Longarm pressed his momentary advantage. "I trusted you, and got ambushed because of it."

Ki felt very guilty indeed. His ploy had sent Longarm deep into Canvas Town, far from help. He hadn't meant for Longarm to be wounded, of course, but the fact remained that Ray and Musty might not have found him if Ki had not directed him into that wild part of town.

Longarm watched and waited as Ki worked his way through the ramifications of his actions. *Sometimes the only way to crack the toughest nuts is to let them ripen awhile in their own hard shells,* he thought. He struck a match and puffed alight his cheroot. He blew a shimmeringly perfect smoke ring, and winked at Jessica.

Ki was about to acquiesce to Longarm's wishes in partial payment of the debt of honor he had brought upon himself by deceiving the lawman. But when he looked up to see that big, swaggering, mustached Longarm flirting with Jessie, he felt blossoming in his chest on envy whose thorns were as sharp as the meanest Texas cactus. He stamped off, calling over his shoulder, "Jessie, I will wait to speak with you in the foyer."

Longarm watched him go. He shook his head and sighed.

"I just don't understand what's gotten into him," Jessie murmured.

"How can you *not,* woman," Longarm chuckled. "That man is plainly head-over-heels in love with you."

"No!" Jessie said, startled. "No, Longarm," she now said it slowly and seriously. "That can't be. You see, Ki and I, we grew up together. He came to my father when he was little more than a boy. His skills as a warrior were already honed. My father, worried about my personal safety, sort of hired Ki to be my companion and bodyguard. I was just a few years younger. Ki taught me some martial skills, and watched over me." She paused, to stare searchingly into Longarm's eyes. "To say that Ki was *hired* by my father grossly devalues the transaction. Ki pledged his services to my family, to me. There's no question that he would give his life for me if necessary."

"All the more reason for him to love you," Longarm insisted.

"That's *our* concept of love, but not the samurai's concept." Jessica blushed. "Ki and I could never have a real love affair. He could not allow that to happen. His sense of honor and duty would not allow it. Ki's love for me must be totally selfless. His life must be dedicated to protecting me. His vow of service to my father allows for no less than that."

"I'm beginning to understand," Longarm said slowly. "If he and you were, uh, *together* as man and woman, it'd confuse things. He'd be your lover, and not your...samurai."

"I love him very much," Jessie smiled. "But our love must always remain chaste. I would never tempt him, for I know that if Ki should lapse from the selfless love he holds for me, thereby allowing his vow of total protection of me to lapse, he'd be forced to commit *harakiri.*"

"Excuse me?" Longarm blinked.

"Harakiri is another name for *seppuku,"* Jessica said.

"Ki told me about *seppuku,"* Longarm said. "That's suicide, right?"

Jessie nodded.

"But what's this other thing, this...'hairy carey?' I disremember Ki saying anything about that."

"In Japan, it's a rather vulgar term," she said. "It means 'belly-slitting.'" Longarm frowned, puzzled, and she went on. "I don't really like to talk about it, but...well, in *seppuku* the suicide rips open his belly with his own sword and pulls out his entrails. Two long cuts, like this..." She drew her hand first across her own abdomen from one side to the other, then upward from pubis to breast bone.

Longarm grimaced and gave a low whistle. He said, "Lordy, these Japans don't do anything halfway, do they?"

"Only samurai are allowed this sort of death," Jessie replied. "It's considered a great honor to die this way. The physical pain means nothing. The greater pain would be in Ki's soul at the knowledge that he'd failed me, and failed my father. That would dishonor him and all his ancestors. The only way he could restore that honor would be through *seppuku,* but he would still have failed, and Ki would never allow himself knowingly to fail. For him to make love to me would be betrayal, the deepest of failure. No, it could never be. He is a true samurai, completely and utterly."

Jessie stood on tiptoe to peck a feather-light kiss upon his cheek. "I think it's not Ki's love for me you're concerned about," she teased sweetly. "I think you're just jealous."

"I won't deny it, Jessie," Longarm said softly, feeling his heart pounding. They stood like that for a moment, as close as a man and woman could be, fully dressed, and in public. Longarm grew dizzy from the perfume scent rising from her cleavage just visible where the undone buttons of her silk blouse allowed the sheer material to gape open. "Go find out what Ki has to tell you," he said, his voice sounding too thick in his ears.

Jessie laughed, and Longarm hurried her on her way with a light and loving pat across the round swell of her ass, so nicely but demurely emphasized by the snug green tweed of her skirt.

"Wait for me here," she winked.

Longarm watched the eyes of every man in the crowded room follow her walk, and he fought down the irrational jealousy he felt. *Relax, old son,* he chided himself. *There ain't enough bullets in the world to shoot all the men who find themselves mesmerized by Jessica Starbuck.* A lot of the cowboys lining the hard wooden benches were passing around pints and flasks of hard stuff. The governor was babbling on about something, up there at the podium, but everybody was clearly waiting for Jessie to reassure them concerning their financial and personal security. How the hell was this young woman ever going to handle it all? Longarm thought about her vow to continue the war begun so long ago between her father and his European enemies. *What some man ought to do, old son, is rope in that female and make an honest wife out of her.* Longarm flicked the ash off of his cheroot. *That's what some damn fellow ought to do,* he thought. *Except that he'd then have to spend the rest of his life taming her—and Jessie would most likely give as good as she got. But hell, that don't sound like a bad life, at all.*

Of course, a man couldn't go traipsing around the West risking his life to enforce the law if he had a wife and maybe a family waiting for him at home. Billy Vail had often said that a man of Longarm's experience ought to be overseeing the work of others and not riding out himself to match his gun against riffraff.

"Whoa, old son!" Longarm laughed, so loudly that several nearby fellows turned to look at him. *Let's eat this apple one bite at a time,* he thought. If he didn't wrap up this case mighty quick, he and Billy would be looking for work, never mind promotions. With a sigh of relief, Longarm turned his thoughts back to the present. The depths of his feeling for Jessie surely did frighten him some.

She was talking with Ki now. As he waited for her to return, he thought over what she'd said.

Well, the girl was only partly right. She'd told Longarm a little something about Ki's past while they were waiting for Doc Brown to finish patching him up. Ki was only half Japanese, of course. His daddy was a true-blue, hot-blooded Yankee. Come to think of it, his Japanese mama couldn't have been an unemotional cold fish, not the way she'd chucked everything to marry the man she loved. Ki's sense of honor, his pride, his sternness—all of that had been forged into him by the harsh, stoic samurai code. But Ki's heart was as warm-blooded, passionate, and loving as any man's; Longarm could tell that just by looking at the fellow, and the way he looked at Jessie. What a war there was going on inside the man! And it was a war Ki could only lose. How long before his heart beat itself to tatters against the warriors steel-clad code, or before that code shattered into gleaming shards against Ki's heart?

Jessie came back into the hall, but there was a determined intensity in the way she brushed by Longarm on her way up the narrow aisle to the front of the room. She sashayed up that aisle like she owned the place. Thinking about it, Longarm was amused. Most likely she *did* own the place.

He began to elbow his way toward the front of the hall. He made good time. As usual, folks who had a mind to complain usually swallowed their gripes when they saw who it was that wanted to get by.

Ki seemed to materialize out of the mob just as Longarm

reached the front of the hall. The expression on his face was earnest and troubled.

"Longarm, what I told her upset her greatly. I myself don't understand the significance—" He was about to say more, but both he and Longarm were distracted by a momentary disturbance.

One of the cowboys sitting in the front row reached out for a handful of Jessie's backside as she began to climb the steps leading up to the speakers' platform. The drover was clearly drunk, the situation far from serious, but both Longarm and Ki took an instinctive step forward to come to her aid. They were too slow.

Jessie, smiling, intercepted the cowboy's lurching grasp. She took his wrist in her two hands and twisted. The cowboy yelped in surprise as he found his entire body following the direction Jessie had set for him with just that one twist of his wrist. He landed flat on his back on the floor, looking up—totally flummoxed—into the laughing faces of his chums.

"It is called *jujutsu,*" Ki said, anticipating Longarm's query. "A good defense form for a woman. Leverage means more than strength." He winked. "Perhaps *you* would like to learn *jujutsu,* eh, Longarm?"

"Old son," Longarm replied honestly, "I'd learn anything you've got to teach."

The governor was still trying for some semblance of order, but now the crowd was so far gone on whiskey that not even the appearance of Jessie on the platform could quiet it down.

"I'm sorry," flustered the governor to her, pounding his gavel.

"You've been away from the heartland too long," Jessie laughed. "That itty-bitty hammer of yours is going to get us no attention."

Before the nearby Texas Ranger could react, she'd plucked a revolver from one of the holsters crisscrossing

192

his waist. "This is a Texas gavel." She pointed the pistol toward the ceiling and fired a single shot. The blast echoed loudly.

The noise in the room ceased abruptly as all heads turned toward the platform. Jessie handed the smoking revolver back to the chagrined Ranger. There was an ugly black hole in the ceiling, and flakes of plaster were still wafting down like an early snowfall.

"Now that I've got your attention," Jessie began, shouting out her words loud and clear, "let me straighten a few things out, because right now I don't have a lot of time. It's no secret that my daddy staked about every one of you, and it's no secret that these days, now that my daddy's gone, you're all wondering just when those notes are going to be called due."

She paused then, to let every man in the hall ponder his own financial situation, and how he could keep his outfit going and still meet his commitments at the loan desk of the Starbuck bank.

"Miss Jessie! Your daddy understood that we'd need time to be able to pay it all back," one of the ranchers shouted out. "Give us a straight answer. When will those loans come due? I—"

A chorus of agreeing shouts drowned out the rest of what the man had to say. Jessie held up her hands to silence them.

"The answer is never." She watched the stunned men trying to absorb what they *thought* she'd said. "The Starbuck holdings belong to me now. Your notes belong to me. Just as my daddy built this town to honor my mama's memory, I'm going to do something to honor my daddy's memory. All of you will be receiving your notes back, and they'll be marked 'paid in full.'"

As the hall erupted into cheers, the governor, looking a sickly shade of green, hissed, "Young lady, this is not what I advised you to do this afternoon." He glanced uneasily at the crowd, but they were all shouting and stomping their boot heels to beat the band. There was no danger of their overhearing his stern lecture. "You have no right—" he started to say, but cut himself off as Jessica glanced sharply at him. "What I mean is, not even the Starbuck empire can function without the cooperation of local and federal government agencies."

"Is that a threat, Governor?" Jessie drawled.

"It's a warning," the man said grimly. "I already explained all this to you. If you don't properly divest yourself of your Starbuck holdings, you're going to leave yourself wide open to the kind of senseless violence that struck down your father—"

"I've just found something out, Governor," Jessie cut him off. "I've just found out that my suspicions were correct, and that my father's death was far from 'senseless violence,' as you put it. My father was murdered in a premeditated act of revenge. I now know what manner of weapon was used against him, but that's not really my concern. I know who killed him, and I know exactly why. The violence is not going to stop, Governor, not after tonight, when I kill the man who was directly responsible for my father's death, and not for a long, long time. My father's enemies were—*are*—many. Their goal is to wipe all traces of the Starbuck name from the face of the earth. I will not let that happen."

The Governor, gone suddenly pale, opened his mouth to say something, but Jessie had turned back to the podium to face the crowd.

Longarm, standing just below them, had not been able to hear their exchange through the noise coming from behind him. But as he watched the governor stand sweating, looking for all the world like a hooked fish just pulled from the water, flopping about, totally out of its element, Longarm thought, *Gov, you may be wearing an expensive suit, and you may be the highest office holder within a thousand miles, but you've got the look I've seen on countless men, from cow thieves to murderers.*

"The governor seems to be troubled by something," Ki murmured beside him.

"He looks guilty as hell, don't he?" Longarm said through pursed lips. "Old son, that apple we've been nibbling has gotten pretty well gnawed down to the core. Just what the hell did you tell her?"

Before Ki could answer, Jessie began once again to address the crowd. "I ask only one thing in exchange: that we pull together to make the roundup the biggest and best ever, even by Texas standards!" After a roar of applause, she continued, "The cattle we sent East have been promised to Europe. We're going to help feed the world. Now there are some good old folks in Europe, folks like us, but there are also some who'd like to see our roundup fail, so that they could buy up our land. They're quite willing to let their own people go hungry if it'll mean our land values get depressed and we have to sell cheap, just to stay alive ourselves. It's damned villains like these folks I'm talking about that had my father killed, because they saw his death as the first step in establishing their own cattle spreads right here in Texas!"

"One of them fellas came 'round to talk to me, Jessie!" A rancher shouted. "A blond man, talked real funny. Hell, I thought I'd have to sell just to meet my debts—" He climbed unsteadily to his feet, obviously drunk. "Until tonight, that is. Ya-hoo!" He pulled his pistol, intending to blast a companion hole to the one Jessie had put in the ceiling, but as his gun bobbed and waved in drunken circles, less boisterous neighbors disarmed him.

"After the roundup, we'll all have our profits!" Jessie declared. "You'll all be able to put that money back into your outfits. Our herds will grow. We'll be able to keep what is ours, what we've worked for. Texas for Texans. Texas for America!"

This time the cheers that went up were deafening. Longarm, standing next to Ki, fought to make himself heard. "Son, you've got to fill me in on what's going on." Longarm watched the governor suddenly scurry from the stage. "Strange, you'd think a politico would want to stand up there absorbing some of that cheering and clapping."

Ki pointed. "Even his Texas Ranger guards have been taken by surprise."

Indeed, the two Rangers were still on the platform as the governor quickly descended the steps to disappear through a side door.

"He left like a man wanting to get away from something nasty that might be happening," Longarm mused. Right then he got one of those *feelings* down along his spine. A man couldn't learn to have those feelings; all he could do was survive enough sticky situations to develop the facility. "Ki! Get up there and get Jessie off the platform—" he began, but stopped. Ki couldn't hear him. The samurai had already launched himself toward the podium. Longarm saw Jessie's eyes lock on to the approaching form of her bodyguard. Her smile faded...

She scanned the faces of the crowd until she saw Longarm. Then she pointed over Longarm's head, to the bank of opened windows. "There!" she screamed.

Longarm whirled, his Colt in his hand. Outside, in the dim glow of the street lamps, there sat mounted on a horse a figure garbed in a canvas duster. The long coat effectively hid his form. His hat was pulled down low over his brow, and he wore a bandanna mask over the bottom half of his face. Some sort of rifle was resting across his saddle, its barrel pointed toward the windows.

The mystery rider raised his weapon to his shoulder. Longarm did not have a clear shot; too many people were between him and those damned windows!

Then the rider fired his weapon. *And fired, and fired, and fired it—*

There was a high, chattering snarl as the weapon's muzzle spouted blue fire. The upper windowpanes rattled in their frames for a split second before the hail of bullets shattered them, spewing splinters and knifelike chunks of glass into the hall.

Longarm threw himself to the floor shouting, "Get down! Get down!" to whoever was still calm enough to listen. The men in the hall were tough, but none had ever experienced such firepower before. The gun kept on firing, chewing a line of bullet holes along the wainscoted walls, bursting wall-mounted oil lamps, so that flaming oil fell into the stacked furniture. Smoke and tongues of flame began to rise.

"Fire!" somebody screamed, only adding to the panic. The men, most of them drunk, were stumbling and falling to the floor, none of them hit, but all panic-striken as they waved their hands in front of them like picnickers trying to ward off a swarm of angry bees.

From out of the corner of his eye, Longarm saw Ki leap from the floor to the platform, easily clearing the six feet necessary to sail over it, scooping up Jessie as he began his descent to the other side. A split second later the firestorm of lead splintered the podium that Jessie had been standing behind into kindling. One of the Texas Rangers had thrown himself from the platform, but the other had both his guns drawn. He was a brave man, furiously returning the mystery rider's gunfire above the heads of the huddled crowd.

The line of bullet holes chewing up the paneling behind the platform abruptly dipped. The black holes being punched into the wall changed to red as they skipped across the chest of the Ranger. The man was jolted backward like a boxer absorbing a fast series of jabs. His revolvers clattered to the floor as he slumped against the wall to slide slowly down into a sitting position, his eyes wide and disbelieving as he stared first at the blood seeping from the holes scattered across his shirtfront, and then at nothing, as he died.

Ki, meanwhile, had Jessie safely cradled in his arms as he plunged downward toward the floor. At the last second Ki twisted around, so that Jessie was above him as they slammed onto the hard planking. He'd straight-armed her so that he'd absorbed every bit of the shock of their landing. A lesser man would have been knocked senseless from the impact. But Ki had her safely huddled in a far corner of the room before Jessie had even figured out just how she'd been spirited out of harms' way.

During the time the rider's weapon was trained on the hapless Texas Ranger, Longarm had begun to make a move for the door. The rider had spied Longarm's movement, and now the seemingly endless stream of bullets was chewing up the floorboards just behind the lawman's heels.

The rider had been aiming high on purpose, Longarm realized. He only tried to kill those who attempted to return his fire, or in some other way attack. Except for when he'd shot at Jessie. If Ki hadn't managed to snatch her up out of the way, the rounds that had turned the podium into sawdust and splinters would have cut her to pieces as well.

The fire, now burst into full flame. The meeting hall was fast filling up with choking smoke. If something wasn't done, and in a hurry, Longarm realized, a whole lot of smoke-blinded, half-drunk men would find themselves running like a herd of stampeding cattle, straight into that rider's incredible gun.

Longarm swung around the doorjamb, crouched low, feeling the hot wind of those rounds as they buzzed by, far, far too close. He took a bellyful of splinters—and was grateful that was all he took—as he slid along the wood-plank sidewalk, just trying to get to a place where he could at least fire back effectively.

Another came loping around the corner. He was dressed the same as the other man, and his weapon was the same as well. The gun's wooden stock was shaped to hook over the user's shoulder, as it took both hands to fire the weapon.

The riders, like Indians, used their knees to guide their horses. Two hand cranks, one on either side of the gun's breech, worked the action, reminding Longarm of the foot pedals on a bicycle he'd seen in Denver.

The two riders rode in a long circle, raking their guns back and forth along Main Street, shattering windows and tearing up walls and doors. A third rider joined them, just as the roof of the Cattlemen's building burst into high, orange flames.

The three riders—drunk with power—began whooping and shrieking like Comanches. Their guns chattered on, stripping the box-planted trees of their leaves and bark and boughs as their weapons filled the air with a high whine. The burning building cast an eerie, flickering crimson light on the scene as the flames crackled loudly. Sarah had been ravished. The town named after Starbuck's wife had been raped. Sarah, along with its fine schools, picket fences and proud, church steeple, had been turned into Hell.

Shiloh, was all Longarm could think as the sky became stained with flame. *Shiloh,* and how futile all attacks were against a Gatling gun...

Longarm, still pressed belly-down against the sidewalk, saw Farley and two of his deputies come running toward the riders. They were firing their revolvers as they ran, which meant that they didn't have a hope of hitting anything. One of the riders turned his weapon on the trio. The rounds kicked up dust, and then the two deputies began to flail the air, jerking and twitching like men suddenly struck with the palsey. The rider, laughing, flicked the barrel of his gun like a hose, and like a hose's nozzle, the gun sent a stream of lead splashing Farley's way. The town marshal's pistol went flying as he twirled in the air to come slamming down into the street.

All three riders had watched the local lawmen go down. Longarm used the distraction to launch himself off the elevated sidewalk and into the street, toward the men.

"There!" screamed one of the riders. "Get him!"

Longarm managed to snap off one shot before the hail-storm of bullets came his way. He back-pedaled desperately, trying to outrun the rounds kicking up dust spouts inches in front of his toes. He lost his balance in his haste, and sprawled backward to land flat on his back, the wind knocked out of him, his Colt a yard out of reach.

The trio of riders cantered toward him. They turned their guns on a water trough just beside Longarm, laughing as their rounds send gouts of water into the air, turning the trough itself into a leaking sieve.

"That's what we're going to do to you, lawman," one of the men laughed. "Join the others," he told his two companions. "This part of town will burn good. Those poor bastards in the Cattlemen's building are fried crisp by now. They were afraid to come out, I guess."

The two riders turned their horses and rode away toward Canvas Town. The remaining man angled his weapon down toward Longarm.

The tall deputy fumbled for the derringer behind his gunbelt buckle, knowing, even as he did so, that his last-ditch attempt to save himself was useless. He shimmied back, desperate to put even another inch between himself and that deadly gun.

Laughing, the rider began to fire. He stitched the rounds into the dirt between Longarm's widespread legs, inching the barrel of the gun up so that it would eventually be centered on Longarm's crotch.

Longarm waited for the hot bite of lead to smash into his groin and then dance its way up his gut, chest, and head, to split him cleanly up the middle, just like a melon.

★

Chapter 14

"There!" Jessie cried, pointing over the heads of the crowd, toward the window.

Longarm had been shouting something, but Ki didn't bother to listen. He'd known that the only chance he had to get Jessie out of the hail of bullets was to perform the leaping part of a *mae-tobi-geri,* a flying, front foot-strike. Normally he would have kicked out twice at an opponent at the apex of his six-foot leap, but this time he stretched and arched his back like a pole-vaulter, gaining precious inches of elevation. As he locked his arms around Jessie, he jackknifed his legs toward the far side of the platform. It was that power-snap wrung out of his thighs, knees, and calves that gave him the momentum to clear the platform's breadth, while his stomach and back muscles strained to lift her off her feet.

He'd landed hard on the wooden floor, taking the jarring impact of their combined weight along his spine. Jessie did not touch the floor until he set her down lightly. Tomorrow his flesh would be a mass of bruises, but bruises always healed. The throbbing pain in his shoulders and lower back he ignored. Pain was all in the mind...

The fire was licking up the walls and blackening the

ceiling. The smoke was so thick that he could not see the far side of the hall. He saw Longarm dash through the door, drawing the awesome firepower of the rider along with him.

Jessie was coughing and rubbing at her eyes. "We've got to get these people out," she managed to say.

"You go out the back way," Ki ordered. "I will see to it that they follow. If they go out the front, they will be exposed to that gun."

"I'll help you," Jessie said.

"No!" Ki shouted. He leaped to his feet. Gathering a handful of the back of her tweed jacket, he lifted her up as if she were a kitten being hauled into the air by the scruff of its neck.

"Bully!" she pouted.

"Will you please go!"

"Longarm is out there by himself, Ki. You've got to—"

He nodded distractedly and propelled her on her way with a hard shove against the small of her back. When he saw that she was safely through the door that led to the back hallway of the building, and the rear door, he turned to ponder the situation in the crowded meeting room.

Several of the men, huddled beneath their benches, made a break for the front door. They ignored Ki's shouts, but he was able to cut them off. The first man, fear-crazed, tried to swing at Ki, who deflected the fellow's clumsy uppercut with a circular block and, as lightly as possible, drove his fist into the man's solar plexus.

The rancher collapsed back into the path of the other two men. As they hauled their friend to his feet, Ki said, "You will be shot if you go this way. Go out the back. It is safe!"

They nodded vaguely, and headed back the way Jessie had gone. Others, seeing what Ki had done, and hearing his explanation, turned toward the back door as well. A few stubborn souls still tried for the front door, but Ki stopped them by quickly whip-snapping burning pieces of furniture into the doorway, effectively sealing it off so that now there *was* no front door. Spreading the fire was of no concern to Ki. The flames had penetrated the walls, and had grown to claim the roof timbers. The building could not be saved.

Now that there was someone telling them what to do, the ranchers and cowboys filed out of the building, with few of them panicking.

Ki waited until the last of them were out of the room, then dived through one of the wide-open windows, the glass of which had been shattered away by the gunfire. He saw one of the riders mow down the deputies and Farley, and saw Longarm take advantage of the riders' distraction by rushing toward them.

It was a valiant attempt on Longarm's part, but a man can often be both brave and foolish at the same time. Longarm managed to squeeze off only one ineffective shot before he was swept off his feet by the return barrage of gunfire.

The three riders toyed with the marshal by shooting up a watering trough just beside him, and then two rode away, leaving one to finish the job. Ki saw Longarm kick his heels into the dust, trying for purchase to push himself away from the bullets rushing toward him between his legs.

For one moment Ki thought, *If I let him die, there will be no danger of his stealing away Jessie—*

The thought flickered through his mind even as his right hand automatically plucked the *shuriken* throwing blade from its sheath and hurled it at the rider's back.

His throw had been hurried, without proper time to aim. The blade missed the man's heart, burying itself high in the rider's left shoulder. Still, the shock and pain of feeling himself stabbed, forced the rider to take his hands from his weapon, so that it stopped firing. The gun did not fall to the ground. It looked to Ki as if it was hooked over the man's shoulders...

Ki reached for another *shuriken*, but before he could send

203

it flying, the rider wheeled his horse hard around, and rode off in a flat-out run, squealing all the while like a scalded pig.

"You all right?" Ki asked when he reached Longarm.

"You saved my life," Longarm said as he got to his feet. "Another second, and—"

"I have merely repaid my debt of honor to you," Ki admonished, looking away. "Earlier this evening I got you into danger by sending you to Canvas Town. Now I have gotten you out of danger."

"Damn, old son," Longarm said dryly. "For a minute there, I thought it was because you liked me. I didn't know you were playing bank teller with that honor of yours."

Ki merely shrugged. "Let us see to Marshal Farley," he said. Longarm retrieved his Colt and followed Ki, muttering oaths beneath his breath.

Farley's two deputies were stone dead, but the town marshal had gotten off lucky. Only one of the .25-caliber rounds had hit him. He had a broken rib or two, but the round had been deflected outward so that the wound was clean. Doc Brown would have an easy time of it patching him up.

Ki helped Farley hobble along with them while Longarm gave him a clean handkerchief to press against his wound. They wanted to take the marshal directly to the doctor, but Farley would have none of that, not until he knew that everyone who had been in the Cattlemen's building was safe.

Now that the gunmen were gone, citizens were coming up for air. Bucket brigades were hastily organized—not to save the Cattlemen's building, for, as Ki had surmised, it was a lost cause. The bucket brigade worked hard just to keep the flames from spreading to the other nearby structures.

The men who had been at the meeting were sitting huddled behind the now-smoldering ruins of what had been their town's pride and joy. Their eyes were red from smoke, and they were tired, but unharmed. Farley's quick check showed that three men had lost their lives: his two deputies and one of the governor's Texas Rangers.

One other of Farley's deputies came running up, braking to a startled halt as he surveyed the destruction. "Jesus," he gasped. "Marshal Farley, you've been wounded!"

"I'm all right, Harry," Farley grumbled. "What's your report?"

"The rest of the town is all right," Harry muttered. "They kept their attack confined to Main Street and Canvas Town. Canvas Town has been torn up just about as bad as this. A few boys were hurt, but nobody's dead. Just about everybody, drunk or sober, had the presence of mind to hug the ground."

"Makes sense," Longarm observed.

"What does?" Farley asked sharply.

"The way they handled it," Longarm replied. "Some of them terrorize the cattlemen who do the hiring, and some scare the bejesus out of the boys who need the jobs. Reckon you'll find that a goodly number of those cowboys-for-hire are going to seek out healthier regions to make their living."

"The tactic of intimidation," Ki said quietly.

"It'll be harder for you ranchers to run your roundup without your free-lance drovers, right?" Longarm called out.

The men nodded, grumbling dejectedly. "It might just be damned near impossible," one of them offered harshly.

"Come on, now!" Longarm argued. "That's not Texas talk!" He looked around. They needed Jessie to inspire them. But where was she?

"Maybe we do need the army, or at least the Texas Rangers," another man said.

"Well now, the Rangers are an ungodly distance from Sarah," Longarm shouted. "Except for the two left who belong to the governor, and they've got to stick with him."

205

He pulled out his wallet to show them all his badge. "But I'm federal, boys. Working out of Denver. We'll catch those bastards, that I promise!"

The men all looked up, clearly heartened by the fact that there was somebody to stand between them and the horror they'd just experienced.

"Longarm, I thought you wanted to remain undercover," Farley whispered.

Longarm shrugged. "Those two who braced me in Canvas Town knew I was a federal marshal. So did those riders just now. It seems the only folks who didn't know have been the good ones." He gave Farley a hard look. "I sort of thought it was you who spilled the beans."

"No way," said Farley indignantly.

Ki stepped between them. "I found out it was Higgins," he said. "He figured it out the day you rode with us to the Circle-Star. He saw the U.S. brand on your horse."

"I see." Longarm smiled at Farley. "I owe you an apology."

"Forget it," Farley laughed, with no real humor. "I've got bigger things to worry about, like putting my town back together."

"It was brave of you to rush those riders," Longarm added.

"Bullshit, sonny," Farley spat back disgustedly. "It was plain stupid. The lives of those two men who got killed following my orders will be my sorrow to bear for a long, long time." He looked expectantly at Longarm. "Well, you're the ranking law. I don't know how to handle this. Should we form up a posse, or what?"

Just then the governor approached, followed by his two remaining Ranger bodyguards, who still had their guns drawn. "Terrible thing, terrible!" the politician muttered. "I hope no one besides my man was hurt."

"Two of mine, as well," Farley replied. "You can put

your shooters away, boys," he told the Rangers. "Party's over."

"Where is Jessie?" Ki asked.

"She came our way," one of the Rangers said. "We had her horse with ours, and the governor's buggy. She took it and rode like the devil. Where, I can't say."

"I bet I know," Longarm said.

"She's trailing those riders, of course," Ki agreed. "We must get after her!"

"A posse it is, then," Farley said.

"No!" Longarm cut him off. "You boys all have horses?" he asked the ranchers.

"Ours were all in the stable," one of them shrugged. "If they're all right—"

"They are," Farley interjected. "We were by the hotel, and the stables are near there. Your animals weren't touched."

"Then you men guard your herds," Longarm said. "I can travel faster on my own." He paused. "Except that my horse was tied outside the saloon," he added.

"If it was that chestnut gelding with the McClellan saddle, you're out of luck," Farley said. "He was shot dead by those bastards, along with all the other mounts tied up along that stretch."

Ki swore softly. "My horse as well, then."

"Hell, boys, take two of ours," one of the ranchers said. Two drovers hurried off to retrieve Longarm's and Ki's gear in order to saddle up two other horses.

"How are you two going to face down all those men?" Farley demanded. "My deputy here just told me half a dozen men shot up Canvas Town. That makes at least nine of them, and all armed with those"—he looked helplessly about him—"whatever they are . . ." he trailed off.

"Coffee grinders," Ki said softly.

"Huh?" Farley looked confused.

"It does not matter at the moment," Ki continued. "We must either stop Jessie or rescue her if she has been captured. If they have her, a show of force would be useless. One or two men, who are clever, would be much more effective in safely freeing her." Ki looked at Longarm. "And saving Jessie is our first concern. Agreed?"

"Me and you," Longarm nodded. "Agreed."

As they started off, Longarm told the governor, "You'd better telegraph the army, after all. They can get here sooner than the Rangers."

The governor looked doubtful. "That would mean martial law, after all. I've made campaign promises..."

"You've got no choice," Longarm said impatiently. "Farley here doesn't have the manpower. The ranchers have to keep their cowboys watching over the herds in case those riders try to butcher the cattle with those"—he looked at Ki—"coffee grinders."

"Why would they want to do that?" the governor asked.

"To prevent the cattle from going to market, and in that way bankrupt the cattlemen," Ki said. "If tonight's attempt at terrorizing the ranchers fails, the next step may be simply to destroy the cattle."

"With those weapons, nine men could do it easy," Longarm muttered. "And I've got a nasty feeling there are more than nine."

"This is foolishness!" the governor exclaimed. "I suppose you believe that poppycock about Europeans trying to take over the cattle industry. That Jessie has some fool notion, and you boys believe her!"

"It is the truth," Ki said. "Earlier this evening I encountered one of the foreign men Jessie spoke of."

"Probably a businessman," the governor grumbled.

"This man and I struggled," Ki pressed on. "He was no businessman, but a professional killer. From him I obtained proof, which I turned over to Jessie."

"What kind of proof?" the governor asked cunningly.

208

"This I do not know," Ki admitted. "But the items had great significance to Jessie."

"There you are, men," the governor called out. "I wanted to look out for her because of my friendship with her daddy. But she's going too far—"

"Longarm, we are wasting time," Ki said disgustedly.

"Don't you use that tone of voice with *me*, boy," the governor warned.

"All of you!" Ki shouted, addressing the ranchers. "You know what you owe the Starbuck family." He turned to point at the governor. "You owe this man nothing!" Turning back, he shouted, "Will you stand by your debts of honor to Alex Starbuck, for what he has done for you in the past, and Jessie Starbuck, for what she has given you this night?"

As the ranchers nodded and called out their agreement, the governor told his two Rangers, "Arrest that slant-eyed bastard."

What happened next was too fast for even Longarm to see. One moment the two Rangers were bracketing Ki, and the next they were on the ground, one clutching at his throat and coughing, the other on his knees, his forehead pressed against the dirt, his arms wrapped around his rib cage. Ki had only seemed to flex his muscles; the hand movements had been just a blur . . .

The governor stood quietly as Ki plucked the Ranger's pistols from their holsters and tossed them away. The politician opened his mouth to say something, but then thought better of it.

"If you do not send for the army, as Longarm asks, I will come back and kill you," Ki said calmly. "You might surround yourself with guards. It will not help. At night, just before you drop off to sleep, you will hear a sound. You will open your eyes to see me standing over you." Ki smiled. "Do you understand, Governor?"

The Governor looked at Farley, who seemed suddenly occupied with his gunshot wound. He glanced at his two

Ranger bodyguards. One seemed to have slipped into un-consciousness. The other tried to get to his feet, but then collapsed with a long, low moan of pain.

Licking his dry lips, the governor mumbled, "Why, yes, I understand."

"Longarm?" Ki walked away.

"Right. Farley, if he doesn't call in the army, you do it. We'll leave a trail a blind man could follow."

He followed Ki around to the front of the burned-out building, where their two horses were standing ready. Long-arm checked his rifle to make sure it was in working order, and was about to mount up when Ki stopped him.

"I must return to the Circle-Star to get what I need to battle these men effectively. For me to come with you now would be a waste. I have only a few throwing blades."

"What about that?" Longarm asked. pointing at Ki's gun-belt.

The samurai only shook his head. "I will be several hours behind you. Save her if you can, but if you get into trouble, know that I will save you both." He offered a sardonic grin. "This time, *I* will be your ace-in-the-hole."

"Mine or Jessie's?" Longarm asked sarcastically.

Ki turned away in pain and consternation.

"You love her. Admit it!" Longarm demanded. He grabbed Ki's arm and spun him around. "You love her," he repeated softly. "And you know that I do as well. Admit it."

"My friend," Ki began plaintively, "that my jealousy is so apparent is my shame, but know that I blame you for nothing. It is not a matter of my admitting what is true, but of living the life I have been given. Your love for her steals nothing from me. I cannot be robbed of what I can never have. Longarm, save her if possible. In exchange I will rescue you both, even if it costs me my life."

Longarm watched him swing himself into his saddle. As

Ki wheeled his horse around, he called down, "I swear to save you both." He rode off.

Longarm mounted up and loped off in the direction of the mystery riders. His one slim hope was that he could catch Jessiē before the riders caught her. Men like those wouldn't kill a pretty girl like her right off. No, they would take their time...

If those riders have harmed a hair on Jessie's head, he vowed, there won't be anything left of them for Ki by the time he catches up...

★

Chapter 15

It had been easy for Jessica to slip away during the confusion. When the two riders rode out of town, she was mounted up and ready to follow them. She'd pulled her Colt .38 rig from her saddlebags, and strapped the gunbelt around her waist. In her riding jacket's pocket was the strange pistol Ki had earlier turned over to her, and that newspaper clipping that explained so much.

The clipping told of the origins of the awesome weaponry that had been turned upon her town; Longarm would be interested in that, no doubt, since it was now clear that those same guns had been used to cut down her father. But what was important to Jessie was that she now knew who had ordered those guns turned on her father.

Ki had missed it during his cursory examination of the foreign-made handgun, but that was understandable. A family crest, the symbol of European nobility, would mean nothing to a man raised in an Oriental culture. As for the initials WD, the monogram of ownership carved below the family crest, the design had been cleverly worked into the filigree, and besides, no one could know what those initals stood for. Her daddy had told no one but her, and she had told no one at all, not even Ki. That way, when the opportunity to avenge her father's death presented itself—as she'd always known it would—she would have time to kill the man before anyone interfered.

Time to kill the man, Jessie thought as her horse followed the trail through the dark night. But not much time. Both Ki and Longarm would be on her heels by now.

Ki and Longarm—she loved them both, in totally different ways. But neither of them could understand the depths of her passion concerning this feud that had destroyed the Starbuck family. She had to be the one to kill the blond man, the owner of the pistol. It was fitting. It was the wheel of *karma,* making one more complete cycle as it spun around and around, endlessly.

And after it's done? What then, Jessie? she asked herself. *You are a woman, made for love, not for killing...*

She slowed her mount, to ascertain that she was still on the trail of the riders. It wasn't hard. There was a sliver of moon to see by, and the riders, confident, had made no effort to camouflage their direction. Jessie knew the area surrounding the Circle-Star spread. She had already surmised that the riders were heading toward an old grouping of buildings situated at the base of a marble quarry. The ramshackle compound of buildings, long abandoned, had once been occupied by stonecutters digging out the marble used in the construction of several buildings in Sarah. The marble had run out very quickly. Once sufficient stone had been dug out for Sarah's needs, the operation had been closed down. But there was wood for fires nearby, and a pure water well. It would be the ideal spot to hide a gang of men.

Jessie rode on. She had been careful earlier, letting the third rider pass her while she kept herself and her horse concealed. This third rider, once he'd joined the others up ahead, would make at least a half-dozen men she was following, and maybe more than that. She couldn't be sure how many horses were making the jumble of tracks, but she could certainly tell that the number was considerably greater than three . . .

When the third rider had passed, Jessie had heard him moaning as he tried to clutch at something sticking into the back of his shoulder. There was a dark, shiny patch running down the back of his canvas duster. It had looked like Ki's work.

That Ki would help Longarm, Jessie had no doubt. What she had told Longarm about her relationship with Ki was true. She looked up to and worshiped the man as if he were her older brother. But sisterly love was one thing, and passionate love was quite another. Longarm was the only man she had ever truly loved, as a woman . . .

Mrs. Custis Long . . . The thought made her giggle out loud. She scolded herself for acting so silly while engaged in such a dangerous activity as trailing a band of armed outlaws. That alone was proof enough to her that Longarm had wrought miraculous changes!

Mrs. Custis Long . . . Longarm wouldn't be an easy stallion to rope, but if there was any woman on earth who could do it, it would be Jessica Starbuck. She'd never known anyone remotely like him, except for her father, perhaps, and of course Ki. She'd let this vendetta rest in exchange for Custis Long's love and companionship for the rest of her life—let it rest after this last violent night, for she fully intended to avenge her daddy's murder by the coming dawn. Then she would docilely accept Longarm's rebuke and use her womanly wiles to turn his anger around into passion. They could begin a new phase in both their lives, leaving their days of hatred and violence behind as they made love and began to make plans for their future together.

Mrs. Custis Long . . . Lord, wouldn't that be something. Not that there wouldn't be problems. A man like Longarm would most likely stomp the first man who referred to him as Mr. Jessie Starbuck, but after Longarm had taught all such men their manners, and told them that a fellow didn't need wealth to be a real man, things would smooth down. But she'd still have to reconcile her role as this proud but poor man's wife with her duties as the head of the Starbuck business empire.

One thing she could do would be to assign control of the day-to-day decisions to her daddy's trusted advisors. Why not? They were making most of the decisions now, she only reserving the final say on the most important ones. She and Longarm could concentrate on the cattle business. He knew cattle. He could take the Circle-Star over and run things, the way a man ought to . . .

Jessie giggled once again as she let her horse pick its way along the narrow trail through a dense grove of pecan trees. The biggest problem she and Longarm would have would be managing to leave their bed long enough to see that business was taken care of—

"You hold it right there, lady!" came a shout from Jessie's right.

She peered into the darkness, but whoever was calling to her had himself well hidden among the tree trunks and shadows of the night-dark grove. She set off at a gallop, her Colt .38 in her hand. Damn! She'd ridden right into a trap! Ridden into it mooning and daydreaming over her lover like some silly adolescent—

"I said hold it!" the man yelled at her. He was one of the riders dressed in a canvas duster, his hat pulled low, his face masked by a bandanna. That strange weapon that the newspaper article had dubbed a "coffee grinder" was resting across his saddle. The rider was not trying to kill her, but head her off.

"Back off, or I'll shoot!" Jessie warned.

The man just laughed. "Cool down, little lady," he said, smirking, as her horse instinctively slowed to avoid colliding with his.

"Laugh at me, and you're a dead man," Jessie swore. This was one of the men who had tried their best to destroy

216

the town her father had built in her mother's memory. Who knew how many citizens of Sarah had been killed by this man alone? Who knew whether it wasn't this man who had willingly obeyed the order to ambush her father?

"Don't you threaten me, you bitch," the masked rider spat. "I know what you need." He reached out to grab the reins from her.

Jessie shot him once, in the chest. The man gasped in surprise, then fell off of his horse. One boot stayed caught in his stirrups, so that when his panicked horse trotted off, it dragged the rider's body behind it like a sack.

Another mystery rider broke cover to intercept her. His "coffee grinder" was also secured across his saddle, but he'd drawn his revolver from beneath his duster.

"Don't kill her!" somebody else shouted. "The boss wants her alive!"

Jessie leaned forward over her saddle and rode hard. Her one chance was to get through the grove and into open country where she could goad her horse into a flat-out run. She was lighter than the men persuing her, and her horse was fresher. There was a good chance she could outrun them.

As the second rider closed in, Jessie fired at him. He groaned, dropping his pistol as he slumped. His mount slowed in confusion as its reins went slack.

The end of the grove was in sight. Jessie began to think that she just might make it. No other riders were trying to stop her. She holstered her Colt and concentrated on riding.

Blue flame suddenly licked out. The harsh, nasty, chittering sound of a "coffee grinder" enveloped her, and her horse screamed in pain and terror as the bullets stitched along its belly and hindquarters, literally disemboweling it. Jessie kicked free of the stirrups as the horse, eyes rolling upward, began to stumble. She jumped clear as the horse somersaulted forward to crash to the ground. It quivered, its stiff legs kicking in the air, and then lay still.

Jessie broke her fall the way Ki had taught her, slapping the ground with her arm and keeping her body curved, to roll with the impact. The strong tweed cloth of her jacket and skirt, and her high leather boots, protected her from cuts and scrapes, but her momentum had been such that she lay stunned. She was conscious, but the wind had been knocked out of her. She protested feebly, and tried to struggle as men bent over her, stealing away her Colt and taking the foreign-made handgun from her jacket pocket.

"What are our losses?" muttered the man who seemed to be in charge of the party. Through dazed eyes, Jessie had a glimpse of him standing above her, wrapped in his duster, his weapon's long barrel jutting up into the sky.

"She killed the first and lung-shot the second," came an answering grumble from somewhere beyond her field of vision. "Damn, that girl can shoot."

Jessie smiled. "You bet I can," she began, but her voice faded; talking was just too much effort. She tried to hoist herself up on one elbow to get a better look at her captors, but even that slight movement set her head to spinning. She flopped back down and closed her eyes. The spinning increased, tightening into a fast downward spiral. The blackness behind her eyelids deepened—

Mrs. Custis Long, she mused giddily. Well, it looked as if thoughts of marriage had been a bit premature. *If you want me, you'd better save me, Longarm,* she thought, but then even thinking became too difficult, and she lapsed into a dream that faded into darkness . . .

"She's passed out," one of the men looking down at her said.

"Get her across one of the horses," the leader instructed. "One of you double up for the rest of the ride."

Two men hoisted Jessie's limp form up, and set her belly-down across a saddle. One of the men furtively tried to slide his hand beneath her skirt, but before he could, he felt a

218

rough hand gripping his coat collar and pulling him backward.

"None of that now," the leader gruffly reprimanded. "You know he's waiting for her."

"Just wanted a little feel," the other rider shrugged.

"Is that what you want me to tell *him?*" the leader asked.

Shaking his head, the man hurried off. "Let's go, then," he said hastily.

"We'll have plenty of time for taking our pleasure after he talks to her." The leader pulled down his bandanna mask, to reveal a scarred, unshaven face and a mouthful of broken teeth just now split into a dog's grin. "He'll give her to us, till he's ready to slit her throat." He turned toward his own horse, calling out, "Let's ride!"

★

Chapter 16

Longarm rode hard until he came to the pecanwood grove. Even before he'd reached Jessie's shot horse, he'd smelled the harsh, throat-drying tang of cordite handing in the air.

He dismounted, pulling his Winchester from its saddle boot and levering a round into the chamber. Everything looked quiet, but he reckoned it had looked quiet to Alex Starbuck the day he was ambushed, and to Jessie, who, from the looks of things, had been ambushed just a short while ago. Alex Starbuck had been killed. Was Jessie dead?

Longarm felt a sick feeling building in the pit of his stomach.

Don't think about it that way! he told himself. He squared his shoulders. *Don't think about her that way.* Right now he had to be a professional manhunter, a lawman, just like always.

Over his years as a deputy U.S. marshal, Longarm had built up a tough shell to protect his own heart. Maybe Jessie was hurt—maybe she was even dead, he mused grimly as his eyes traced the line of bloody bullet holes puckering the horse's carcass. Maybe he himself felt like grieving.

But he wasn't going to. He was going to get on with doing his job. That was the difference between foolish amateurs like Jessie and Ki, and professionals like himself. A professional lawman knew enough not to take *anything* personally. A lawman couldn't afford to love anybody. Hell, he couldn't afford even to *like* anybody. People close to a lawman had a way of getting hurt, and the problem was compounded when those people were damned amateurs playing this professional's game of manhunting.

Jessie—an image of her as she'd been that one blissful night, in front of the fireplace, came into his mind. Longarm felt his loins stir. It made him want to laugh, or maybe cry, he wasn't sure which. He was surrounded by danger. He was forced to contemplate the awful possibility that she was dead or dying. He was a man who knew the many faces of death and violence better than he knew any man or woman. He lived by the gun, and he would most likely die by it, and yet—

And yet, as callous as he was trying to be, as cold and as cynical, just the thought of her, as she'd been that night in his arms, forced him to swell and fill the front of his pants. Just the thought of her proved to him that he was a flesh-and-blood man, alive, and that there was goodness in this hard-as-nails world . . .

She was not dead! Longarm suddenly knew it, the knowledge as certain as his ache to touch Jessie, to hold her in his arms. She was not dead, and so he would find her and have her again. And God help any man who had touched her . . .

Longarm froze as his horse whinnied softly, snorting and tossing its head. Now he suddenly knew something else, as well. He was not alone in this grove.

Horses had a way of calling to each other, especially at night, when the darkness combined with a steed's instinctive tendency to run with a herd, and in that way gain safety from the world of predators that craved horseflesh. His borrowed mount was an experienced cow pony, but it had already been panicked by the carrion smell of Jessie's dead horse.

Chances were, the horses of the ambushers surrounding him were not too thrilled about being in such close proximity to one of their own kind, dead. Longarm figured that there were at least two ambushers. In situations like this, two men had a way of comforting one another. One man alone, waiting in the darkness to ambush, had a way of becoming jumpy.

Longarm wanted to get it over and done with. If he started things off, maybe he could get his bushwhackers to reveal their locations by returning his fire.

Longarm fired into the woods at random, at the same time crabbing sideways into the trees. He saw a flash of blue fire as one of those "coffee grinders" opened up, sending rounds tearing into the corpse of Jessie's horse. The gun was positioned across the trail directly opposite Longarm. The damn fool was counting on his awesome firepower to keep Longarm pinned down and unable to fire back. That tactic could work, but only if the gunner was positive as to the location of his target.

Longarm brought his rifle up to his shoulder and fired once, aiming just above the blue flicker coming from the weapon's barrel. He caught a glimpse of that flashing muzzle rising toward the night sky as the gunner fell back. Then the blue flame winked out and the chattering gunfire ceased.

Longarm caught only a glimpse of this because he'd already begun rolling fast away from his position. He was just in time, for three shots from a more conventional weapon, a rifle, plowed into the fallen tree trunk he'd been hiding behind. He saw the muzzle flash this time as well, but held off firing back. Chances were, the man had already moved from his position. If Longarm fired now, he'd hit nothing, and give away *his* new hiding spot.

There was another reason he did not fire back. He wanted

223

one of these men alive, and he'd already shot the first. He needed to know what had happened to Jessie, where she'd been taken. Blindly following the trail left by the other riders' horses could easily lead him on a wild-goose chase, or right into another ambush.

He heard his man moving through the undergrowth. The fellow was trying to circle around him and come up from behind. Longarm began to move silently to cut across the other's path. He ran parallel to the trail, to avoid the chance of making any unnecessary noise.

The rounds thudded into a tree behind him, even as he heard that firecracker chatter. That damned gunner with the "coffee grinder" wasn't out of commission after all.!

"Pin him down for me!" screamed the other ambusher. The man operating the "coffee grinder" answered by turning the cranks on his weapon. This time he restricted his fire to short bursts as he moved and bobbed, weaving in and out among the trees, so that Longarm did not have a steady target.

"There he is!" shouted the man across the road as he sent a burst of rounds Longarm's way. "Hurry up! Finish him off! I'm hurt bad! The bastard hit me before!"

Longarm rolled and twisted on his belly like a snake run over by a wagon. He tried to ignore the bullets kicking dirt into his face. *A miss is as good as a mile,* he reminded himself.

He twisted around as the man on his side of the grove came rushing at Longarm from behind. If Longarm fired at him, he'd exactly pinpoint his own position for the other gunner. Longarm was between the two men, cut off front and rear—

Longarm smiled. It just might work . . .

Leaving his rifle behind, Longarm hurled himself up to run toward the man who was rushing at him. Confused by Longarm's tactic, the man brought up his own rifle and levered off several rounds, but he'd aimed too high. Before he really knew what had happened, Longarm had managed to thrust himself beneath the other's field of fire.

Meanwhile, the man operating the "coffee grinder" was trying his best to cut Longarm down by sending a steady stream of fire after him. The bullets nipped at the lawman's heels like a pack of hungry wolves. The weapon fired fast, all right; what Longarm was hoping was that the hellish thing fired *too* fast.

The rifleman realized what was happening, and dropped his gun to wave in panic at his crony across the road, but it was too dark for the other man to see clearly. As Longarm veered sideways to dive into the brush, the hail of bullets continued along the trajectory he'd set.

"No! Stop!" wailed the rifleman as he zigged and zagged, trying to get out of the other's arc of fire, but he was too late, as was the gunner, who immediately stopped cranking his gun but not before several rounds had peppered his partner's torso. The man fell backwards to lay spread-eagled on the ground.

Longarm listened to the rattle coming from the shot man's chest, and had no doubt that the fellow was just moments away from dying. That left the gunner across the road.

Longarm prepared to move for his life as he called out, "Give it up!" He waited tensely, fully expecting to have to dodge another barrage, but none came. "I'm a federal marshal. You're alone now, and you're wounded! Let me help you!"

Longarm slid sideways to wait for an answer, but none came. *Damn,* he thought, *hope the poor bastard hasn't gone and died on me.*

Off to his left, he heard his horse. The animal had trotted back the way they'd come at the first sound of gunfire. Now it was about fifty feet away. Longarm, his eyes grown accustomed to the darkness, could make out the horse's silhouette against the trail so fitfully lit by that miserly portion of moon. The horse seemed to have calmed a bit.

It was beginning to browse the tender shoots beneath the trees that bordered the road.

The horse seemed no longer to feel the tension it had shown just before the gun battle had started. Sometimes an animal knew better than a man when the fight was all over and done with.

Longarm found splatters of blood where the gunner had been. He'd managed to drag himself and his "coffee grinder" off into the woods on his side of the road, but from the quantity of blood the man was losing, he wasn't going to get far. Longarm traced the man's path by following the trail of bent and crushed grass and undergrowth. The fellow was crawling, but Longarm kept his Colt ready and his concentration focused. A man didn't need much life left in him to let the hammer down on a revolver. More than one lawman had gotten himself killed by blundering into a dying outlaw's gunsights.

On the other hand, Longarm couldn't afford to close in on the man too slowly. The fellow might get to his horse and make a break for it, or he might curl up and die before Longarm had a chance to question him.

When he finally caught up to him, the fellow was sitting propped against a tree. He was wrapped in that same sort of canvas duster worn by the riders who'd attacked the town. The long coat didn't make the man look nearly as menacing as it had those others. This poor bastard looked like a collapsed rag doll. His knees were drawn up and his head was lowered, his hat tipped forward over his eyes, just like one of those Mexican fellows who liked to take a noontime siesta. Except that this man's siesta was going to last a long, long time.

The ambusher had lost his "coffee grinder," but he held a revolver loosely clasped in his right hand. At the sound of Longarm's approach, he raised the handgun to wave it in the marshal's general direction.

"Throw it away, old son," Longarm told him gently. He

kept his Colt centered on the huddled form.

The man did throw it away, quickly and briskly, as if getting rid of his gun had been a great idea he'd been waiting for somebody to suggest. "Good riddance—" he began to grumble, but whatever else he wanted to say was lost in a fit of coughing and groaning.

Longarm crouched down beside the man, and quickly checked him over for hidden weapons. To do that, he had to open the man's duster, and that revealed the full extent of his gunshot wound. The .44 slug had caught the man full in the belly. He was as good as buried.

"How am I, lawman?" the ambusher asked craftily. "Am I going to make it?"

"I'd say so," Longarm nodded. "You'll be fine."

"Then I'd say you're a fool or a liar." The man turned his head to spit out a mouthful of blood. "And from the way you foxed me and Terry, you sure ain't a fool..."

"Neither are you, old son."

"My name's Lucas Conrad," the man said. "Make sure they get it right on my stone." He peered up at Longarm's face. "Just who the hell are you that killed both me and Terry?"

"My name's Custis Long. I'm a deputy U.S. marshal. Lucas, we both know you ain't got a lot of time left. Tell me what's happened to Jessie Starbuck. Where has she been taken?"

"U.S. marshal...Shit! They must of known...and they only left us two to stop you. They said it was going to be that Chinese fellow—"

"Japanese, half Japanese," Longarm corrected. "He's a man who deserves to be called what he is, just like you deserve your rightful name on your stone."

"Reckon so, Long, reckon so..." Lucas laughed weakly. "Or maybe a man just naturally feels generous when he knows he's dying. Say, you did kill Terry?"

"You killed him," Longarm replied.

"Maybe so," Lucas agreed resignedly. "But you tricked me into it. Them 'coffee grinders' work real good, but I reckon they ain't meant for close-in, eye-to-eye fighting."

"Where's the gun?" Longarm asked. "I wouldn't mind taking a look at it."

"Don't know," Lucas muttered. "Heavy bastard. I left it in the woods somewhere after Terry got killed. Don't matter, though. Danzig's got twenty-five of them tucked away, every one of them hand-forged by that fellow Brader..." After another coughing spasm, Lucas continued, "There's twenty-five men... well, maybe just twenty now... but all of them are gunslicks brought in from other parts of the country. Me, and Terry over yonder, we was just cowboys who got in over our heads. Maybe that's why they picked us to stay behind and cover the trail..."

"They made a bad mistake, then," Longarm said. "You leave your best, not your worst. I'll make them pay for what they did to you, Lucas." He then added politely, "And I'm rightful sorry that I've killed you like I have."

"Don't hold no grudge agin you, Long," Lucas shrugged. "A man decides to play poker, he can't go blaming the other boys for wanting to win. Say, Marshal, you got a smoke on you?"

Longarm gave him a cheroot, and struck a match to light it. As Lucas inhaled, he was again struck by a fit of coughing. This time, Longarm thought it was the end. The man's eyes fluttered, and his breathing became irregular.

"The girl," Longarm demanded. "Is she all right? Where'd they take her?"

Lucas snorted. "All right! She's a damn sight better than all right. Pretty thing, but powerful ornery. She killed two of us before we cut her horse out from under her. Danzig— he's that foreign fellow, hard to understand him—anyway, Danzig wanted her taken alive..." Lucas paused.

"Say what you've got on your mind, Lucas," Longarm coaxed. "I don't hold you responsible for none of it. Maybe if you tell me, the Lord will look favorable on you. It's His law you're going to be judged by."

"You believe in the Lord?" Lucas asked softly.

"Don't rightly know if I do, old son," Longarm answered truthfully. "But then again, I've never had a .44 slug nested in my belly."

Lucas laughed. "Lead does have a way of bringing a man around to the religious way of thinking..." The cheroot fell from his lips as he wrapped his arms about himself and squeezed tight. "Oh, Jesus, Long. It hurts something awful!"

"Say what you've got to say," Longarm urged. "Before it's too late!"

"It's that this foreign-born fellow, Danzig, hates that girl something *fierce*. He wanted her taken alive so that he could kill her himself. I almost don't mind dying now, 'cause I ain't sure I would've had the stomach for what's going to happen to that little lady. Danzig's got some old boys working for him who've been promised a go-round with her before Danzig kills her. Those boys don't mind cutting up an unwilling gal to make her lay still, you know, Long? Hell, those kind of men *like* it when they can mix some serious hurting in with their loving."

"Where did they take her?" Longarm asked through clenched teeth.

"An old quarry set in among a bunch of hills. You'll hit it right enough, if you just follow along this here trail."

"Don't sound like Danzig is too worried about being tracked down," Longarm mused out loud. "Now, twenty-odd men armed with those 'coffee grinders' could most likely hold off any local opposition, but not the army..."

Longarm glanced at Lucas for his opinion, but the man was all finished talking. His breath came slowly, and then faded altogether in one long, hoarse exhalation. Longarm gently closed the dead man's eyes and stood up.

"Well, Lucas, what I think is this. Your ex-boss ain't

worried about the army because he knows it ain't coming. I'm starting to smell a rat in this here situation, and I'm starting to think I know who it is. I'm going to need your duster, old son. I mean to get near enough to that quarry where they've got Jessie without starting an all-out shooting war..."

He stripped the man of his long canvas coat, and wiped off as much of the blood as he could with handfuls of leaves. "Lucas Conrad, I do pledge that if I live through this, I'll see to it that you get your headstone, with your name carved on it all right and proper. Rest easy, old son. You helped me right fine."

Longarm turned and walked back through the woods to gather up his Winchester. He never even paused to examine the body of the man named Terry, but simply walked on toward his horse. The duster that would be his ticket to reaching Jessica was folded over his arm.

His plan was to dress himself up in the coat and identify himself as Lucas Conrad to whatever sentries were on duty. Chances were good that he could pull the ruse off long enough—in the darkness—either to get past the guards or else take them out quietly, so as not to alert the whole camp.

As he approached his horse, the animal turned its head in the direction opposite him, the way out of the grove. Longarm, eyes narrowed, stood quietly. *There couldn't be more ambushers around,* he decided. *They would've gotten mixed in with the fighting by now, for chrissakes.*

"You're just talking to Lucas and Terry's horses. I hope," Longarm muttered. He wished he still had the army gelding. He's spent some time with that horse, and had been learning how to read the signals it gave. This animal was still a puzzle to him.

He hauled himself up into his saddle and goaded his horse hard toward the encampment Lucas had talked about. He had to hurry. There was no telling when this Danzig character would decide to throw Jessie to his dogs. He hated her, Lucas had said. Hated her so much that he wanted to be the one to actually kill her. And Jessie was looking to kill the man who'd done in her father. What was the link between these two? Were they both just caught up in this generation-spanning feud? Was Danzig just a soldier fighting for the other side? Or did he have a personal reason for wanting her dead?

Just as Longarm reached the end of the grove, he saw the flickers of movement on either side of him in the shadows. He pulled hard on his mount's reins, twisting the horse sideways and forcing it to rear up, but it was far too late to try and make a break for it back the way he'd come.

Longarm heard the reedy whistling sound as the lariats came drifting down, their loops cinching tight around him, pinning his arms to his sides. The two cowboys dressed in canvas dusters kneed their horses out of the woods to trot backward, jerking upon their ropes as they rode. Longarm was jolted out of his saddle. He hit the ground hard, and was dragged, jouncing and jolting along behind the two, for perhaps one hundred feet before there came a shouted command for the two riders to stop.

Longarm, only half conscious, heard the sound of horses' hooves approaching. He tried to move his arms to reach his Colt, but the lariat loops were being kept tight. He was helpless.

"We will not skin him now, but save that pleasure for later," said a thickly accented voice.

Longarm stared up into a face topped with a close-cropped fringe of golden blond hair. The man's eyes were pale blue, and a thin red scar ran the length of one cheek. This man did not wear one of the canvas dusters, but instead a suit of black.

"Herr Long," the blond man began, "do you play chess?"

Longarm let his eyes close. "You're Danzig, right?"

"At your service." Danzig straightened up to click his heels. "Do you play?"

"I have," Longarm muttered. "It ain't my favorite game. How long you been waiting for me?"

"Since you arrived. I placed my two men back there to occupy you for a while, and then lull you into thinking you were in control. I knew you'd easily defeat them."

"So you sacrificed them," Longarm said slowly. "I get it. You sacrificed a couple of pawns."

"Precisely, Herr Long!" Danzig beamed. "I have sacrificed two pawns to capture the first of Jessica Starbuck's two knights!"

"And the other?" Longarm asked.

"The Oriental," Danzig said grimly. "I have a special score to settle with him. I will take him alive, just as I have taken you."

"Why go to all that trouble?" Longarm began.

"To hurt her!" Danzig cut him off. "To make her suffer. I want her to know that everyone she cares for has been destroyed by Wulf Danzig. I want her to know that I have won, that I have wiped the scourge that is the Starbuck family from the face of the earth. Then, and only then, shall I give her to my men, before I personally slit her throat."

"Herr Danzig?"

"Ja, Herr Long?"

"I'm starting to understand why everybody thinks you're such an asshole—"

Danzig kicked out savagely, the tip of his boot thudding against Longarm's head. He brought his foot back to kick again at the still form, but hesitated and then got control of himself.

"I must not kill him too soon," Danzig growled. "You two! Take his gunbelt and his coat. Search him carefully for hidden weapons. Hurry!" He smiled. "Jessica is waiting for her knight to arrive. We must not disappoint her!"

★

Chapter 17

Longarm opened his eyes to see Jessica's face just above his. She was staring down at him with concern. He was lying stretched out on the floor. Jessie was cradling his head in her lap and pressing a cool, damp cloth to his forehead.

He tried to sit up, but the pain that began throbbing in his temples forced him right back down. He tensed his neck and shoulders against the worst of it, and once it had passed, he allowed his head to nestle upon Jessie's soft, warm lap.

"Rest easy," she soothed. She dipped the cloth into a pan of water, then wrung it out before replacing it across his forehead. "You've got a bad bruise. "She traced it lightly where the discoloration ran along the front of his ear, but even that made him wince. "Sorry. There's no bleeding, but you've been unconscious since they brought you here."

"How long..." Longarm paused to clear his throat. "How—"

"The whole night. It's about ten in the morning. You kept going in and out..."

"Damn." Longarm sat up again, but this time very slowly. He took the cloth from Jessie and gingerly dabbed at his head. "Owww! And my side hurts too..." He looked around. They were in the one windowless corner of what

233

seemed to be an old supply shack. Around them, locking them in, were two floor-to-ceiling partitions of steel grating. The door to this cage was held shut by a short length of chain and a padlock. The other walls had windows, and pegs from which hung saws and rope, picks and shovels, buckets and mallets, and other tools and hardware. All of it looked rusty, as if it had been out of service for a long time.

"Any water to drink?" he asked.

Jessie pointed him toward a bucket in which a ladle floated. Longarm drank deeply, then poured a cup of the cool, fresh water over his head, to refresh himself and wash away the last of the cobwebs.

"Where are we?"

"At an abandoned stonecutting quarry," Jessie explained. "This particular building was their tool shed, and in this cage they kept the payroll and stonecutters' valuables."

"When they brought you here, were you able to get an idea of the layout?" Longarm demanded. He'd gone to the door of the wire cage to examine the padlock.

"Well, I was knocked out when they—"

"Are you all right?" Longarm asked anxiously.

"Shhh," Jessie scolded. "I know the layout of the compound. I've been here countless times. Used to play here as a little girl, before my father got wind of it. He considered all these old buildings too dangerous. Near this building is a cookhouse with a well in back, another shack like this where they used to store blasting powder, a long, barracks-style bunkhouse, an office, and a stable. At one time this place housed fifty men, but I doubt if there are that many here now."

"Between twenty and twenty-five," Longarm said. "But most of them are professionals. Gunmen hired and brought here by Wulf Danzig." Longarm glared at her. "Just who the hell is this jasper? Why'd you chase after him in the first place?"

"Why don't I start at the beginning," Jessie said mildly. "Did Ki tell you about the things he gave me just before the meeting began?"

"No, only that they meant something to you, but he didn't know what." Longarm reached for a cheroot, and realized his coat was gone, as well as his gunbelt and derringer. His pocket knife was in his coat, as well. Its second blade, filed down into a pick, would have made short work of that padlock.

"He brought me a pistol and a newspaper clipping. The clipping was in German, and the pistol would have meant nothing to anyone but me. I've seen this model of pistol before. Have you ever heard of the Mauser brothers?"

Longarm was about to shake his head, but decided against it. "What do they have to do with Danzig?"

"Well, they're considered among the finest gunsmiths of Europe. The pistol Ki had brought me was a Mauser. It's a model of revolver called the Zig-Zag, because of a groove etched into the cylinder. A pin on the gun's frame travels along this zigzag groove, rotating the cylinder as the pistol is fired. The zig-zag is a popular gun. The Mauser brothers' designs are as common in Europe as Colt's are in America. But this particular Mauser was a special edition, commissioned by one family. When I saw the gun, there was no mistaking the special finish, the custom filigree work on the grips not to mention the family crest or the individual monogram of the owner."

"The Danzig family," Longarm mused. "And I assume you knew this weapon belonged to Wulf Danzig?"

"Yes." Jessie's eyes darkened to a hue resembling the Texas sky when it is suddenly overwhelmed by gray storm clouds. "Wulf Danzig, the man responsible for my father's death."

"I still don't understand," Longarm complained. "What meaning did this special-edition Mauser have for you? Why do you and Danzig hate each other so?"

"There's a pistol just like Wulf Danzig's in my father's gun collection," Jessie said. "Remember that I told you my father had killed a young fop in Europe? A young man who was the son of the baron who had ordered the runaway-carriage attack?"

"That was the incident that took your mother's life," Longarm said quietly. "Your father killed the man's son for revenge, just before his own ship set sail. He had the boy's monogrammed handkerchief sent to the grieving father, along with a Starbuck business card."

"My father took something from that young fop besides his handkerchief. He took the man's pistol. It was a Mauser Zig-Zag, a pistol identical to the one Ki brought me, except for the monogram. The initials on my father's Mauser are KD, for Kurt Danzig."

"And Wulff Danzig—" Longarm began.

"Is Kurt Danzig's son. He was just a child when my father took his father's life."

"To avenge your mother's death," Longarm concluded. "And now Wulf Danzig has killed *your* father to avenge his *own* father's death, and now he wants to kill you, as well."

"The feud continues," Jessica mourned. "The wheel spins around and around." She reached out to press her fingers against his bearded cheek. "I thought loving you could make it end, but it never will, not until the last Starbuck is dead."

"Or the last Danzig," Longarm said cynically. "The Starbucks ain't exactly been innocent victims. Up till now, your family has given as good as it got."

Jessie frowned. "It will get worse. Danzig wants me dead for personal reasons, but the people for whom he is working are very pragmatic."

"Because of that book your father left you," Longarm said sadly. "Because of that book they figure you're dangerous."

"They know I intend to use it to foil and frustrate every one of their schemes to expand their influence in this country. They know I will fight them the way my daddy fought them."

"Well, right now Danzig's got us," Longarm reminded her. "What was the newspaper clipping?"

"I've still got that," Jessie said, digging into her skirt pocket to extract the folded square of newsprint. "It tells of one John Brader, an expatriate American gunsmith who sold his Gatling-style gun to the—"

Jessie broke off as the door to the shack swung open. In stepped Danzig, accompanied by a short, fat, balding man dressed in a blue velvet suit and a garish satin vest.

"That's John Brader," Jessie announced.

"Now how did she know that?" the fat man wondered out loud to Danzig.

Jessie held up the clipping, then balled it up and dropped it to the floor.

"Well, you're a rude girl," Brader frowned. "Never mind that clipping. I have extras."

Longarm took in the gray wisps of Brader's hair, his glinting spectacles, his blunt, callused fingers, and the sharp tang of cordite that seemed to emanate from his skin and clothes. "You're the man responsible for these 'coffee grinders,' I take it?"

"Indeed I am, young man," Brader beamed.

"But you're American," Longarm said. "Why are you working for a foreign power?

Danzig laughed. "Go on, Herr Brader. Tell your story," he coaxed, his blue eyes lit with malice.

"I'll have you know, Deputy Long, that I gave my country every opportunity to appreciate me," Brader began. "I was an officer of the Union Army during the War. Because of my experience and expertise in weaponry, the Army saw fit to call upon me to evaluate Richard Gatling's designs. The Gatling gun was clever, that I will concede," he sniffed, hooking his broad thumbs into his vest, "But nothing I couldn't beat on my worst day."

237

"So why *didn't* you beat it?" Longarm demanded.

"I did! I did beat it! I worked on my designs until I had a gun comparable to Gatling's in every way. I used every cent I had to build my prototypes. They were the same weight as Gatling's, used the same ammunition, but they could outshoot anything he had to offer. They were more reliable as well, Deputy. My guns didn't jam nearly as often as *his*."

"This was right after the War, I take it," Longarm interjected. "Bad time to try and peddle armaments." He shrugged.

"I demonstrated my prototypes to the army and the navy." Brader stopped. He was shaking with fury. "The United States government, Deputy—your employer—was not interested in what I had to offer them. They came up with some cock-and-bull story about having already spent their budget on building up an armory of Gatling guns. But I didn't believe that. I knew that someone, somewhere, had been paid off. It was bribery and corruption working against me! There could be no other explanation as to why my far superior designs were turned down!"

Longarm said wearily, "Your designs were most likely turned down for exactly the reasons the government gave you."

"Bribery, corruption," Brader staunchly insisted.

"Bad timing, you mean," Longarm said. "Stubborn stupidity on your part." Longarm laughed. "If you were in the service, you should have known better than to try to interest a peacetime government in expensive weaponry. What did you think they would do, throw away all those Gatlings they'd already bought?" Longarm's expression turned to one of disgust. "And for all of your bragging and crowing, you let that one disappointment defeat you."

"No I didn't!" Brader snarled. "I took my plans and prototypes to Europe. They appreciated me! The British Royal Navy bought my guns, and other armed forces are

238

even now getting ready to commit themselves to large purchases."

"Let me guess," Longarm said. "Danzig's organization has generously decided to fund your factories, am I right?"

"That is correct," Danzig said stiffly.

"And what about the 'coffee grinders'?" Longarm asked. "Aren't you going to give your own government first crack at the plans for those, Brader?"

"Actually, no plans exist," Brader said slyly. He tapped one finger against his bald dome. "Except up here, that is. Oh, there might be some specifications and parts lists lying around somewhere, but they'd be meaningless without my overview. No government has yet seen my guns. No one even knows about them, except those who may have seen them in action, and Danzig here. He furnished me the funds to hand-build my prototypes. I personally built every 'coffee grinder' we have, and they are all here."

Danzig rested his hand on Brader's shoulder. "It is the innovation of the century," he said in genuine admiration. "Essentially, it is a one-man Gatling—"

Brader shrugged off Danzig's hand and began to pout like a small boy.

"Pardon, Herr Brader," Danzig smiled. "What I meant to say is that it is essentially a one-man Brader gun."

"Damn right!" Brader declared. "I reduced the weapon's weight by chambering it for a small, .25-caliber round—after all, making lots of little holes in a man is the same as making one big one—and by holding the number of barrels down to just two. The cranks are opposed, so that when one barrel is firing, the other is ejecting its spent casing. A magazine fits into the weapon's breech. The gun weighs no more than two Winchesters—certainly a reasonable enough weight—but the fact the gun hooks over the user's shoulders helps to make it even easier to carry and fire. With my gun, one man has the firepower of ten men, and ten men have the firepower of one hundred!"

Danzig laughed. "We have twenty-five of these weapons, Herr Long, and enough ammunition and magazines for each."

"Enough to do what?" Longarm replied. "What do you think you're going to do with your nasty toys? Take over Texas?"

"In a manner of speaking," Danzig said.

"Never happen," Longarm said flatly. "Twenty or twenty-five men, even armed with those gadgets could never hold the entire state."

"They don't have to," Jessie broke in. "They don't have to *steal* Texas, Longarm," she explained. "They can buy it, lock, stock, and barrel."

"An apt phrase." Danzig ducked his head in appreciation. "You are indeed your father's daughter."

"As you are your father's son," Jessie said evenly. She turned to Longarm. "They can keep the cattle from reaching market, which would mean the ranchers would not get paid."

"That would mean they could not meet their obligations on the notes held by the Starbuck bank in Sarah," Danzig added. "Their land, their herds, their businesses—all of which they have put up as collateral—will be seized."

"Except that Jessie freed the ranchers of their obligations," Longarm pointed out.

"Verbally, perhaps," Danzig shrugged. "But she did not put anything to that effect down on paper, am I correct?" The Prussian looked at Jessie, who sighed and looked away.

"And now she never shall. You must realize that neither of you will leave this place alive," Danzig said.

"I think we will, Danzig," Longarm shot back. "I'm a federal deputy marshal. I turn up missing, and folks start to look for me."

"Not this time, Herr Long."

"I left instructions that the army be sent for."

"The instructions will not be followed, Herr Long."

Brader giggled. "They still don't understand," he said.

240

"Understand what?" Jessie asked slowly.

"That the governor himself is in cahoots with these two," Longarm said grimly. "It fits, Jessie. Why he pulled the strings way back in the beginning to keep the army out of the area, why he's shown such an interest in your business affairs."

"Oh, Custis," Jessie said faintly. "I've given him power of attorney—"

"The governor was in on it from the beginning, all right," Brader confirmed. "It seems your daddy had decided—rightly—that the governor would make a lousy senator. So the governor helped us get rid of Alex Starbuck, in exchange for financial backing for his campaign."

"He has the connections to see to it that he becomes the executor of your estate, Jessica," Danzig said. He will see to it that the ranchers' holdings are foreclosed, and that they are sold to my people at a fraction of their true worth. We will have control of Texas's cattle industry, a foothold in American commerce, and a senator who will do our bidding from that point on." Danzig smiled. "He is a handsome, articulate man, the governor is. Perhaps one day he will be your country's President."

"And what do you and Brader get out of this?" Longarm asked.

"Brader gets wealth, and revenge on a country that spurned his genius," Danzig replied. "I will also receive wealth, but more importantly, I will have the satisfaction of knowing that I was instrumental in grinding the Starbucks into extinction. Not only will Jessie die by my hand, but the empire her father built will, for all intents and purposes, fall into the hands of her father's enemies. I will live in your father's home, Jessie," he continued, staring at her with a mocking grin. "I will control the governor as if he were a puppet, and I will rule over your father's people and his town."

"Brader, don't spend your money yet," Longarm snarled.

"And you, you Prussian fruitcake," he spat, addressing Danzig. "You haven't won yet."

Danzig paled with fury. His eyes frosted over like ice, and the long scar down his cheek pulsed visibly. "I could kill you both right now," he said. "But I will wait until the Oriental is caught. I want to see the sorrow in *her* eyes when you and he beg for mercy. I want to see her cry when I kill both of you." Danzig moved closer to the wire mesh. "Then, Long, do you know what I shall do with her? I shall give her to my men to be used like a whore!"

"That's because he can't do the job himself," Jessie laughed scornfully. "And he'd better not try, or I'll—"

But Danzig, sputtering incoherently, had turned on his heel to stride out of the shack. Brader looked reproachfully at Jessica.

"You mustn't make him angry," the inventor warned. "He can be very cruel indeed if he's angered."

"He might kill us twice," Longarm said laconically. "You're as nutty as he is, Brader. Run along."

"He can make it *seem* like he's killed you twice," Brader squeaked in rage. "He can make it feel like you've died a thousand deaths. And I hope he does!" With that, the short, fat man hurried out of the shack, shutting the door behind him.

Longarm turned to Jessie and enfolded her in his arms. "You were great."

"All show," she murmured. "I'm petrified." She kissed him and then asked softly, "What are the chances that someone else might telegraph for the army, or make contact with your superiors in Denver?"

"Not too good, I'm afraid," Longarm answered, hugging her. "Farley's a good man, but not the type to go over the goddamned governor's head. The way we left it before I set off after you, the governor was to telegraph for the army, while Farley and the ranchers organized their men to protect their herds. But twenty-odd professional killers armed with

242

those infernal Brader guns will be able to cut through those cowboys like a hot knife through butter. Hell, most of those drovers never drew their Peacemakers against anything but coyotes."

"Ki will help us," Jessie said. "You need a shave, your beard is scratchy," she giggled as Longarm planted kisses along her neck and cheek. "But your mustache is nice and soft," she murmured as she nibbled at his lower lip. Suddenly she pulled away slightly, still staying close enough, however, for him to rest his hands on her hips. "Darling," she breathed, "there's a time and place for everything..."

"And we'd sure as hell be in a different place if you'd listened to me," Longarm scolded. "What got into you to set off after Danzig by yourself? You were sure to be captured."

"Well, you got captured too," Jessie said.

"That's different!"

"Oh, really?" she laughed. "Explain that to me!"

Longarm thought fast. "I wanted to get captured. It was the only way to get to you."

Jessie stared skeptically, but slowly her eyes widened with adoration. She pressed her head against his chest. "I see. How brave of you." She bit her lip to keep from laughing.

"Now we have to find a way out," Longarm said absently, most of his concentration captured by the softness of Jessie in his arms, the fragrance of her hair.

"Yes, dear." Jessie tucked her fingers into his back pockets.

"But I'm still riled at you for breaking your promise," Longarm said firmly, trying his best to ignore her teasing touch. "I thought you said that it was very clear that I was in charge of doing the apprehending."

"I said it was clear," Jessie nodded, a mischievous smile forming on her lips. "I never said I was going to *listen*."

Longarm made a sound that was somewhere between a

growl and a groan. "And I also said you needed a spanking!"

Jessie stroked the hard bulge filling the front of his trousers. "Sounds like fun," she said sweetly. "But shouldn't we get out of here first?"

"We've got a little problem there," Longarm mused, letting go of her. "We've got nothing to pick that lock with, and no weapons. We're also surrounded by a band of armed, professional killers."

"Ki will help us," Jessie repeated. "He'll come tonight, close to dawn, when the enemy is most relaxed."

"That still don't get us out of here," Longarm frowned. "Good as he is, he can't take them all by himself."

"Did you say you knew how to pick a lock?" Jessie asked.

"Sure," Longarm shrugged. "Especially one as easy as that padlock, but I need something to stick into it. My pocket knife has a filed-down blade that'd do the job nicely, but they've taken it—"

"Will this do?" Jessica interrupted, removing a pin from her hair.

"Son of a bitch," Longarm chuckled, taking it from her.

"As for a gun," Jessie murmured, looking out through the mesh to make sure they weren't being scrutinized, "I think this will help." She hoisted up her skirt to reveal, high up on her shapely thigh, a black elastic garter. Sewn onto it was a tiny holster in which was a derringer. She drew it and handed the little gun to Longarm.

"Didn't they search you?" Longarm muttered, astounded.

Jessie shrugged. "To a point."

"*I* wouldn't have passed up a chance like *that*," he smiled. The derringer was a twin-barrel .38. Its grips were of ivory, and engraved upon them was the Circle-Star brand.

Longarm handed it back to her. "Put it back in that interesting holster of yours," he remarked. "Or, if you'd rather, *I* will—"

"Let's keep our minds on our work," Jessie suggested wryly, slipping the derringer back into its hiding place.

Longarm tucked the hairpin into the band of his hat. "Tonight, toward dawn, we'll pick that lock and head for that shack you told me about, the one where they once stored explosives. I'd wager that's the building Danzig is using for his armory. We've got to destroy those weapons, Jessie."

"But what if tonight is too late?" she asked. "What if Danzig decides to raid the herds today?"

"I don't think he will," Longarm began. "First of all, *he* doesn't know when Ki is going to attack. When I was taken, Danzig was there, in person. Capturing Ki will mean that Danzig's fun can begin. He hates you more than he cares about this business scheme. He knows the army isn't coming..." Longarm nodded. "My guess is he feels he can afford to wait until he's captured Ki and has us all locked up. Then he can ride out with his men to do his dirty work, knowing that he's got his revenge to look forward to, all nice and neat."

"I guess you're right," Jessie sighed. "Anyway, we need the cover of darkness, and the confusion Ki will cause, if we're to succeed in destroying those weapons." She left the last part of her thought unspoken: *And if I'm going to kill Danzig...*

★

Chapter 18

Ki waited for night to fall before he began his final approach. He'd left his horse two miles back, in order to close in on foot. He'd changed his clothes, donning his old, worn jeans, his collarless cotton shirt, and his soft leather vest with its multitude of pockets.

He'd selected his weapons with care. With him he had his bow and two leather quivers. In one quiver was packed an assortment of twenty-five arrows. The other quiver held twenty-five arrows all of one kind. Ki could only hope that Longarm would remember what Ki had told him days ago.

That Longarm was with Jessie, Ki had no doubt. The story written with blood in the pecan grove had been easy to read. Both Jessie and Longarm had struggled valiantly, costing the enemy dearly for their capture, but prisoners they now were—

Unless they were already dead.

If one was, they both were; of that also, Ki was certain. Still, he refused to allow that particular possibility to take root in his mind. For one thing, forlorn heartache had no place in a samurai preparing to do battle. For another thing, be the two alive or dead, his plan of action would remain exactly the same. He would disrupt the enemy's camp,

247

disabling as many of them as he could. If Jessie and Long-arm were alive, they would reveal themselves to him in some way. Ki would then aid them in making good their escape, and the trio would retreat to some sanctuary. Jessica would then express what she wished to accomplish next, and Ki would do his best to carry out her desires.

On the other hand, if the two were dead, Ki would sooner or later come across some evidence proving this. At that time he would stop his random attack to concentrate on finding the one he had earlier struggled with, the blond foreigner. He would kill this man, for he was sure Jessie would desire as much, and then he would go back to battling the rest of those who had sided with this foreigner, until they managed to bring him down. If Jessie was dead, he would fight with the ferocity of a man who does not care what happens to him. It crossed his mind that he probably ought to stay alive long enough to carry out his threat against the governor, should that man disobey his order to send for the army; buy if Jessie was dead, what was the point? If Jessie was dead, would it not be better to die where she died, and hope that her spirit, her *Kami,* lingering near the scene, could watch proudly as he wrought havoc upon her enemies?

The how and when of dying were always tricky matters, Ki knew. Better to wait for more facts about the situation before attempting to ascertain the proper etiquette in this case . . .

Rock outcroppings encircled the quarry compound. Ki knew them well. In happier times, he and Jessie had explored and climbed these "baby mountains." As soon as he had surmised which way the tracks were heading, he'd known instinctively that the deserted stonecutting site was the hideout of the mystery riders. There was water there, and timber for fires, in addition to the obvious shelter for men and horses that the deserted buildings could provide. Those high rock walls, broken only by the single trail that led into the shallow canyon, created a natural fortress around the collection of buildings.

Fortress or prison, Ki thought, smiling to himself. It depended on who controlled the walls...

He could not afford the luxury of a preliminary reconnaissance. True, it was a dark, nearly moonless night, and he would have the advantage of stealth surprise, but he was only one man against what he was sure would be many sentries. Some might be amateurs, but most would be professionals, men quite experienced in the art of killing and staying alive despite the efforts of other professionals.

In all, it would be a pleasure, Ki thought, for a samurai's greatest pleasure is fighting. But it would not be easy. The only thing he could think to do was to make his way as best he could toward the center of the compound. If and when he found Jessie and Longarm, he would begin to divert the enemy's attention from them by drawing it upon himself. Until then, he would just infiltrate, striking at the enemy as he went.

He checked the glittering array of *shuriken* blades and stars lining the inside pockets of his vest. In addition to these, he had the pair he carried in the two sheaths strapped to his forearms. Both his bow and his *shuriken* would be useful for distance killing, but he carried one final weapon for close work: a *nunchaku.*

Normally, Ki would have depended on his *te* techniques, but his enemies were many and his time was short; the *nunchaku* would help to even up the odds.

Next to the *bo,* or staff, the *nunchaku* was Ki's favorite weapon. This was because its original effectiveness was derived from the fact that it appeared to be only a harmless farm implement, a tool of the common people. The Okinawans had originally used the forerunner of the *nunchaku* as a grain flail. It was only after Ki's own people, the Nipponese, had confiscated all of the Okinawans' real weapons that these proud people developed *te,* and *kobudo,* the art of using tools as weapons. A *nunchaku* consisted of two sticks of varying lengths attached together at one end by a few inches of braided horsehair. Ki owned many different sorts of *nunchaku*. The one he now carried was a *han-kei,* or half-size version. Instead of the two halves reaching approximately from his palm to his elbow, which was the traditional length, the two sticks were each only seven inches long, and flat on one side, so that they fit smoothly together. The *han-kei* form of nunchaku was easy to carry; Ki kept it tucked into his jeans like a dagger. With it, Ki could effectively perform virtually every *te* block and strike, but with the extra power brought to the techniques by the hard wood of the *nunchaku's* handles and the centrifugal force generated when he whipped that handle around on the end of its horsehair braid. Flail-like blows from the weapon could shatter a man's bones. Thrusts could smash his face or throat. A finger, wrist, or other joint caught between the two sticks would crack like a pecan shell in a nutcracker. The only *kobudo* weapon that Ki considered superior to the *nunchaku* was the *bo* or staff. But its five-foot-plus length made the *bo* too cumbersome a weapon for the sort of fighting Ki had to do this night.

Ki began to climb the rocks. He would cut a path through the first line of sentries. He would then situate himself to have a clear view of the compound, and then wait for the hour or so before dawn.

It was just human nature, he mused philosophically. That first gray glimmer rising up in the east had a way of comforting men, what with its full promise of another day of light and life on this earth. Men on guard during wartime—even professionals—tended to relax a bit with the first hint of dawn. Some clock inside them seemed to command it. Long ago, Ki had taught Jessica this curious thing. If she was still alive, she would know that the hour just before dawn would be the time to make her attempt at escape, that that would be the time when he would come to help her.

His bow strung across his shoulders, his twin quivers of arrows riding on his hips, Ki climbed the rock face as quickly and quietly as an ape. His climbing techniques were, after all, based on those of the monkey. A samurai soon learned that his bare toes could flex and bend to grip like fingers. A samurai who became a *te* adept also learned the art of sticking, of shifting one's center of gravity this way and that countless times in a moment, so that falling became unlikely. Down and up are, after all, relative terms, and Ki merely reminded himself that to the climbing samurai, down did not exist. Besides, the tall rock was part of the world, and who could fall off the world?

Ki's fingers slid up to hook themselves over the top of the outcropping. He flexed his elbows, biceps straining, to support himself as he peeked about to see if a sentry was anywhere nearby. There was no one. Ki quickly hauled himself up and darted into the shadows cast by the tumbled boulders.

The interior slopes of the ring of outcroppings surrounding the compound descended much more gradually. A man did not have to climb, but could walk down these rock-strewn hills. From his vantage point, Ki could see sentries, alone and in pairs, scattered about. Evidently he was expected! None of them that he could see were armed with those "coffee grinders," but such a weapon was not really appropriate for this sort of sentry duty, where there was no clear, agreed-upon field of fire for which a man was required to be responsible. Ki also noted that the large clumps and piles of rocks and boulders strewn about the landscape kept the various sentries from being able to see one another.

Ki smiled. All in all, things were working out well. The path down toward the fires that glimmered in and around the compound's buildings was a maze. Guards stood here and there at various turns and twists of that maze. Ki would traverse it, removing the guards as he came—

The gun barrel pressed behind his ear was as cold and

251

hard as the slab of granite upon which Ki was leaning. He groaned inwardly. He was off balance, in no position to attempt a *te* counter-move.

"You even *breathe* fast, little brother, and I'll blow your head off," a deep, calm voice said. "You're carrying a bow, little brother. I'll show you a trick my father taught me."

Ki felt a strong hand tug him up into a standing position. The bow strung diagonally across his back and shoulder was removed as the twin quivers were plucked from his waist.

"Now cross your arms across your chest, little brother," that deep voice instructed. "Do it like you were a shy maid who'd suddenly lost her blouse."

Mystified, Ki did as he was told. That gun was still drilling itself against his head. Then the bow was wiggled back down over his torso. This time the tough, tempered wooden part was in front, across his chest. The curve of wood pinned his arms and hands tightly in the position where he'd been ordered to place them. The string was now across his back. The man behind him gathered up the spare inch of slack and twisted it away by slipping a handful of arrows beneath the string and turning the shafts like handles. Ki felt the circulation in his arms being cut off. The man tucked the arrows through the string a final time, so that the pressure cinched them into place. Ki's upper limbs were now immobilized. The bow stretching horizontally across his chest, and extending for two feet on either side of him like wing bones, was nothing from which he couldn't break free, but doing so would take a little time—

More than enough time for his capable adversary to shoot him dead.

"You can turn around now, little brother."

Ki turned to confront a giant of a man, at least six and a half feet tall. He was built like a grizzly, with long, massive, muscle-slabbed arms. His torso was barrellike, and seemed to make up most of his length. His legs were as squat and thick as two tree stumps. Even in this faint light, Ki could see that the man's skin was of dark hue. He had a large, strong, hawklike nose that protruded from a craggy face long ago pitted by smallpox. Two black, glossy braids framed that face. The braids reached down to the man's thick shoulders.

Ki, curious, peered up at his assailant. His was not a cruel face, nor a particularly nervous one. It was a warrior's face.

"This is a quite interesting use for a bow," Ki remarked quietly. "How did you come by this technique?"

"Like I said, my daddy taught me. I'm a full-blooded Apache, little brother. That's how we used to take other tribes prisoner. 'Course, all that was before my time."

"Very effective," Ki remarked sadly. "What is your name?"

"Hell, little brother, telling an Apache name takes a lot of time. And we—or maybe just you, little brother—ain't got that much time." The big Apache raised his revolver in salute and grinned. "Just call me Joe."

"Joe, my name is Ki."

"Short for something, I'd wager," Joe said shrewdly.

"But we don't have the time," Ki smiled.

Joe was scantily dressed in a sleeveless leather vest and a loin cloth that left his stubby legs bare. Around his belly hung a wide leather gunbelt from which dangled a holster. A sheathed bowie knife hung like a pendant from around his neck. He wore no hat and no boots. Studded metal bracelets extended up Joe's arms from wrist to elbow. Ki knew that those bracelets would act like armor, reinforcing Joe's forearm smashes during hand-to-hand combat.

"I compliment you on the way you crept up behind me," Ki said politely. He purposely kept his voice meek. It was important that Joe feel confident enough to holster his pistol. Ki could not afford to let his adversary fire even a stray shot, for that would alert all the other sentries.

"Hell, little brother," Joe smiled. "I go barefoot, just like you." He pointed to his feet with his revolver, and then, absently, slipped it back into its holster. "Apaches have feet tough enough to crush rocks, to flex cactus spines till they're as soft as an old man's prick. Apaches are born man-trackers. Little brother, I began my training as a little boy."

"So did I, Joe," Ki murmured, fascinated despite his predicament. He knew that he would have to do his best to kill this man who would try to kill him. But for now, before the killing started, he was content to share a moment with his peer.

"When I was just ten, I had to creep up and pull the tail feathers off a partridge. When I was twelve, I had to snatch a rattler and bring him home alive. When I was thirteen, I had to count coup on a grizzly bear, and live to tell about it." A look of amusement flashed across Joe's face. "No offense, little brother, but sneaking up on you was a mite tougher than the rattler, but a lot easier than the bear."

Ki bowed his head in acknowledgement. "Why did you leave your people? Why do you serve villains?"

Joe's face grew hard. "My people are no more. I was trained to be a warrior, but the Apache nation has left fighting behind. The men have become squaws, as the squaws have become whores. But I must fight. It is all I know. With no people to fight for, I fight for money. I don't care for what cause. There is no longer any cause that can interest me."

Ki stood silent for a moment, contemplating what he had been told. "It is a pity we are on opposite sides. We are much alike."

"Maybe you're right, and maybe you're not," the Apache grunted. "But you're on the button about that last fact. We're on opposite sides. Which brings this conversation to a close, I'm afraid, little brother." He drew his pistol. "Sorry about binding you up like that with your bow. I mean you no disrespect. I only did it 'cause I heard you were a real feisty fellow, real fast, and real clever with your hands.

Now, Mr. Danzig said to bring you in alive if possible, or dead if we had to." The giant smiled. "I'd just as soon it was alive. It'd cause me some troubled sleep to have to kill you, little brother..." He shrugged. "Well, let's start on down." He gestured with his pistol in the direction he wanted Ki to go.

Ki watched the gun turn from him, down toward the compound for one instant. He brought up his right knee to strike out with a snapping forward foot-strike. His rigid toes slammed into Joe's wrist, catapulting the revolver up over the Apache's shoulder.

Both men stood quietly. They regarded one another as the handgun clattered against the rocks.

"So be it, little brother," Joe whispered. He moved in fast, his arms held wide, attacking like the grizzly he so resembled. He was fast, but Ki was able to sidestep the attack. As Joe lunged past, Ki performed a *yoko-geri-keage,* a sideways snap-kick. He kept his back and head straight throughout the kick, raising his striking leg until his knee was in line with his waist. He brought his foot back, cocking his leg until it was next to his other knee. When his foot slashed out, its outside edge was angled like a knife blade toward the front of Joe's knee.

The Apache was able to twist his body around at the last moment, so that he took the powerful kick on the back of his knee, instead of upon his kneecap, which would certainly have been shattered like a fragile china plate by the force of Ki's blow. In this way, Joe was able to escape real injury, although Ki's foot, driving into the back of his knee joint, forced him down into a kneeling position.

Ki danced forward, sending a third foot-strike slamming into the side of the Apache's face. Joe shook it off and rose to his feet, forcing Ki to retreat.

The big Indian spat a mouthful of blood. "Ain't that a kick in the head," he grinned. "You're right fast with your feet as well as your hands," he observed wryly. He scrutinized the bow across Ki's chest, trying to evaluate how securely his opponent's hands remained pinioned.

He must not notice the bow's tips, Ki willed. He began to weave and dip in order to distract the man.

"I could call out for help," Joe said with a ghastly red smile. The blood still flowing inside of his mouth had stained his teeth. "I could do that, you know, little brother."

"But you will not," Ki said matter-of-factly. "This night was destined. Have we not both been trained as warriors from childhood?"

"We have, little brother," Joe said, moving in. "Ki, I salute you." He brought up his bracelet-armored arms and attacked.

"I salute you, Apache samurai," Ki whispered. He ducked beneath Joe's first clawlike swipe, but the bow extending on both sides spoiled his timing and balance.

The Apache's second forearm swipe caught Ki across his back. He felt Joe's bracelet studs gouge deep furrows into the leather of his vest as the sledgehammer blow knocked him forward, clear off his feet. With his hands pinned across his chest, he was unable to break his fall. He landed hard, and slid several feet across the jagged stones.

Ki felt his own blood—hot and wet—seeping down his lower spine. He'd purposely landed on his back, letting those arrowheads bite through his clothes and into his flesh, so as to avoid damaging the bow. He would need it later on. Assuming there was going to be a later on . . .

The Apache came lumbering toward Ki. "I'm going to stomp you, little brother," he huffed.

Ki scissored his legs wide, then locked them closed around Joe's massive legs. He swung his hips, letting his higher leg apply most of the pressure. The scissoring, levering action toppled the giant to the ground.

Ki scrambled to his feet, but Joe was right behind him. Ki twirled, trying to get a spare instant to prepare another kick, but the Apache was so close behind him that the two men resembled one dog chasing its own tail.

If only he could get far enough away to turn one of the protruding tips of the bow extending across his chest toward the Apache, Ki thought desperately. Then he could use what Joe had noticed about his strange bow. The bow's secret. The bow's tips were bound in leather to disguise—

Joe locked Ki in a bear hug. With his arms tucked against his chest, there was no way Ki could alleviate the terrible pressure squeezing his rib cage, locking in his lungs, forcing him to exhale endlessly. Time was running out. He could not inhale enough to breathe!

Ki rammed his knees into the other's groin. Joe groaned with pain, but only tightened his grip.

Ki felt his vision funneling down to a small circle of sight. He kicked at Joe's bare legs, but those two massive limbs resisted the kicks the way columns of stone resist a chisel. Ki had no time left to continue hacking away at his enemy by inches...

Joe straightened up, lifting Ki off of the ground. Now, ironically, the only thing keeping Ki's rib cage from being crushed and splintered was the barrier of the bow between the two men.

"As I saluted you in life, I now salute your death," the Apache grunted. "I will carry your bow to remember you."

Ki's face was pressed against the sheath of the bowie knife hanging from the man's neck. *If only his hands were free!* His face was slick with his own sweat and the sweat that ran down Joe's bare chest and belly.

"The bow will be yours," Ki whispered. "Alive or dead, you shall have my bow!"

Joe heaved Ki up to get a better grip on his twisting, kicking, sweat-slippery body. Ki used the momentum imparted to him by the Apache to add to his own strength as he butted hard with his forehead against Joe's nose. The

Indian gagged in agony as his nose was flattened by the force of the impact. Blood squirted down out of both of his nostrils. Ki butted him again, this time smashing Joe's front teeth. The Indian's bear hug loosened. Ki wiggled free, and then back-pedaled away.

Joe soundlessly wiped away the blood and spittle from his ruined face and attacked once again.

Ki, wobbling on his feet, waited until the last possible instant and then turned sideways, to present the tip of the bow toward his onrushing foe, as if it were a spear.

Which it was!

Ki braced himself, then sprang sideways toward the big Indian. The bow's tip caught the Indian's belly, puncturing through his flesh with an initial crunch, followed by a long, wet, sliding sound. Before Joe could stop himself, he'd run himself through. The bowstring stretched on the curved wooden bow only deepened and extended the wound, sawing it wide.

Joe's chest actually touched Ki's shoulder. His bleeding belly was flush against Ki's side. The bow had come out his back, tent-poling the Apache's vest.

Joe's mouth opened to speak, but he no longer had the strength to form words. His eyes, only inches from Ki's, asked his silent question.

"The bow's tips are of sharpened steel, camouflaged by a thin leather covering," Ki said.

The Apache's legs buckled beneath him. Ki braced himself and twisted to withdraw the bow as Joe's lifeless body fell away.

"Alive or dead," Ki repeated, "you shall have my bow, and now you have." He stared down at the corpse. Steam rose from the gaping crimson slit in the Apache's belly.

Ki, having regained his breath, stood a moment in concentration, and then began to flex the muscles of his back. Moments later the string broke. He caught the flexing bow before it could fall to the ground.

His muscular contractions and expansions had set his own wounds bleeding again. His bow was also bloody. It would have to be cleaned.

He wandered toward where Joe had tossed his quivers of arrows. The few that had kept him bound seemed all right. He would restring the bow—he always carried an extra string—and then find a place where he could rest and regain his physical strength and spiritual equanimity.

"Joe, I am sorry you had to die," Ki addressed the Apache's body. "Tonight, many of my kills will be made in your name. I beseech your *Kami* to wait and watch, and see what your little brother can accomplish!"

He dragged the corpse between two large boulders and piled smaller stones upon it, hiding it as best he could. Ki doubted that any passing sentry would find it before morning, and by then it would not matter.

Gathering up his possessions, he hurried away to find a place where he could safely rest for a few hours. Soon it would be time to begin the final attack.

★

Chapter 19

"What time do you reckon it is?" Longarm asked.

"About fifteen minutes later than the last time you asked," Jessie remarked, amused. "Calm down. You've been pacing back and forth like a tiger in a zoo." She was sitting on her folded jacket, leaning against a wall, doing her best to relax and rest.

"I know we're supposed to wait until just before dawn," Longarm growled, "But I've had enough of being cooped up. Besides, I want to take a look around to make sure those Brader guns really are in that old powder shack. I've got to put those guns out of action if we're going to stop Danzig."

Sighing, Jessie climbed to her feet. She put on her jacket and raised her skirt to draw her derringer. "Let's do it," she said, smiling.

"Let's do it," Longarm repeated. He took her in his arms to kiss her once. Then he went to the door of the cell. From his hatband he removed the hairpin Jessie had given him. "I think I'll keep this in my hat from now on," he said as he went to work on the padlock. "It's a handy little thing to have around."

It only took him a few moments to pick the lock. He set

it aside and removed and then rewrapped the short length of chain so that it would fall smoothly from its position with just a shove on the door. Next he reset the padlock, but only through one link.

"That will fool the guard for the moment we'll need," he said, evaluating his work.

"There are two of them out there," Jessie pointed out.

"Well, all we can do is hope only one will come in," Longarm said. He stretched out on the floor. "If both come in, do your best to keep them both covered. I'll only need a second."

He and Jessie exchanged looks.

"Ready?" he asked.

She nodded. "Guard!" she called. "Help!"

Presently the door to the shack opened, and a man stuck his head in. "What's going on?" he demanded.

"He just fainted dead away," Jessie whimpered, pointing down at Longarm's still form. "I think his head is hurt bad."

Laughing, the guard sauntered into the shack. Jessie, her heart in her mouth, watched the building's door, hung crookedly on its hinges, swing slowly, slowly closed.

"What do you want me to do about it?" the guard asked. He stepped up close to the wire mesh in order to peer down at Longarm.

"He needs a doctor!" Jessie demanded, approaching the guard from her side of the mesh.

"No doctor here, lady," the guard said, and began to turn away.

Jessie jammed the derringer up against the mesh so that it was aimed point-blank at the shocked guard's head. "That's too bad," she hissed. "Because if you make one sound, you're going to need a doctor right quick!"

Longarm was already pushing against the cell door. The chain snaked to the floor. Coming around behind the guard, Longarm drew the man's Colt out of his holster and tapped him behind the ear with the weapon's barrel. He caught the man beneath the armpits before he could slump all the way to the floor. He half carried and half dragged the unconscious guard into the cell, then hurried out.

"What's next?" Jessie asked, at his heels.

"Wait here for a minute. I want to take care of that other guard."

Longarm crept to the door and slowly inched it open. The remaining guard was sitting on a crate, with his back to the shack. He was huddled over a small campfire, and was wrapped in a blanket against the night chill.

Longarm left the shack and walked directly up to the guard. He made no attempt to quiet his footsteps. His hope was that he would assume it was his partner, returning to the comfort of their fire.

"What was the trouble back there?" the man muttered over his shoulder. "Everything all right?"

"Just fine," Longarm said, and hit him over the head with the butt of his revolver.

As the guard fell back, Longarm caught him and dragged him back to the shack. Inside, he handed Jessie the guard's gun, and chose the corner of the cage area farthest from the door of the shack to prop the man up. Next he put the first guard beneath the other's arm, and wrapped the blanket around both. He tipped their hats down over their faces and stood back to survey the scene.

"Are they supposed to be us?" Jessie giggled as she, reholstered her derringer and checked the load in the revolver.

"They might fool somebody who only bothered to glance in through the shack's door, or a window," Longarm shrugged. "Come on!"

They locked the guards in the cell and then left the shack. They kept to the sides of the buildings and hid in the shadows, but were fortunate in the fact that most of the men not on sentry duty on the surrounding slopes were, it seemed, sleeping in the bunkhouse.

"Lead the way to that powder shack," Longarm told Jessie. He had his gun at the ready, but was depending on staying out of sight of any stray guards. If they had to fire a shot, the whole camp would come down on them.

"This way," Jessie whispered. She tugged him toward the center of the compound, close to the other campfires.

Longarm dug in his boot heels. "Are you sure?" he demanded suspiciously. "Damn! Why don't we just drop in on Danzig for a shot of schnapps, or whatever? I'd think the stonecutters would have kept their explosives on the outskirts of the compound, in case—"

"Oh don't be a mule!" Jessie scolded, exasperated. "They kept their powder where they could keep an eye on it, against thieves!"

Longarm stared at her. "Oh." He nodded. "Well, then, let's get going!" he demanded.

"Men!" Jessie seethed. "I had to fall in love with the most bullheaded—"

"You get what you deserve," Longarm cut her off. He peered around the corner of the cookshack. "The coast is clear. Let's move!"

They scurried across the dark open space, and were halfway to the shack's door when, from around the building's corner, there came strolling a shadowy figure. The man struck a match to light his cigar. Its flare made Longarm and Jessie's eyes ache.

"Stay here!" Longarm hissed, and strode toward the man. He repositioned his stolen gun in the hip pocket of his trousers, angling the butt to make it seem as if he were wearing his gun in a high-cinched holster. Longarm's hope was that the fellow would glimpse his silhouette—a man in a hat, with a gun on his hip—and assume he was just another recruited gunslick.

"Who is it?" the man growled as Longarm approached. The match winked out as it fell to the ground.

"Hold that light!" Longarm called. "Oh, shit. Got another match, old son?"

"Sure," the man replied. His hand was still splayed over his own revolver's butt, but he had not drawn. Now he relaxed as he saw that Longarm's gun was still "holstered." He pulled an another match from his shirt pocket, and struck it against the sole of his boot.

Longarm waited for that blinding flare, and for the gun-slick's eyes to be fixed on the flame as he brought it up, cupped in both hands, to light Longarm's cigar.

"Where's your smoke—" the man began.

Longarm drove his left fist into the man's belly, just above his belt buckle. As the man grunted and doubled over, the wind knocked out of him, Longarm connected with a right cross, catching the man on the tip of his jaw, just below his ear. The gunslick fell to his knees, then slumped.

"We ought get him out of sight," Jessica whispered, coming up behind Longarm.

"I know that," he said. "It's a question of where. I guess we'll just dump him behind the shack." He pulled the man behind the building, relieved him of his sidearm, and left him there.

When they reached the door of the shack, they found it locked.

"Well, that's no big surprise," Longarm said. He reached into his hatband and withdrew Jessica's hairpin. He inserted it into the lock and turned it. He felt some resistance in the lock's mechanism and applied more pressure. The pin broke off in his hand.

"That's no big surprise, either," he said. "What now? I could likely kick the door in, but I don't reckon that would be a very good idea, and I don't want to be out here much longer."

"Come on," she said. Grasping his hand, she pulled him

around to the back of the shack, explaining as she went, "I told you Ki and I used to explore around here. Well..."

She knelt down and pulled at one of the vertical planks that made up the walls of the building. It moved to one side, not much, but enough for a person to crawl through and get into the shack.

"Woman," Longarm said, "you've come through again. Let's go. Ladies first."

He held the board aside and let her crawl in first, then he followed. It was a tight fit, and he had to go in feet first so he could hold the board aside. He might not have made it, but Jessica grabbed the seat of his pants and pulled, and he squeezed through with a startled curse.

"Where'd you get muscles like that?" he asked her.

She shrugged. "Just leverage," she replied.

Longarm struck a match.

"Where'd you get those?" Jessie asked. "Oh, from that man you knocked out, of course."

"Of course," Longarm said absently, looking around as the match's tiny fire inched toward his fingers. "There! A candle stub. On that shelf. See it?"

"Got it!" Jessie tilted the candle's wick into the sputtering match's flame. It caught.

"That fellow only had the one match," Longarm sighed. He looked around the interior of the shack. Several piles of stacked wooden crates, half-covered with canvas tarps and old, motheaten woolen blankets took up the center of the floor. Leaning against the windowless walls were the "coffee grinders." Longarm counted twenty. That meant four of the weapons were being carried by guards outside. Longarm's count assumed that the one carried by Lucas Conrad was even now beginning to rust somewhere back in that pecon grove, the site of the decoy ambush.

Piled in one corner of the shack were several wooden crates of .25-caliber rounds. Other boxes held fully charged magazines for the Brader guns.

"They're all here, except five," Jessie said excitedly.

"Except four." Longarm explained what had taken place earlier in the evening. "Now all we have to do is figure out a way to destroy them." There was a prybar standing against the wall, and he used it to lever up the lid of the crate containing the bullets. "It's going to take a while, but I guess we can build up a charge by emptying the rounds and gathering up the gunpowder."

"Longarm," Jessie called softly. "Here's a box filled with powder!"

Longarm hurried over. It was true. Brader had stockpiled loose powder, ingots of metal, and bullet molds to make his own ammunition.

"Why would he bother to go to all this trouble?" Jessie mused out loud, staring down at all the reloading paraphernalia.

Longarm thought about it. "I seem to remember that one problem concerning Gatling guns is that a soft lead-nosed bullet can get bent out of whack, jamming up the gun's firing mechanism. If Brader's guns work on the same notion—and from what he's told us, I suspicion they do—he can't depend on finding store-bought ammo to suit his needs. He's got to hand-load his own rounds for the 'coffee grinders.'"

Jessie set to work tearing a strip from one of the old wool blankets. "Do you think this cloth will burn?"

"Well enough," Longarm remarked. "I'll tuck one end of the strip into the powder by poking a hole through one of the waxed-paper sacks it's in. And I'll leave just enough sticking out to give us time to get away from here." He sprinkled some gunpowder onto the wool fibers to insure a good burn. "It's not the most dependable fuse in the world," he shrugged. "But it's the only fuse we've got."

"And now we wait," Jessie said. "We've got another hour until Ki attacks."

"*If* Ki is even here," Longarm added.

"He's here . . ."

"Assuming that he is, how will we know when he's started?"

Jessie smiled. "We'll know," she chuckled. She set down her gun and shrugged out of her jacket.

"Well, all we can do now is wait," Longarm said, his voice growing thick. He watched Jessie take off her hat and toss it to the floor. She kept her big green eyes on him as she removed the pins remaining in her hair. Then she gave her head a toss, to let down her shimmering mass of copper-gold tresses. Next she unbuttoned her blouse and took it off. Her breasts jiggled with newly found freedom. Her nipples swelled erect in the cool air. She unbuttoned her skirt and stepped out of it, to stand before Longarm entirely nude, except for her boots and that holster high up on her thigh.

"It's a shame to waste this time we have together," she murmured seductively. She patted the top of the crates piled up in the center of the floor. "All these tarps and blankets make a nice, soft little bed for us."

The flickering candlelight emphasized and delineated the lush curves and swells of her magnificent body. Longarm rushed forward to gather her up in his arms. Their tongues entwined as his hands felt the heat her flesh was generating.

"Oh, Custis, you're the only man I've ever loved," she whimpered, twisting in his embrace to rub her hips against the taut tweed of his fly.

Longarm picked her up and plopped her down on the cushioned tops of the crates.

"I think you better keep your boots and that holster on," he said. "Keep that gun handy, just in case." He gestured toward the door, then began to undress himself. He took off his shirt and hat, but only lowered his trousers and cotton longjohns until they were bunched around his boot tops. He set his revolver down beside Jessie's head, where it would be within his easy reach in case of a sudden intrusion.

268

"I'm sorry about being only partway undressed," Longarm began, "and about leaving that gun there, but I've got no holster, an —"

Jessie reached out to tickle his jutting member with her fingernails. "Yes, you have, darling," she said, spreading her legs.

Longarm wasted no time. He was hard as stone and dying to slide into her. He hopped up onto the crates, stretched himself out over Jessie, and penetrated her deeply, to his full length. He withdrew teasingly, until he and she were linked only by the merest kiss of their flesh, and then slammed fiercely into her again.

Jessie bit into his shoulder to keep from crying out in delirious ecstasy. Longarm wanted to prolong the sensations, but he could not keep from hurrying. The constant danger of discovery spurred him on, and truth to tell, he found making love surrounded by all those long, gleaming gun barrels downright inspiring.

Beneath him, Jessie shuddered and let out a tiny birdlike cry. She wrapped her legs around his waist and thrust herself up to meet him. When he came, it was like all those Brader guns going off at the same time.

They rested in each other's arms. Longarm was still nestled inside Jessie.

Twice they thought they heard somebody fiddling with the door, and twice they held their breath, half naked, locked together like Siamese twins, both of them pointing their guns toward the noise. No one intruded, and after both false alarms they giggled like naughty adolescents hiding from their parents.

It was not that they considered their predicament unserious. On the contrary, they both fully realized that they could be discovered and killed at any moment. Accordingly, they were hell-bent on enjoying every moment of whatever amount of living was left for them. Right now, that meant enjoying each other.

"Dynamite," Longarm said.

"Mmm, yes indeed," Jessie said, then realized that he was not looking at her face, but over her shoulder, and he seemed surprised.

She turned her head to see what he was looking at. During their lovemaking, one of the blankets had shifted, revealing black lettering stenciled on the crate beneath: DANGER! DYNAMITE! STORE IN A COOL PLACE.

"I'll be damned," he said. "We've been making love on a bed of high explosives!" He withdrew from her and they dressed, and he used the prybar to take the lid off one of the crates on which they'd been lying. It was filled with neatly packed cylinders covered in thick waxed paper.

"Look around," he told her. "There's got to be blasting caps around. Probably on the far side of the shack . . . .There! Under those sandbags!"

In the opposite corner of the small building was a pile of sandbags. Longarm knew that blasting caps were always stored away from the charges they were intended to ignite, and that seemed the most logical place. He removed a few of the sandbags, and sure enough, underneath was a single crate of caps, packed in sawdust. Each had a short length of fuse attached to it. Longarm took several of the caps and inserted them into the ends of some of the sticks of dynamite at the other end of the shack. Then he put the lid back on the box of explosives.

"Why did you do that?" Jessie asked.

"Because I'm about to light this cheroot, and I don't want any stray sparks or ashes setting this stuff off before we're ready."

"Where'd you get that?" she grinned.

"Same place I got the matches. That old boy lying behind this shack ain't going to feel like smoking for a while. He lit the cigar, and puffed its tip into a ruddy glow.

Jessie shuddered. "I think you broke that man's jaw."

"Hope so. That'll mean I won't have to try and kill him.

A broken jaw ought to be painful enough to keep him out of the action."

Jessie watched Longarm's face. "You don't like to kill, do you?"

"Few men who've killed like it," Longarm frowned. "Mostly the only folks who do are those that never have, but have strong imaginations." Longarm puffed on his cigar and watched her, hoping that what he'd said had gotten through the layers of hate and anger she'd built up since the murder of her father.

"Like me—that's what you're thinking," Jessie accused. "But you're forgetting something. Earlier this evening I did kill, for the first time. I shot two men in that pecan grove. One I shot dead, the other I wounded badly. He may be dead now, for all I know. I didn't like doing it, Longarm, but I knew why I had to." She shrugged, and her eyes grew wet with tears. "I'm not saying it was right or wrong, I'm just saying that—"

From outside there came a hoarse shout: "They got away! Search the camp for the prisoners!"

"Uh-oh," Longarm muttered. "Here we go. You've got that gun I gave you?"

"Right here," Jessie answered. Her voice was harsh, her throat dry. "Remember, if anything happens . . . well, I love you . . ."

"Nothing's going to happen to us," Longarm assured her. "And I'll save saying how I feel about you until I can prove it," he winked.

He grabbed his gun, and gathered up the sticks of dynamite to thrust them into his back pocket. Just then the door to the shack was kicked in by one of Danzig's men. He stood, his gun in his hand, blinking stupidly at them in the candlelight. Jessie yelped in shock and fear.

Longarm whirled to whip off a shot the man's way. The round chewed a piece of the doorjamb, chasing the outlaw away. As he backed out hurriedly, his boot heels caught on

271

the threshold. His gun fell to the floor as he stumbled out of sight.

Longarm snatched up the fallen gun and held it in reserve as he pegged a shot out through the door. There were targets aplenty. Men—many of them just awakened and still dazed with sleep—were scurrying past. Longarm took his time and fired again. One of his targets clutched at his side and pin-wheeled to the ground.

Jessie took cover on the other side of the doorway. She fired her revolver twice, missing the man she was aiming at both times.

Longarm couldn't help smirking at her. "Need spectacles?" he asked as he sighted at a man crawling across the roof of a nearby building, and fired. The man howled in pain, and slid down the steeply angled shingles to fall somewhere out of sight.

"I'm used to my .38!" Jessie muttered. "This gun you gave me is a .44!"

"Typical of a woman to complain," Longarm laughed.

Jessie swore an oath from between clenched teeth. She gripped her gun in both hands, drew a steady bead, and squeezed off another shot. This time the target she'd been plinking at let his pistol drop as he slumped across the barrel he'd been hiding behind.

"If I use both hands I can steady my aim," she said. "I can handle it."

"Never thought you couldn't," Longarm replied.

Just then one of the gunslicks fired at them. His round slammed into the doorjamb just inches from Longarm's head.

"Do not return their fire!" Longarm and Jessie heard Danzig scream, his accent made thick by anger and frustration.

"Oh, no! My guns!" Brader chimed in. Longarm and Jessie could not see him, but they could hear the helpless flutter in his voice. The pudgy inventor sounded like a mother wailing over her babies trapped in a burning building.

"So that's why they're not shooting back at us," Jessie observed.

"They know what's in this shack," Longarm chuckled. "As much as they'd like to shoot us, they can't risk a bullet hitting that dynamite behind us. Their "coffee grinders" would be blown to smithereens."

"Yep, for now it's a Mexican standoff," he remarked, puffing on his filched cheroot. "They can't shoot us, but we can't escape, either. We'd never get out through that hole fast enough to make a run for it. We'd be spotted for sure."

"Ki will divert them," Jessie said quietly.

"Well where the hell is he?" Longarm began.

As if in answer, the night air was suddenly filled with a shrill wailing screech. The sound ended abruptly with a dull thud, followed by a shout of pain.

From out of the darkness a man yelled, "I've been hit by a fucking arrow! Indians!"

"I could never forget that sound!" Longarm laughed with relief.

Ki slid down the rocky slope, firing a barrage of "death's song" arrows as he went. He had twenty-five of them packed into one of his quivers. He aimed at a visible target when he could, but for now, just getting the special arrows singing through the darkness took precedence. From his vantage point he had clearly heard and seen the gunfire coming from that windowless shack. The enemy had surrounded it, taking heavy losses as they did so, but they were not returning fire. Clearly there was something valuable—other than Jessie and Longarm—in that shack, something that could be damaged by shots. Longarm and Jessie were safe for the moment, but they were also trapped. Ki wanted to give them a chance to escape, so he kept his dreadful rain of screeching arrows arcing through the night. The technique was called *inagashi*, or "flight shooting." There were many Nippoese bowmen who could fire thousands of arrows—all of them accurately—during a twenty-four hour period.

He raced about beneath the covering cloak of darkness, firing "death's song" as he went. The enemy had been thrown into confusion by the volley of wailing arrows. It was the same tactic of intimidation that had worked so well, so long ago, in Ki's own country. He hoped desperately that Longarm had remembered the story Ki had told him, so that he could put Ki's diversionary tactics to good use.

Ki kept careful watch around himself as he attacked. Up above on the slope, he had left one other man dead to keep Joe's *kami* company. Ki had come upon the man quietly, and snapped his neck before he could make a sound of alarm. Now his head twisted around like a rabbit's as he kept careful scrutiny of his surroundings. His bow made little noise, and there was no muzzle flash for the enemy to zero in on, but all it would take would be one moment's carelessness to put himself in the sights of another's gun. Now that he knew Jessie was alive, he could not afford to become injured—or killed—until he knew she was safe.

Ki fired another "death's song." This one wailed its way close to one of the men keeping his gun trained on the shack. Ki hurried away, but not before he was spotted.

"Get him!" he heard the blond foreigner scream. *"Alive or dead—get him!"*

Ki spun around the corner of the cookshack, smack into two of the outlaws, one of whom was armed with a Brader gun. Here a large campfire had been built and kept burning to warm food and drink for the men who had been on watch. Ki had lost the advantage of darkness.

He backed out of sight around the cookshack's corner, just as a pistol round send wood chips flying from the place his head had just been. The man armed with the "coffee grinder" began to fire. His chattering weapon sent blue flame and a rain of lead Ki's way.

Ki shielded his eyes from splinters and crabbed sideways, out from the shelter of the shack, to let an arrow fly. It caught the man firing the "coffee grinder" in the belly. He screamed, and jackknifed in two, the "coffee grinder's" long barrel somersaulting the man forward, over onto his back, where he lay convulsing.

Meanwhile, Ki had let go of his bow in order to throw himself upon the ground. The remaining man fired again, in panic, trying to slow Ki down, but the samurai had a *shuriken* star slicing through the air halfway to its target before the gunslick could get off a third round. The star caught the man in the forehead. He looked cross-eyed at it and began to reach up automatically to pull it out, but then he dropped his gun and pitched forward on his face, burying the star yet deeper.

Ki retrieved his bow just as three more of Danzig's men came careening around the corner to see what all the shooting had been about. Ki went down on one knee to fire off four arrows as many seconds. The last man of the three managed to throw himself back the way they'd all come. The other two went down, two arrows in each of them.

From behind Ki there came two others. Now there was no time to fire an arrow, and they were too close for *shuriken*. Ki charged in between the two, to confound their attempt to use their pistols. He knocked one of the men to the ground by slamming his bow against the side of the outlaw's head. He turned to jab at the other man with the bow's sharp tip, but the string became entangled with the man's pistol barrel as the outlaw used his gun to block the jab, and the bow was torn from Ki's hands.

Ki stepped in quickly and dropped his adversary with a "sweep lotus" kick to the fellow's chin. He next pulled his *nunchaku* to meet the renewed attack of the first man, the one he had felled with a swipe of his bow. This one's pistol was far out of reach, but he had managed to grab Ki's bow while the samurai was busy with the other outlaw. Now the man moved in toward Ki, warily swinging the bow before him like an ax handle.

Ki kept the *nunchaku* whipping in front of him in a figure-eight pattern. His opponent had bashed in more than his fair share of skulls with ax handles and clubs, this Ki could tell, but no matter how the outlaw bobbed and weaved, trying to land a blow with Ki's bow, the swinging *nunchaku* kept him off balance and at a distance.

Still, the advantage of time was with the outlaw. More men would arrive to aid him at any moment. Ki knew he had to end this stalemate, and fast!

The outlaw feinted with a quick stab of the bow's point toward Ki's chest, but Ki easily blocked it, falling back into a single-footed stance as he parried the jab with the right handle of his *nunchaku*.

The man jumped back, thinking he was out of Ki's reach. He brought the bow up and swung it back over his shoulder and then around, trying with all of his might to knock Ki's head off his shoulders. Ki did not even have to take one step forward, but merely brought his right arm around as if he were trying to chop at the man's neck with the edge of his hand. His arm was too short to make the distance, but the *nunchaku's* length gave him the reach he needed. He held the weapon at one end and whipped the other half into the fellow's neck. The bow fell from his stunned opponent's hands, but before he could utter a cry of pain, Ki had closed the distance between them to deliver an elbow strike to the man's chin. Ki kept the *nunchaku* braced along his forearm to strengthen the blow.

The brawler was now out on his feet, and just in time too. Ki heard footsteps stomping his way. He locked the *nunchaku* beneath the man's chin, and held his sagging form up as a shield against the onslaught of bullets sent his way.

Ki felt the rounds thud into the man's body, which was now dead weight.

"Damn it!" one of the gunmen swore. "Don't get near the bastard. Surround him!"

Ki staggered backward, but he couldn't move at more than an awkward shuffle with the dead man's weight upon him, and letting his shield drop would expose him to the others' guns. But there was really no choice in the matter. In another instant he'd be surrounded anyway, and then the man's body would be useless. He let go his grip, and as the corpse fell away he reached for a throwing star, even as he realized it was a futile gesture. He might get one more of the enemy, but then—

The sky seemed to light up, and the awesome clap of noise came close to bursting Ki's eardrums. From somewhere on the other side of the cookshack, clods of earth and rocks flew up. From that same direction there also came angry shouts, and the terrified whinnying of horses. The men who were about to fire at Ki flinched at the explosion, and all heads swiveled toward the direction of the blast. By the time they looked back, Ki was gone.

"Ki's keeping them busy from one side," Longarm told Jessie inside the armory and explosives shack. "We've got to attack from this side. For that, we need mobility!"

They could hear the banshee wails of Ki's arrows. Next came Danzig's furious commands to his men to hunt the archer down.

Longarm nodded in satisfaction. "Good, he's dividing his forces. This is the best chance we'll have!" He tossed Jessie the extra revolver and told her to keep watch to make sure they were not suddenly overwhelmed in a rushing attack, then hurried over to the collection of "coffee grinders." He fetched two of the weapons, along with extra magazines.

"Think you can handle one of these?" he asked anxiously. "I'm going to need covering fire."

"Looks a little heavy for me," Jessie said dubiously. "Help me shove a couple of those dynamite crates over to the doorway. I can rest the thing on them—"

"And also guarantee that they don't shoot back!" Longarm grinned. "Great idea!" He shoved a stack of two crates into position, and set the Brader guns upon them. Only the bottom crate held dynamite. The top crate was filled with bullet molds, but Longarm figured one was plenty to keep Danzig from risking an explosion.

Fortunately, Longarm had seen enough Gatling guns to quickly puzzle out the odd weapon's mechanism. He showed Jessie how to turn the cranks, and how to reload a clip into the breech, although with two guns primed and ready, he didn't think she'd have to reload.

"What are you going to be doing?" Jessie asked.

"I'm going to go blow something up," he said mildly. "The bunkhouse over yonder looks like a good target. I'll try for that, while you keep me covered with these. I'll run out and throw a stick in that direction. Then I'll come back to work the guns so you can get out—"

"What's the point of that?" Jessie interrupted.

"So I can light the fuse on the dynamite."

"I can do that!" Jessie groaned. She reached up to pluck the cigar out of Longarm's mouth, and then took a few puffs to keep it going. "Not as good as your cheroots," she said, making a face. "Now you take one of these 'coffee grinders' along with you, find cover once you've tossed your stick of dynamite, and give me cover fire to get out of here. I'll leave one stick with a longer fuse burning in here, and throw the other at Danzig and his men just before I make my break for it." She grinned at Longarm. "It's a better plan than *yours!*"

"Can you throw?" he asked skeptically.

She looked at him disgustedly. "Just go," Jessie ordered, "before I decide to forget to give you cover fire!" She gave him a quick kiss. "Be careful," she whispered, as he handed her the three dynamite sticks.

"You too," Longarm warned as she handed him back a stick with a lighted fuse.

They both listened to the sound of shots coming from the other side of the bunkhouse, near the cookshack. Their eyes locked—Ki had been cornered.

Longarm shoved his pistol into his waistband, grabbed a Brader gun, and made his break for it as Jessie began to twist the handles on the remaining gun. The weapon shuddered and shook on its precarious carriage of wooden crates, but the steady stream of bullets—coming *at* Danzig and his men for a change—was more than enough to make them huddle behind their cover.

Longarm ran about twenty yards to a nearby clump of tumbled boulders, and let his stick of dynamite fly. It fell short of the bunkhouse but made a satisfying explosion, nevertheless.

He propped his "coffee grinder" across the rocks, and began to fire. He had a better angle to work from than Jessie did, and he managed to make his burst count, hitting two of the outlaws as the rest scurried around to put something between themselves and Longarm. Jessie, meanwhile, kept firing. Her logic was sound—between them they had Danzig's men trapped in a murderous crossfire—but Longarm cursed her nevertheless. What she'd forgotten was that there was nothing to keep the band from returning *his* fire. Rounds from rifles, pistols, and the Brader guns controlled by the enemy were ricocheting into the rocks. The whine of the bullets whizzing off reminded him of the sound Ki's arrows had been making. Despite the fusillade, Longarm kept firing. His chances, as well as Jessie's, rested on his keeping Danzig's men from being able to take the time to aim.

"Do it, Jessie!" Longarm mumbled to himself. The sky was turning gray with dawn's light. Every moment she waited increased their chances of being shot.

A stick of dynamite flew tumbling out of the shack, to land squarely amidst the half-circle of Danzig's men. It exploded with an orange flash and a roar, and men were sent sprawling in all directions.

Longarm cranked off what remained of the rounds in his "coffee grinder" as Jessie scrambled to the shelter of the rocks he was hiding behind.

"Told you I had a better plan!" Jessie teased.

"You wouldn't have thought of it if you hadn't been learning stuff off of me," Longarm countered. "Give me back my cigar!" He stole the smoke out of her mouth, and went back to raking Danzig's forces until the Brader gun clicked emptily. "Shit!" he fumed.

"Brought you a present," Jessie said sweetly, offering him two more magazines for the weapon. "You don't have to thank me."

"The guns!" Longarm heard Brader shout. He watched the short, fat man waddle as swiftly as he could toward the shack.

"He's out of ammunition!" Danzig crowed. "Attack them now!" His men began to break cover.

Longarm ignored Jessie's proffered ammo magazines, and instead put his hand on the top of her hat, pushing her flat to the ground. He threw himself on top of her, angling both of their bodies as close to the sheltering boulders as possible.

He'd been prepared for a huge explosion, but what occurred literally took Longarm's breath away. The noise was the least of it. The ground beneath them seemed to heave up and then back into place. The shock wave tore his own hat off of his head, and then the air itself seemed to disappear.

Seconds later, after the worst of the debris raised by the blast had fallen—most of it far beyond Longarm and Jessie—he raised his head to gaze dazedly around.

His ears were still ringing from the thunderous noise, but still he could hear the cries and moans of men lucky enough to have been merely wounded by the blast. They had followed Danzig's command to attack, just moments before the explosion took place. Danzig's band of professional gunslicks, caught in the open, had been chopped to pieces and now lay scattered among the wreckage.

On the shack itself there was nothing left but bits of flaming or charred wood. Brader had unquestionably perished in the blast, Longarm knew.

He rose to his feet, brushing himself off, and then helped Jessie up. Both he and Jessie drew their pistols, but held them uncertainly. There seemed to be nobody left to point their guns *at*. Those men not killed were lying crumpled and broken, crying for help.

Off to their right they saw Ki pop up from behind another rock. He grinned and waved at them, and then hurried to their side.

"It is finished," he said.

"Reckon so." Longarm nodded. "Any men still up in these surrounding hills will be taking off for greener pastures. This fight is over. Jessie, we—" He broke off abruptly. "Where *is* she?"

"Find the foreigner, and we shall find her," Ki sighed.

Jessie didn't bother to search through the rubble for Danzig's body. If he was there, all well and good. If he wasn't— and her instincts told her he wasn't—she thought she knew where she could intercept him.

She made a beeline for the corrals, a fully loaded double-action .44 in her hand. She got there in time to see Danzig leading a saddled horse out of the stable. His black suit was tattered and torn, and his face was smudged from the blast, but otherwise he seemed untouched by it. Obviously he had not followed his own orders, but had been careful to keep himself behind protective cover during the explosion.

An early-morning breeze fluttered Danzig's coat, revealing his holstered brace of Mauser pistols. In his left hand he held one of the Brader guns.

Jessie understood it all perfectly. The murdering Prussian intended to escape with his prize. Other gunsmiths could calibrate the parts of the weapon and duplicate Brader's invention. Danzig could rebuild his arsenal and start this nightmare all over again.

"You're not going anywhere," Jessie called out, leveling her revolver at him. "Except to hell!"

Danzig moved with serpentine quickness. He let the "coffee grinder" fall as he crabbed sideways to put his startled horse between himself and Jessie. The animal bolted away, but by then he had his own pistols drawn and cocked.

Jessie crouched down, and held her gun with both hands. *I could have shot him twice by now,* Jessie thought. *Why haven't I?* Was it Longarm's restraining influence? Longarm understood honor and justice, but that was precisely why the lawman would want her to do her best to take this man alive...

"You cannot do it, can you, *mädchen?*" Danzig sneered. His blue eyes were bright with hate, his thin, bloodless lips were pulled back in a canine snarl. "I shall win!"

"I'm telling you to drop those guns," Jessie warned, doing her best to keep her voice calm and steady, doing her best not to show her own feelings of anger and disgust, flaring within her. How she itched to pull the trigger and blast Danzig into oblivion! But Longarm expected better of her, and she would not let him down. She would *not* lower herself to the level of this animal she had in her gunsights.

"I'm not going to kill you, Danzig," she said. "I'm going to turn you over to Longarm. Now drop your guns!"

"Do as she says, Danzig," Longarm ordered, coming up behind Jessie. His own gun was out and pointed at the Prussian. "There's no way you can get us both."

"Certainly not all three of us," Ki added, standing on

Jessie's other side. A *shuriken* star lay balanced on his fingertips, ready to be thrown.

Danzig shrugged and smiled. "I am indeed outnumbered," he said. Slowly he lowered his own pistols and let them drop to the ground.

"I'll take it from here," Longarm told Jessie as Danzig walked toward them.

Jessie nodded, lowering her own gun. She kept her eyes on Danzig, knowing him and instinctively distrusting him. It was this instinct that allowed her to cry out her warning in time.

"Longarm! Look out!"

Danzig had dropped to his knees. A third pistol had almost magically appeared in his hand, snatched from his waistband. "Whore!" he screamed, aiming at Jessie.

Both Longarm and Jessie fired at the same time as Danzig. The reports of their three guns sounded as one. The two slugs hit Danzig in the chest, knocking him backward so that his own shot went astray. Nevertheless, Jessie was certain she'd heard Danzig's round sizzle past her ear.

She, Longarm, and Ki approached the still body. Danzig's dead eyes glared up at them. Jessie bent to pick up the weapon Danzig had fired at her. It was her own, .38-caliber, double-action Colt, the one her father had given her.

"I should have known," Jessie murmured. "Of course he would take my gun with him to add to his collection. It was to be his trophy."

Unbidden, Ki had gone to fetch Danzig's brace of Mauser pistols. He showed them to Jessie, then pocketed them.

"And I'll add those to the gun collection in my father's study." She turned to Longarm. "We've got to destroy that last Brader gun. "Men already do an efficient enough job of murdering one another."

Longarm just nodded. He stood beside Jessie, and together the two of them emptied their pistols at the infernal gun until the last of Brader's weapons had been turned into a useless mass of broken steel and splintered wood.

"Now it really is all over," Longarm told her. "Your war is finished. You've won."

Jessie did not answer. She walked silently to the ruined gun, removing a lace handkerchief from her pocket as she did so. Longarm, close behind her, could see that the Circle-Star brand had been embroidered in one corner of the fabric. She dropped the hankie above the weapon. It landed on the wooden stock of the "coffee grinder," and before a breeze could flutter it to the ground, Ki pinned it in place with a swiftly hurled *shuriken* throwing star.

"Danzig's confederates will come here to investigate what has happened," she said by way of explanation. "This will tell them that the war will continue." When she turned to look at Longarm, there were tears in her green eyes. "I'm sorry for what it is going to mean to us. But I'm going to carry on my father's fight, wherever and whenever I can."

★

Chapter 20

Longarm sat sprawled across the threadbare green plush of the railroad car seat. It was late morning, several days after that night of carnage at the quarry. He was on the first leg of his journey back to Denver.

Without Jessie.

As the car rocked and swayed across the New Mexico border, Longarm adjusted his cross-draw rig. He'd found his own guns—his Colt, his double-barreled, .44 derringer, and his Winchester—along with his holster, in the quarry office.

Jessie had begged Longarm not to mention the governor's role in the plot against her father and the state of Texas. It would damage the state's spirit and the cattlemen's morale to know that one of their own had turned against them. In any case, nothing could be proved against them. In any case, nothing can be proved against him with Danzig dead, and Longarm had already wired a brief message to Vail, informing him that everything was well in hand, the case was closed, and he'd report in person as soon as he arrived in Denver.

"I still don't understand you, Jessie," Longarm sighed. They were back at the Starbuck ranch, in Jessie's bed, where they intended to remain until it was time for Longarm to catch his train out of Sarah the next day.

"It's not like you to decide to let a man like the governor get off scot-free," he continued as the blushing Myobu served them a delectable meal she'd carried up to the bedroom on a laquered tray.

"He's not going to get off scot-free," Jessie said. She sent Myobu away and sat up, letting the sheets fall from her. She poured them both cups of hot tea laced with Maryland rye, and picking up a fork, she began to feed Longarm.

"I can feed myself," he laughed.

"I know, but is the duty of a geisha to do everything for her man," she insisted. She reached down between Longarm's legs to give him a loving squeeze. "And I mean *everything*. Open your mouth."

"Yes, ma'am!" Longarm said obediently. He knew a good thing when he had it.

"Anyway, the governor will be punished. I sent Ki—"

"Oh, no!" Longarm moaned. "I'm warning you, if you sent him to kill the governor—"

"Of course not!" Jessie said. "You've taught me a lot," she continued docilely. "Killing is a last-resort measure. I understand that now."

"Then what's Ki going to do?"

"Well, he'll go to the capital, and visit the Governor late one night. He won't hurt him, but merely give him a good scare, inform him that we've got enough evidence to get him sent to prison in disgrace, and suggest that he resign his office and retire from political life." She smiled. "Once Ki lets him know that he'll be keeping tabs on the governor from time to time, I think the man will get the message and do as he's told."

"I'm sure he will." Longarm shivered. "I hope Ki doesn't get caught—"

His remark was interrupted by Jessie's silvery laugh. He

had to smile along with her. Ki ever getting caught at anything was sort of a silly thing to worry about.

"And you still insist on continuing this vendetta?" Longarm demanded. "On following those leads in that notebook left to you by your father?"

Jessie's face went suddenly grave. "It's something I have to do." She reached out to caress his cheek. "Because of you, I no longer hate, and I thank you—and love you—for that. And for *other* things. But I've got to fight my father's—and this country's—enemies."

"Just you and Ki, against all the forces those bastards can marshal?" Longarm shook his head. "It's too much."

"I won't be alone," Jessie reassured him softly. "Don't forget, all across the nation there are Starbuck offices I can call upon for assistance. Ki is already hard at work designing a special wagon to carry everything I need, and his arsenal of special weapons. He's been referring to it as our 'vengeance wagon.' We'll be able to ship it along with us on trains, and then rent horses whenever we need them. I don't know if we'll use the wagon all the time, but we'll have it when we need it."

"And you'll have me when you need me," Longarm promised, embracing her. "I hope you know that."

"I do," she swore, kissing him. "I love you, Custis. I wasn't a virgin before you met me, but I love you, and when you're ready, and I'm ready, I expect you to come and make me your wife for good and ever!"

"Here now," Longarm pretended to scold her. "I'll do the proposing." He grinned. "When I'm ready, and you're ready, I expect you to let me marry you for good and ever." He looked into her eyes, wanting to say more, but before he could speak, she pressed her finger to his lips.

"But you're not ready yet, Longarm."

"No," he had to admit. "No I'm not."

"And neither am I," she replied.

287

The lacquered tray clattered to the floor, but neither of them really heard it. They were too wrapped up in each other to let anything disturb them.

Longarm was startled from his reverie by a breeze blowing through the railroad car's opened windows. A marvelous scent had suddenly reminded him of Jessie, but what he had smelled was only a meadow of wildflowers growing alongside the tracks.

Smiling to himself, he pulled a cheroot from his pocket and lit up. Soon enough he'd be back in Denver, reporting to Billy Vail, and most likely getting saddled with another case.

Jessie had been right. He wasn't anywhere near ready to settle down. But when he was, he'd plant his roots alongside hers. Until then, Longarm knew that his tracks would cross Jessica Starbuck's whenever possible.

She was good, both in bed and in battle. But there were still a few things Custis Long could teach her...*both* places.

Watch for

LONGARM IN THE BADLANDS

forty-seventh novel in the bold
Longarm series from Jove

Coming in September!

and

Here is a
SPECIAL PREVIEW
from

Lone Star On

The Treachery Trail

first novel in the hot new
LONE STAR series
from Jove

Coming in September!

The crew hesitated, giving her hard, belligerent looks, then slowly settled back on the benches. In the tense hush that followed, Jessica sipped her coffee and thought how they all must be silently wishing she'd go away, preferably straight to hell. Well, she wasn't about to go; she was going to stay and find out how many of *them* were going to go.

Draining her cup, she returned their glares and said, "But in another sense, you're through. Through for good."

One of the feistier hands protested, "Lady, it's not—"

"Miss Starbuck, if you please. And yes, it is."

"Miz Starbuck, okay, but it's not right to fire us now. We came back and worked all day, like you wanted. It's not fair."

"I don't have to fire you. You're firing yourselves, with all your hurrawing on the ranch's time and money. And the rustlers are firing you too, by raiding and looting till the Flying W is stone broke, and Ryker can take it over as a favor." She leaned forward, sternly eyeing the shaken crew. "Ryker says he's planning to form a combine out of the ranches he buys, and you know what that'll mean? It'll mean most of you'll be canned, and those who aren't will have to work twice as hard for half the wages."

Another puncher shrugged. "Nothing we can do to change it."

"That's where you're wrong, dead wrong. You're going to start tomorrow dawn, by weeding out the stock of everything four years and older, and shipping them to Starbuck. We need them like the plague, but it'll help pay your wages, help keep you *hired*. And I want a couple of you to take some Giant powder to the west end of the valley, where the stream flows down out of that long canyon. I found plenty of tracks heading up it, and the cows didn't get there by straying."

The second puncher nodded, brightening. "Not a bad idea. A little blasting up in the rocks oughta close that gap to rustlers."

"It'll also dam the stream," Jessica continued. "It'll form a reservoir to provide extra water for the herd, and for crop irrigation."

That startled a third hand. "Crops? We're not sodbusters."

Jessica favored him with a flinty smile. "It's not hard to learn. And you'd better, because that whole section by the canyon will be fenced off for native hay and maybe some sugar beets. What you don't use for the ranch will be sold as another source of income."

By now the entire Flying W crew was gaping attentively at her. Daryl as well was studying her in wonderment. She was moving fast and decisively, this Jessica Starbuck. She was ramrodding hard—which, though unsettling, was also generating fresh enthusiasm.

And then she dropped the bomb. "You're going to need a foreman, what with Nealon gone—and from what I've seen so far, good riddance—so I'm going to ask Toby Melville to stay on awhile, as guest of Mrs. Waldemar. From now on, you'll take your orders from him."

There was an outburst of voices, including Daryl's: "But Je—"

She shushed with a wave of her hand. "Listen, Toby

Melville's forgotten more about ranching than most of us will ever learn. And you all get along with the Spraddled M crew, don't you?" When she wasn't contradicted, she forged on: "The two spreads will remain separated. I'm only talking about banding together till we've licked the rustling. A common herd can be defended by fewer men, freeing others for nighthawking—and fighting."

A fifth hand balked at this. "Fighting, like in shooting? Not me. I was hired to nurse cows, not toss lead."

Jessica nailed him with steel-cold eyes. "You're hired to side the Flying W, a fact you've managed to ignore." Surveying the others, she added, "You're bogged down and sinking fast, and if you hope to save your ranch and your jobs, you're going to have to lay your brains and guts and, by God, all your loyalty on the line."

"By damn, I've heard all the manure I plan to," a puncher way in the back sneered, "and the only reason I say 'manure' is on account of a female's present. Leastwise, she *looks* like a female."

Daryl stiffened. "Hold on, watch your tongue there."

The third Flying W hand who'd spoken now chimed in, "Yeah, Wylie, ain't no call to—"

"Shut up, Croft," the man called Wylie snarled. "Maybe your spine is made outta smoke, but as for me, I've had my fill of bein' lectured at by strange wimmen." He got up from the table, a dark, squat man with a barrel chest and black, beady eyes. "I'm doin' nothin' till Mez Waldemar tosses these troublemakin' talkers offen the ranch. If anybody else feels the same, come with me."

The two burly punchers who'd been flanking him on the bench rose and fell in, swaggering behind Wylie as he began shouldering his way toward the door. Apparently his close buddies, they laughed when he glared at Jessica and taunted, "Yeah, if I craved preacherin', lady, I'd go to Sunday school." Then, turning to Daryl and Ki, he added, growling, "Step aside, 'lessen you wish to get busted apart."

293

Almost to the front of the table now, he drew abreast of Croft. Foolishly, Croft shifted on the bench and reached out to place a cautioning hand lightly on Wylie's arm. "Simmer down, Wylie," he said. "Hear them out. Maybe these folks've got something to—"

"Leggo!" Wylie wrenched away from Croft's hand as though it were a snake biting his arm, then pivoted and shoved his palm flat into Croft's face. "I'll learn you to shut up!" he snarled, and mashed Croft's head down into his dinner plate with a dull, meaty crunch. Dazed and half-blinded, Croft reeled to one side and began falling off the bench, and Wylie drew back his right foot to kick his boot into Croft's unprotected belly. "I'll learn you good!"

Ki reacted before the kick could land. With an odd smile that masked his anger, he launched himself at Wylie, who immediately turned to meet him with fists. Ki ducked Wylie's first and last punch, catching the puncher's outflung arm and angling to drop to one knee, swinging him into *seoi otoshi*, the kneeling shoulder-throw.

Wylie arched through the air, over the heads of the seated men, and came down on the table, atop the meat platter and the bowl of mashed potatoes. He sprawled there, dazed and breathless.

Even before Wylie hit, Ki was swinging around in the cramped space between the bench and the wall, to check whatever Wylie's two friends might be up to. The nearer one was charging him with arms outstretched, as if he were tackling a drunk in a barroom brawl. Ki chopped the edge of his hand down at his nose. He purposely held back a little so he would not break it, but it struck forcefully enough to hurt like hell, and tears of pain sprang into the man's eyes. Ki followed through by kicking the man in the side of his knee, collapsing him to one side. He caught his right arm, crunched down on it with his elbow, and then brought his own knee into his hip.

The man dropped to the floor, leaving the way clear for

Wylie's second pal to lash out at Ki with his wide leather belt. Ki had already seen this second one slide off his belt and fold it double, which was one of the reasons he'd had to dump the first man, for now he was able to step over the first man and catch hold of the second one's right arm and left shoulder with his hands. At the same time, Ki moved his right foot slightly in back of the man so that as the fellow began tumbling sideways, Ki was able to dip to his right knee and yank viciously. His *hizi otoshi*, or elbow-drop, worked perfectly; the second man catapulted upside-down and collapsed jarringly on top of the first man, flattening them both to the floor.

And Wylie, face purpling with rage, launched himself off the table, a well-honed bowie knife clutched in his right hand. "I'm gonna carve you apart!" he bellowed, slashing at Ki.

Ki calmly stepped aside and then kicked up with his callused foot. His heel caught Wylie smack on his chin, so hard that Wylie flew backwards onto the table again. This time he sprawled cold on his back, staring sightlessly up at the rafters and cobwebbed ceiling of the cookshack.

The rest of the Flying W crew gaped at Wylie, his two moaning pals, and then at Ki with stunned disbelief. They said nothing.

Jessica broke the silence. "If these three want to quit, then they can quit. If any of you others want to quit, you can. Or you can stay. It's up to you, but make up your minds. As I said last night, I don't have the time—and the Flying W doesn't have the time—for you to sit on your butts. Either start kicking or packing."

The feisty hand who'd first spoken, now spoke up again. "Well, boys, I reckon Miz Starbuck might have something. She sure has a powerful persuader, and she's got me convinced. We gotta pitch in and stop the raidin', else we'll all be grub-lining. 'Sides, none of us is safe from a bushwhack bullet, lessen we do rare up and fight back."

"Okay, count me in."

"We gotta do something, I see that now."

"Sure, we couldn't face Miz Waldemar if we didn't."

A consensus of agreement quickly swelled from the crew, including the one who'd refused to fight. "Might as well," he growled, moodily building a smoke. "Guess it don't make no difference how I bleed, fast or slow. I'll be dead here anyways."

Diplomatically thanking the men for their splendid co-operation, Jessica rose and left the cookshack. Ki followed, amused as ever by how much she was her father's child, equally as competent as Alex Starbuck had been in defusing and mastering tricky negotiations.

LONGARM

Explore the exciting Old West with one of the men who made it wild!

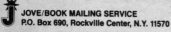

LONGARM

Explore the exciting Old West with one of the men who made it wild!